MUSTANG

A NOVEL OF WORLD WAR II

also by

JOHN J.

DWYER

Stonewall

Robert E. Lee

When the Bluebonnets Come

The War Between the States: America's Uncivil War

The Oklahomans: The Story of Oklahoma and Its People

Shortgrass

MUSTANG

A NOVEL OF WORLD WAR II

JOHN J.
DWYER

TIREE
PRESS

an imprint of
OGHMA CREATIVE MEDIA

OGHMA

C R E A T I V E   M E D I A

Tiree Press
An imprint of Oghma Creative Media, Inc.
2401 Beth Lane, Bentonville, Arkansas 72712

Library of Congress Cataloging-in-Publication Data

Names: Dwyer, John J., author.
Title: Mustang/John J. Dwyer.
Description: First Edition. | Bentonville: Tiree, 2019.
Identifiers: LCCN: 2018942270 | ISBN: 978-1-63373-428-9 (hardcover) |
ISBN: 978-1-63373-427-2 (trade paperback) | ISBN: 978-1-63373-429-6 (eBook)
Subjects: BISAC: FICTION/Historical/World War II |
FICTION/War & Military | FICTION/Action & Adventure
LC record available at: https://lccn.loc.gov/2018942270

Tiree Press trade paperback edition May, 2019

Cover & Interior Design by Casey W. Cowan
Editing by Dennis Doty & Gil Miller

For my father, Sgt. John Adams Dwyer (1923-1958),
U.S. Army, Pacific Theater, 1943-1946.

"Be strong, saith my heart; I am a soldier; I have seen worse sights than this."

–Homer, *The Odyssey*

PART I

ENGLAND

"My beloved is mine, and I am his."
—Song of Solomon 2:16

ONE

MARCH, 1943
SUFFOLK COUNTY, ENGLAND

The first sign Lance caught that he might be in real trouble was his initial night at the Suffolk County air base in East Anglia near the little town of Beccles. Originally a Royal Air Force field, the English had turned it, and dozens of others, over to the Americans as the latter's presence grew on that pastoral enclave of fields, streams, marshes, plains, and villages in far eastern England that jutted into the North Sea and the past.

A poster on the wall outside the crescent-shaped Nissen hut, Officers' Mess Hall Number Two featured a smiling, movie star-handsome, American aviator and the words, "Who's afraid of the new Focke Wulf?", a take-off on Disney's *Three Little Pigs* song "Who's Afraid of the Big Bad Wolf?"

"Lookee at that," Lance pointed to a large sheet of butcher's wrapping paper someone had pinned onto the poster under the question. It read, "We are." at the top, and two long columns of signatures rolled down below that. "Reckon ever officer in our 299th group signed it. Includin' the group commander, Tavington." He turned to Waddy. "You think they sayin' them FWs got 'em buffaloed?"

Waddy broke into a smile and slapped him on the shoulder as they headed into the mess. "Well, if they are, we gettin' here jist in time to yank they chestnuts outa the fire for em!"

It felt like the old days, when he and his best friend and Sigma Chi fraternity brother yanked chestnuts out of the fire for the Oklahoma Sooners football team. They defeated Texas, Nebraska, and a slew of others, and co-captained the first great team in school history in 1938.

Waddy made it seem not so long ago now, not nearly so long as having loved and lost Mary Katherine, or the past year traversing basic, primary, and advanced B-17 Flying Fortress, or Fort, training with Waddy and their spunky Sig brother and all-conference OU wrestler Trigger McCurdy.

Course, Sadie was long before that. Hard to believe it was going on eight years since he last saw her the day he left home for OU. Her voice broke and she rushed past him and back into the house, her bronzed, half-Chickasaw cheeks darkening as she slammed the screen door so hard something inside fell and shattered on the floor. You'd have thought it was he that broke her heart rather than the other way around.

They'd just heard that Will Rogers and his buddy, Wiley Post, had died. Wiley taught her to fly at age thirteen and later gave her the Curtiss Robin. She flew it, the day they met, when she rescued Lance from her galloping, rifle-packing fiancée at the last-ever Duncan-Marlow football game. She was a cheerleader for Marlow, and he, a star player for Duncan. The game ended scoreless when the two towns emptied the stands and brawled.

What he still remembered most, though, was her tackling him under the moonlight in her pasture just a couple nights before that, after good ol Jeb, his mustang and best friend in the world, ran her big white thoroughbred into the ground. He was eighteen and a thoroughgoing Mennonite and Sadie was the first girl he ever kissed.

Well, the first girl ever kissed me....

"What're you smilin' at, Parson?" Trigger hollered, hitting him in the head with a roll that was way harder than Mama baked on the Roark spread where he grew up. That was outside of Duncan, on the old Chisholm Trail in southwest Oklahoma, back before the Dust Bowl, the Depression, low cattle prices and boll weevils drove his parents and so many others out and away to California and elsewhere.

Eating with Trigger and members of their crews, he didn't feel like a stranger even though he'd just arrived in England. The shortgrass country, where he had lived his whole life, was half a world away. The more veteran aviators—usually boasting stints at Beccles of between two and six months— were generally tolerable toward him, Waddy, Trigger, their crews, and the other rookies. Several were friendly—a few aloof. He noticed one beefy pilot, his crush cap angled up against the black hair that encased his olive-complexioned face, eyeing them but not joining in the conversations. After a few minutes, the man stood and walked past them to leave. As he did, Lance extended a hand to shake his.

"Keep it to yourself," the man snapped in a sharp New Jersey accent peppered with the worst vulgarities. "You Okies are gonna get yooz cheeks shot off before we get a chance to know yiz."

"Don't mind Cappuccio," a fresh-faced Midwesterner named Risinger said a moment later. "I'm guessin' you fellows can hit a baseball?"

"Why yow," Waddy said. He had been OU's heavyweight conference wrestling champion and first-ever consensus football All-American, before becoming the renowned "Iron Dodger" for Brooklyn's NFL football team.

"Good, we'll have a game tomorrow if—"

A strange, unearthly voice booming somewhere outside interrupted him. A collective groan from the room's non-rookie patrons followed.

"What the hey!" Waddy blurted.

"Means we gotta fly again tomorrow—in the morning—the early morning." Risinger's countenance appeared considerably diminished by the strange, grating voice from outside. "Not you neophytes, but the rest of us."

"So, what is that dang thang?" Waddy canted his large square head toward it.

"That's the Tannoy," Risinger said. "Latest brainchild of the brass. They string speakers throughout the base, in trees, on rooftops, you name it. Comes on to announce whenever we fly the next day."

"Three days in a row!" one man slammed his plate down on the metal dining table, scattering Spam and beans like stray calves in a shortgrass norther.

"Had a rough one today," Risinger barely spoke loud enough for Lance, Waddy, and Trigger to hear. "Sub yards at Bremen. First run on 'The Fatherland' itself. Problem is, the Jerries are starting to shoot back. Seemed like they had a thousand flak guns firing at us."

As he lay on his cot after lights out, in the Nissen hut where he shared one of the two little rooms with Waddy, he thought of Mama's recent letters from Bakersfield, California. They spoke a lot of Daddy and how he worked as hard in the Lockheed factory as he did in the oil patch where he'd lost two fingers roughnecking.

Wonder do the letters leave out that heartache, lost dreams, or the bottle have wrenched Daddy's faith from him?

Only in an offhand moment did the letters reference the colossal machine toward which his labors contributed—the same Flying Fortress he now flew. "Reckon we are all serving Caesar now," she had concluded that letter. An unusual twinge of bitterness revealed itself in the stiffness of the normally-flowing words her hand wrote.

I promise, I'll make ye proud, Mama.

His eyelids grew heavy.

You'll be so happy....

—

The next day, he learned there was something more despised than flying a mission into Germany. They were ordered to fly, rousted out by Kupchak the waker for the flying officers with his flashlight in their faces at 1:30 or 2:00 in the morning to shower and eat powdered eggs and bacon fat before going to group briefing. They dressed out, hitting the flight line with their crews. They sat, engines idling, then taxiing for an hour or more before taking off, risking their lives in a thirty-five to forty-five-minute climb to altitude and the assembly point through scores of other planes and cloud cover. They headed out over the North Sea, then were ordered back because bad weather conditions were now predicted sometime, somewhere—over the target in continental Europe, en-route, on the way back, later at Beccles, or anywhere.

"Rather spend the rest of the war over the IP than on that God-forsaken flightline," a roughhewn tail gunner flung his headgear, parachute, and Mae West jacket onto the equipment truck when the bombers returned just after sunrise. "Cripes, let's go eat breakfast again after the retards interrogate us."

—

When Bob Patton rolled into the Beccles base that morning, pretty much the same thing happened as when he showed up anywhere else. Folks took note of the tall handsome man with the yellow hair and cobalt blue eyes and the bearing that came as natural to him as it was impossible for most. They soon reckoned they wanted to be part of whatever he was part of.

"Bullet Bob Patton!" Waddy hollered when he, Lance, and Trigger saw him saunter into their officers' mess for breakfast. He had the six-foot-four-inch Patton in a bearhug and up in the air before the Chickasha, Oklahoma, native remembered who Waddy was.

Gathering himself and sprouting the winning smile that had new Oklahoma Governor Robert S. Kerr's political machine already wooing him toward the oil and gas business, Patton extended his hand.

"I know we've met, but—"

"Aw, jeez, Bob, '38 All State football game," Waddy, two feet away, blasted him with his booming voice.

The cobalt eyes sparkled. "Yeah, I remember. You put me out o that game—

though I don't actually remember that part." Waddy and the gathering cluster of men around them hooted their laughter.

"Yeah, well," Waddy said, "that's after you run straight past me fer one touchdown and threw right over me fer a couple more."

After a round of introductions, Waddy turned to Lance. "This gonna be our squadron pitcher fer hardball. Hey Bob, you still with the Yanks?"

"Yankees?" a voice sounded from several tables away. *New York Yankees?*

Patton blushed with embarrassment. "Aw, I was only with 'em for a year till my rotator cuff played out on me."

"With em?" a voice called from a different table.

"Well, I was with their Single A Minors team for a year and their Double A for two years 'fore I went up," Patton said.

Lance could see the Chickashan trying to divert the attention from himself. Then Patton looked right at him. "I'll never forget'chu. You knocked us out o the conference championship single-handed, on our own field. We never did stop you all night."

"That lanky galoot?" a navigator standing nearby pointed at Lance.

"Shoot yow," Patton said, glad to point the attention elsewhere. "These two yahoos were Oklahoma Sooners. They almost won the national championship couple years ago."

A murmur rippled through the widening throng. He saw Patton's pleasure was short-lived when a bombardier got up close to him and asked, "You play with Joltin' Joe?"

He had to smile at Patton's reluctant idol attitude. Bullet Bob just nodded. Before he could change the topic again, another flyer jumped in, "You did? What was he like?"

And, so it went, until Cappuccio piped up, "So you gonna pitch for us in tomorrow's hardball game against the 303rd?"

"Didn't you hear him?" Trigger glared at him, coloring. "His arm's throwed out."

"Yeah, sure..." Cappuccio's tone was one of *Yeah, I bet he's great, but we'll* never know how great because of course he's not able to show us, even though all his fellow Okies can tell us stories of how great he is and we are supposed to believe them.

Trigger's eyes narrowed. "Hey, listen, you—"

"Naw, it's alright." Patton touched Trigger's arm. "I can go."

"How the heck can you do that?" someone asked. "Your shoulder better?"

How he did it was to parley his ambidexterity into a two-hit game against the 303rd—left handed. This sparked love for him from the 299th, awe from others, and hatred from a few. It sparked some of that from Cappuccio, plus an empty wallet from having bet all he had against the 299th, once he learned Patton would pitch left handed.

"Dumb Okies," Lance heard Cappuccio growl loud enough for him to hear, as everyone left the base's makeshift ball field. Then he launched his own discordant opening to the new Broadway stage play *Oklahoma's* famed theme song: "Ohhhhhh-klahoma, where the dumb . . . come sweeping down the plains."

"Think I'd be a mite bitter if I lost that ability," Trigger said that night to Waddy and a couple of their crewmen referring to Patton's injury as they sank into the army of old stuffed arm chairs littering the Officers' Club.

"Well, I guess you can find out firsthand," Waddy winked as he sipped Coke from a bottle. "He's leadin' a Bible Study in the base chapel this evenin'. It's an 'alternative' to that Catholic chaplain's mass."

This cheered Lance, who had just learned he and the other new arrivals, including Waddy and Trigger, faced at least a month of classroom work and flight training before they flew their first mission. Trying to hide his lingering disappointment about that, he went for a walk past the ammo dumps and the perimeter road that looped five miles around the station. He gazed out at the frosty oak and hawthorn trees stretching away from the base as the rising moon set them aglitter.

Seems like I been in class and practicin' all my life, Lord. Yessir, all right, I know, lean not on my own understandin', but trust You in all things.

Heartened, a spring back in his step, he returned to the Officers' Club. The oddball pair of Cappuccio and his buddy Cochran, a short, stocky nineteen-year-old hailing from the South Carolina Piedmont country and sporting a seemingly permanent chaw of tobacco in his cheek, stood admiring the unclothed image of a Vargas Girl they had just unfolded. More men congregated to admire the Vargas, a bombardier clowning and grabbing himself as he cracked wise about the model's physical attributes.

"She's my date in London this weekend," a navigator mimed his dance moves.

Cappuccio planted a well-placed kiss on the foldout and hooted "I love that combination," at the navigator, graphically extolling the model's charms, and Cappuccio's own male prowess. The group roared their approval.

"Saw Patton after his two-hitter," Trigger winked at Lance and Waddy.

"Yeah?" Waddy asked. "What was he doin'?"

"Walkin' 'crost the top o the Waveney River yonder," Trigger held a poker face, "not needin' a bridge, jist 'fore he turned it all into wine—I mean grape juice."

—

He finally got up in the air a couple weeks later for a lengthy practice flight. He led one three-plane element coupled with another led by Waddy who also led the six-plane flight, while Almond their squadron leader commanded the twenty-plane formation. Aided by Lance and Waddy's flight experience, this and a similar session the next day ran smoothly.

The next mission took place four days later, following three days of the prohibitive, moisture-related, island weather conditions he was already coming to know. Only he and Waddy's flight flew this time, and he realized the necessity of further training. The plane wasn't even high enough for the first oxygen check when a stream of silver stratus clouds emerged from nowhere and enveloped them. He assumed he would get out of them in a minute or two, but they kept going, growing darker and thicker. He heard his brilliant but temperamental navigator cursing through the interphone.

"What the heck, Goldsmith?"

"Aw, Parson," Goldsmith continued the nickname Waddy and Trigger had announced for him. He sighed. *"All right, I don't know where the heck we are."*

"Jesus, Joseph, and Mary," the voice of O'Connor, the Boston Southie, crackled over the intercom from the tail.

After another minute, the stratus thinned, providing maybe four-tenths visibility, but then Goldsmith uttered a profanity.

"We hardly in the air and you lost your... backside already, Goldy!"

Gotta pray for O'Connor's sad mouth! Got his own arsenal o cuss words that seem to rotate with ever sentence. That time, it was like he was waitin' for the chance to jump on Goldsmith.

"O'Connor," Goldsmith tried to sooth. *"I can still see the ground, buddy."*

"Yeah, and you can still see the ocean, too, on your way across it, but that don't mean you know where you are," O'Connor barked back.

He shifted in his seat and squinted out his little side window.

Dang, they's towns, but who knows which ones they are?

"Any ideas?"

Clifton, the copilot, had none.

"So, what do we do?" O'Connor's voice crackled again.

"First thing is keep the lip to a minimum on the interphone."

A collective *"Whoooooo!"* ascended from all points of the ship and he had to chuckle. "All right, all right. I know I ain't no Captain Bligh, but come on, boys, one o these days soon, we gonna be dogfightin' our tails off and we can't be all a'yakkin' at once."

A few seconds of silence followed before O'Connor cracked, *"What sorta language do yooz guys speak down there in Indian Country, anyhoos, Parson?"*

Patton flew second element lead in his flight.

He's probably the only ship in the squadron doing his job well, cause he's right where he ought to be.

His near wingtip hung mere yards off Lance's starboard one. Patton had no ideas what to do, but he was unhelpful in an encouraging and supportive way.

Hmmm...what now? Think I'll switch from the interphone to the group pilots' liaison channel and radio Waddy for help.

But he wasn't much help either, since he had drifted far enough away due to the cloud cover and other confusion that he couldn't even see Lance's Fort. Trigger still flew alongside Waddy.

When he detected Goldsmith's anxiety and that the only use he had for his sextant was to slam it on his little plotting table up front in the greenhouse, he decided to head home. No one objected, which might have been the first unanimous verdict his crew had yet accomplished on anything, in the air or on the ground.

One of the first people he saw when he stepped onto his hardstand back at the base was a sheepish Trigger, who had already returned, somehow ahead of Waddy. A sudden, new, but not unusual sprawl of fog and cumulus had only furthered the confusion. They just shook their heads at each other as a young orderly appeared to let them know Group Commander Tavington wanted to see them in his office.

"What are you men going to do against the *Luftwaffe* when you can't even find the urinal in the friendly skies of England!" Tavington raged at them, Patton, and one of the three other pilots and their co-pilots five minutes later in his office.

He marveled at how the man could still communicate so crystal clear a message amid a vulgar apoplectic fit.

"Did nothing you've learned in all these months stick in your mottled brains? Pitiful!"

With his vaguely aristocratic nasal accent and impeccable attire, he had wondered whether Tavington was English, but this shouting and his inflections rang distinctly American.

He's from somewhere back east, I reckon. But he's one Dapper Dan. Dapper Dandy. Dandy Dapster Dan. And lookee at that fancy black-faced chronometer he's sportin'. Looks like it does everthang but shoot out the weather forecasts for our flights. I'll bet he wears a white silk scarf when he flies.

Just as the smile he was suppressing threatened to break open across his face, Waddy hustled through the door, his enormous frame barely fitting through it, his co-pilot nowhere to be seen. Tavington took one look at him, shook his head, scowled, and stomped out, hollering over his shoulder, "I'll be up there with you tomorrow, you cretins, and you better have your act together or I may have some new infantry recruits for our North Africa invasion!"

After a miserable debriefing, a miserable supper, and a miserable evening, he slept soundly until Kupchak rousted him and the others from their slumber at 5 a.m. They could fly anytime during the day, but 299th Group Command wanted them conditioned to the even-earlier rises that would come with flying missions over France and Germany.

When they got to briefing, they learned Tavington had gone to Wing headquarters. Those meetings and a 299th mission to Kiel—*I'll swan, that's the name o one of our Mennonite towns in western Oklahoma the Council o Defense made us change in World War I*—prevented any other combat mission-seasoned pilots from accompanying them. Tavington left orders for Patton to fly lead.

"That sorry piece o..." O'Connor's rude anatomical references and aspersions against Tavington's manhood provided a bodyguard of colorful verbiage to the Southie's assertion that the CO had his tail between his legs.

That was because he had something else somewhere else that it shouldn't be, Utah Cade the flight engineer and top gunner coarsely observed in a voice dry as the Monument Valley sands where he grew up and as rarely heard as rain in those parts. He liked Utah, not least because the ranch hand and horseman had managed to get a stained, weather-beaten cowboy hat all the way to Beccles with him.

Patton—more specifically, his navigator—fared no better than Goldsmith had the day before in keeping track of his course and objectives.

Startin' to see how continually this English fog, rain, heavy clouds, and just plain wet air, none of it conducive to orderly flyin', are affectin' our efforts.

Today, they conspired to scatter the planes even before they had climbed to the assembly point for another short run over friendly territory. Risinger suggested the disturbing specter that France had even more capricious weather for flying than jolly old England.

Tavington had not returned from his "Wing meetings." Risinger told him and his Oklahoma pilot buddies these were taking place at a young RAF prisoner of war's cozy bungalow in Great Yarmouth, twelve miles east on the North Sea coast, with the airman's lonely and lovely wife. Thus, Lodge, the Ground Exec, conducted today's chewing out. An officious little man— or "pint-sized..." according to O'Connor—he delivered as much heat as Tavington, but with even less gravitas. When Lodge headed straight for lunch at the officer's mess, Trigger asked Waddy, Patton, and him to accompany him on a pressing errand.

As Axis Sally welcomed the recently-arrived 299th Group to England over the Tannoy—unsettling information for a sensual female Nazi radio propagandist to possess—the somber trio followed Trigger up the dirt trail into the grove where the officers' hutments squatted, shielded from view in case of a German air attack.

"Why should you lay down your lives for England, the most arrogant and rapacious imperial power since Genghis Khan and his yellow Mongolian hordes?" Sally proceeded, her voice honeyed with seductive allure and no trace of accent.

He remembered a letter from Mama telling him Daddy had asked a similar question.

"How'd that witch know we jist got here?" Waddy turned back and shot Sally a lewd salute.

"Shh!" he stifled a laugh.

Unlike the pilots, Tavington and Lodge had their own rooms. Apparently expecting that Lodge had wisely locked the door to his, Trigger produced a metal instrument with which he popped it open. As his colleagues looked on in shock, he strode straight to Lodge's cot and loosed both number one and number two on it from his own bomb bays.

"Well, I guess if it worked for ye on the Beta House, it oughta work here," Waddy encouraged his Sigma Chi brother as they hurried gleefully from the premises.

TWO

Tavington still hadn't returned the next day, and nothing had come forth from Lodge about his sullied abode. A rough mission to the North Sea sub pens at Wilhelmshaven overshadowed such matters, anyway. Two more Forts went down and six suffered significant damage, emptying out all but one cot in the rooms either side of Lance's.

"Hellacious air defenses around those sub yards," Risinger leaned against the cheap plywood bar in the smoke-filled, colored-bulb-lit Officers Club after supper. He lit up a Chesterfield and tossed back a jigger of Vat 69. "And doubt we're doing anything, anyway. Krauts got those pens sunk in concrete halfway down to China."

Lance blinked.

That's what's different bout Risinger and the others, been flyin' combat for several months—they're around my age er younger, some of'em several years younger, but it's like they got a shadow over their face er somethin' that makes'em look years older. Risinger is twenty-five, like me—but he looks thirty-five.

"How long since you flew your first mission?" Lance's voice was creaky.

"Six months to the day tomorrow," Risinger poured another jigger and sucked down a long draught. "And five more to go."

He felt like Brock or one of the other Nebraska Cornhuskers had just put a shoulder into his ribs in their epic conference championship game back in '38. That was the game he won for the Sooners on the final play when he ran a fumble back ninety yards for a touchdown after Waddy had decked the ball carrier. Waddy, sipping a beer, noticed his look.

"You okay, Buckwheat?"

He just nodded.

Risinger glanced around and lowered his voice. "Look, fellas. You didn't hear this from me, okay? But they're sendin you guys up soon—real soon."

"The heck you say," Waddy slammed his drink down.

"Hey," Risinger quieted him.

"I got a bombardier can't hit his backside if ye hand it to him on a platter," Waddy's voice was an emphatic hiss. "Lance here, his navigator's good nough with numbers to prolly memorize the phone book, but the man couldn't find the drain in a half-filled bath tub."

He found himself quite speechless.

"It ain't good, I know, boys," Risinger said, expletives peppering his words, "but we're gettin' our schnozzes shot outa the sky. That blasted hutment of ours has almost completely turned over twice since I been there—and we haven't even begun regular missions over Germany yet."

Lance and Waddy stared at him, blinking at the string of expletives he garnished his words with.

"There isn't anybody else, fellas." Risinger's handsome ruddy farmboy face appeared earnest. "We're the pioneers, the wedge-busters. Everyone's rushed through." His brown eyes, gone from warm to wary, darted around and he lowered his voice. "Besides, I got it on good authority, if we don't get some notches on our belt, Roosevelt's gonna just let Churchill and the Brits roll those of us ain't already gone to Africa up into their own air force and their nighttime bombin'."

Still don't fancy this notion of fellow-travelin' with "The Brits." Plenty o history with'em as Irish crushin us and recent history as Mennonites gettin' dragged into their wars. Plus, it's lookin' more and more like high rankers' brainstorms and schemes means soldiers' hides.

Waddy considered this for a moment. "Gee whiz. Guess we better git our sad sacks ready."

A few minutes later, Lance strode alone past the Admin buildings.

Gee, wonder if somethin' from the bar 'sides lemonade might help this poundin heart. Wonder what sorta intel they conjurin' up in that building, and what sorta ops they hatchin' in that one yonder.

He headed across the still golden-brown centerfield of the airdrome, over the mile-plus-long diagonally cut runways, past a camouflaged Brit gas lorry and trailer headed for the Fort hangars, and beyond the far perimeter road, until he finally reached the barbed wire fence on the east end of the air field.

He gazed out over the flat lime fields of young barley that rolled toward the River Waveney a few hundred yards away.

Dang, that looks a lot like home.

He closed his eyes and drank in the fresh aroma of eventide. A hint of the Waveney sweetened the breath his nostrils drew in.

It could be Little Beaver Creek jist yonder beyond the alfalfa, er haymow.

It was a pleasing thought, not without feeling, but despite the challenges of war, he liked where he was, what he was doing, and what he looked forward to accomplishing.

I been sorta driftin' fer quite a spell now, Lord, but I think I'm finally gettin' back on track, specially with Bobby Patton and his example and his Bible Study. Meetin' nearly ever night now, fer either Bible study er prayer er both. Bob is the genuine article. I remember our senior year at Duncan High when Chief blocked the extra point after Bob's fourth touchdown pass and we won by one point. We knocked his number three-ranked Chickasha team out o the conference, and maybe state, championship race. Plus, I'd tore up his shoulder—Oh no, that's prolly what sunk his career with the Yankees! He was hurtin' so bad he had tears in his eyes and his arm in a sling, but he called us all out to the fifty and led us in a prayer o' Thanksgiving to the Lord fer all we had and that we could play like we jist had.

Quanah "Chief" Bailey was the fatherless, rough-hewn Comanche who was his best friend in high school and Bullet Bob Patton was the best high school passer he had ever played against or seen.

He looked up to a beautiful metallic blue sky.

Thank you, Sir, fer placin' such a man as Bobby here to help me. And some o' these other boys, the Christians that're actin' up cause they far from home and lonely and scared, they findin' they way back to You, sir. And some o' these others, that never knew, why, some of'em are listenin', maybe fer the first time ever. And some like Cappuccio...

He chuckled.

...well, we jist keep prayin' for 'em, sir!

For a moment, no sound reached his ears, not even from the base sprawling behind him.

Hmmm—that faint noise—like the wagons some o the old timers used to drive into Duncan on market day Saturday.

He looked off to his left, where came a slender girl of nineteen or twenty with a bramble of light auburn hair flaming crimson in the sun's shining death throes. She pushed a wheel barrow piled with sweet potatoes, sugar beets, and turnips along the fence line toward him.

One o them "Land Girls" the English been draftin' from all over the country to work on the farms.

The sweetness of her face caught his breath. She wore a worn navy cardigan and a slightly frayed gray skirt that hung to a few inches below her knees.

Land Girls ain't royalty.

As she came near, a constellation of happy freckles presented themselves to him, as if to introduce the most disarming and gentle of smiles he had ever beheld, which seemed to trigger the sparkle of her gray-green eyes.

"Where ye takin' them sweet taters?"

"To Mr. Bond's barn." Her voice was as calming as Mama singing him Daddy's favorite Irish lullaby, "The Castle of Dromore," when he was a child.

He catapulted up and over the barbed wire fence, dropping softly down onto the black dirt path beside her as her eyes widened in merry surprise. Only then did he realize how short she was, perhaps five feet tall.

"Oh, my goodness," she said, looking up at him. "You are quite tall." She blushed, perhaps concerned with embarrassing him. "Of course, many of you Yanks are so." She looked down at the ground and seemed nearly to curtsy in deference.

"Well, that's okay," he heard someone with his voice saying. "Cuz you're cute!"

"Cute?" she broke into a giggle. "I suppose that is an American manner of complimenting a girl?"

He felt stupid. "Uh, yes, Ma'am—I mean, uh, yes, it is."

She giggled some more, with no malice. "So at least you didn't call me 'Sweetie' like some of your fellow... Yanks." She noticed the perplexity on his face. "Oh, I didn't mean offense, sir. I—"

"Aw, I know ye didn't. It's jist that—well, where I come from, that word— Yank, er Yankee—ain't exactly a compliment. But I'm learnin' y'all call us all that over here."

She pondered him as the final gush of sun swabbed a coral brush across her smooth unlined face and he felt his heart pound in a strange fashion. "You're a funny stick, aren't you, Cowboy?"

Now his heart jumped. "Well—why'dju call me that?"

"Why, because I can tell you're from Texas," she said, the first trace of a glint sneaking out despite the sun's momentary illumination passing from her face.

"Hey, I ain't from Texas.," he said. "I'm from Oklahoma."

She started. "Oh my, I meant no offense." Now the glint had blended with the sweetness.

"Oh, I'm sorry, " he said. "I didn't either. It's jist that...."

She canted her head in a manner that reminded him of Sadie. "So, is Texas not exactly a compliment, either, where you come from, Cowboy?"

He knew then he needed to guide the wheelbarrow to whatever destination she intended for it.

"Can I?" he motioned such.

"Oh my," she seemed, surprised and impressed. "Yes, of course."

"Hey, buddy, what're you doin' out there?" an unwelcome American voice hollered. He turned and saw a strapping, white-helmeted MP standing on the running board of a Jeep, another sitting at the wheel. "Get your hide back in here—*sir.*"

"Roger that," he gasped a bit, his eyes shooting from the girl to the loaded wheel barrow. "Uh, sorry bout that…Ma'am. Can I come say howdy this Saturday?" He couldn't believe the words came out of his mouth. While his comrades, aside from Waddy and Patton, chased everything stuffed in a skirt and drank everything that was illegal back in Buckle of the Bible Belt Stephens County, where he was from, his most audacious adventure had been leading his Group to the Wing's Spring flag football championship.

"Yes," she smiled as he sidled back toward the fence.

"Where do ya live?"

"In Beccles. Little Chickasaw—that's the name of the house—on St. Anne's Way."

"Chickasaw? Like—the Indians?"

"Of course, silly."

He reckoned her family had some property after all, with a house name, as seemed common around there for the nicer homes. When he reached the top of the fence, she called, "But what is your name?"

He stopped, straddling the barbed wire. As the MPs gazed, he answered, "Oh, yeah. Lance. Lance Roark. What aboutchu?"

"Sarah Johnston."

"Well, all right then, Sarah Johnston," he said, clambering down to the ground on the other side. "How bout 10 a.m., Saturday?"

"Ten o'clock it is," she gave a snappy confident nod. Then she turned and plodded away, pushing her wheelbarrow.

He reckoned the MPs as the culprits, but he still marveled at how everyone from Cappuccio to Waddy could be gigging him about his "wee little Land Girl" by the time he reached the Officers Club just a few minutes later. The lesson he had taught in Patton's Bible Study the night before helped him stay poised when Cappuccio's little South Carolina sidekick blurted a vulgarity regarding Sarah's diminutive stature. The fact that Cochran wasn't even tight spurred him to pity him the more.

Not to be outdone, Cappuccio unleashed a barrage of lewd, explicit sarcasms that managed to encompass everyone from Bronson, who was a pilot and the biggest man in the 299th, to Sarah, to Lance, to Cochran's high school English teacher.

Feeling his "Irish" rise, he marveled at the persistent "lowest common denominator" nature of such exchanges and reckoned the better part of valor at that point was to bid a good night to all and find his bunk. There, he lay in the dark for several minutes smiling at the corrugated ceiling, saying his prayers, playing and replaying his few seconds with Sarah over and over in his mind, and smiling.

This is the most I've smiled lately....

—

The fragrance of blooming daffodils filled his nostrils and his soul as he rode into the sun-warmed little market town of Beccles on a base bicycle. He peddled over the Waveney Bridge and south the few blocks into the town center, where St. Michael's Church's 800-year-old stone tower loomed over the open-air vegetable market, the Fish and Chips shop, the Woolworth's Department Store—*Gee, we got one o them in Duncan*—the Regal and Odeon Cinemas, and other small businesses.

From there, he swung southeast along Blyburgate, which led into the newer "outskirts," such as they were, for a village of less than ten thousand souls.

Dang, I forgot to hit the PX for a hospitality pack. He was cross with himself to the point of tears.

Thought of it right after meetin' her, but since our typical fine breakfast this mornin' o powdered eggs, pancakes, and fried Spam, I've thought o' nothin' but her. Maybe they got'em a big spread after all—their house is named "Little Chickasaw,"—and don't need our goodies.

He shook his head as though debating someone else.

Nah, they all need what we got. This country's bout got the life choked out of it.

His eyes lit up as he spotted the Moll Confectionary to his left. It sat beside railroad tracks crossing the street, immediately beyond which the recently and partially built block that formed St. Anne's Road ran to the right, alongside the tracks. A middle-aged man bent over a broom and swept the pavement fronting the little store. He rode over to him.

"Mornin' to ye."

The short man eyed him. "Texas?"

He chuckled and reached out a hand. "Oklahoma. Lance Roark, sir."

"Percy Moll," the man sized him up. "Knew a couple of Oklahoma chaps in a previous, uh, detachment here."

"Yeah? They done already?"

Moll's eyes flickered, then he swept some more. "Yeah, they're done. Somewhere over Holland."

A jolt of startled sorrow coursed through him. "Oh."

Golly, why'd I ask that?

Even though the USAAF had established a twenty-five-mission limit for American bomber crewmen a couple months earlier, he had learned that no one had yet successfully completed the full twenty-five. It wasn't the sort of information you'd read in the newspaper or hear on the radio.

Think I better get my mind off this subject.

"Thinkin' to git me some candy and other goodies fer a friend."

"Sure," Moll pulled up his broom, turning to enter the front door without looking at him. He followed him into the store.

"Smells great in here." The door jingled closed behind him. "Like Christmas."

"Anything in particular, you want?"

"Hmm," he pondered the question. "Whadduya usually—whaddu they—"

"Who's it for?" Moll asked in his straight-on way. "A girl?"

"Well, yessir," he blushed.

"Someone round here?"

"Yessir. Matter o fact, I think she lives right down St. Anne's yonder."

"Oh? What'd be her name?"

"Sarah. Dang. Ye know I can't even remember her last—"

"Johnston?" Moll's whole countenance lit up. "Is it Sarah Johnston?"

"Why yeah, sure is," he nearly broke into laughter.

Feels swell just bein' in a conversation where er name's spoken. What the heck's gotten into me?

"Well, Leftenant Roark, tis nothin' too good for that lass," Moll swept out a much larger sack than the one he held and added numerous items to it, and to a second large sack. "Lives at Little Chickasaw, round the bend and down the end of St. Anne's."

"Whaddayu mean?"

"That girl is the cream of the crop, lad," Moll's words came faster than before, "sweet, with a heart of gold. Works with the urchins, the street waifs—what we got round here—and over in Lowestoft, too, and helps the old folks. Why, she tended this store you're standin' in for a fortnight or more when I came down with tuberculosis and the Misses had to tend me in that rat-eaten hospital. All, with every manner of tragedy striking her own kindred through the years. Yes," Moll handed the stuffed sacks to him, "nothing's too good for Sarah Johnston." The gray eyes narrowed again. "And nothing's too bad for the bloke that treats er less than the princess she is. Follow me, Yank?"

"Why, yes, sir. I mean no, sir. I mean, you can count on me to treat her ever manner o good, sir, and you can hold me personally accountable." He didn't realize he was backing up until he almost crashed through the blackout-curtained glass front window.

Moll cracked his first semi-smile. "I speculate she'll be all right with you, son." He hustled around from behind the counter. "Here, allow me to open that door for you."

Back out on the sidewalk, he balanced the sacks as he climbed onto the bicycle. "Thank ya again, Mr. Moll, sir." He noticed Moll's eyes growing distant, and when the man spoke, his voice was softer.

"I stood on this very sidewalk a month ago as one of those Focke-Wulf hot shots with the bright yellow noses tore into a group of Flying Fortresses," his voice was as solemn as Lance's heart was gay. "He must have hopped onto them from Normandy as they crossed back over the Channel from a bomb run. You have to credit the Jerry, he had some sort of spunk. Followed an entire formation here by himself, paying no heed to their guns or what Spits or other fighters might have come against him over our skies." He paused and stared up at the peaceful linen blue sky. "Standing right here, I saw three of them go down—one right next to the Common."

Dear God in heaven....

When Moll looked at him again, his eyes held something different. "Be good to our Sarah, lad. And take care of yourself."

THREE

Halfway down St. Anne's Road appeared the name "Chickasaw" engraved on the gate fronting an elm, cedar, and pine-rimmed lot that covered at least an acre.

Gee, nice spread.

His impressed whistle spooked some of the cluster of blackbirds blaring their own claim to the property.

They are well-to-do. He pulled the bike over and started to climb off. *But Mr. Moll said it was at the end of St. Anne's. They both said it was Little Chickasaw. Aw, that's prolly their idea of a joke.*

He shook his head and stepped off the bike. Just then, a red-faced little yardman appeared across the gate.

"May I elp ye, lad?"

"Oh, why yes, here to see Sarah Johnston."

"Down the way, Little Chickasaw," the man motioned, looking away as though he had often given the same directive.

"Oh, sorry," his face flushed. "Thank ye, sir." He climbed back onto the bike and rode on. The homes lessened in size until the road veered off into open country. Right there, as a train whistled north into Beccles to his right, was Little Chickasaw. Red roses, tended with care, wound their way up slender trellises both sides of the front door. A happy thrush peeked around them at him. He assayed that the small stone structure could contain no more than a kitchen, living room, and one bedroom.

"I know it's small for a bungalow with its own name," Sarah told him as they left Little Chickasaw on their bicycles a few minutes later. "But me da, 'e always had quite large plans for us—dreams, really, I realize now—and those included our moving up St. Anne's into the real Chickasaw house, which you no doubt saw en route here."

A couple of boys bicycled past them from the other direction. They stared popeyed at him in his forest green American airman's uniform and cap.

"Hello, Dale and Michael." Grinning, Sarah glanced back at him. "I believe you—and your uniform—have a couple of new admirers."

He looked back and saw the boys had stopped their bikes on the street. Talking to each other, they looked toward him.

"Yes, I'll be hearing all about this—most likely from their older sisters." Her amusement was plain in her voice.

As they rode past Chickasaw without noticing it, an exhilarating feeling swept through him, and he had no more control over it than he had over the Germans knocking another bevy of the group's Forts out of the sky the day before. The latter meant he, Waddy, Patton, and Trigger would fly their first mission Monday morning.

He and Sarah waved and exchanged greetings with Mr. Moll as they turned left past his sweet shop and headed back toward the town center.

Gee, does he sweep that sidewalk all day?

She burst into giggles, looking back. Dale and Michael were following them at a respectful distance, along with two more riders their age.

He looked at her and they both laughed.

"I warned you—big, tall 'Yank'!" They laughed some more.

"So, where we headed?"

"You'll see," she hid a new smile.

They pedaled through the town as a slight mist appeared. After growing up on the dry, scalding, wind-blown Oklahoma plains, he delighted in the moist, cloudy England that infuriated Army Air Forces personnel from top to bottom. He reared back his head, closed his eyes, opened his mouth, and let the mist soak into his face and onto his tongue. "Ahhh!" He couldn't help exclaiming as Sarah giggled at him.

"You like our wet conditions, I see!"

Soon they arrived at the Waveney docks, the bridge out of Beccles into Norfolk County just beyond.

"That's a strawberry of a young lass you're escorting today, Yank," the dock manager unmoored a small craft with an old outboard motor and handed him a pair of oars.

"So sorry," she tried to ignore the compliment, "there's no petrol to be had."

He grabbed the oars, delighted for the workout and the chance to perhaps show off a bit for her. He rowed them around the first bend of the Waveney, sprinkles dappling the dark quiet water. "So, this y'all's boat?"

"No, we had a boat, but Mum sold it to... help out after Da passed."

"Oh, I'm sorry, I didn't mean to—"

"No, tis all right. Mr. Wade back there, he's a very kind man, like so many in Beccles have been to Mum and me. He lets us use his boat anytime we wish."

"Oh, it's his boat?"

"Yes. He has had to sell the others he himself owned, the nicer ones. Twas through the help of other townspeople he even has the little boat now."

The light rain lifted as they talked, and he rowed. He couldn't believe it was past noon when they arrived at a small verdant clearing spread inside one of the little river's many bends.

"Gee, this day is flyin' by and I wish it'd slow down," he climbed out of the boat and helped her ashore, then handed her the picnic basket.

"Your little care packet," she spread a quilt and a lunch of cold sausage, tomatoes, and bread. "Crikey! Some of my friends have received such treats from other Yanks—other Americans—but tis my first time!"

As she started to bite in, she noticed him hesitate.

"Uh," he indicated the cause with a slight motion.

It prompted her as he had hoped. "Oh, yes, of course," she bowed her head, and clasped her hands.

After he prayed a short prayer brimming with gratitude toward God and thankfulness for his new friend they ate, and he asked about her father.

"He had such dreams, such aspirations for our family... for me, in particular."

"What sort of aspirations?" he was enthralled, the base, the Forts and the war consigned to a different and forgotten universe.

She looked at him. "No one has ever before asked me that question." She swallowed and looked out at the Waveney as another little boat, only the third they had seen during their idyll, headed back toward Beccles, an elderly couple both rowing. "He called me his princess and said every energy, every talent he owned were devoted toward giving me opportunities and blessings he had fallen short of having." Her voice grew raspy. "He said the greatest of these was the happiness in my face."

They both sat for a few moments, nothing sounding but the light lapping of the river against the bank a few feet away.

"Minds me a lot o my daddy." Some part of his brain was aware that never had the greens of trees, the fragrance of flowers, the twittering of orange, gray, and milky white English robins impressed his senses with more clarity, as though forming a portrait frozen in time and framed around him.

"Oh?" her interest piqued, snapping out of her distractedness.

It took long enough to tell that story and answer her questions about it, including Irish-Catholic Daddy's conversion to Mennonitism at age twenty-two after meeting Mama. He told of his Grandpa Schroeder, a church elder and preacher who suffered stinging persecution during World War I for not supporting America's fighting involvement. He spoke of Mama and Daddy's heart-wrenching migration to California, following the loss of the family farm, his friendship with and mission among the Comanche Indian tribe and his long-held intentions of devoting his life's work to them. He spoke wistfully of the shortgrass country. It was nearly two when they boated back toward Beccles.

As they did, the low scudding clouds melted away and he saw for the first time the true beauty of the river and the country around it. Then he found himself telling her of flying and the Mennonites, how the humble and valiant Matthew Haury, who had founded his family's church had won the Cheyennes to Christianity through His and Christ's blood and the refusal of both to shed it. She told him of helping tend the hurt and dying in the hospital eight miles over at Lowestoft on the North Sea, after the Germans bombed the town's dock area the year before. She told him how she wept for two full days after returning home, but when she stopped weeping, she knew she was now a nurse and would be the remainder of her days.

"So, why are you a Land Girl?"

"Because we need the extra shillings," her face was open and transparent. "Mum was in the other room when you arrived because she was weary and embarrassed to be seen afflicted with a palsy, unable to stand or walk or sit or any particular thing for long, only capable of bits of work at most, much to her chagrin. And I do it because England needs all of us, needs me, if she is to survive this terrible ordeal."

"I thought Land Girls was drafted."

"Drafted?"

"You know, ye git a letter from the gubment, sayin' ye gonna work for 'em."

She smiled. "Ah yes, well, tis true, though...." She stopped and pulled a chocolate, coconut-stuffed Bounty candy bar from the stash he had brought from the sweet shop. "Some of our boys are quite as resentful of, as grateful toward Yank soldiers, because you make thrice the pay they do." She un-wrapped the candy, her freckles seeming to emerge in a fuller sort of glory across her cheeks amidst the pastoral setting, though the glowing gray-green eyes were what held him mesmerized, they and the soft sing-song of her voice, in which a periodic flair of brogue asserted itself that was different from the other girls of Suffolk.

"Well...."

"One of our boys would really harbor a fancy for a girl to afford such a bountiful package of overpriced wartime delicacies," she said, her eyes glinting at him as she popped the first of the Bounty's two halves into her mouth, chewed it with relish, her eyes closing, then swallowed it. He watched the full transit, including the gentle gyration of her milky white throat, tardily noticing her eyes on him, as well as her smile.

"The government exempted me from farm service due to my nursing work, but I volunteered—twice, actually—and I work from midnight until eight o'clock in the morning at the hospital in Lowestoft, then on Mr. Price's farm by your airfield in the afternoons," she stored the second half of the Bounty away for another time, then locked her eyes onto his. "Among other reasons, my uncle lost his legs when a U-boat sunk his destroyer off Scapa Flow, my best friend from Beccles fell defending Singapore against the Japanese, and my closest cousin drowned when a Nazi bomb burst a water main and flooded the underground London tube where she was sheltering with her family during the Blitz."

He blanched. "I...."

"I do try not to hate them," her eyes misted. "Mum reminds me we are to pray for our enemies and those who persecute us, and that helps to calm me."

All he could think to do was look down at the neatly folded, bright blanket she had laid across the soft ground for their picnic.

"All the same, the acts they have committed have brought you here," acceptance and hope again filled her face, her voice sweet and soft, becoming of her diminutive stature, but like it, steeled with quiet strength.

"Your... accent," he didn't quite know how to ask.

She giggled and grabbed an overripe grape. "Me mum, then, she's Irish. I myself was born in Dublin."

He stared at her. "Gee, Sarah. My great-great-grandpa and his brothers, they come to Oklahoma, back when it was Indian Territory, from County Kildare, next county over from Dublin."

"Kildare, is it? Me mum is an O'Neill."

"Daddy's side's O'Rourke," his voice grew excited.

She grinned at him, then with a bit more lilt to her voice even than before, "Sure it is."

After a long time more, just before the angry young man with the cane, bandaged head, and Royal Air Face uniform shouted at them back at the Beccles quay, the sensation struck him of having lived through this experience, this conversation, before. Mary Katherine.

Then, his lips formed another word and his throat nearly spoke it.

Sadie.

A sorrowful feeling ebbed through his body, until the RAF fellow intervened.

"So, is this the one?" he pointed at Lance while almost screaming at Sarah.

"No, Andy, he doesn't even know him."

"Well then, who is it? Where is he?" The man was handsome, athletic and, he gauged, about his own age.

"Andrew." Wade, the dock manager, touched his arm gently.

"What do you want?" Andrew's emotional and physical pain was obvious.

"Please, come, let's go to the Hotel Waveney for tea and biscuits," Sarah interposed herself.

"I don't care for tea or biscuits!"

"Hey, buddy," Lance reacted to a terrible vulgarity of Andrew's toward Sarah, stepping toward him.

"I want to know where my wife and that Yank are!"

"Please, Andy," Sarah tried to reason with him, gently restraining Lance.

"Get away from me, you tramp!" His eyes were wild. "Yeer all tramps!" Then he collapsed to his knees and onto his buttocks and began to weep, gasping more vulgarities. "The whole country... our women, our girls, our wives—yeer all betraying us."

Goodness gracious—poor fella—that's awful.

"There's a good lad, now," Wade said, with obvious affection and sympathy, bending down and patting Andrew's shoulder. "All will be well, lad, you'll see, all will be well."

Sarah motioned Lance away with her.

"Low grade reprobates," he heard Andrew say before unleashing more agonized vulgarities as she took his arm and hurried him off. "With their candy and their dollars and their nylons and liberty leaves, in our very homes and neighborhoods. Some religious nation, some bunch of Christians they are! Mr. Wade, I know chaps who've lost their girls to African Yank soldiers up at Norwich—Negro Yank soldiers! Oh, we've lost more to them than they could ever save for us!"

The last sounds he heard of Andrew were long, guttural sobs.

—

Euphoria filled his heart as he bicycled over the Waveney bridge and back to the base just before dark.

She likes me, I know she does.

"Me!" he shouted to a wheat field rolling away from the hedgerows bounding the winding road. "And I'm gonna kiss er next time, see!" He unleashed a Rebel Yell of such magnitude that a flock of blue nuthatches fluttered up out of a tree and away over the field. "Thou hast put gladness in my heart, more than in the time their corn and their wine increased!" That provoked a bellow from a cow near a red barn on the other side of the road. He laughed at the animal. "I may take her back to the shortgrass country, and you with her!"

The mood at the base was less sanguine. Another rough mission into the Ruhr River Valley industrial colossus of western Germany had bloodied part of the group, and the rest of it had run into a Mixmaster of flak and Messerschmitts over the sub pens on the French coast at St. Nazaire.

Risinger's cheerful demeanor was absent as he shoved a chair out of the way and strode to the bar in the smoky Officers Club. He downed one shot of whiskey and called for another. He turned to Lance and Patton, "We're killing more French than we are Germans and we still ain't laid a glove on those pens, or even the supply chain for 'em."

"But the briefings say—" Patton began to object.

"The briefings are a crock!" Risinger cut in, his voice low and dangerous. "The ravings of fools tryin' to clean up the disasters of our intrepid leaders' theories and visions of grandeur. Well, gentlemen," he tossed back a third slash, "they're cozy in their castles around East Anglia with their Limey tarts—did you know some of them have bells on their nightstands provided by Wing to ring when they want servicing? The men fighting this war are paying for their mistakes with their own blood, along with the poor slugs we're supposed to be liberating."

Lance and Patton stared at one another as Risinger stalked out.

Dang, sounds like Rise means to curse his way all the way back to his sack.

He and Patton both knew their first mission was the next morning, assuming the damp, capricious English weather held. Thankfully, Sarah refused to be shouldered out of his thoughts, and as he and Patton walked silently back to their hut in the chilly spring evening air, thoughts and visions of her filled his mind and heart.

I do believe I could fly my Fort, which my salty crew has voted to name and paint Hellfire and Brimstone *in my honor, to France er even Germany and back under my own power, without engines, if it meant gettin' to see her again one minute sooner!*

FOUR

Kupchak stepped into his hut and stared at him. He looked up from his lamplit desk where he had his worn old King James Bible open to Psalm 91 and gave him a cheerful smile. "Why, ye look surprised, Kupchak."

"Well, I never yet seen a man already up and at it when I came to wake him, whether awake or asleep—and you look like you been at... that... for a while." Kupchak struggled to regain his composure. "Most men—all men, sir—they squeeze every last second o sleep out o the night before they has to get up and face... well, face what they got to face, sir."

Lance smiled at him.

"Plus," Kupchak said, "they sure's he—uh, heck, sir—got no smiles on their face, especially before their first mission."

He was not sure what to say.

"You's been different though, Lieutenant, ever since you got to this here base," Kupchak said. "And you's different now, too."

"Well, the Lord, He's already got my days numbered, Kupchak. And if today's my last—well, I hope it ain't, but if it is—then I reckon I be goin' to a lot better place than this'n anyhows, buddy."

Kupchak half-shook his head as he moved towards the sleeping Waddy on the other side of the coke stove that cut but didn't kill the hut's damp four a.m. spring chill. "And that's just it," he said. "Lotta joes gets over here with their Bibles and some even talk about Jesus some, for a while. Butchu—you seems to actually believe it. Like He's really there for you, sir. Lieutenant Clifton, up and at 'em, sir, time to hit the showers."

"Well that's cuz he is, Kups," he said. "He's always there." He paused. "He can be there for you too, buddy."

"Aw," Kupchak raised a hand, "That's all right, Lieutenant. Glad it works for you, but me and the Big Guy upstairs, well, we got our own understandin', see, Lieutenant?"

"Yeah? What's that?"

"Well," Kupchak said, with more confidence. "Me, I does my part down here, and Him?" He shot a glance upward. "He does His up there."

After he left, Lance looked back down at the yellowed pages of the Bible his Daddy had given him when he turned twelve.

Time fer one more drank. "*Thou shalt not be afraid for the terror by night; nor for the arrow that flieth by day... A thousand shall fall at thy side, and ten thousand at thy right hand; but it shall not come nigh thee.*" *I'm ready, sir.*

—

Most of the chatter and jocularity during breakfast in Officers' Mess Number Two came from men who had not yet flown a mission. This included his own non-com turret gunner, the muscular little Chicago Pole Ripkowski. That surprised him, because "Rip", since the initial assembling of *Hellfire and Brimstone*'s crew back in the States, had been one of its quieter members. Conversely, his waist gunners, Musso and Rodriguez, who had traded fists with local villagers, ground crewmen from another squadron, and each other, and jabbered incessantly, spoke hardly a word. O'Connor, meanwhile, as spunky as those two, if prone to even more violent yet less frequent outbursts, chatted no differently than he ever did, seemingly oblivious to the significance, and danger, of the day.

Who can figure how a man'll hannel a tough situation?

He consumed the familiar powdered eggs and silently thanked God for both His protection and the calming assurance of it.

Soon they filed past the MPs into the corrugated metal briefing building. The B-17 group's eighty-plus officer crewmen—pilots, co-pilots, navigators, and bombardiers—found seats in the metal folding chairs that filled the large room, arranged somewhat like a non-sloping theater. The men of *Hellfire and Brimstone* sat near him. A dark gray curtain spread behind most of the slightly raised stage at one end of the room. He saw his luminescent watch had just hit four a.m. when Lodge called the group to order.

"The first item of business is the Venereal Disease epidemic sweeping our base and most all of the others in East Anglia." Lodge held a poster aloft. "It is not the first time we've discussed this, and you will recognize these warnings, since they have been posted outside both the enlisted men's and officers' messes, as well as the Officers' Club, for some months now. Now gentlemen, the mounting toll this is taking on us...."

Lance had heard it before and he didn't need to be persuaded. *Everone from Risinger to Cappuccio's caught some form of it, and Trigger's real sore now and gettin' examined today by the base flight surgeon... if you can call him a surgeon with a few hours o first aid instruction durin' college and basic training.* He glanced upward as Lodge droned on. *Lord, I pray Your best for these men, sir, that they'd... Lord, hep'em to be the sorta men worthy o their own Sarah's. Hep me to be that sorta man.*

Tavington, sporting an immaculate olive uniform, topped by a cream cravat, strode to the stage as Lodge pulled back the curtain. He saw an enormous map of Europe. A scarlet thread ran from Beccles across the English Channel, into northern France, to an airfield halfway between Paris and the Channel.

"Le Chezvous—not a bad first outing for you new squadrons," Tavington intoned, indicating the destination with his pointer. "And there is light fog over East Anglia lifting, remarkably, as we speak, and clear skies until this evening over all of western and central Europe." An overhead projector threw the image onto the wall of an airfield and its adjacent buildings as Tavington continued. "Intelligence only last night reported a large number of gleaming new 109s—insofar as the Germans are capable of producing anything resembling a new version of the ancient beast—sitting on the ground at Le Chezvous awaiting dispersal to coastal defense positions. You'll not have to travel far into France, you'll have the Spits covering you most of the way, and we suspect this will be a complete surprise to Jerry, as our British friends say." The positive response that greeted this announcement demonstrated more verve in a few seconds than he had witnessed from the group since he rose an hour ago. "Stations at 0530, start engines 0540, taxi at 0550."

"Dang, he sounds like a limey." Lance couldn't suppress a smile at Waddy's whisper, genial face, cockeyed leather-billed flying cap, and loose demeanor.

It's good to be goin' into battle with Wad again.

Confidence and thankfulness filled him as he spotted Patton and Trigger in other seats down the row.

Too bad ole Cactus Face and Long John ain't here, too.

He wasn't so sure about his co-pilot, Clifton. That was one man who said little in normal doings and nothing today.

Don't wanna be unkind to a brave man, but I ain't decided yet, sir, even though we flown together fer months—but not yet in combat—if that fella's a cool, "slim customer," er....

Or a feigning incompetent.

Reckon I'm gonna watch him close to make sure, specially up in the air durin' missions.

Next, the pilots and co-pilots stayed for their own briefing while the bombardiers and navigators went to other huts for their own. The sergeant gunners, meanwhile, headed out from their own briefing to suit up and collect their ordnance. Then he and the other officers headed to the equipment room to suit up in their leather, sheepskin, parachutes, Mae Wests, masks, and other accouterments.

"How many kind o mud this sorry island got, anyhow?" Trigger scraped the distinctive gelatinous variety from his flight boots as they walked back outside.

More than any I ever seen.

The cold soupy air enveloped him as usual. Then it was time to shake hands and wish Waddy, Patton, and Trigger well. Waddy lingered a moment as Jeeps waited to take them and their fellow officers to their planes. Clifton, Ripkowski, and Goldsmith already sat in his, some yards away.

"Long time comin'." Waddy said with a smile in the lamplit darkness. They looked one another in the eye for a long moment, best as they could, considering the shadowy conditions. Then they shook hands.

"Good luck up there, Wad," he said, his heart was suddenly full. "See ya after." They both smiled again, nodded, and went to their Jeeps.

When he and his mates got to their plane, he stepped out and walked around it, inspecting it with the crew chief, Red McElroy. For the past few months, he had studied every moment he could, not only the plane itself and his own job as pilot, but those of the other nine crew members. He was pretty sure he knew at least a couple of their jobs better than they themselves did, and that might prove important if things got too crazy once they hooked it up with the Germans.

He saw the sergeant gunners setting up their guns in the plane and pulling belts of .50 caliber bullets out of their ammo boxes. For some reason, at that moment he noticed the enormity and grandeur of his aircraft, which he seldom did. He could not discern the camouflaged coloring and sky-blue underbelly, but the form that towered over him and stretched away nearly half the length of a football field paid mute testimony to the gathering might of the United States of America.

What a magnificent feat by the hand o' man. A wry half-grin tugged at the corners of his mouth. *I reckon the FW-190 is, too, though. I wonder if Cunnel Lindbergh is proud o what we've made o what he did so well.*

Colonel Charles Lindbergh was the most famous and beloved American of the Twentieth Century for his courageous and historic 1927 cross-Atlantic solo fight. That was until President Roosevelt and a powerful company of allies ranging from the famed newspaper columnist and radio gossipmonger Walter Winchell to F.B.I. Director J. Edgar Hoover, unleashed a vendetta on him for many reasons that had gravely damaged his, heretofore, stainless reputation in the eyes of the American public.

Many issues contributed to this "crusade" against the Lone Eagle. Foremost were Roosevelt's long and bitter resentment against Lindbergh for publicly exposing his disastrous 1934 Air Mail Act, and Lindbergh's more recent leadership of the America First movement that had vigorously exposed and denounced the third-term President's secretive machinations to maneuver the pre-Pearl Harbor United States into World War II. "Copperhead," "traitor," "anti-Semite," "fellow traveler of the Nazis," and "Nazi" itself were a few of the remarkable appellations with which Roosevelt and his minions branded the legendary patriot. Chief among those detractors was Roosevelt's acerbic Secretary of the Interior, Harold Ickes.

From a chance 1939 meeting in a White House bathroom prior to his meeting the President with a delegation of Mennonite leaders to advocate for non-combatant roles for the denomination's pacifist adherents should war come, Lindbergh had become a sort of mentor to the lanky farm boy. He influenced many of his career flying and test-piloting opportunities, some in concert with Lindbergh's friend Thomas Murchison, the Oklahoma oil magnate and hard-bitten father of his college flame and now Big Band vocal sensation Mary Katherine— "The Golden Girl with the Golden Voice."

Oh, I reckon the Cunnel's "Mister" now, since the President publicly insulted him a couple years ago and he resigned his commission. Wonder where he is.

A little later, they all gathered around him on the ground a few yards from the plane line in a huddle like back when he used to call defensive signals for the Sooners.

"Well...." He was suddenly at a loss for words. He had watched Morgan, captain of the *Memphis Belle*, namesake of that man's beloved fiancée back in the States—and which had half a dozen missions remaining to get to twenty-five, meaning they could go home—conduct his own huddles.

Not one crew in the Eighth Air Force had yet reached twenty-five before getting shot out of the sky.

He searched for words as his nervous crew fidgeted around him.

I think Morgan does this a lot better.

Then O'Connor, of all people, said, "You wanna say a prayer, Parson?"

He looked up, thinking it a joke. It wasn't.

"Why, sure." He pulled off his leather aviator helmet and the cap and lining beneath it. He repeated some of the lines fresh on his mind from Psalm Ninety-one. When he looked up, the crew seemed calmer. He'd never seen the rosary O'Connor had tucked inside his palm before. "Well, fellas, I ain't got nothin' fancy to say, cept I'm purty proud to be flyin' with ya. If we all keep our heads and remember our jobs, we'll be jist fine." He looked around the group and everyone just sort of nodded and indicated they were with him. "Jist remember—we got each other." He could feel something in those words draw everyone together, though he had no idea what it was.

As they broke up and headed for their stations, he came face to face with O'Connor. Something in his expression prompted the tail gunner to confide in him. "Ah, Parson, don't get the wrong idea. See this thing?" He brandished the rosary beads. "Blacker than the ace o spades, right? That's because I ain't hardly acquainted with 'em. But chu can be sure I intend to get that way."

Interesting....

"So, what would they look like if you were acquainted with em?"

"Well," O'Connor said, "most pious person I ever met was Sister Margaret at my old school back in Boston. They say that lady, when she wasn't feeding the poor or trying to teach us bunch of fools, she was prayin' with folks, for 'em, or over 'em. And her rosary, why the beads on it were purpler than a cluster of the juiciest ripe grapes you ever saw on a vine," O'Connor said.

He nodded as he put his head gear back on, "Hmm."

Strapped in his seat a few minutes later, Clifton and Utah Cade, the flight engineer, checking the instruments and fluid levels, and McElroy and his boys pulling out the wheel blocks, he felt a surge of excitement and anticipation, alloyed by a strange nostalgia and longing for home and all the folks he suddenly missed with an overwhelming sense of loss. He took a deep breath and silently prayed.

"O God the Lord, the strength of my salvation, thou hast covered my head in the day of battle."

Then he shoved open the small port side window next to him and shouted out it, "Clear right, clear left!"

He flipped the starter switch on *Hellfire and Brimstone*'s first engine, the far left of the four, and it whined in response. The engine coughed, sputtered and spewed smoke that rendered the scene darker than it already was.

Danged wet, cold, English weather.

The propeller spun, and the engine burst to life. He flipped the switches for engines two through four and each, in turn, roared to life. He could feel the ship shaking, its power consolidating.

It's become—part of me.

A few minutes later, he pulled the Fort out of its hardstand, taxied onto the perimeter road and along it for a couple hundred yards, then over the runway approach path, and finally onto the mile-and-a-half-long landing strip. Someone fired a pistol a quarter mile ahead to start the mighty column forward.

FIVE

It took nearly an hour for all three groups of the Wing, sixty planes, to form up and head for the splasher beacon down near Scole, which would help direct them south out of England, to the gray-green Channel and France. A sense of pride rose within him as two other groups came alongside them from others of the dozens of American air bases cross-hatching East Anglia.

Recalling how Morgan, Risinger, and others among the better Fort pilots consistently checked signals with their crewmen regarding the latter's various jobs, he started doing so with more vigor than ever before.

"Start your log and check your Morse equipment," he ordered Blevins, the radio operator, through the interphone. "Gimme a position report now and do it ever half hour till we're back."

"O'Connor, oxygen checks?" The tail gunner whose responsibility it was to have each crewman confirm from his own station he was alert and well supplied with oxygen once they hit ten thousand feet responded with a microphone click.

"Clifton, you ain't said nothin' 'bout our gauges." He glanced at his copilot as the four engines roared. "We're leadin' this element, so check if Wad and Patton nestled up to us good." Two B-17s had collided just as the 299th formed during its previous mission. Eighteen of the twenty men on board did not survive. "You got them cowl flaps shut down? And check the liaison and command radio channels."

Clifton's got a lot to do and I'm fraid I need to ask him is he doin' it all. Plus, seems like I got more to do myself than I've ever had before. Ever time I take care o one thang, three more occur to me. Dang, hope I shaved close enough.

Waddy had told him one of the group's waist gunners forgot to shave on a recent mission. What with a high altitude on-board temp of minus-sixty degrees in that breezy part of the plane, enough air had gotten inside the man's mask due to his one-day stubble that condensation formed up, blurred his vision, and caused him to miss a point-blank shot at an FW that screamed past and raked the next Fort with cannon fire, sending it and its whole crew to earth in a flaming orange fireball.

All this, and despite his layers of woolens, alpaca, leather, and insulation, he didn't think he'd ever been as cold—aching, painful cold—as when they reached 20,000 feet crossing into France. At the same time, he felt sweat forming on his forehead, lip, and under his arms.

Gotta calm down. The Lord is my shepherd, I shall not want....

After a moment, he realized the crew seemed crisp and more poised than he felt. Plus, it seemed they were barely past the French coast when they hit the Initial Point.

Looks like ol Lodge was right for once when he told us we'd be over France hardly more than twenty minutes.

He'd already given Remington, the bombardier, the customary control of the plane. Remington would guide it to the drop point with the miraculous Norden electronic bombsight apparatus connected to the cable running from his position in the plexiglass astrodome nose through the length of the plane to the tail.

"Jeez, Parson, not an ME, FW or even a JU in sight, and we're almost to target?" O'Connor asked.

"Shut up!" He shot a look at Clifton, whose job it was to maintain interphone order, including O'Connor's streams of vulgarities and profanities. Everyone knew to keep their chatter to a minimum long before getting this close to a target. Calming himself again, he saw out his small side windows the quilted verdancy of Flanders far below. There wasn't even any flak until after the bombs from the forward squadrons began to explode on the ground ahead.

Sakes alive, we caught 'em with their underoos down, and it's an airfield brimmin' with fighters that're fannin' all over western Europe.

The patchy flak from the Germans' legendary 88-millimeter howitzers, none of it intruding close to *Hellfire and Brimstone*, mesmerized him when he spotted it.

Looks like gray mushrooms openin' up, or dark popcorn apoppin'. Looks so soft and quiet and harmless.

And so, it was, when half a mile or a mile away.

FWs ranged in ranks by the hundreds along the edge of the field as he passed over, smoky explosions bursting up from it.

Dang, now this is doin' good.

His blood raced and goose bumps rippled his chilled skin.

Ever one o them hombres we splat, they's one less contraption gonna bring terror to a whole bunch o our boys—and people that love 'em. I know Mama'll understand once I git to explain it all to her in person.

A pang struck him in his heart as he felt the plane buck when Remington loosed its payload.

When'll that be, though?

A slight concussion from a flak burst not far away jolted him back to attention as they approached the rally point a few miles past the airfield to turn home. "O'Connor, any bandit traffic back there?"

"*Nada, Parson,*" O'Connor responded over the interphone. "*Contrails jackin' with 'em's all.*"

Indeed, the condensation vapor trails from the squadrons ahead of them now filled his own vision, forming a sudden fog that forced him to concentrate on his instrument readings and gauges. "Keep your eyes peeled, Clifton. This might be dicey makin' the curve to head back." He grew tense, remembering there were other crews besides his for whom this was their first combat mission, and reports of midair collisions of Forts and Liberators due to bad visibility were legion.

Good grief, the sweat on my face is startin' to freeze in my goggles, and my feet are numb with cold, even with all these layers o covering. I gotta pay attention to make sure it doesn't cut off my oxygen flow....

After a couple of Psalmic prayers and a few more stressful minutes, he reached the safe point and the formation spread out, diluting the concentration of vapor trails and aiding his vision. Once he had *Hellfire and Brimstone* back down around ten thousand feet several minutes later, the cold relented and he pushed his goggles up.

"That drink looks pretty good, huh, Parson?" Ripkowski hung down over the Channel in his ball turret as they neared the English coast.

"Sure does, Rip!" Relieved, Lance also ignored the mandated radio silence.

"Hey, Parson, think we took a big hunk outa some Jerry on our first mission," Musso said, through the interphone, from his waist gunner station as they lumbered over Dover's gleaming white cliffs. He reported graphically *"Chili Relleno back here, didn't even get a chance to shoot nothing off hisself."*

"And this greasy-headed wop didn't even get to shoot off his own greasy pompadeer!" Rodriguez retorted, radio protocol cast to the wind.

"Pompadeer!" Musso howled with laughter *"What kinda spick word is that? They teach you that down in Chihuahua, amigo!"*

"El Paso, you gangster. Gonna buy you some spaghetti and linguino for surviving your first mission without wetting your scared dago panties. Oh wait, everybody, I think he did!"

"Linguino, you dumb chili pep—"

"Alright, we know y'all love each other, but knock it off." Lance couldn't help laughing. "Save it fer the interrogators in the briefin' room." A couple of the crew laughed.

"Hey, Musso," O'Connor piped up from the tail. *"I'm savin' something back here for that chubby Red Cross squirrel you been moonin' for back at the base. Unless you want it first!"*

Lance calculated that Musso's spirited response may have contained more cuss words than any such outburst he had ever heard, and certainly ranked high for his imaginative usage of the terms.

"Alright, let's observe some interphone protocol," Clifton finally spoke up. So stiff and unconvincing was he, that everyone went silent for a moment, then erupted into convulsions of laughter that even Lance joined.

"Hey, Clifton," Musso was the first to recover. *"I got some protocol back here for you and your Ivy League—"* Lance had to marvel at the velocity and creativity of the man's lewd riposte.

And so it went, as *Hellfire and Brimstone* made its first victorious return to base. Only twenty-four more remained.

"They didn't lay a glove on us." O'Connor said, as Lance pulled the plane onto its hardstand back at Beccles. *"We are some fearless, righteous, mother-lovin—"*

—

Bad weather stood down the 299th for the rest of the week, so most of the other flyers hopped a rare weekend liberty run for London or at least Ipswich, the largest city in East Anglia, forty miles south. Lance grabbed a hospitality pack from the PX, then bicycled into town to see Sarah, the marathon rain pausing as he did.

When he arrived at Little Chickasaw, no one answered for a couple of minutes. He was about to sit down on the little front stoop and wait when the door creaked open and he saw, stooped with a cane, rising barely four-and-a-half-feet high, Sarah's mother.

"Yes, do come in, young man," her voice was a lilting Irish brogue, her eyes the color of Sarah's, her hair the same color as well, though streaked with gray, and her pale, fortyish face, pretty and unlined. It took her many seconds to turn her body in the direction to move toward a nearby chair and more seconds yet to make her way to it.

Golly, poor sweet lady, goin' through all that jist to answer my knock at the door. And what love for her daughter to do so?

They talked of roses and Dublin and the wealth of America as he savored a Russell Stover's chocolate. She spoke of how the handsome and light-footed lad from Beccles had charmed her even as he shouldered an automatic rifle as one of the hated Black and Tans who occupied her unruly section of Dublin, before the English and Irish crafted the Irish Free State—which was neutral in the current war.

"Life never gave him the dreams that filled his heart," there was only a twinge of poignancy on the edge of her gentle voice. "But, I loved him for them and always will." She looked him in the eye. "And he would not suffer his little girl not to be treated as the princess she is."

The steel chains he and Daddy had wrapped around drilling pipes back in the oil patch possessed no more strength than the voice and eyes conveying the message just given.

"Yes Ma'am."

"Your Yank blokes are charming, handsome, and tall, and they have lots of money," she looked him directly in the eye. "Lots of dollars in their pockets. But they are also sex-mad. Far more so than our own lads. Like nothing I've ever before seen." She eyed him even tighter. "I trust, with the religious values Sarah claims you possess, you don't share their... appetites? Or at least their pursuit of those appetites?"

"Uh, oh, no, ma'am." He leaned involuntarily towards her as he spoke. "I mean, yes, I mean, I do, you know, I'm a normal fella, but I don't, I never, I would never—well sometimes, ye know, it's hard, but the Lord...."

The steel in her eyes turned jolly again and her mood sweet as she struggled, with his help, to her feet.

"Sure, and I'm an ungracious hostess not to have offered you tea before now," she seemed to stifle a laugh.

Sarah arrived a half-hour later, tired but excited at his presence. "So sorry to be tardy, but they found an unexploded Jerry bomb next to hospital just as I was leaving for home."

He felt a jolt in his stomach, worry for her physical safety for the first time intruding upon him. He didn't know what to say and so said nothing, but his concern grew as they bicycled down St. Anne's. The reappearance of Dale, Michael, and this time, four other friends bicycling a ways behind them lifted his spirits.

"Hmm... if I didn't know better, I'd be bound they were waiting for us to emerge from Little Chickasaw," she seemed delighted, her eyes glinting, "perhaps to fetch a look at their new idol?"

"Aw, phooey," he waved his hand in dismissal. Then he spotted two of them clutching model B-17s in one hand.

Hah! They're even painted olive like ours.

The escort had grown to eight riders by the time he and Sarah reached the common, an enormous mowed field on the northeast edge of Beccles where people walked, picnicked, and rode horses. His concern for her safety had returned and deepened by the time they laid aside their bikes and walked, the chill mist bracing against his face, their followers gone.

She stumbled in a divot. "Oh, they've been playing cricket out here again."

He caught her arm to help keep her from falling, it just seemed natural to keep gentle hold on it, especially when she nestled gingerly against him.

Goodness, I don't think I've had this feeling since the night Sadie and I fell to the ground in her pasture....Why, I feel like I could end the war with my next mission, bring all the hating parties to the table, if not the altar, for reconciliation, and give Sarah a life o happiness and fulfillment I'm pretty sure she ain't never dreamed possible.

For the next two hours, he told her of his life.

Goodness, I been gabbin' on about myself! I want to hear more about her!

A pale March sun had seeped through the clouds over the train lumbering past Little Chickasaw when two hours later they returned.

He had spoken of everything he could conjure except the worry growing in his stomach about her safety in Lowestoft. And on the road back and forth from here.

She turned a doe-eyed gaze up to him that poleaxed him where he stood on her porch with the scent of roses in his nostrils and the air of reinvigorated hope in his heart. "Somehow," her sweet voice trilled, "when I am with you, I feel as though all the evil deeds ever contemplated by man could not so much as touch me."

To his shock, the kiss that followed—after an aborted first attempt that pecked her nose, causing them both to giggle—was the longest, softest, and surely the sweetest of his nearly twenty-six years of virgin life.

SIX

Hellfire and Brimstone's next flight proved even more of a "milk run", the flyers' term for an easy mission with little danger from enemy fighters or flak, coupled with modest weather and distance conditions, than the first. The target was a Belgian town where the Germans had established a railroad marshaling yard for supplies and troops going into northern France. Only two groups, around forty planes, participated. Trigger had to abort the mission due to his plane's landing gear failing to fold up.

The target didn't seem that significant of a complex to him and he wondered whether the Germans shared the sentiment, since only a handful of fighters contested them, on their return trip after the bombing, and only light anti-aircraft fire opened up on them, wounding two crewmen on one plane and slightly damaging another. All the Forts returned home safely.

The main image he carried back to the station with him was that of a young German pilot's face, his goggles pushed back, flashing down across his

B-17 windshield from one o'clock high in his ME-109 and toward the lower squadron. His eyes had taken a snapshot of the youth's face, nervous, earnest, and determined.

A far cry from the propaganda poster in the Beccles town center of a snarling, foaming "Hun" barbarian machine-gunning women and children.

One of Mama's recent letters—she wrote at least twice a week—mentioned the New Deal had apparently still not solved Oklahoma's problems. *"More folks coming out here now than in the '30s, even with all the boys going for soldiers, and here he's had a whole decade to do something about it."*

Another letter urged him to remember that some of his own kinfolk no doubt wore the German colors. *"Misguided as their cause may be, son, remember that Jesus said to pray for our enemies, and not to return evil for evil. In the situation in which you have placed yourself, surely you should never hate them, son, or even revel in their misfortune. Too many folks around here are so filled up with hate, especially toward the Japanese, it is eating them to pieces. Don't put yourself at cross-purposes with our Lord regarding these supposed enemies."*

Mama. He marveled anew at her. *You the best they ever was.*

Lingering barrage balloons still dotted the mostly-sunny spring afternoon skies off to the west leading into London. He committed again to praying both for the Germans and for as little suffering as God would see fit to grant to all parties, in particular the innocents—Germans and otherwise—suffering under Nazi tyranny, as well as those living under British and American bombs. The Brits were apparently wreaking devastating carnage with their night bombing on German cities.

Ole Wad was right when he told me 'bout the difference 'tween the Brits' style o bombin' cities and our bombin' military targets. Thank you, Lord, fer puttin' me in a country wouldn't never do the other. Thank you fer not puttin' me in a situation to hurt my conscience, sir.

He glanced up and back at Waddy, off his starboard wing, and remembered something else his old buddy had told him between games of flag football on the station infield a couple of days ago. It had been when Beccles' weather was fine but a thunderstorm system covering most of western Europe had grounded the 299th. Patton, for all his pious modesty, seemed to have friends sprinkled through all sections of Army Air Forces hierarchy. He had told Waddy that the dramatic destruction of German cities by the British campaign of night bombing was having significant impact on the Allied air chiefs. It especially contrasted with the withering damage the Germans were unleashing on the American daytime bombing crews. Bomber Command head, Arthur "Bomber" Harris, had convinced the British leadership, up to and including Churchill, that the Allies should mesh U.S. Eighth Air Force operations with— "Under, I reckon they mean," Waddy had said—the Brits' night campaign. And Churchill had nearly convinced American leadership, including Roosevelt, "to lay down for it." Waddy had been indignant.

"Bunch o peckerwoods. Patton said he wouldn't fly such missions, jist a droppin' bombs on cities full o folks down below. Killin' women and children like his own little girl back in Chickasha, with nary a mind to who ye hit, and neither'll I." A chill apart from the twenty-three-thousand-foot height he saw still registering on his altimeter rippled through him as he remembered Waddy's next words. "Bobby, he said them Limeys fixin' to start droppin' incendiary bombs on folks, too. You know, bombs that jist burn ever thang up, mostly people, cause they ain't gonna burn concrete and stone and metal and steel buildings."

He had shaken his head, not believing the "good" side would commit such acts. Waddy didn't really, either. They agreed it was probably just potential acts that would never happen.

Fog socked in East Anglia when they got over it, but Operations had lit the fuel-filled pipe that ran all the way around the station, outside the perimeter track, and he could see the fountains of fire leaping twenty-five feet into the hazy air through intermittent holes in the pipe. He felt confident he could have landed using just his approach instruments even if he had Clifton, who appeared to have developed a nervous tic in one eye, blindfold him. His enthusiasm waned, however, when he saw a Fort ahead of him skid off the landing strip and crash into a storage shed. Squinting through the eerie maw, he saw ambulances, men on bicycles, tow trucks and firetrucks converge on the shed like an old Oklahoma land run.

Several planes had to make a couple extra passes and one even flew to Seething, the next station north, about halfway to Norwich, but the accident inflicted nothing more than a few bumps and bruises and everyone else landed safely.

After he touched down and taxied in *Hellfire and Brimstone,* he caught Clifton staring at him. "What is it?"

"Nothing," Clifton pulled off his interphone mike and detached both his electrified suit from its power cord and his oxygen supply.

"Naw, really, what is it, bub?" He was curious if he had erred.

Clifton shook his head. "Well… sir, the way you put her down, any time, in any conditions, the way you fly her. It makes me a little jealous, to tell the truth." He glanced out his side window. "Look at that. Half the squadron—those that are even at this landing strip—are still circling." He grabbed the flight clipboard, turned his attention to the dash, and began flicking off switches and taking readings, saying nothing else.

That evening, Clifton read a book in his hutment, but the rest of the 299th were lords of the universe, at least in the Officers' Club. Sober, Lance found he had a knack for winning poker hands from scotch and soda-swilling fellow officers.

"You're either the luckiest or the cheatinest poker player I ever seen," Cappuccio complained, sweeping the full house he had just had bested by a straight flush off the scuffed, green-sheeted table and onto the floor, along with a blizzard of penny, nickel, and dime chips.

"Had me some good teachers back at the OU Sigma Chi house," he said, winking at Waddy and Trigger.

Cappuccio got up and headed for the bar, Cochran and another friend accompanying him. "Honest to God, can't trust a man refuses free Scotch."

"Huh?" Cochran stared at him as they walked off.

"After the post-mission briefings," Cappuccio added his own complaint, "that Bible-thumpin Okie, he don't take it, even when it's offered free."

He noticed, as he had before, the handsome, chiseled face of Clarke, another of the table's losers and a pilot in one of the other squadrons, staring at him with mirthless blue eyes. "Parson," the man gave a wry smile and spoke in barely more than a whisper. No one seemed to notice this but Lance, who smiled at him. It did not have the same winning effect on Clarke that it did most folks.

The Tannoy intruded on their fun with a ten o'clock announcement eerier-sounding even than normal with the stout breeze that had kicked up outside. It proved more unwelcome than eerie, as the 299th had a second straight mission scheduled in the morning, and this one was a marathon return to Wilhelmshaven, Germany.

"Well," Waddy grinned, "We jist kick their tail tomorrow like we did today!"

He noticed that the newer officers, like himself, laughed, but Risinger and the other more seasoned ones displayed a variety of expressions, none of which could have been mistaken for smiles.

—

Back in the chilly hutment, he sat at the small metal desk he and Waddy shared and wrote to Sarah by the light of the lone dim bulb hanging from the ceiling. Recalling he owed Mama a response to her latest letter, he mused on what Sarah might be doing at that moment.

Is she in bed asleep, listenin' with her mom to one o them funny English radio comedies she loves, workin' in the hospital at Lowestoft, er maybe on her way to and from one o those places?

The image of her slender, petite body flashed into his mind and he shook his head and forced himself to think of her kneeling at the ancient stone Anglican church in the Beccles town square the Sunday before on the crocheted kneeler her grandmother had knitted. Then he remembered the milky white glow of her slender exposed knees. He thought he might have to slap himself to shake off the sensations invading his body, but he commenced instead to write to her of his optimism that "together our two countries are doing such good. And you know I wasn't raised to love England, nor was I raised to believe in or certainly fight in war, or even participate in the governments that wage it. But somehow, when I think of you, when I'm with you, when I think of us two together, I get the feeling there ain't nothing we can't accomplish when we are doing it together."

He stopped writing and stared without seeing at the mountain of laundry he and Waddy had piled in a corner, his heart speeding up.

It all comes back to us bein' together, Sarah and me. Sarah Johnston Roark. I don't want to ever be without her again.

The revelation, as overwhelming as it was sudden, unleashed a rush of blood through his head. He smiled, then laughed out loud.

Just then, Waddy rambled through the door, barely fitting. "Aw, look atchu!" he teased with a grin. "I seen that grin on you even durin' your post-mission interrogations. You in love with that little girl in town, ain'tchee!"

He started laughing out loud and couldn't stop and Waddy couldn't, either. "I know, buddy, I know how ya feel!" Waddy nodded laughing. "I love my Maggie girl so much sometimes I—I feel I'm fixin' to bust wide open into a field o daffodils!"

His brow crinkled. "A field o...."

Then they were laughing again, hollering, Rebel yelling.

"She a good lil gal, ain't she?" Waddy was suddenly serious.

"Aw Wad, she's the best."

"But," Waddy's brow furrowed a shade. "What about...?"

"Mary Katherine?"

"Naw, the Indian girl, the flyer."

"Sadie?"

"Well, yow."

"What about her?"

"Well, she's the one ye always loved, I could tell that from the start."

"But'chu never even met her. Heck, I ain't seen her since I knowedja," his voice grew softer. "And she's long married and got her kids."

For a moment, they just stood there, all of a sudden both aware of the many years and shared miles between them.

"Aw, she's a great girl, buddy." With a whoop, Waddy was bearhugging him and lifting him off the floor. "Gonna take ye home a war bride! And a dang fine lookin' one, too!"

"Hey, hold it down in there, lovebirds, we tryin' to study!" Trigger shouted from the next room.

"Hey, I'm gunna come in there and study my boot up your tailpipe, Trigger McCurdy!" Waddy darted toward Trigger's room laughing.

—

As they breakfasted the next morning in their officers' mess, Trigger stared at the mound of egg shells Schmitty, the rough-hewn head cook, frequently displayed at the serving line.

"What is it?" Lance noted Trigger's scowl as he was spooning down some runny oatmeal.

"Why, that—" Trigger pointed at the cracked egg shells. "Jist figured it out… in between loogeyin' and blowin' his snot into the food of us that cracks wise with him, he been flashin' them broken shells 'bout half the days we been here, givin' us to think he got us real eggs, 'stead o that powdery dung." He looked over at Waddy, a couple seats away. "That sewage taste like real eggs to you, Wad?"

"Heck, no!" Waddy chortled as he folded a clump of the gelatinous mush into a piece of toast and woofed it down.

"Hey Schmitty!" Trigger summoned the cook, jumping to his feet. "Where you git them shells, jackleg? Under your mama's dress?"

Schmitty, flushed with anger and embarrassment, fired back a string of expletives at the "Okie." A chorus of howls cut off his next sentence. "I—hey— you bunch o spoiled—"

The first round, metal plate fired at Schmitty took out the egg shells, which showered over him. The second one splattered him with oatmeal from a nearby kettle. The third one, flung by Waddy, hit him in the forehead and knocked him over a cart loaded with empty glasses, which crashed to the floor shattering, a stone cold Schmitty landing atop them.

"Sheesh," Trigger jumped up and down in excitement. "Good shot, Wad."

"Dang," Waddy shrugged, embarrassed. "I didn't mean to hit him." Even with Schmitty down, a volley of plates zinged at the serving area. One nearly took the head off a skinny young man sporting an ill-fitting uniform that was sans insignia and markings. He looked vaguely familiar to Lance, and he ducked just in time to avoid getting a new part in his sandy-colored hair.

While he and Waddy hurried to check on Schmitty, even as more plates flew, and raucous laughter and shouts resounded through the tin hut, he nudged Waddy and pointed, "Hey, Wad, don't that guy look familiar?"

"I dunno," Waddy looked around the raucous scene, "but them experienced crews don't hardly grunt in here, and they're takin' the opportunity to let the badger loose."

When they reached Schmitty, they saw a round greasy pancake laying over his sleeping face.

"Shoot, happiest I ever saw that rascal," Waddy jerked a thumb at the fallen cook. When Schmitty emitted a snore, he and Lance laughed. Waddy looked over at the skinny young man, his eyes flickering and said, "Yeah, sure, that's old Cronky, our OU radio announcer, ain't it?"

"Hey, Cronky!" He hustled to him with Lance in tow.

Twenty-seven-year-old Walter Cronkite's eyes widened in surprise. "Why— Waddy," relief taking hold of him. "And Lance? What the—"

He and Waddy bear-hugged Cronky front and back, squeezed him till he grunted and hollered for mercy, and lifted him up and down off the ground.

"Why, ye ole sharper, Cronky!" Waddy grabbed his arm as Lance fetched Cronkite's hat off the floor and mashed it back on his head. "What the heck ye doin' here?"

Billowing with pride and joy at seeing the familiar faces, whose collegiate gridiron exploits he had broadcast on Oklahoma City's WKY Radio in his first job after graduating from the Sooners' arch rival University of Texas, he had a still-evident Lone Star drawl that seemed too deep and robust for a man of his diminutive size. "Well, boys, I'm writin' for the United Press now, and they sent me over here to cover the war. And now I volunteered to fly with the Eighth and tell folks back home what y'all are up to."

"Dang, Cronky," Lance directed him toward the Schmitty-less serving line, "why don'tcha fly in one o our planes? We'll show ya how it's done!"

"Aw, I'd like to, boys, I sure would," Cronkite grimaced, spooning himself some of Schmitty's "eggs", "but they got me lined up to fly with some guy name o Clarke."

"Oh," Lance traded glances with Waddy.

"Know him?"

"Uh, yeah, sure."

"What's he like?"

"Uh, well, he's a real experienced pilot, only got a mission er two left, so he must be good, cuz—" He looked around as they got back to the table and dropped his voice. "—well, hardly no one round here's made it to their twenty-fifth mission yet, and he bout has."

Cronkite's eyes widened as a glass of orange juice halfway to his mouth halted in transit. "Well—what about'chu boys? You gonna make it to your twenty-fifth?"

"Well shoot, yow, Cronky!" Waddy slapped him so hard on the back that he spit out a mouthful of eggs. "Lance and me, we always git er done!"

Just then Lodge, the Ground Exec, appeared. "Oh, there you are," he eyed Waddy and him warily. "Mr. Cronkite, I'm sorry to say Captain Clarke has, uh—"

"He has him the clap's, what he has!" Trigger couldn't stop himself from shouting from several seats away. "From that heel-clickin' Piccadilly Commando with the snappin' dalmation he wall-jobbed last liberty!"

A chorus of laughs cascaded down on Lodge from everyone in earshot.

"You mean she wall-jobbed him," Cappuccio's tone directed more toward Trigger than Clarke or his paramour.

"That Trigger's gittin' crazier longer we over here," Waddy dropped his voice and spoke, only half-jokingly.

"No," Trigger was on a roll now, "he got her down to a pound-and-a-half."

"Yeah, on his fourth vertical," Cappuccio offered a barking laugh.

Tiring of the technicalities, Trigger unleashed a middle finger at Cappuccio.

Cappuccio's buddy Cochran piped up and returned fire at Trigger, giving his utmost to put his entire upper body into the obscene gesture he threw to the Oklahoman's declarations.

"That'll be enough!" Lodge trained his gaze on Trigger, who had jumped to his feet in a flash and stepped toward Cochran.

Recognizing himself as the focus of Lodge's anger, the five-foot-six-inch Trigger clenched his jaw, then shot Cochran a murderous glance, muttered, "Sawed off piece o—," and returned to his breakfast.

Lodge turned back to Cronkite, who was uncomfortably awaiting what was next—breakfast, orders, or a mess table brawl. "We need to reassign you to…"

"I'd like to go with Lieutenant Roark here," Cronkite pointed at Lance.

"Uh," Lodge hesitated. "Well, Lieutenant Roark's only flown—"

"I flew sub-huntin' missions in the Gulf fore I ever got over here, sir," he sat up straight. "Me and Wad both."

"We're already acquainted, sir," Cronkite indicated Lance and Waddy with a gesture. "It'd be a comfortable setup, and—well—you and I are both already sorta out on a limb on this with my higher-ups back in the States. I think this'd help it run smoothly, Sir."

Lodge didn't appear pleased with anyone at the table, and he felt all their eyes on him, regarding a matter that wasn't his doing nor preferred by him.

"All right, Roark, get your crew and meet Cronkite and me in the briefing room in ten minutes."

SEVEN

Feels like we jist kicked off fer a big game back at OU.

His adrenaline raced as they rumbled northeast over the North Sea, the first hint of light setting the distant horizon aglow. Flying in the "Coffin Corner," the lowest, farthest back, and most dangerously-exposed squadron of the entire two hundred-bomber stream was no thrill, however. Flyers also referred to it as the penalty box, the shooting gallery, walking the plank, and No Man's Land. Risinger and others had shared numerous horror stories about it.

Lodge told Trigger, of all people, that Tavington was so upset about a journalist for one of the world's greatest news organizations flying in the spot most likely to get him killed that he pleaded with Wing Command to scrap the mission, to no avail.

"Ole Lodge left cussin' that the most important objective he had today's to git ole Tavingschmuck a bottle to his office in hopes o keepin' him halfway off his duff as they watch the claim board," Trigger said, spicing his words with the usual colorful expletives. "Almost startin' to feel sorry for Lodgepiddle, with what he has to put up with from that gilt-edged prima donna. Almost."

It was also Lance's first trip to Germany itself. He had overheard the cocky Clarke and a couple other veteran pilots grumbling to one another in the equipment hut a little while before about "when our idiot leaders will pull their heads outa their chutes long enough to realize their sacred doctrine of the mighty Fortress not only winning the war for the Allies, but doing so without fighter escort over Germany, is worth less than the blood of one lost crewman," which was immensely less blood than the flyers felt was being shed to expose the falseness of the theory.

British Spitfires, American P-47 Thunderbolts, and twin-engine P-38 Lightnings accompanied them into France on those raids, but they hadn't the fuel to reach Germany, and none were along this morning as the Eighth Air Force took the sea route to the sub docks on Germany's northern shore at the far end of the North Sea, nearly to Denmark.

Top o' all that, Bob Morgan and his Memphis Belle, *now jist three missions from goin' home, their group got bombed by JU-88s flyin' over'em t'other day! Them Junkers couldn't do jack against us if we had Thunderbolts er even Lightnin's flyin escort. Good gravy, what'll them boys come up with next to throw at us? Plus, this about as cold's I ever been in my life, colder even than them other missions.*

He looked out his small side window, reassured.

There's Waddy, though, on my port wing, Patton just above and behind, and Trigger's down there, jist below in the basement. If anybody can succeed in the Coffin Corner, it's us.

Their three-plane elements comprised the standard six-plane flights and twelve-plane squadrons. The Forts in each level of formation were cantilevered and echeloned in tight and meticulous sets that aimed to provide multiple fields of fire in every direction, as well as covering fire for one another.

"*Mind me to tell ya somethin' we git back tonight, Pard,*" Waddy broke in, as if on cue, over the liaison channel.

He looked over at him again and saw his head bobbing.

That ole coot's laughin' his tail off about somethin'.

He shook his head. "Roger that."

Wonder what's goin' through that overactive brain o' his now?

Ole Cronky sat in the jump seat just behind him, ready to report on their doings like he had that golden year in Norman when the Sooners showed the country how tall, lanky, rawboned, small town and country boys from the Southern Plains could pack a wallop hard enough for anyone in the land to feel.

"Thanks for comin' along with us, Cronky!" he said an hour or so later, just after rather reluctantly turning over the controls to Clifton and detecting the copilot's lack of enthusiasm at the presence of their visitor. He hollered over his shoulder through his oxygen mask, eschewing the interphone, so that no one else could hear them. "So, who ya workin' with now?"

"United Press." Cronkite, too, had to shout to be heard over the roar of the Forts.

"What?"

"United Press."

"Oh, UP? Gee, ain't they the top news service?"

"Well, along with the AP."

"So why didja, Cronky? Git in the middle o' all this, I mean."

"It's tough back home for folks. Rationing, separations, and now— a lotta folks are startin' to get visits from those uniformed messengers. But you boys are doin' great things over here, and I want to tell people 'bout the good that's happening, to give'em hope."

For a moment, he and Lance stared at one another through their goggles with affection and thanksgiving at having once again crossed paths. When Lance noticed Cronkite's mask quivering and the clear plastic portion fogging, he realized his own body was aching clean through from the cold. He eyed the cockpit thermometer.

Good gravy, seventy degrees below zero. Are all these boys feelin' like this? Dang electric flight suit ain't much help now. And half of'em ain't even workin' at any given time.

The ache and the ensuing sensation of stabbing, all-over agony, prompted a strange momentary urge to panic at the unearthly cold, the pain, the inescapability from it, and its long probable duration today. He prayed.

Help me git my mind off it, please.

He shifted in his seat and opened his mouth to thank Cronkite, but O'Connor piped up from the tail on the interphone.

"Tail to pilot, who's got the stick up there, sir?"

"Pilot to tail, radio silence, please," he said, irritated.

He had grown increasingly nervous about Clifton, especially since learning after a practice flight briefing a couple days before, that the man had a mere fifty hours in the air. "Well, pretty close to that, anyhow," Clifton had said. Lance had dozens more.

Not even countin' all the other flyin' I done. We're so desperate to give the Germans some sorta fight somewhere before they win the war without us even bein' all the way in, that we rushin' everthang and everbody through the system too da—uh, danged—fast. Pressure, pressure, pressure, from everwhere, at ever level.

Yesterday O'Connor cornered him. "Musso told me waist gunners in adjoining planes make a show of adjusting their 'chute harnesses when they see Clifton flying."

"Well, how the heck they know when he's flyin?" he asked.

"For the love of G—uh, sorry, Parson—no offense meant. You're a cowboy, right? So, can one of your horses tell the difference when you get on him with spurs and what all, kicking his tail and riding like a bat outa hades, and when some jackleg dude like me gets on who ain't never ridden nothin' but the Merry-Go-Round at Coney Island?"

He was at a loss for words.

"Criminy, Parson," O'Connor looked as earnest as he'd ever seen him. "You fly this thing like some Dapper Dan playing a concert piano. You ain't flyin' the lead plane, but we never feel you jockeying your throttles to adjust our position, even though we know you're constantly doing it. Smooth as my brother's little baby's hiney. That cretin riding shotgun with you flies it like he's takin' a sledge hammer to the throttles. Waits 'til he's in the exact position he has to be before jerkin' forward or retarding the throttles. A blasted rookie, he is. Like ridin' through the sky on a—" Lance winced at the cursing he knew was coming. "see-saw, uh, Parson—sir."

Then he thought of the eruption—*eruptions*—in the Mess Hall—the *Officers' Mess Hall*—at breakfast. Patton had told him on the Jeep ride out to their planes that two of his own sergeant gunners had slugged it out in the enlisted men's club the night before. One of them suffered a fractured jaw and would miss at least a month's worth of missions, meaning a green man would have to be replaced with a greener man.

Boys're strung tighter 'n old saddlebags scorched in the sun. How many other guys on my crew ain't ready? Musso? Already had concerns about both Goldsmith and Remington. I don't even know enough about Rodriguez to have an opinion on him.

Was this what it was like to get hit over the head with a telephone pole?

I gotta pay better attention to 'em on practice flights and dang sure on missions. I gotta talk more to 'em on the ground, have my own briefings with 'em. I think Lodge or Tavington, stupid as they are, or somebody, said to do that, anyhow. No, it was Risinger said to do it.

All of a sudden, a rare sense of being overwhelmed swarmed over him, then *Hellfire and Brimstone* jerked him forward at another of Clifton's inelegant course adjustments.

Goodness gracious, is it all too much?

Before he could descend, shivering, further into the slough of despondency, a Messerschmitt BF-109, gleaming black as midnight, slashed in from out of the fast-ascending sun and fired a .20-millimeter cannon burst that jolted the plane and knocked its Number Three engine dead. Despite his intensive and ongoing fighter identification training, the 109 screamed by so fast, he barely saw it.

Clifton shouted an expletive, looking out his window with bugging eyes at the yawning holes in the engine and its lolling propeller blades.

Lance flinched and corrected the plane's course, Clifton willingly relinquishing the controls. If he could have interpreted the wordless thoughts flashing through his mind, they would have registering something akin to: I never actually thought we'd git hit.

"Heads up, boys!" he said through the interphone, spotting a squadron of JU-88 twin-engine fighter-bombers banking down toward them in echelon, again from out of the sun. "Six JU-88s comin' in from one o'clock high. Hit 'em, boys!"

"See 'em, Parson!" Utah up in the top turret and Goldsmith the navigator called in unison.

Hellfire and Brimstone jerked as every gun on her seemed to open up at once. Tracer fire hurled in from the 88s, then they flashed by, not so blinding as the black 109—

—*Where is that joker?* he forced himself to keep a steady course, curses rising in his throat, and aligned with the squadron above and ahead—

—but plenty fast.

Jist like first playin' college ball, gotta git used to the speed o' this game, and quick.

He glanced at Clifton, sitting stiff as a statue, sweat streaming down the edges of his mask. "Quit spectatin' and start callin' 'em out, Clif!"

It was all happening so fast. More 88s appeared, and the faster, shiftier, more dangerous ME-109s as well. Most of the crew seemed to be reacting well to its first real dogfight, their shouts clamoring over the interphone.

"109 comin' your way, O'Connor!"

"Squadron of 88s coming up at us!"

"What position, Rip?" he said, irritated at the ball turret gunner for not specifying and Clifton even more for not doing so.

"Twelve-o'clock low, sir!" Ripkowski said, excitement turning his calm response into a shout.

"Five Card Stud *just took a direct hit, sir, on fire!"* Rodriguez's voice crackled on the interphone.

"Any 'chutes?"

"Don't see any, sir—no wait, there's two, three—oh—Madre Mia!"

"What is it, Rodriguez?"

"She just blew up."

"Here come those 88s!" Ripkowski had to yell to be heard over the rattle of his guns from below.

The firing became general again.

"Y—you're doing good, sir," Clifton said, looking straight at Lance. *"Don't know how—"*

"Thanks, Clif, but keep spottin', and keep your eyes on our instruments."

O'Connor shrieked.

"What is it, O'Connor?"

"Oh, my God, Parson, I just shot off a piece of Hail Mary's *vertical stabilizer!"*

"Our Hail Mary?"

O'Connor's sigh took the place of what he knew would normally have been a sarcastic, and no doubt obscene, response. Instead, *"Yes, sir."* The shaken Southie sounded near tears.

"Well, that mighta been me, O'Connor," Utah said, his voice forlorn.

Before he could process this further, someone screamed, *"Watch it, Musso, there's that black ME—"*

Clifton shouted another profanity, looking out his window.

Loud machine gun fire sounded, the plane jerked again, and someone screamed over the interphone.

"That dirty—" Lance couldn't identify the shouting voice.

"Musso!"

"Did you get him, Rip?"

"No, he got away," Ripkowski replied somberly, breathing hard. *"Oh! That black 109 just blew up* Betty Grable's Boys!"

The cold still burrowed like dull dirty scissors into his insides, but he felt sweat dripping down his face and realized the inside of his goggles were starting to fog.

Oh, God, Jesus, no, please.

"Rodriguez, how's Musso?" he asked.

"He's down, sir, he's hit, can't tell where, he's alive, but hurtin'." Rodriguez replied.

He continued speaking in Spanish, worry filling his voice, and words like *"mi hermano"* and *"mi amigo"* streamed out.

Clifton stared at him, pale, his eyes wider than ever, but he wondered what his own shaken face looked like. He rubbed the outside of his goggles with his glove and wondered what to do. He turned to Cronkite.

"Cronky, don't suppose you can hannel a fi'ty?"

"Actually, they made us test out on it before we could fly."

"God bless ye, buddy!" he wanted to kiss him. "Well, ya mind gittin' back there and grabbin' Musso's 'til he's up again? Left waist. You know where."

"Got it," Cronkite gave a firm nod, unstrapping himself, jumping up, and turning to head back through the plane.

"Cronky!" He had to scream, since Cronkite was off the interphone. "Grab that bottle o walk-around oxygen er you'll be dead 'fore ye git to the gun!"

Cronkite's eyes widened. He nodded thanks to him, grabbed the plastic bottle from a small shelf near his jump seat, snapped it on, then headed back.

His eyes landed on Clifton, staring toward the ceiling window, the co-pilot's eyes starting to roll back in his head.

"Clif? *Clif!*" When he didn't answer, he shook his shoulder and saw the hose hanging disconnected from his oxygen mask. "Dangit!" He leaned forward, reconnecting it. Within seconds, the rebreather bag resumed moving, indicating Clifton was taking in air, and he regained his sensibility, looking at him, nodding, and turning back to the instrument panel.

"Keep that thing plugged in! Dang it!"

"*Tighten up the formation, men,*" Colonel Rossiter from Wing, flying in the lead plane, said over the liaison channel. Rossiter had nearly twenty missions of his own and he sounded calm as a cow chewing his cud. "*Save your ammo, we've got a long way to go, boys. Fire in short bursts.*"

Utah shouted words he didn't want to hear, from up top. "*Four FWs coming around from one o'clock level, sir.*"

He knew Krauts like Hartmann and Barkhorn were racking up the greatest numbers of aerial combat victories in history while flying ME-109s, but he also knew the newer, bigger, but easier-handled, radial engine FW-190 was a combination aerial tank and arsenal. Despite its armored muscle, it could accelerate, climb, strike, and roll like a flying ballerina. No other fighter he knew of had its firepower—twin machine guns in the upper engine cowling, 20-millimeter cannon in the wing roots that each fired seven hundred rounds a minute, and two more cannon farther out in the wings.

And here come the jokers, right when I see we're losin' power and speed jist like I thought, and I'm gunna have to try and feather number three.

Feathering turned the propeller blades toward the wind to minimize drag, similar to coasting an auto with a dead engine to a stop.

"Look at this, sir," Remington the navigator said from the nose.

Clifton gasped.

The four FWs headed straight for the Americans in a chain, wingtip to wingtip, the pilots exhibiting unflinching control, poise, and determination as top, front nose, and side nose guns opened up on them from the entire bomber group.

Wouldja look at that....

As the fighters neared, their level just higher than his, he sighed with involuntary relief. *They're goin' for the squadron jist above us.*

"Not too far to go with it feathered?" Clifton asked, referring to number three.

"What else can we do but bail?"

"But what if the engine runs away?"

"Clif, there ain't no good choice—" he cut himself off as the FWs came roaring in, machine guns and cannon blazing. He saw pieces splintering off one FW wing, though it kept flying. Then he saw—*felt*—a Fort above and just ahead explode in a ball of flame, and another one's wing fall off. For a moment, debris and smoke—and a torn, trouserless leg—filled the sky around him.

Remington cursed loudly as most of the amputated wing sailed right at them, then fractured into two chunks that whooshed to either side of them.

"Criminey," Cliff said emphatically as he and Lance ducked.

Still freezing cold, but feeling sweat trickling down his face, as well as having an overwhelming urge to pee but with no way to get up and go, and blood rushing through his head, he tried to calm himself. He realized the fighter attacks, especially the brazen FWs, had disrupted the group's formation even before he heard Rossiter shouting to tighten it up. Nonetheless, he set about adjusting the pitch of the Number Three prop and harnessing the wind, so the prop would slice through the air with ease, offsetting the loss of the dead engine and stopping its drag. He had to accomplish all this without the blades spinning out of control and flying off the wing, perhaps with the engine, very possibly into the nose, cockpit or another section of the plane, a not-infrequent occurrence.

Now, colder than ever and sweating all the more, he threw all his mental and physical energy into feathering the engine. Twice he almost lost control of the plane, then Goldsmith, cool as a cucumber, announced, "Approaching IP, sir."

Consumed by the mortal peril of the ravaged engine, he didn't know whether to thank or curse God at the announcement. The German fighters disappeared, though he expected to see them, or others like them, on the journey home.

Just as he realized he must drop out of the formation and become chum for the flying sharks, he heard Clifton say, "You've got it, sir. It's feathering. Perfect, sir!"

He had no time to process this welcome and life-saving announcement, only to follow Remington's coordinates and shift toward the IP that Rossiter had just reaffirmed.

"There it is, sir," Remington said.

"Pilot to bombardier, you flyin' the airplane now." He released the controls to Remington and his Norden automatic piloting bombsight in the nose. "She's all yours."

He sensed something amiss just as the dark gray popcorn began popping all over the sky.

"Where'd all this flak come from!" someone shouted with four-lettered emphasis from another plane, not realizing he was on the liaison channel. *"It wasn't this bad before."*

"Shut up about that flak!" Rossiter's voice seemed cold as ice.

When a shell burst, not far away, and rocked the plane, he nearly peed his pants. His relief at not doing so was temporary.

I already did.

Horror followed on the heels of embarrassment when he remembered how a waist gunner in the 298th died a screaming death when all his privates froze from the same cause, after his urine burnt out his electric flight suit.

But I ain't back there in that howlin' crosswind, standin' and shootin'. Please God—

A loud, now-familiar buzzing sound interrupted his plea.

"Bomb bay doors open," Remington paused. A few seconds later, *"Happy St. Patty's Day from Roark and O'Connor, Adolf."* The plane jumped with the release of five thousand pounds of ordnance.

God, I'm gunna jist trust ye with my pee, sir—and that You'll take care o me, sir.

He glanced up through the top window where he saw more debris sailing past in the windstream. Remington returned control of the plane to him at the safe point on the other side of Wilhelmshaven and he turned with the formation back toward the sea and home.

Who knows if we'll do any damage even if we hit them bunkered fortresses?

He looked down at the distant ground as explosions rippled across it.

From what Patton's connections at Wing say, only thang these fool's errands are accomplishin' is killin' the brave crews that fly 'em.

Musso was unconscious but stable, the rest of the crew shaken but all right, though Clifton looked worse to him than Musso.

"Okay, Clif?" he stayed off the interphone, choosing to shout instead. The copilot nodded unconvincingly.

A half hour later, Utah said, *"Squadron o' ME-110s eleven o'clock high, comin' right in at us from the sun."*

"What's with all these twin-engined fighters?" O'Connor asked with an expletive over the interphone.

The 110s were faster than the JU-88s and nearly as fast and more heavily armed than the ME-109s. They spread out across the Group like a canvas and dove in. The air came alive with the blasting of a couple hundred 299th Browning machine guns. *Hellfire and Brimstone* shook.

"ME-110 diving from eleven o'clock—" Clifton said. Before he could finish, Utah sprayed the fighter's cockpit area from long range with a hail of .50-caliber bullets and the plane flipped over, out of control, and screamed straight into the path of another of the attackers. The two exploded into an orange fireball that peppered the plane with debris and nearly knocked Waddy's out of the sky as the other 110s zoomed past.

"Did you see that!" Remington was jubilant his words spiced with an unusual display of profane passion. *"Utah got two of em!"*

O'Connor shouted his crude approval from the tail.

"Heckuva shot, Utah," Goldsmith said.

"Ya alright, Wad?" Lance used the liaison channel to check on his wingman.

"Never better, Pard," replied the familiar voice.

More JU-88s joined the fight as it continued across the North Sea and the ME-110s returned.

"How's Number Three, Clifton?"

Please let it be good, Lord.

"She looks fine, sir," Clifton replied. "—and instrument readings fine."

"Don't wait fer me to ask, ya hear?" Before Clifton could answer, he asked, "Cronky? Rodriguez? Cronkite alright back there?"

"Yes, sir," Rodriguez said, *"I told him if he don't give them fifties a break, he gonna melt them both down."*

He laughed. Blevins the flight engineer appeared just behind him.

"What in the Sam Hill are you doin' here?" He had to shout over the engine noise.

"Well, thought I better check on that third engine," Blevins replied.

"Git back to your station and man your gun, bub! Have ye noticed we in the middle of a dogfight?"

"But—"

"Sir?" someone said over the interphone.

"Git!" He jerked his thumb at Blevins. "We'll letcha know if we needja!"

"Sir?" the voice crackled again.

"Yeah, what is it? *Who* is it?" He grew more irritated as he felt his thighs and groin growing colder still where his pee had spread. "Say it, man!" Then the electric heater wiring in his suit shorted out, delivering him a brief but agonizing shock.

He screamed perhaps the first profanity of his life, and certainly the first with any witnesses besides God.

"Right waist gun to pilot. That ME-110 at three o'clock level, sir?" It was Cronkite. *"He seems to be shadowing us, just taggin' along out there."*

"Good eye, Cronky." Trying to catch his breath and shake off the multiple painful sensations down around his privates, he squinted out Clifton's window. "Dangit, Clif, you shoulda made that call." The fighter-bomber zoomed ahead a mile or more, then curved toward them. "Wait a minute. Is that a 110 G-4?" He grabbed his binoculars and what he saw sent a jolt like a stabbing knife through him. "Yeah, he got a rocket slung under him! He's comin' in at—"

That was all he got out before the 110 fired an air-to-air rocket that exploded in front of the plane with a deafening roar, staggering it in mid-flight. His ear drums felt like they might burst from the concussion. Thankfully, the plane flew on, but the Plexiglas nose out front was smoking.

"You boys alright in the nose?"

No answer.

"I think the Jerrys lit out for home, sir," O'Connor said.

Finally, Remington answered from the nose. *"Sir, that rocket blew a small hole in the nose and Goldsmith's trying to plug it up."*

"What's he usin'?"

"Uh, his gloves, sir, from one hand."

"What? Tell him to put his gloves back on, all of em! It's minus seventy degrees up here!"

"Yeah, Goldy," he heard Remington tell the navigator, *"put your gloves back on. Goldy!"*

"What is it?" he asked alarmed at Remington's profanity-laced eruption.

"The glass is jagged around the hole, and—" Remington began. *"—Goldy!"*

Now screaming sounded in the background.

"Take the plane—and engine check," he said to Clifton, unstrapping himself and his hoses, grabbing a walk-around oxygen bottle, and squirming down the cramped little passage leading from the cockpit to the Astrodome nose. From the moment he got into the passageway, he could feel the Arctic rush of air from the snowball-sized hole the rocket shrapnel had punched in the nose. Goldsmith was writhing in agony on the floor behind his Norden, screaming. Remington was trying to get hold of his damaged hand.

Oh my—

Half the mass of the navigator's hand—flesh, muscle, and bone alike—was gone, part of it stuck to the jagged hole in the Plexiglas, part of it on the floor in frozen lumps, a piece stuck to the Norden.

Lance shouted the worst profanity, realizing he had left the first aid kit under his seat above. He hurried back up, got it, and returned. Goldsmith was howling like a wounded coyote. The first thing he did was ram a little morphine syrette into him. When the navigator kept screaming, he stuck in another.

"Sir?" Remington was hollering through the din of engines, rushing air, and machine gun fire. He realized he was staring transfixed in horror at Goldsmith's hideous hand. He pulled a mustard plaster from the first aid kit and applied it as best he could.

"This kit ain't got diddly," he said, "and nobody taught us what to do with what it does have."

Thankfully, the morphine along with the shock had calmed Goldsmith. Lance bit his lip, then another jolt hit him.

"Git his gloves back on him! He'll lose the hand."

He saw Remington's expression. *Right, lose it? He's already lost it.*

"Okay, let's tie it off so we can save his arm." He took his own flying scarf and did so.

Goldsmith gazed up at him with deep and pure gratitude.

"It's okay, podnah," he patted the wounded man. "Ye gotcher self a million-dollar wound. Jist hang on. You goin' home a hero, buddy."

EIGHT

Bad flying weather in England and worse on the Continent grounded the 299th for the next week. He managed to get liberty that weekend to see Sarah, though it required returning to the station to sleep each night. The hours with her were more than worth that small price. Moll had ordered him to stop into the store each time he came to visit Sarah, insisting it be on the way to see her and not after. The shopkeeper always had a bag of goodies, ostensibly for him, though as he got to know Sarah and her mother better, he concluded it was Moll's way of encouraging and picking up tidbits of information from him, while ferrying the goodies to the Johnstons.

He knows they too proud to take gifts from a neighbor who's also strugglin', plus he knows I can buy most o' this sorta thang at the base PX.

He found himself allowing extra minutes on his stop by Moll's to chew the fat with him. It had been a long time since he'd had an older man he respected and really liked such as Daddy or Pastor Schroeder to talk with about the matters of life. Moll was a motherlode of knowledge about the customs and people of Suffolk.

There's Patton, too, but now he's in that other squadron and with all his own activities, includin' his evangelistic ones, I don't see that much of him. And I ain't that comfortable with his blunt approach to folks with the gospel, even though he smiles while he's doin' it.

Before he could reach the front door of Little Chickasaw, Sarah flung it open and rushed into his arms. They hugged, then kissed long and with much passion. It seemed as natural as breathing.

I should marry her! Then I would always have a friend and someone to be with and talk to, and ain't no one—since Sadie—I can talk to like this. But would she have me?

As he pondered that, her fresh feminine fragrance, sans perfume, filled his nostrils and head.

Oh Lord, I could have every bit of all of her the way I want it right now. Oh Lord, I gotta stop this er I'm gonna tackle her onto the livin' room floor right now!

Then, thankfully, they were sitting on the Johnstons' frayed little couch and talking. Actually, Sarah was talking, about what she had been doing, fun things she wanted to do—dreams—America and American things and Americans and him.

Her talk cheered him for many reasons, not least because it meant he wouldn't have to dance around the increasing rudeness toward him from Cappuccio and Cochran, or the continued icy stares from Clarke, or about his post-Wilhelm-shaven interrogation that led to Clifton's sacking as co-pilot, or Goldsmith's agony and amputation, or the... *experience* Wilhelmshaven proved to be.

In fact, he thought he was doing a good job of keeping his recent experiences away from both Sarah and himself until, after a couple hours, she touched his wrist and asked if he was feeling well. When he assured her he was, she gently asked if he was perhaps a bit fatigued or... preoccupied.

"Oh, I do hope I'm not proving a bore, Lance," she now held his wrist, her thin brow furrowed. After he assured her she was the least boring thing in his life, she shook her head, "But I must be an awful bore to someone who has experienced and accomplished all that you have, being a sports star and cowboy on the range and courageous aviator saving me and Mum and my whole country from evil." The emotion and force of her own words caused her eyes to water and prodded her to snuggle against him.

Her mother coughed long and jaggedly from her room.

"Oh," Sarah sat up with regret, but rose and headed toward the coughing. "I fear she's taken pneumonia."

On the bicycle ride back to the station, he realized Mrs. Johnston's cough had been a Providential one.

I was ready to tear that little Shetland sweater off her. I gotta ask her to marry me. But what if somethin' happens to me? What if I'm killed, er—some o these fellas lose their family jewels up there, or the use of em... they wish they were dead. That one fella in the 298th did shoot hisself. And... everthang I saw on that Wilhelmshaven mission...

Gratitude swept him as he looked up into the overcast sky, which started spitting chilly drizzle.

Nah, I gotcha, sir. Ye'll protect me like ye always do, 'specially when I'm doin' Your will. Oh, if only Mama could meet Sarah and her mom, she'd understand how much God wants me to protect them and all the innocent folks over here. It's true, Your ways are inscrutable and beyond understandin'. Ye don't like violence to settle things, but Ye don't like divorce, either, Ye hate it, and yet, long time ago, Ye started allowin' it 'cause of our own hard hearts. And if ever in the history o the world You've allowed violence to stop wicked men, it's now, sir. I'm sure of it as I am that I love that little Irish-English girl—Daddy'll laugh at that—and that I am gunna marry er! In fact, regular as she is at that stone church in the town square and the way she does good works and prays and tries to follow You, I know You'll approve, and where she falls short, I'll help her, and all the ways I fall short, she'll help me. Oh, I love You Jesus, and I love that little girl Ye made fer me to take care of and make happy and make lotsa babies with!

He was laughing and whooping so that he barely saw the oncoming gasoline lorrie headed for the station in time to keep from getting run over by it. Climbing out of the hedgerow into which he had careened and wobbling his bent bike back onto the road, he laughed as the rain poured in torrents.

On the eighth night since the Wilhelmslaven mission, Lodge stopped him as he rose from his interrogation table after another practice sortie that included his new copilot Palmer, a Pennsylvania Quaker, and his new navigator Maier.

"So, your reports on the new crewmen sound good," Lodge said in his rapid-fire way.

"Yes, sir. Them six missions Maier already flew with the 296th have helped, and he's near as steady as Goldy and got him maybe a smidge more of a nose for it."

"For what?"

"For where he needs to go."

"I see," Lodge clearly didn't. "And Palmer?"

"Young, like most, but solid, quick to learn, and smart. I like'em both, sir."

"Hmm," Lodge muttered, rising up and down on his toes, as if trying to look him eye to eye. Giving up on that, he sighed, "Well then, carry on," as he himself hurried off.

—

After supper, a game of pool, and tossing the football around in the landing strip infield, he and Waddy lounged in their hutment, Waddy reading the *Stars and Stripes* newspaper sports section, he, an article on a promising new long-range fighter escort plane the British had commissioned North American Aviation to produce for them. The plane potentially offered the distance and muscle no other Allied fighter yet possessed to take the bombers all the way to their target, even in Germany, and home, and with blazing speed at least fifty miles per hour faster than anyone's best current fighters, plus unsurpassed maneuverability.

The article made clear that the British and especially the American air barons had not yet surrendered their long-held doctrine that the right bomber—*The Flying Fort*—could handle whatever German opposition came against it, return safely home, and win the war before American boys had to set foot on Continental Europe.

I've heard it all along and believe it myself. Lately, though— since Wilhelmshaven, really—I wonder. Trigger calculates that of all the 299th crewmen who've flown missions so far, they averaged no more than ten completed before being shot down or otherwise incapacitated for further missions. When Waddy and me hooted him down, he got ticked and said, "Hey, hot shots, Risinger figgered it and he made it out only a little over six missions."

All this, not least Trigger's unusual seriousness, put him to thinking. *Whatever the math, most of us ain't gonna finish twenty-five missions. We may not finish near that. 'Course, wonder if I'm a shade more open to listenin' since Wilhelmshaven.*

Just then, the familiar crackling static of the Tannoy coming to life sounded, followed by a deep, sonorous, familiar voice. *"Gentlemen of the esteemed 299th Air Group. The difficulty in understanding the Russian is that we do not take cognizance of the fact that he is not a European, but an Asiatic, and therefore thinks deviously,"* said the voice.

"The Russian?" Waddy asked, about to burst into laughter.

"We can no more understand a Russian than a Chinese or a Japanese—that is, a sawed-off little slant-eyed, yellow-faced, scum-suckin' Jap—" the voice continued with gravity, *"—and from what I have seen of them, I have no particular desire to understand them except to ascertain how much lead or iron it takes to kill them. In addition to his other amiable characteristics, the Russian has no regard for human life and they are all-out sons-o-whores—not to mention barbarians, incestuous rapists, fornicatresses, and chronic drunks."*

"Why, it's that ole coot Trigger!" Waddy said, jumping up from his cot. "What the hoot in heck is he doin'!"

"I now return you to your normal duties, men o' the 299th," Trigger said. *"I am General George Patton, and you are dismissed."*

Waddy headed for the door. "That two-headed loon!"

"But first," Trigger said, *"those of you in the clubs, put down your drinks, those of you riding jockey on the porcelain bus, wipe your brains, and those of you in your*

hutments, put down them dirty girly magazines and quit disgracing your mothers! You are now dis-missed!"

—

Lodge pulled back the curtain in the briefing building and revealed the target as St. Nazaire, the Germans' concrete Atlantic Coast U-boat bastion on the west coast of France. Some of the more veteran flyers seemed less than pleased. "Flak City," he heard one behind him whisper with an accompanying obscenity.

"It's where the Jerries introduced their 'Box Barrage' to us back around New Year's," Risinger, sitting next to him, whispered. "One of the largest concentrations of big guns in the world and they trained the whole kit and caboodle on a field five-hundred yards wide and one thousand feet deep and every one of us had to fly right through it. Nearly half the planes that flew that day took serious hits—or worse."

As the morning proceeded, from Kupchak waking him till he, Waddy, Patton, and Trigger rode weapons carriers with their crews out to their planes, an increasing heaviness and tightness gripped him—and an increasing awareness of what, since Wilhelmshaven, he knew could lay ahead.

Throughout his life, he had been able to put bad experiences and images behind him with prayer. Now, remembrances from the last mission—black, oppressive and terrifying as that 109 that had opened the action that day—began to assault him. His prayers turned back the remembrances and held them at bay—until one would spring up from nowhere, at random. He would douse it with more petitions to God and it would recede—but not permanently. He began to look up scriptures to apply to them.

He now knew that same black as midnight Me-109 joker had closed out the action that day at St. Nazaire, as he attacked *Hellfire and Brimstone* at Wilhelmshaven. Blazing in from the rear of the bomber stream, where every American eye that could see it was turned, and with a couple dozen chattering Brownings trained on him, five minutes after the last German fighter besides himself had departed, he chewed up the tail and tail gunner of Risinger's wingman with machine gun blasts, laid a scorching trail of fire into the top of his Fort, killing several more crewmen, then veered his plane just enough to riddle the Number Two engine fuel tank and explode the plane. Next liberty, Risinger would have stood up as best man at his wingman's wedding in Cambridge, the next county to the west.

He felt the first creeping sense of something more than dislike toward another human being. He said a quick prayer that he and his crew might have another chance to confront the black 109 and avenge what was apparently a large and growing number of American airmen.

"Risinger told me he's spoken to men from other groups who've seen that black 109," Patton told him one morning as they readied for a practice flight. "Seems he's known as the Black Knight. Guess he favors makin' that last pass like he did against us. Think he's shot a lotta Forts and Libs out o the sky."

He sighed as he pulled on his flight gear.

Alright Lord, jist lemme me face him, sir.

This prayer seemed much more grudging than the previous one. By the time he had his Fort—a different one than *Hellfire and Brimstone*, which wasn't yet ready to fly after the punishment it took on the previous raid—on the flight line, he felt sick to his stomach.

The shotgun sounded and when his turn came to take off, he saw the Catholic chaplain between the landing strip and the forest green command tower, looking like he was blessing each plane and crew as they took off. He was airborne with his new navigator Maier, his new copilot, the Quaker kid Palmer, and Musso's temporary waist gun replacement, and halfway to the splasher beacon before Rossiter, again riding in the lead plane, announced the scrapping of the mission due to probable bad weather moving into southern and eastern England within the next few hours.

What? It can't be. We're ready. We been through—why this preppin', then scrappin' is as bad an experience, if not worse, than combat itself. That hour on the flight line like to wiped me out.

A stream of profanities revolved through his mind, followed by a half-hearted apology to God for them.

"So, the weather here's good, for once the weather over the whole continent is good all day and night, but we might run into something back here when we land!" O'Connor shouted with the typical obscenities. "I'd a sure sight rather take my chances going into the drink or crashing into an East Anglian hayfield."

"Quiet on the interphone," Palmer said in a calm but firm manner that, to his surprise, silenced O'Connor.

He glanced over at the new co-pilot. Clifton'd never hanneled that situation.

A wry smile formed under his mask.

Turning back felt like choosing to turn and leave Sarah when he didn't have to. *'Course, I might can see her, dependin' on how long that weather that's costin' us a mission sticks—why, yeah! But that means another day, or two, maybe another week, maybe more, farther away from finishin' our twenty-five missions and bein' with Sarah all the time. Why can't we git credit for a mission, anyhow? We done our part, went through the gittin' ready, the awful waitin' on the flight line.*

Then the worst thought of all struck.

Why am I countin' toward when I can git out o here? I been countin' toward bein' here for more'n a year and I only flown three dang missions. I been countin' toward makin' a difference in the world my whole life, and now I am.

How little was now under his own control, even his own emotions and hopes.

—

March became April and the flowers dappled the rolling Suffolk hills as the sun warmed history's most colossal aircraft launching ground, host now to over one hundred thousand American air and ground personnel. He and his buddies flew four missions over the next couple of weeks. These included a couple of milk runs, a Nazi distribution facility for Swedish ore in Norway, and the previously-cancelled St. Nazaire run. He encountered heavy flak on the Norway mission, and that plus a hornet's nest of ME-109s at St. Nazaire.

Hellfire and Brimstone, back in action for the latter two missions, suffered no damage in Norway and only a minor pattern of shrapnel holes in the fuselage behind Rodriguez's left waist station at St. Nazaire. Six bombers went down out of the one hundred twenty the division threw at the base, though, two more ditched in the Channel, and four more suffered Category E designation—unsalvagable for further use. Once again, nearly half suffered serious damage, *Hellfire and Brimstone* and others with lighter hits not included in that total. Maybe worst of all, Waddy told him as they readied for shuteye the next night, "One o Patton's new pals in intelligence, one o them boys lives down in the hole under their building by the west gate, told him we ain't cracked them concrete pens for squat yet at St. Nazarene or whatever, nor any of'em on the Baltic, neither."

"The Eighth burned down the whole city o St. Nazaire, though, didn't we?" he said.

"Yeah, we got rid o all the folks' houses, but we ain't hit their bloody subs a lick," Waddy said. "They still out there runnin' roughshod on everbody's ships."

"And we still bein' their guinea pigs," he said, for the first time wondering if it was true.

"You heard that, too?" Waddy asked.

"Yup."

"Patton told me they got'em 'bout as many fellers workin' in ops and intelligence and what-not as they do us flyboys and our ground crews combined," Waddy said, speaking faster. "He said he saw some o their wall charts and table maps and graphs and calculations, and they still just figurin' out what works with how many of us and to where, and what's worse, they still convinced our Forts're gunned up enough not to need no fighter escorts when they start sendin' us into the heart o' Germany. I can't hardly believe that, can you? You see them FWs and 109s swirlin' and whirlin' and how the Sam Hill we supposed to hannel packs of'em like we ain't never seen when we git into Jerryland?"

"Like that black ME son of a gun," he said without mirth.

"Shoot, yeah, like him," Waddy said. "You see what he done to Risinger's wingman on that Wilhelm—"

"Yeah, and Luckadoo told me he saw the peckerwood nearly crash into one o them boys in the low squadron, 'fore he emptied everthang he had into their nose and cockpit."

They both lay quiet in the cool, clammy dark.

Sheesh, I'm tired—there goes Wad again about that black 109—Believe I've heard him curse more in the few weeks we been flyin' missions than I did the four years we were at OU—

—

The weather socked in the 299th the next two weeks. The first liberty he had, Sarah was in Lowestoft the whole weekend tending wounded civilians from another raid on the port city and unable to visit. Surprised at how disappointed, even despairing he was, he waved off Trigger's, and Cappuccio's, invitations for the liberty bus to London, as he always did. He returned to his old pushups and running regimen to try and shake off his depression and recited verses from Proverbs 31 he was memorizing about the godly woman he had long prayed for. He attended a couple of Patton's Bible studies, and he tried not to imagine what lay under those modest Land Girl dresses.

After another raid in northern France in mid-April, he finally saw her again. His tension and recent nightmares melted away at the sight and feel of her, especially when he perceived her own pale and worn expression.

"What is it, Sarah?" he asked gently after they had bought some small items for her mother at the Woolworth's store in the town center and enjoyed fish and chips on a table outside the small shop.

"Now we shan't discuss my small matters," she said, smiling.

"Hey." He reached across the little wooden table and held her hand. "Ain't none o your matters small. What gives?"

She blushed and looked down. When he saw her hidden chin quivering, he slid around the table to her side and embraced her. She wept softly into his shoulder.

"It's okay, darlin'," he said, "it's all okay. I'm gunna make sure it's always jake fer you, and safe, and you ain't never gunna have to worry 'bout bein' alone er scared again."

She looked up at him, tears streaking her open, pretty face. "Oh truly, Lance? "Do you really mean it?"

Then he kissed her softly and held her some more. "Oh, Lance, dearest, I fear my heart has broken into a hundred pieces," she said in a whisper, facing behind him, her head resting against his hard shoulder. "I—I just don't understand how civilized human beings can commit such acts toward one another. Barbarians in Africa or the South Seas or even Russia, that is fathomable, but—well, many Englishmen actually have German relatives, and many more, Germanic roots. Many of the common people derive from the same Saxon stock as the Germans."

"Yeah, us, too," he said, his voice hollow. He held her, then rocked her softly. He wanted to ask what had happened, but dared not.

"I've seen too many blasted homes and dead children and ruined dreams." Her voice broke, and she sobbed into his shoulder, her head feeling hot to him and her eyes wet. "My own mother has taken such a turn downward I fear she may not remain long with us—with me. I am so very tired, Lance. Oh, if not for you, my true love, I fear I should prefer heaven to here," she buried her face into his shoulder again.

They held one another for some minutes and ate no more fish nor chips. He felt her soft auburn hair.

It's time to ask her. I—

Then her head lifted and she said, alarmed, "Oh Lance, love, I'm late for giving Mum her midday medication and treatment."

They hurried on their bicycles to Little Chickasaw and found Mrs. Johnston ill and wan. The only conversations he and Sarah had the rest of the day and evening and through the night regarded how best to tend her mother. Dr. Payne came, did the little he could for the semi-delirious woman, and told Sarah her mother might have weeks or hours or minutes yet to live.

"Much depends on whether this fever breaks."

The embraces Sarah allowed him to share with her, intermittent as they were, salved his worn soul and body like no medicine or other remedy could. Pondering her revelations outside the fish and chips shop, he realized with more clarity than ever before the value, the cruciality, of his service.

It's like ever time I go up, I'm personally standin' between the Jerries, and Sarah and her mama.

It was around 3 a.m., and he watched her press a cool wash rag to her mother's forehead and listened to her sweet voice soothe the woman, who now looked so small. He stared at Sarah's unkempt hair, unmade face, and crinkled old dress, the collar and sleeve ends worn and losing their color.

She is altogether beautiful in ever way, Lord, and there is no blemish in her. Oh please, please, sir, spare her mama, least fer a spell. What a daughter she is. What a mother she'd be. What a helpmeet.

Just before 6 a.m. the fever broke and Mrs. Johnston began to breathe and sleep with calm, her bed as soaked as though someone had dumped buckets of water over it. Then Sarah slept for a few hours in a chair beside her and he on the frayed couch in the living room.

They all woke when Mr. and Mrs. Moll appeared at the front door with food.

"That Yamamoto bloke who led the Pearl Harbor attack, you Yanks got him," Moll said to him as they stood in the front room while the women went to Mrs. Johnston. "Tracked him, shot him down in an aircraft, killed him." He placed a gentle hand on his shoulder. "I think it's some sort of sign, Lance, me boy. I think it's the turning point. Years ago, Mr. Churchill spoke of the end of the beginning. I think this is the beginning of the end."

—

So spent was Sarah in the few hours that remained to him with her, he did not ask her what he wanted to. Soon, he was bicycling back through and out of town.

I'll git back over here in a couple weeks.

Dazzling fields of canola flowers glowed yellow before him into the distance. *I'll ask her then.*

He knew the crucible they had shared the past day had bonded them like nothing else could have. Watching, helping, and supporting her had filled him more than a night of passion could have. Her embrace of him on the front stoop, just before he departed, the roses redolent, had deepened his conviction and thrill.

God created her fer me and me fer her!

As he pedaled closer to the station, however, and the sky cleared as if for the sun to bow out for the night, a heaviness came over him about not finding a way to ask her. He remembered Mary Katherine and Mount Scott, and her father's "messenger," Culpepper, and the rain and the mud-spattered Mercury. Mere hours before he planned to take her to the top of the Wichitas and ask her to be his wife, word reached the Post Oak Mennonite Mission in the far reaches of the shortgrass country. Harry James wanted her in Chicago the next night as his famous swing band's new female vocalist. It had been Mary Katherine's otherworldly rendition of "Somewhere Over the Rainbow" which her father arranged for her to sing with James's orchestra—while lead vocalist Frank Sinatra watched admiringly—that wondrous evening he spent with her at the Skirvin Ballroom in Oklahoma City that had begun it all and won her the job.

All her emotional healing and spiritual growth those many months—more than a year—as their friendship, then love, blossomed—her changed heart and goals, the privilege and plenty she intended to lay down to follow him wherever he went, including and especially to serve the Comanches he loved as a ministering couple. It had all vanished in the twinkle of a rain-drenched, tear-filled eye. She had become the revered "Golden Girl with the Golden Voice," one of the greatest and most beautiful stars of the age, even as her father's inattention, her mother's coldness, her own ancient wounds and increasing dependence on liquor mounted alongside her fame.

Mary Katherine left, never again to be the same fresh-faced girl with all the hope in the world, and bound for a later, subtle rejection by him, which she sealed with her own subsequent and irreversible misdeed. She had been his and God's, then Harry James and his friend Tom Murchison and his courier Cliff Culpepper called, and Quanah Parker's Christian widow To-pay told him, as the storm roiled. *"I'm over one hundred years old and God just took that girl away from you—Quanah Parker follow long, hard, bumpy road—and To-pay. But we all sinners and we need it to break that sin we don't even see sometimes, and that ole devil, Satan, in us. So, even church folk need it, even good Christian folk. Now, you goin' to follow that road."*

He thought of her words more and more as the months and years passed. They visited him again as his heaviness roiled into anxiety, then agitation, anger, and finally, desperation.He pedaled past the repair hangers with the whirring engines of Forts receiving the urgent ministrations of their ground crews, so that the division might enlarge its next mission strength.

Parking his bike outside the mess building, he lifted it into the air to hurl it against the wall. At the last instant, it seemed to him as though the Holy Spirit himself tided over him with a wave of calm. As he lowered the bike, Cappuccio and Cochran passed him, smirking. He took a deep breath.

We got time, time to talk, and anyways, I think I know how she feels like no other girl before.

Peace and trust filled him, shunting out the other emotions, as he headed across the landing strip infield toward the grove where lay his hutment.

A couple hours later, shortly after he reckoned the Division commanders would have seen their twenty-hundred hours weather report for England and the Continent, he recognized, barely, Trigger's now-scowling voice over the Tannoy.

"Let us have a dagger between our teeth, a bomb in our hand, and an infinite scorn in our hearts. A nation of spaghetti eaters cannot restore Roman civilization! Tomorrow you will take the bombs into your hands and heave them down the flak-snarled halls of fire at the insolent, incorrigible city of Bremen! I am Benito Mussolini, and you are dismissed to your fetid huts!"

Paralyzed in mid-push-up in front of his bed at the fearsome sound of the name, he heard a pilot at the other end of the hut holler the Lord's name in vain.

No one heard "Mussolini" chuckle, *"Or perhaps Berlin or even Rome!"* Fortunately, Tavington was raking in a healthy cut from the contraband generated by Trigger and Massie, the group's cartel founder who worked in Operations when he wasn't orchestrating peach shipments from liberated Italy, strawberries from Fascist Spain, and real eggs from the Norfolk farm whose matron and at least one daughter he was personally rewarding in full. Otherwise, the group commander would have suspended Trigger from flying, pending an investigation, and delayed the date of his coming promotion to first lieutenant.

As it was, Tavington tongue-lashed him, ordered him never to mention, even in jest, a possible mission destination, and directed him to double Tavington's shares of cartel stock—at half the share price, even if Trigger had to make up the difference himself, which he found a way not to do. Tavington also expected a weekly fifth of Cutty "on the house" until Trigger completed his twenty-fifth mission.

Had they heard of Trigger's stunt, the generals at division headquarters would have been nearly as upset as the 299th's flyers were the next morning.

"Bremen," he heard a pilot a few seats away growl amidst the bitter groaning of nearly everyone who had flown previous missions to the day's just-announced destination.

Goodness, I never even heard Long John Starr er Cactus Face Taggart, back in our Sooner locker room, say some o the words these boys are usin'.

NINE

April 17, and I can't believe how cold it is in this cockpit.

The airborne group curved south on the North Sea coast near Wilhelm-shaven. A different sort of chill rippled through him. *Recognize those landmarks down there from that earlier mission.*

Keeping such gigantic machines formed within a few yards of one another whilst flying across seas and continents, when at any instant death-dealing enemy fighters could assault them took all the concentration he could muster.

And them air barons, they still believe the B-17 can fight its way, unescorted by fighters, to even the worst German targets and back.

He would have let Clifton take the plane for a spell or two, but Palmer's inexperience made him too nervous to let him have it.

Maybe on the return trip after they were back out over the North Sea and past the safe point.

Black flecks appeared far ahead, growing in clarity and number.

Palmer, who, as co-pilot without the wheel, should have spotted them first, finally said, "Is that more B-17s, sir?"

"Nah," he said, his sphincter muscle coiling. "That's a flak field waitin' on us at Bremen."

Palmer turned to him to say something, then his expression turned quizzical. When he said, "Sir?" he looked at him and an unnoticed icicle formed by the breath discharged from his oxygen mask, and running from the mask all the way down to his seat belt, cracked and cascaded onto his leg and the floor between Palmer and him.

Before he could take that in, a flock of gray-black FW-190s screamed down out of the sun, guns blazing. As the Forts returned fire, he said, "Pilot to crew. Gitcher eyes open—and start callin' out numbers and positions o' Jerries, Palmer."

They came at the formation from the front, rear, and every other direction. The plane was past the IP and Remington had control of it. He fought down an involuntary sensation of terror and panic, such as he had not experienced before or even during Wilhelmshaven. Palmer was saucer-eyed, his view darting every which way. "Palmer, what's that?"

"Sir," Palmer said, turning out his starboard window and announcing over the interphone, "Six, no eight ME-109s at three o'clock level, moving—"

"Pilot to crew, they movin' forward, boys, 'spect they'll be comin' in at us in a minute from twelve o'clock level," he said, cutting in.

One burst of flak narrowly missed them out his window, then another peppered the starboard fuselage, jolting the plane. A Fort spun flaming out of sight in the squadron ahead of *Hellfire and Brimstone.*

"Everbody all right back there?"

A chorus of voices signaled yes.

"Flak just missed me, Skipper, but I'm okay," Musso replied, back in action and full of game. *"Uh—right waist gunner to pilot."*

He heard shouting in Spanish over the interphone.

"What is it, Rodriguez?"

"Sir, Musso's shooting at the flak," Rodriguez said, over Musso's cursing.

"Musso," he said, frustrated, "you know better'n to waste your ammo like that."

Something exploded into an orange fireball directly ahead of them amidst Risinger's squadron. Some of the planes around it skittered off their Norden-piloted paths. *Dang, boys're panickin' and takin' their planes back from the bombadiers.*

A tornado of smoke and debris startled him as it flew past and into his plane.

He heard Remington in the nose shout just as something cracked his own front windshield. His eyes widened, and he held his breath, wondering if the wind would blast in. But somehow, the glass held.

For the next hour, first the flak then the fighters again continued the assault. This was way beyond the scale and intensity of Wilhelmshaven or anything he had heard about, but he had to keep his mind and strength on piloting the plane, staying tight in the combat box, and retaining command of his ship with a rookie co-pilot and navigator.

He barely heard Remington announce, *"Bombs away, squareheads."*

He couldn't keep from hearing O'Connor's ringing shout that included the increasingly-used obscene derivative of Focke Wulf. *"Tail gunner to pilot, scored me a Woof!"*

A brief burst of laughter and cheers erupted from the crew over the interphone amidst the din and dread.

"Top gunner to pilot, confirm that kill, sir," Utah said.

A half-hour out of Bremen, Messerschmitts, Focke-Wulfs, and Junkers still screamed in like groups of blazing dragons.

Dang, I messed up my chaffholder—more'n once.

Something was amiss inside his jacket, too.

My own crap's backed up through the chute almost to my shoulders. Weak and sick, he prayed to God for strength. *Don't think I've seen this many Forts go down in my other ten previous missions combined—eight, I mean.*

Disgust filled him at the remembrance of the cancelled missions.

After thirty more horrific minutes, the fighters finally relented. Then, one final phalanx of FW-190s, a half-dozen strong, wing-to-wing, spread directly ahead of the formation and charged.

"What the—" Palmer said.

"Six FW-190s comin' in, twelve o'clock level," he said for him.

Maier shouted the Lord's name in distress as he opened fire from the nose. Amidst all the sound and fury and the stench of burning gas, cordite, sweat, and smoke, Utah methodically pounded away up in the top turret with his twin fifties.

"Give it to 'em, Utah!" he said.

Here they come, Lord. The Lord is my shepherd, I shall not want, he leadeth me into green pastures—

The roar grew deafening and the wing of yet another Fort blew off just ahead of *Hellfire and Brimstone*. Explosions sounded from other directions and he saw one FW coming straight for him.

Oh, Lord, he gunna ram right into us, er shoot us to pieces.

He saw the tracers of a covey of bullets as they sang over the top of the cockpit. Then a hail of fifty-cal bullets from Utah's guns blasted apart the FW's spinner, propeller, cowling, engine, and cockpit, and the plane swerved wildly up and over him, then exploded into a thousand flaming pieces.

Numb and shaking, he offered up a prayer of thanks that had no words or coherent thoughts as the remaining FWs headed home. Just then, the black ME-109 came screaming down from the now-westward-leaning sun and unleashed a furious barrage on the Fort ahead and to the right of him—one of whose engines burst into flames—and sent a stream of fire into *Hellfire and Brimstone*, rocking the plane as voices shouted over the interphone.

He called out to God and ducked away. Terrified, he swerved directly into the path of Trigger's *Jesse James*. He jerked the steering yoke to the right and Trigger swerved to the left. His plane clipped a chunk off *Jesse James's* right wingtip—maybe about a foot—but both planes straightened and leveled out, then proceeded forward.

"Dang there, Parson," Trigger said over the liaison channel.

"Sorry 'bout that, Trigger," he said, wondering if the refuse had crawled up a little closer to his neck.

He glimpsed the black ME barrel-rolling away and back toward home as

Rodriguez's agonized voice screamed over the interphone, *"Left waist gunner to pilot—black* diablo *blew Musso's head off!"*

—

Even the MPs out front of the interrogation and briefing building looked wary as the surviving crews, raccoon-faced from the crusted dirt and sweat painted on their faces around where their oxygen masks had been, slogged in under a cold drizzle and a dark late afternoon. Rain drummed on the corrugated tin roof as the officers mumbled their reports like monotoned drones. He and most of the rest answered what was asked, but their brains could take them no further. The interrogation officers had to pull out of them what had happened piece by bloody piece. He explained with equal clarity and dispassion the weather conditions on the mission, the handling of his plane, and his wrapping Musso's severed, gelatinous head in his, Lance's, leather helmet, gently carrying it to the ambulance, and handing it to the sorrowful attendant. He did not mention Rodriguez weeping like a child and trying to take the head from the ambulance man.

After completing his report, he strode toward the Red Cross counter, thanked the chubby girl for the shot of Scotch, and declined it, but for the first time it tempted him. It might dull whatever horror now pressed in against the numbness. Dismissing the thought, he took the proffered Mars bar and a mug of steaming coffee, then made the usual stops at the equipment room, his hut, the showers, and the Officers' Mess Hall Number 2. That room proved as quiet as the interrogation and briefing building.

After a couple of minutes, Waddy and Patton joined him, Patton patting him gently on the shoulder as he got to the table. He barely noticed and did not respond. No one said anything besides "Pass the salt" until Waddy mumbled with a mouthful of beans, "Hear Risinger bought it?" He heard it but did not process the meaning till he woke up at 2 a.m., not to Kupchak's jostling him and shining a flashlight in his face, but to the sounds of a pilot down the hall screaming in his sleep.

———

He ain't Jeb, but he'll do.

The vague notion wafted through his numb mind as he and Sarah rode a couple of stumpy plow horses from the farm of Moll's brother twenty miles southwest of Beccles into the tiny, chestnut-tree festooned village of Stradbroke. They had traveled with Moll and his wife in the Molls' ancient little Singer Junior motor car for the day's outing during his next liberty, on the Saturday exactly one week after the Bremen raid.

Twice, Moll narrowly avoided collisions with other vehicles careening around narrow, curvy country lanes. He recognized such driving as a practice among the English and wondered whether he might survive twenty-five bullet, cannon, flak, and ice-infested bomber missions only to meet his demise on a pastoral Suffolk road.

"So strange," Sarah said as their horses clomped past century-old stone cottages. When he did not respond, she continued, "Only a few miles away, death looms, ready to fall at any moment from the sky—roaring, flaming, bloody death—yet here, we might almost be traversing Eden."

"Hmm," he replied without enthusiasm, barely glancing at her.

"Oh, Lance, dear." She reached to him from astride her horse. "I am so sorry for whatever happened on that last—horrid—mission. I do so want to comfort you and make you happy."

He turned and searched her face. As the soft spring breeze tousled his sandy colored hair, his expression, though weary, softened and endearment tinged his eyes. "I know ye do, darlin'." He squeezed her hand, pulling it to his mouth, and kissing it. "And I'm so thankful and so lucky—that you're my friend. I jist gotta trust the Lord, that He'll bring me through it and won't gimme no more'n I can hannel."

She gazed at him as though marveling. "I've just, never before, known a person who speaks of the Lord as though He is so intimate an acquaintance, even friend," she said. "I—I hope some of it will 'rub off' on me as Americans say."

He leaned toward her, wrapped a muscular arm around her tiny waist, pulled her to him, and put his lips to hers. The tolling of a bell nearly startled them off their horses. He whirled around, his ears ringing. The stone church tower was one of the tallest and most impressive he had ever witnessed, a hundred and twenty-five feet high and no more than a hundred feet away, across a greening old graveyard.

"Goodness gracious."

"Oh, Lance, darling, do let's go in!"

"Aw, I don't know—"

But she was off her horse, tying it to a nearby traffic sign, and hurrying toward the massive oaken front doors. He chuckled, shook his head, and followed.

"They say a great man served as vicar here in the late 1800s," Sarah whispered, as though not to intrude, when they got inside. Her eyes gazed up and around the oaken arches high above as they walked down the center aisle, winged by dark polished wood pews and stone pillars.

"Yeah?" he said, heading for the shiny cherry pulpit that looked down and out over the sanctuary. "Who was it?"

"Rylie, I think," she said, watching him as he mounted the winding staircase up to the pulpit. "No—Ryle."

"Ryle?" he asked, startled anew as he looked out at her and placed his hands on the sides of the pulpit. "J. C. Ryle?"

"Why, yes," she said, "I think that was it. How could you know that?"

"Oh," he said, looking down at the pulpit, life surging back through him and empowering his voice. "Yeah, this looks like where he was! Know what's carved around this here pulpit, right where the preacher'll see it when he looks down at his Bible?" He looked back out at her. *"Woe to him who preaches not the gospel of our Lord Jesus Christ."*

She stared at him. His attention returned to the carving and the pulpit.

"Lance?" she said softly, the cavernous building carrying her lilting voice to him.

"Yeah?"

"Do you realize I've never heard a lad—a man—speak such words other than in jest? Not even the vicars around here do so."

"Huh? Whadduya mean?"

"They say this used to be a very religious country." She walked slowly toward him, the prismatic beauty of the sun cascading through the Scripture-laden stained glass to one side snaring her gaze. When she reached the stairs, she climbed them til she stood alongside him in the pulpit, bordered by the crescent-shaped rim with Ryle's enduring declaration.

His face had hung slack all day. Now energy animated it. He gave her a small grin, then turned, glanced again at the carved words, looked out over the room, and gripped the sides of the pulpit. His voice boomed, "Behold, I am the Lord, the God of all flesh—is there anything too hard for me?" He paused an instant, glanced at her with a wink, then concluded, one fist thumping the top of the pulpit, "And God did it!"

When he turned back to her, her eyes glittered in the reflected colors of the sun-splashed stained glass and her chest seemed to roll a bit like the tide he saw the day he and Waddy went to the beach at Aldesbury. Her lips had never looked fuller or moister, and she said, "Lance, dear, I love you with all my heart and I've never loved another."

His own heart thumping with power, he swept her into his arms at the pulpit and kissed her mouth, her cheeks, her chin, her neck and—

"I say, cheerio, may I help you?"

They turned, startled yet again, to see a thin, tallish man of sixty with a thatch of silver hair and a clerical frock walking toward them.

Missed, lost, and blown opportunities through the years and the girls sped through his mind—Sadie—Mary Katherine—and he asked in an echoing voice, "Will ye marry us right now, sir?"

—

The kindly vicar had lived through four years of this war, four of the "Great" one, and, as it turned out, a couple in South Africa with the Calvinistic Boers at the turn of the century. He didn't need much persuasion to perform the ceremony, and in a manner, that, if somewhat condensing the majestic Anglican wedding ceremony, retained the spirit and beauty of it.

Upon Sarah's final, "I do so promise," life not only full but fuller than ever he could have imagined it filled him and he kissed her lips long.

"Pastor?" he asked after, blushing, "er, Father, sir?"

The vicar laughed merrily, his blue eyes twinkling.

"Well, sir," he said, pulling several English pound notes from his pocket and handing them to the older man, "can you watch our horses fer jist a spell? I don't reckon they got the game in 'em to do much more'n munch them wildflowers sproutin' up in your churchyard where we tethered 'em, but, well, Sarah and me need to go run and do somethin' real quick-like, then we'll be right back."

The vicar laughed the more, seeing that the young husband and wife had already backed several feet toward the front entrance, hand in hand, giggling. Rightly interpreting his mirth as approval, they turned and raced at a full run out of the church, leaving the hulking doors wide open.

The vicar's delighted hoots had barely ceased echoing through the mighty old structure when he and Sarah dived onto a shrub-concealed patch of clover in the rear of the graveyard, at the foot of a cherry tree whose ancient, blossom-festooned boughs stretched like protective arms over them, dappling them with fragrant white blossoms.

The blood so rushed to his head at the enormity of the situation and the beauty of Sarah's smooth supple ivory body at last revealed and offered to him, that at the moment of consummation, sensing withal the thoroughgoing pleasure of God Almighty, and overwhelmed with gratitude—*You saved me for her, sir, through all the years and all the close calls, and through no doin' o my own!* He lost his sight for a few seconds and nearly fainted. By then, transported by her own rapture, Sarah did not even notice, and when his ardor soon resumed, their cries could be heard at the church and their deep passion recognized.

—

When they returned some hours later to Little Chickasaw, Mrs. Johnston was asleep. Sarah, her face possessed by joy, asked him, as he battled to stymie the giggles that kept trying to escape from him, to sit a moment on the couch. Then she walked to a set of book cases in the hall between the living room and her mother's room. He saw her searching a minute for something, then, her face brightening in recognition, pulling it out and bringing it to him.

"*Exposition on the Book of Matthew,*" he read aloud from its cover, "J. C. Ryle." Surprised, he opened to the front pages. "London, 1856." He looked up at her, his green eyes blinking in amazement. "Where'dja git this?"

"My father's father," she said. "He died when I was little, but they say he— well, he may have been the last man around our family who spoke—who believed—as you do, darling."

He pulled her down and laid her on the couch and again demonstrated how he loved and desired every inch, not just of her body, but of her soul, yet only to fill it to overflowing with joy and contentment.

I wonder how many days we can just stay—like this—with each other if we plan it out!

She giggled, laughed and screamed his name, delirious and tossing in escalating waves until she took the ravenous lead, *imago dei*, oblivious to her sleeping mother in the next room, oblivious to anything at all outside. The only world that mattered to either of them now, was that within their few feet of soft, sacred couch.

TEN

He sprang up from the couch the next morning, leaping into the air with joy and nearly knocking himself out when his head struck the low ceiling. Mrs. Johnston felt thrilled when they accompanied her breakfast in bed with their matrimonial announcement.

"We goin to church this mornin, honey, to praise the Lord fer His goodness and leadin' us to each other in the middle all this craziness!" he said to Sarah, wrapping his arms around her waist and swinging her up and around in Mrs. Johnston's bedroom, as the coughing, but delighted woman hooted with pleasure.

"Lance, love, tis true," Sarah said that afternoon as he led her to another pastoral setting for their lovemaking, a secluded spot behind the Beccles Common, albeit this time with a thick woolen blanket beneath them. "You boys from the Wild West are a bunch of outlaws!" She screamed the final words in delight as he discovered new spots of enchantment on her body. "You boys from Oklahoma and Texas! Is Oklahoma part of the Texas country?"

He growled at that and nuzzled and nibbled the more.

"You-all!" she mimicked him with glee.

When finally, they lay satisfied in one another's arms as the late April sun warmed them, she looked at him and said, "Dearest, there is something about which I've wondered for the longest time. Will you not think me foolish if I ask it?"

"Course not."

"Well," She bit her lip. "Actually, I have two questions."

"One," he said, kissing one side of her neck. "Two." He kissed the other side.

Squealing and squirming, she flipped at his hand, giggling. "Stop, silly boy, you are bad!"

"Okay," he said, affecting chastisement. "What're these questions?"

Drawing in a breath, she said, "Did you ride the stagecoach to school?"

"The what? The stage—"

"Yes—don't Americans, especially in Texas, I mean in the West, ride the stagecoach lots of places?"

He examined her face, as though an irony or silly message lurked somewhere, but found none.

"No, you, silly goose!" He tickled under one of her arms, "I ain't never rode a stagecoach in my life! We don't have stage coaches any more." He paused. "Though they is an old one parked out there in the Post Oak Mission church barn."

"So, do you want to hear my second question?"

"No," he said, rising to his feet, lifting her squealing body from the blanket, tossing her over his shoulder on her back, then spinning around and around in the sun and breeze, the taut muscles rippling across his tall, lean body.

"Did you wear a six-gun to protect yourself?" She screamed and laughed so deliriously she began to choke as he continued to spin. "Lance! Stop! Lance!" When, finally, he wobbled dizzily and slowed, she asked, shuddering with more laughter, "Did you wear a pistol and shoot all those other bad Yankee boys like you with it?"

Ignoring his dizziness, he spun quicker again. "Yankee? I told you I ain't no dad-blamed Yankee, girl! And I ain't from Texas, neither! I'm from Duncan, Oklahoma, and the shortgrass country and that's a million miles away from the dam—uh, from the Yankees!"

"Oh!" she said, surprised but giggling as he kept spinning her petite body, "You said a curse word, Lance Roark, Husband! For shame!"

"Okay, uncle." He fell to his knees, huffing and puffing, spilling her back onto the blanket. "I give. You win. My legs're no match for your mouth, ye little Limey vamp!" Then he fell onto her, tickling her again in the usual places and some new ones as she writhed and squealed.

"I shall have to tell your poor mum what a bad, bad boy you are, Lance Roark!" she said as he covered her again.

—

He bicycled in to the station the next evening just as Waddy and Trigger came roaring in from a pub in Beccles.

Waddy slapped him on the shoulder. "Hey, Podnah!"

"Dang, you boys smell like a brewery," he replied, smiling.

"That ain't all ole Trigger nearly smelt like." His old friend shook with laughter.

"Hey, you shut up, Wadster." Trigger staunched a smile and took a pull from a half pint of bourbon.

"I ain't never seen that brand before," Waddy said. "That some o that cartel booty you rakin' in?"

"Cartel?" Lance asked.

"Yeah," Waddy said, cradling Trigger's neck with one arm, then balling up a fist and rubbing the top of his head with the knuckles of his other hand. "Trigger and ole Massie runnin"em a full-blown bidness from right here in our lovely station, Podnah!" He got louder and rubbed harder as Trigger tried without success to get loose. "Shippin"em oranges from Algeria, 'maters from Portgual, and whoppin' cantaloupes from Morocca! Ain't that right, Trig!"

Finally squirming loose with a full-throated shout of pain, Trigger said,

"You inbred gorilla! You try that again, I'll git me one o' them Sicilian mobsters our Eye-talian partner knows to snuff your lard butt out!"

All three of them stood mute for a moment as that sank in, but within seconds they were quaking with laughter.

"Look, he jist tryin' to take the limelight off his own sorry married hide, Lance," Trigger said.

"Me?" Waddy's omnipresent grin widening as he yacked at Trigger. "Flirtin' your young Okie tail off with that tall Limey drink o water all night—cute fer him, too, Parson," he said, turning his attention to Lance, "when this ole blue hair granny smokin' a pipe proceeds to tell me, 'That girl's the worst —awright, she didn't say —'She's the worst *girl* your friend could possibly git involved with.' Then she proceeds to describe her like she worse'n one o them Bela Lugosi vampires. So, I ask her how she knows all that, see? Well, what the Sam Hill, she rears back, blows out a mouthful o' smoke and says, 'Cuz she's my Royal Navy son's wife, when he been in the Pacific goin' on three years!" Then he turned back to Trigger and said, "Say, gimme a pull on that high-dollar Limey firewater ye got'cherself there, bub."

He reckoned he would wait a day to tell Waddy the matrimonial news, and he would insist his buddy tell no one else at the base.

—

Several things grew clear over the next couple of months. One was, due to the rainy weather, the group was lucky to fly one non-practice mission a week.

At least one that counts. He shook off a twinge of bitterness. *Course, that's givin' our new right waist gunner, Jackson, a chance to git his ducks in a row. Not that he's short on confidence.*

Killing Germans seemed about the only thing that fired up Jackson as much as his ardent evangelical faith. Son of a World War I combat veteran and Alabama Baptist pastor who cheered Alvin York's idea to execute Lindbergh as a traitor. The grandson of missionaries to India, Jackson quickly clashed with

O'Connor and the tail gunner's running stream of lewd sarcasm toward the Army and toward the Army Air Force's high command.

"Whadduya 'spect from a godless Papist?" Jackson asked him one evening as they walked toward the base chapel for the evening's Bible study and prayer meeting, led by Patton and the new Protestant chaplain. "And how in tarnation can Patton stomach ministerin' with that cigarette-suckin', whiskey-'bibbin' apostate of a so-called minister? I knew the Methodists were goin' downhill, but that boy done plowed hisself halfway to China."

He tended toward agreement with Jackson regarding the chaplain and O'Connor, though he liked and respected the latter, but he remembered Waddy telling him of a conversation in the cold showers in which Jackson shook his head regarding "the Satanic-inspired pacifism o the Mennonites and Quakers. Praise God we got us a pilot and co-pilot what broke loose o them devilish bonds and doin' a lotta good now."

Jackson, meanwhile, had been shouldering arms since he popped his first squirrel at age eight.

And he's the most accurate gunner I've had yet, maybe the best in the squadron. We'll see if that holds when he's got the Germans blastin' away at him. Though I suspect it will. Anyhow, ever time we go up on real missions, more o the boys don't come back.

Fewer and fewer faces he knew returned to enjoy the Officer's Club's new mahogany bar, courtesy of Trigger, or the mess hall, and more and more huts lodged new men from the replacement crews that had begun shipping in. Trigger—who himself had narrowly escaped death on the previous mission when a golf ball-sized chunk of .88 shrapnel took off the left side of his helmet but did not scratch him—said one bed a couple huts over held its fourth flyer since the 299th arrived in January.

And another thang—they's boys round here still laughs and smiles and cuts up, they just ain't many can do it sober, now.

Thanks to the attrition and their own hard-won experience and skill, by the end of June and his sixteenth counted mission, he, Waddy, and Patton had each been promoted to first lieutenant and received squadron commands in the group.

Attrition, indeed. Out o the dozen Forts in the squadron when Wad, Patton, and me flew our first mission, only one crew 'sides ours is still flyin'.

In five months, German fighters, flak, a runway crash, a mid-air collision with another Fort that was shot up and spiraling toward the earth, and a pilot's mental breakdown had taken out all the others.

I wonder how Roosevelt'll explain such casualty rates, if they don't change, to the American people. I assume he continues to deceive whenever he sees fit to do so. And it ain't like the Eighth's a bunch o' bozos up here with no idea what we're doin'. A blind man could see we got us the cream o' the nation in this air corps, even if some of 'em ain't exactly my best buddies.

And did the worst nightmares of his life that began shortly after Bremen typically accompany such promotions in rank? Or the stinging, aching shingles that appeared behind his right shoulder a couple weeks later? Or the tremors in his left hand that started a few days ago?

Sojourns with Sarah every week or so, along with Patton's Bible Study and the Sunday morning Protestant service Patton helped lead in the base chapel, somewhat steadied his nerves. He counted not just the days, but the hours till his next rendezvous with his secret wife. He labored to force her from his mind on mission days, however, because death loomed at every turn, even with his full powers of concentration. Divided attention would kill not just himself, but the rest of his crew and perhaps others.

Letters and occasional care packages from Mama, Grandpa Schroeder—who remained kind and supportive in his writing despite the disappointment and embarrassment of his pursuit of a military, even combat, role in the war—and Klassen and a couple other friends from the old family church near Corning remained welcome, though an odd, indistinct sense of distance from them had lately grown.

Almost like I'm readin' letters written to somebody else, somebody with a life sorta familiar, but different from mine. Somebody that didn't have the wife I ain't told the folks back home about either, even Mama.

He couldn't shake a queer sense that telling them about it might jeopardize it.

A week into July, a marathon curtain of clouds over England and Northern Europe abated long enough for him to complete his seventeenth mission and start his eighteenth, until engine troubles forced him to abort over the Channel and return to base. So strong was his desire to notch the eighteenth, it took the combined urgings of Palmer, Maier, and Utah all but threatening to mutiny for him to turn around.

"You okay, bud?" Utah asked as they climbed down the front hatch and out of the plane. Other than that, all he detected was a glance from Palmer.

When he himself gave a largely-accurate description of the sequence in the post-mission debriefing, Palmer, seated next to him, seemed satisfied and nothing more happened, other than the intelligence officer's low-key comment, "You've been doing this long enough to know you're making decisions like that for ten men, not just one, right?"

"Yes, sir." As seemed increasingly the case, however, his thoughts were on not just those ten, but—

—*'specially one little lady—sir.*

After the cloud cover returned for a couple of days, during which time Trigger delivered a box of fresh grapefruits to Waddy and him, courtesy of his thriving cartel, the entire Eighth Air Force stood down, all liberty suspended, in preparation for something Patton had heard whispered "would be really big."

One night as he and Waddy shot pool in the OC, the Tannoy crackled to life.

"Hello, North America, Germany calling," the robust English-accented voice of Trigger bellowed through the speakers across the base.

"Lord Haw Haw," Waddy chuckled with weary amusement.

Time was, he woulda been howlin' at this.

Trigger's most comical reindition yet unfolded. Scattered laughter gradually rose into hoots—*seems sorta stilted tonight*—across the OC as the flyers recognized the imitation of the infamous Irish-American William Joyce. Along with the leggy, sensual Axis Sally—also an American—Joyce was the best-known of the Nazi radio propagandists.

"To say the British Empire is in danger today would be a feeble understatement,"

Trigger concluded in the snorting English accent Joyce affected while on air. *"Last month alone, the German forces sank one, er—one aircraft carrier, one cruiser, three destroyers, and a number of, uh—smaller vessels. And—they damaged two battleships."*

"Two—battleships!" a tobacco-chewing co-pilot howled with gleeful epithets from the other end of the club.

"The British Empire is weak and scattered all over the world," "Lord Haw Haw" rambled on. *"It has yet to perceive the plight into which they have allowed Churchill to lead it. It must pray the fearsome flyers of the United States Army Air Forces' 299th Group, those few who still fill their cold, clammy bunks tonight, rise up and smite the Hun from the smoking, flaming, iron-filled skies over Northern Europe tomorrow morning!"*

"Well that's a first," he said, pocketing the eight ball and winning the game.

"What is?" Waddy tossed down his cue, then tossed back a final mug of weak wartime English beer.

"Trigger made that announcement drunk on his kiester."

"Well who in their right mind'd send us where we fixin' to go, sober?" Waddy said, heading for the door.

—

"Men, the Eighth has been fighting, bleeding, and dying for nearly a year to take the fight to Hitler," Lodge said the next morning at briefing. "And we— you—have been the only ones doing so. Well today, we begin giving Hitler more fight than he ever wanted. We are going beyond the Rhine—way beyond—and we are going to hit him where it hurts."

"Little peckerwood finally git past puberty?" Waddy whispered to him in their seats halfway back in the large room. "Actually seems to have a pulse today."

He didn't hear any jokes when Lodge jerked back the curtain to reveal the scarlet thread stretching from Beccles to, "Hamburg, gentlemen."

"What the—?"

Miscellaneous other mutterings and epithets accompanied the exclamation, as well as at least one soft whistle of incredulity.

"That's right, men," Lodge said. "The second-largest city in Germany and the largest port on the European continent. The Brits have been plastering it right along, but today we're going after it, and unlike them we're not going for homes, schools, and churches, we're going to take out some of the biggest aircraft engine production facilities and U-boat plants in the entire Third Reich."

The many implications of Lodge's brief, spirited announcement spun his head. Gradually, the sensation grew of a dagger plunging through his solar plexus.

So far it is, much farther than we ever gone before.... Hamburg's ack-ack is fearsome and the whole danged Luftwaffe'll git a shot at us by the time we git there and back.... We bombin' a city full o people, Nordens er not, ain't nobody can drop no pickles in barrels from twenty-five thousand feet....

His head drooped to his chest and he barely heard Lodge announce how their new auxiliary tanks, or "babies," would allow the rugged P-47 Thunderbolt fighters to escort the Forts most of the way to Hamburg, and others to rejoin them for most of the trip home—

Worst of all, now I'm worried 'bout gittin' back to Sarah. Now that she's in my world—now that she fills my world, my heart, my future—well it's like she took the sword I wanted to use to smite the Krauts out o my hand. I can't seem to hate nobody now—'cept maybe the jokers issued these orders.

—

The sentiment carried forward to Hamburg, where the towering gray curtain rising into view an hour before they reached the city was not clouds, but smoke from the British pulverizing it the night before, and tens of thousands of feet below was—*Gotterdammerung.*

Lord, what is happening to them—folk? That ain't the German military fillin' that city down there.

"Right waist gunner to pilot, only with thine eyes shalt thou behold and see the reward of the wicked," Jackson said, as Remington loosed their own five-thousand-pound payload.

ELEVEN

AUGUST, 1943

"It ain't big, but I'll git her a bigger one when we git back to the States," he said to Waddy one sunny morning a week and one mission after they flew four times to Hamburg in six nights. Waddy admired the ring Trigger had gotten him for a steal through the cartel.

"Heck you say, it's plenty big and plenty purdy, too," Waddy said. "I think ye oughta show it off to the boys at breakfast, maybe light a spark under 'em so's they'll get off their cans and get their own gals."

"Nah, I don't wanna make a scene," he said. "But—you can start tellin' 'em after I bike off fer Beccles in a little while. And, thanks fer keepin' it quiet, Wad. Really appreciate it, pard. I think I come closer to spillin the beans than you did."

"Yup, ole Trigger sure come through this time, Podnah," Waddy said. "How's his squirts?"

"I don't reckon good." His grin faded. He hadn't mentioned to Waddy the base "flight surgeon's" tentative declaration of the painful, pimply skin rash spreading behind his own right shoulder, across his right chest, and on the back of his left hand as shingles, and the Doc's prescribing of calamine lotion for it. "Guess on the way back from Hamburg, after it got cold again, some of it froze between his cheeks and a hunk of his, uh, sphincter, come out with it when he got back here. They played heck sewin' it up."

"Sweet Nellie Bly," Waddy said. "Why, he didn't say nothin' to me."

"Well I don't expect he's goin' around braggin about it," he said. "'Sides, I got at least three boys in my own crew poopin' their brains out ever day now."

"Yeah, I noticed that stocky little ball turret gunner o yours looks a little frail these days," Waddy said. "Who else?"

"Blevins my radio man and O'Connor."

"Really? Smart-aleck tail gunner?" When he nodded, Waddy thought for a moment. "Sorta been rough since Bremen, ain't it?"

He said nothing.

"That why Trigger was in the hospital fer a few days? Wadn't no virus?" Waddy asked.

"'Magine so."

"Stupid cracker," Waddy said. "Why the heck he not tell anybody?"

"Only way I knew was Patton told me private-like to pray for him," he said. "Guess he's only one Trigger asked to sit in there a spell with him."

"Patton's the prince o the whole Eighth," Waddy said.

"He said the hospital stint give Trig time to gin up more cartel bidness," he said. "Had his gophers and couriers runnin' in and out. Patton thinks they got planes from the Eighth, Ninth, and that new Fifteenth all transportin' product for 'em."

Waddy chuckled and shook his head. "Crazy moron. Well, like he always says, 'Rich folks gittin rich off this war, why can't I?' No matter what he rakes in, it ain't too much fer gittin' your keister shot off." He glanced around, saw the door to their room open, got up and closed it, and came back, his voice low. "Say, buddy, you hear anything 'bout that Ploesti raid other night?"

"The Ninth, Liberators?" he said. "Oilfields in—"

"Romania." Waddy nodded and looked around again. "Yeah, that's it. You hear what happened?"

"No."

Waddy ground his lip for a second then said, "One o Patton's buddies in Division Intel told him if you could imagine Dante's Inferno a'flamin' and spread out a couple hunnerd miles crosst the sky, well that was Ploesti."

"Whadduya mean?"

"Guess they sent several groups o Libs up from Libya, nearly fifteen hunnerd miles each way, crosst the Mediterranean, over nine-thousand-foot-high mountains in eastern Europe. Krauts busted their code and was waitin' on our boys." Waddy paused for a moment and he was tempted to tell him to stop, but like not turning away from a horrible automobile accident when he knew he should, he said nothing. "Went in at two hunnerd miles an hour, fi'ty feet above the ground—"

"Fi'ty feet?"

"Fi'ty feet," Waddy said. "Formations got shook up by crashes en route, aborts, giant cloud columns, and navigational errors. One group flew clear to Budapest, then back. They come in from all directions. Patton's buddy said Jerries got more flak guns round Ploesti then they do Berlin. And thousands o' machine gun nests and rapid-fire cannon, stuck on roofs, out o' windows, inside haystacks, fer miles in ever direction o' Ploesti. Our boys had eighty-eights shootin' *down* at'em from surroundin' hills."

They heard a pilot shout a profanity from the next hut over.

Waddy paused again and took a pull from a half pint of whiskey Lance had not noticed. He glanced at his wristwatch.

Seven hunnerd hours. He felt a pang.

Absent-mindedly licking his lips, Waddy added, "We was droppin' time-delay bombs so's we wouldn't blow ourselves up, only we blew up planes comin' in behind us. Our incendiaries were blowin' up oil tanks jist by hittin' 'em, and we was so low, the flames shot up and torched the Libs comin' up after. Tops o' the tanks was flyin' through the air and slicin' other planes in two."

His shingles started aching, stabbing his upper right body clean through. He tried to rub them, but that worsened the pain. He uttered an expletive, his head canting downward.

"Looks like we may o' lost forty percent of our planes and men," Waddy said, taking another pull.

After a moment, that sank in and he looked up. *"Forty* percent? O' five groups? In one mission?"

"Sheesh, let's go git us some o' that four-star breakfast, *amigo,"* Waddy said, stashing away the half-pint.

—

A bit of life had returned to the Officers Mess as the weeks passed since Bremen, but nothing like before that raid. So, the loudness and anger in Trigger's and Jackson's voices as they argued surprised him.

"Tellin' ye it's true," Trigger said, with a mouthful of powdered eggs, showing no ill effects from his wound other than perhaps the size of his temper.

"Yeah?" Jackson shot back, sweeping a *Stars and Stripes* newspaper up off the table and brandishing it. "Well, why ain't nobody done said nothin' 'bout it yet in here?"

"You think they gonna plaster somethin' in there 'bout a bunch o' jigs flyin' million dollar fighter planes 'round Europe against the best air force in the world—'cept fer us, o' course." Trigger's jaw flushed crimson.

"What is it?" Waddy asked as he and Lance sat down.

"I heard from some folks, lot higher up the food chain than this numbskull, Army's latest brain-belch is a bunch o' colored boys flyin P-51s as escort for Fifteenth Air bombers in Italy." Trigger's disbelief was apparent.

"What?" Waddy asked, startled.

"Tuskogee Air Group er some such."

Jackson shook his head. "Lettin' darkies fly million-dollar machines! Next thing ye know, they'll be letting 'em pilot Forts and Libs!"

"Or monkeys," someone a few seats down the table said, to snickers.

"Day they jam one of those African baboons in the pilot's seat of a Fort is the day I switch sides," O'Connor, in the OC for a moment to bring Lance some aspirin, said. "Need to deal with 'em same way we do in Boston. Screw up anything they do, anywhere they go."

He had to marvel, even if in sadness, at the passion, hatred, and imagination with which O'Connor lathered his blitzkrieg of racially-inspired vulgarities which followed.

"What do you say, St. Patty?" Waddy called to Patton, sitting several seats down, quietly eating oatmeal. "Tween the Jerries and the coloreds, who'd you side with?"

Patton lowered his spoon and thought for a moment. "Well, the Jerries are givin' us plenty o trouble over here, but the coloreds are liable to give us even more trouble than they have before back in the States once the war's over— 'specially if the Army lets 'em fly airplanes—which by the way I hear they might be." His brow furrowed as he struggled for an answer. Finally, his face lit up. "How 'bout we don't side with either of 'em, wallop Hades outa the Japs, and all go home?"

More than a couple of heads nearby nodded their agreement all through Patton's comments.

Sarah'd say side with the colored boys for sure, but no way Sadie ner Mary Katherine would.

Just then, one of the hulking MPs stepped inside, strode to Trigger, and spoke into his ear.

Trigger bellowed a joyous obscenity, rose to his feet, and addressed the entire room. "Boys, don't say ole Trig never done nothin' for ya. That is, if ye'd care to join me in the OC, after ye gag through the rest o' this dung and partake o' the first on-base craps table in the entire bloody division!"

A solitary "What the hell?" from Cappuccio preceded the loudest and throatiest cheer he had heard since long before Bremen.

—

By the time Trigger—excusing himself twice during the set-up to run to the bathroom—had his craps table operating with a dealer he had recruited from his ground crew and whom Tavington had breveted to technical sergeant in return for a one-time bonus above his usual cartel cut, he had tucked Sarah's ring, encased in a tiny box, into a pocket of his olive colored tunic, grabbed a bicycle from the rack next to the OC, and headed into Beccles.

I'll git her some o' them purty roses from Mr. Moll on the way!

He could barely keep the bike straight as he gleefully peddled through the warming sunshine that cascaded down from the cloudless azure sky. Lush amber fields and green pastures spangled with yellow daffodils that seemed to smile with delight stretched away to both sides from the road. The closer he pedaled to the Waveney bridge, the more his heart swelled with joy, and the further the pain of the shingles and the memory of missions, and all they were, receded.

"With gladness Thou hast filled my heart, more than in the time their corn and their wine increased!" he said toward a little garden warbler singing in his high quick chirping way atop a nearby hedgerow. The plump creature quieted and eyed him as he sailed past, then resumed his ancient song. The melody expressed his own feelings better than any sound he could utter.

He waved to Mr. Wade the dock manager as he pedaled over the bridge into town. *The entire world looks brighter and clearer than ever it done before, 'cuz o her! I hear keener, see sharper.*

"I even smell better!" He inhaled the redolence of the town center's fruit market, fish and chips frying, and popcorn sizzling in the lobby of the Regal Theater, whose front doors stood open in the August daylight.

And I bet I can smell me some o them Bounty candy bars in Mr. Moll's store from out here on the road if I sniff real close!

He wheeled up to the store, chuckling until Moll came out the front door carrying a large package, then stopped dead in his tracks, anvil-faced at the sight of him.

Moll's eyes welled over with tears. A moment later someone with a shuddering, cracking version of his voice was saying, "O my dear, dear lad, I tried

116   *John J. Dwyer*

giving you a ring at the base on the telephone, but they said you had just left. You see, my boy, she—our—your—Sarah—well—"

Only later that unending dark night did he digest the part about the German observation plane shot down by a Hurricane crashing into the hospital where she was nursing injured children, killing the pilot, doctors, nurses, other women, children, and Sarah Johnston Roark, aged twenty, land girl and daughter, nurse and wife, of Beccles, Suffolk, England.

She and an unborn baby, two months in her womb.

TWELVE

Once word got out—through Waddy—about Sarah and him, the honchos at Division assigned the crew of *Hellfire and Brimstone* ten days at one of its new rest houses, this one up in Norfolk, not far from the Wash. The plane was out of commission again, anyway, having taken a pounding from both fighters and flak guns on the Hamburg missions.

The rest house occupied a sprawling estate manor relinquished for the war by its owner to the Army Air Forces. It offered everything a young man whose wife had not just been killed could wish for. The billiards, ping pong, swimming pool, basketball, tennis, croquet, library, juke box, and especially the American nurses, some of whom were attractive, would have made the stay delightful indeed.

But day after day, he ate so little that O'Connor, now knowing like the other flyers what had happened, said without mirth, "Come on, Boss, you're tall and skinny as your pal Lindbergh now. Jeez, you turn sideways, you're gonna vanish into thin—uh, flipping Limey air."

He mostly stayed curled up in a ball in his bed as thoughts and visions of Sarah and their union hurtled in and out of his mind. He must have drunk a hundred glasses of lemonade and his shingles disappeared. He appreciated the army doctors and psychiatrists who tried without success to reach him, and by the time the ten days were up, he was ready—no, for the first time since the beginning of his missions—*eager*—to get back in the air. A preoccupation with killing Germans on the ground and in the sky, began to grow within his aching bosom.

He forgot to take his Bible back to the station with him.

—

Tavington spoke privately with him when he returned. The group commander expressed his heartfelt condolences and asked whether he would like more time off, perhaps even a thirty-day furlough back to the States.

"I can rotate in your seat with Palmer, the Air Exec, and another officer I know who's available," Tavington said with a solicitousness he had never before seen from him. "I've been seeing to it I get more hours up there with you—with the Group."

"No, sir, but thank ye, sir," he said earnestly, having heard as much from Patton, but still numb and chilled as he'd been since he heard the news of Sarah. "I think it'll do me good to get back to bidness. Otherwise...." His voice and gaze trailed off.

"We can also use you in Operations for awhile," Tavington said. "You've got a keen sense of such things, and that's not just my opinion."

"I'd ruther git back flyin', sir. I promise I won't let ye down."

Tavington studied him. "All right, Roark, I had already determined to keep you on the ground for a while longer, but—well, some big doings are afoot and it's 'all-hands-on-deck' as they say. I can, darned sure, use one of my—best—squadron commanders helping to lead them."

His eyes widened. Neither Tavington nor anyone else in command above him had ever expressed such a sentiment. He leaned forward a bit in his metal chair. "You'll git the best I got, sir. Better'n ever before."

"Like before is good enough." Tavington rose from his chair to conclude the meeting. "But you're going to fly at least two practice missions before you go anywhere farther than jolly old England." Detecting a trace of alarm in his face, he added, "Don't worry, the doings to which I referred won't pass you by. That first practice run will be this afternoon. But Palmer is going to instruct you on his responsibilities, because I want him taking the plane twice what he normally would, and I want you and him prepared to switch roles on a dime, at any time."

He stifled a wry grin.

I knew Palmer's job better'n he does now before he ever flew his first mission in Hellfire and Brimstone.

But what he said, with a snappy salute, was, "Thank ye, sir, ye won't regret it."

—

The practice missions the next two days went well, as did a short run escorted by British Spitfires to the *Luftwaffe* airfield just across the Channel in northeast France on August 15. The next day, they flew farther south, to the LeBourget airport outside Paris. Messerschmitts and Focke-Wulfs tore up the more-exposed low squadrons, but the attacks on the high formations where he was proved light, even after the accompanying American P-47s turned back. Just as he reached the IP, however, he winced and felt a cold shudder run through him when he saw a ripple of white smoke puffs just below the plane.

"Cripes, peppered me!" Ripkowski hollered from the ball turret. *"Where'd that come from?"*

When Palmer glanced inquiringly at him, he flipped on his throat mike and said, "Sneaky FW-190 lobbin twenty-millimeter shells at us and keepin' his distance. You hit, Rip?"

"Nah, just pockmarked my turret," Ripkowski said. *"Close call, though. Wait—he bent one of my guns. Other one's still workin' fine."*

"Better check the bomb bay, Utah."

"Looks like a shell exploded here," Utah reported through the interphone a minute later. *"Tore it up down here. Jammed it up, too."*

His body went taut with tension and sweat dripped from his forehead down onto his goggles and froze in the minus-40-degree air, obscuring his vision.

"Can ye jickie it loose?"

Utah tried, then said, *"Too tore up, sir."*

No time to think it through, just gonna stay in formation but not release the payload. All the scenarios that could cause my own bombs to blow up the plane, though—

"What're you going to do, sir?" an alarmed Palmer hollered, off the interphone.

"Utah, do whatever ye can to dislodge what's in the way," he said. "Can ye use some help?"

"Nah," Utah replied in his laconic manner. *"I think I see a way, but it may take a spell."*

"We got the whole trip home," he said through the interphone, then, after flipping off the mike, "I hope."

He thanked God the fighter pursuit was negligible before the Thunderbolts rejoined them, but every second could be his and the entire crew's last in this life. "Want'chu boys to strap on your parachute harnesses," he said. "Make sure ye got'cher life vests on, too."

Palmer flinched at that admonition, unbuckled himself, and reached under his seat to get his vest.

"If Utah can't loosen thangs up down there, y'all gunna start bailin' when we halfway 'cross the channel."

Never, did a three-hundred-mile journey seem so unending. Somewhere during it, he realized he'd had a large bowel movement, and runny feces, now in the process of freezing, had migrated up his back.

Dang G.I.'s.

He prayed in fleeting bursts while lasering his attention on every aspect of the crisis, including ordering Palmer to call over the command channel to ground control for rescue planes.

Oh, God in heaven, if ever Ye heard a prayer o mine in my life, I pray ye'll git me back to her, sir—I know I'd be with Ye if we blow—but we've had so little time together, I fear how sad she'd be—wait a minute—oh my God—

She was gone.

Another burst of the runs struck him, but the lower altitude had halted the freezing process, and Utah shouted, *"Hot darn, there goes the son of a gun causin' all the trouble, sir. It's gone. Drop'em now, sir, drop'em all."*

Shattered at the remembrance that had escaped him for a few terrifying but beautiful moments, he strained to keep a steady hand on the wheel, eye on his instruments and gauges, and ear on the reports and comments from his crew.

God help me.

It was almost like losing her again. He waited until they reached the Channel to release the remaining bombs so as not to endanger French civilians below. He shared nothing of the glee blaring over the interphone from his crew. Grief overwhelmed him.

"Good job, sir," Palmer said, respect filling his eyes.

He managed a nod, then asked the co-pilot to take the plane. The burning, roiling sensation he had felt several times since she passed tided through him again.

Thank You, sir, that maybe the very next mission You might bring me home. I know Your Word says ain't no marriage in heaven, but I know she's there with Ye and I'll take my chances with that. Know it'll be a dang sight better'n this vale o' tears and sorrow.

—

The next night, just after they turned in following the announcement by Trigger, in the guise of the Japanese Prime Minister, that, *"Tojo veddy happy, send congratch-lations you fo wasting powder eggs, throwing out cold Spam, infecting dip stick in booby trap Limey slime dog,"* he spoke to Waddy across their dark little room.

"Say Wad, you happen to notice what'cher gas load is fer tomorrow?"

"No," Waddy said, "hadn't checked it yet. Why?"

He thought for a moment before speaking. "Ever carried eighteen hunnerd gallons before?"

"Good gravy," Waddy said. "How far that git us, ye reckon?"

"Way I got it figgered," he said, "'bout fifteen hunnerd miles, seven-fi'ty both ways."

They lay quiet for a moment in the darkness, the only sound the distant rumble of planes, likely British night bombers headed for Germany to raise Cain for Bomber Harris.

"Gosh A'mighty," Waddy said, the last words for either of them, though not because sleep came soon.

—

Kupchak rousted them at 3:00 a.m. the morning of August 17, 1943, the date of Lance's twenty-fifth and final Flying Fortress mission. The sense of Sarah's presence carried over a few seconds into the still morning watches from the dream the waker had interrupted. Neither her face nor her body had been within his embrace after all, and he couldn't satisfy his excited condition as he had done those precious few times and as it now begged to be. He wanted to weep, but instead a stabbing cold pain spread through his chest and stomach and for a moment he choked, his throat trembling in pain.

"Oh, Sarah, darlin'," he whispered into his pillow, barely able to restrain himself from shrieking. "How am I ever gunna—" Then the burning tide scalded out the cold pain and he lay there, praying till it passed. It passed quicker this time, partly because the pleasant sensation grew of what he might accomplish against the people who had killed his beautiful sweet bride, the people whose actions had brought him to this far and lonely land in the first place and destroyed so many fine young men and friends he had come to know. By the time prayer gave way to the painless projection of massive good accomplished against massive evil, he felt neither heat nor cold, possessed no thought of life beyond today's mission, and was on his way to the privy hut with Waddy.

"Think somethin' big's afoot fer ya last mission," Waddy, who had two remaining, said.

"Big" was not among the unusually inspired vulgarities flowing from the mouths of the group's flight officers a little over an hour later when Lodge pulled back the briefing curtain to reveal not one but *two* missions for the division to fly this morning. These included the 299th's to Schweinfurt, a little town neither he, Waddy, nor Trigger had ever heard of, and which lay farther into Germany than any mission any of them had ever flown.

"Holy mother o—" Trigger gasped when Tavington, who was giving this briefing himself, announced the group would be over Germany for four straight hours.

"How we going to fly in this molasses, anyhow?" he heard someone behind him ask a neighbor. "Thick as I've ever seen it."

"Straight through Germany, almost to bloody Czechoslovakia," another pilot whom he respected said, and not in a whisper.

Lance sat stunned, disbelieving. *I'm ready to unleash on some Jerries, but what good is it if they shoot us all down fore we even get close to our target?*

Patton's taciturn face, partially obscured by the olive crush cap pulled lower than usual, was less expressive than anyone around him.

Hmm, his copilot looks cool, too.

Soon, he knew why. One officers' cohort and a backup from each group in the entire three hundred eighty-five-bomber attack force had received briefings for the mission since mid-July. Their planes would comprise the group leaders.

Looks like that Clarke's one of 'em, too, either the leader er the backup, dang if that don't look like a smirk on his face, like he's fired up about it all.

Around one hundred fifty of the planes would take off at 0700 for the picturesque Bavarian city of Regensburg to attack a key ME-109 production plant. Over two hundred thirty more would leave minutes later for Schweinfurt, home to the most important complex of ball bearing factories in the Reich.

"With the indispensable role of ball bearings in German machinery and industry of all sorts, should we destroy these factories today, we will shorten this war by six months," Tavington declared. Then he stepped down from the stage, to within feet of the front row of flyers. "Today represents a maximum effort such as we have never before put forth. Every available bomber in the Eighth Air Force will be in the air today. No squadrons will stand down." Just then, he happened to make eye contact with Lance, several rows back. He wondered was it his imagination that Tavington's Brahmin dialect seemed to take on a brief twang as he said, "All four in every group will saddle up."

A few soft whistles greeted that announcement, and he realized there had never been a complete ban on stand-downs. Plus, as if two mighty assault fleets, both flying over seven hundred miles were not enough, somehow the Eighth was mustering smaller diversionary forces against points all over western Europe, from Holland to Marseilles on the French Mediterranean.

His shock gradually gave way to grudging admiration of the audacious plan. *At least, if it works.*

The Regensburg force would draw the brunt of the *Luftwaffe* response, then head over the Alps for North Africa! The 299th and the rest of the Schweinfurt groups, behind the first force but not far, would then peel off toward their destination rather than Regensburg, whilst the *Luftwaffe*, not realizing they comprised a separate attack force, would first be occupied defending Regensburg, then grounded for refueling by the time the larger American force tore into hitherto-unscathed Schweinfurt.

He, Waddy, Trigger, and Patton walked together through the fog-shrouded darkness to the equipment hut. "Well all's I can say is General Custer was a sure thang at Little Big Horn compared to these odds," Trigger cursed outside as he spit tobacco and passed the pouch to Waddy, who stuffed a plug in his own cheek.

"Gimme some o that," he said.

The other three stared in surprise.

"Careful there, bub," Waddy said, tossing the pouch to him.

He stared at it, then looked up at Trigger as they walked. "That's quite a cartel, can git Red Man tobacca over here."

"Yeah," Trigger said, nodding, "and you oughta git'chee Bible-thumpin' hide in on it, too, so's ye can—" His voice trailed off, before he mumbled, "Be set fer after the war."

"Tried it once or twice before, back home," he said, referring to the Red Man, steady and shaking off Trigger's unintended awkwardness related to his lost bride. He stuffed in a large wad and worked it, nonchalant.

Waddy grinned. "Well, all righty, then."

"Say, lookee here, boys, I wanna show ye somethin'." Trigger lead them to his plane, not far away. Armorers swung time-release bombs into position to load into the bomb bay. The 299th and other lead crews would deliver them. They were designed to smash through the ball-bearing factory roofs so that incendiaries from the rear groups would land on the wooden floors and set them ablaze. Trigger pointed out some other ordnance—.50 caliber ammo boxes loaded with a diverse array and voluminous amount of human feces.

"Shoot, Trig," Waddy chortled, "them boxes'll prolly scald out Slamhurst or whatever it is worse'n them thousand-pounders."

Lance managed a wry half-grin, spat a stream of amber juice into one of the open boxes, then strode off to *Hellfire and Brimstone,* which stood ready but battered, patched, pockmarked with the telltale silver shrapnel scars, and dulled from its many experiences since its gleaming debut less than six months before.

They didn't take off at 0700, after all. Long before the Oklahomans got into the air, he and the others watched the mission unravel in front of them. The Regensburg force, drilled on instrument takeoffs and landings for this very mission for months by the famed General Curtis LeMay and his subordinate commanders, headed aloft from other bases through one of the thickest morning fogs he had ever seen. Were Forts flaming back to earth across East Anglia, or not even getting off the earth? Being up there in the soup meant flying blind. So Lance—and the remainder of the Schweinfort armada—cooled their heels, the familiar old fragrance of freshly-cut hay from a nearby field filling their nostrils as the minutes passed.

"Joseph, Mary, and my hemmorhoid," O'Connor bellowed over the interphone as their first hour on the flight line concluded. *"The whole point o this plan is for us to rumble in right behind the Regensburg boys, using them as cover, then hosing*

Schweinstein while the Jerries are refueling. If we're couple hundred miles back, they'll just wail the bejeebers out of us, and they'll have more time to do it then they've ever had."

"Shut up, O'Connor," Utah said, deadpan.

The crew paused, surprised to hear the phlegmatic cowboy take such a stance on anything, especially with so direct a rebuke of a fellow crewman.

"Hey, you shut up, jackass, or I'll come up there and shut you up myself," Ripkowski said to Utah from down in the ball turret.

"Hey, everbody shut up!" Lance said, silencing them. "Must be somethin' up er they wouldn't be holdin us. We can't fly in this soup nohow. Maybe they're bringin' the Regensburg boys back."

Seconds later, orders came to deplane and wait till the fog thinned to take off.

"Morons runnin' this man's air force," O'Connor ranted as they hit the ground. "They kill us every way imaginable, then they finally come up with a plan that might keep some of us from getting screwed, chewed, and barbecued, and whadda they do? Before we even take off, they blow up their own plan and doom us to the most hopeless mission we've ever had!"

As hour after hour passed, his sense of detached numbness evolved into dread. The parade of men stepping behind his plane and others parked along the flight line to pee was continual. He noticed the hands of some of the coolest flyers in the group shaking as they raised cigarettes to puff. Others could barely get the sticks to their mouths. For the first time, he would have asked someone for a cigarette if his mouth wasn't already full of Red Man.

Waddy's hearty guffaws wafted through the persistent fog. He sauntered toward them across slimy little puddles of grease and black oil on his Fort's hardstand and found him and Trigger rolling dice with some other fliers on the apron, Patton watching in amusement.

"All righty, then." Trigger jumped up with a fistful of cash. "Soon's we git the official word this pile o dung mission's dead 'n burried, I'll throw all this in to git the pot goin' at the craps table."

That announcement generated an appreciative response from the dozen or so men gathered there.

"Fer now, though, I got to deliver me a Dear John load over yonder," Trigger added.

Lance turned to follow him. *That boy gunna be the richest man in Oklahoma 'fore he's done.*

Patton took him aside.

"Brother, I just wanted you to know," he said, his words tense and halting in a manner unusual for him, "well, you were the one they intended to lead the group today. If it hadn't been fer—your sweet wife—"

He stared at the man, whom Tavington had also announced as the new Air Exec, second-in-command to the Group Commander for 299th flying business.

He be leadin' some o the briefins 'fore long.

Filled with affection and pride for his friend and former opponent, he unleashed a stream of tobacco juice that splatted onto a grease stain on the concrete several yards away, then followed after Trigger without saying a word. He had to run to catch him as Trigger hurried to make it to the closest latrine. One of the least appealing sounds he had ever heard indicated Trigger got there in time—partly. A few minutes later, when he emerged, Lance sized him up as he continued to chew.

"How much you weigh, Trig?"

"Shucks if I know."

He just stared at him. The little entrepreneur looked way thinner even than he did back in college when he squeezed himself down a full weight to take over for an injured OU wrestling teammate, then won the conference championship.

Trigger shrugged and looked down. "Shoot, Parson, can't even enjoy the fruits o my own labors. The juicier the 'mater, sweeter the melon, quicker it sprays out the other end."

He spat on the ground, then asked, "Jist who's this cartel?"

"Why, it's lotsa folks," Trigger said, "from lots o places. Mericans, Brits, Canadians, other free countries, neutral ones, occupied, Italy—both parts of it."

"Why, how ye know they ain't fascists, even Nazis involved?"

"Why, I know there *are* such folks," Trigger said, to his amazement. "They jist tryin to make a buck, too, buckaroo. And they jist riskin' their skinny selves fer some other fella's orders and money like we are."

"Yeah." His brow furrowed. "But'chu still know they's a difference tween us and them, right?"

Trigger stared at him. "Difference? Tween their leaders and their cause and ours, yeah. But tween us boys doin the fightin' and theirs? Heck, no. They fightin' their keisters off to save it just like we are, Parson. Case you ain't noticed, they fightin' to save their kinfolk, too, from the hellfire and brimstone we droppin' on their heads—no pun intended."

He just spat.

"'Sides, this war's gunna end, we gunna win, and every ole boy's gunna hafta earn hisself a livin afterwards," Trigger said. "So, I reckon we might as well git ourselves on the inside track like these jackasses that got us in this thang, and some o them boys on the other side are lookin' to do the same. So why can't we help each other do it?"

Afterwards? A hard sensation walloped him, bitter this time rather than grief-stricken, and so strong that dizziness overtook him for a few seconds as his teeth ground together.

"Gimme 'nother chaw, Trig." The fog was thinning.

"Dang, Parson." Trigger stared at him, startled.

"What?"

"Never heard ye spew out a word like that before," as Lance helped himself to more Red Man. "Ye been around Cappuccio and O'Connor—and me—too long."

Gee, what'd I say?

"Maybe we, 'specially you, Lance Ro-ark, git lucky and they replace this abomination with a milk run tomorra," Trigger said, gently for him, compassion filling his eyes.

Seconds later, the Tannoy ordered the group to return to the flight line and prepare for take-off, more than three hours after the Regensburg fleet departed.

It suited him fine.

THIRTEEN

No more than a minute after the 299th's P-47 Thunderbolt escorts waggled their wings and turned for home, just east of Eppen, Belgium, more German fighter planes than he had ever seen emerged from every corner of the sky. Within minutes, Forts were in flames, exploding, and dropping. At the same time, a field of broiling shrapnel from flak shells launched from some community below tore into the fleet. Debris of all sorts pelted *Hellfire and Brimstone*'s nose, windshield, wings, and fuselage. His crew quit calling out enemy fighters because there were so many. Every gunner had more than he could track with his own eyes.

"Jeez, pick your poison," O'Connor said in one of the few complete sentences, such as it was, that sounded over the interphone for the next forty minutes. Every utterance brimmed with vulgarities and obscenities. Actually, the Southie had a second a few minutes later—*"Got him!"*—when he laced an ME-110 night fighter that had just shot down a Fort in the group directly

ahead as it passed under it. *"Tell me that cretin didn't have automatic machine guns mounted to shoot straight up!"*

As planes continued to fall, explode, or drop back or drift away with damaged engines, the squadrons of the 299th and the other groups pulled together to close the gaps.

Boys're hangin' tough.

The fusillade his own gunners were unleashing on their attackers shook the plane on its own.

Well into Germany, the attacks from aloft finally slackened for a few minutes, though fresh bursts of flak from the defenders' inimitable .88s far below continued to explode around him every time they passed over a city or town.

"Tail to pilot," O'Connor asked over the interphone, *"Sir, the Krauts got guns in every town in Germany?"*

Utah, also the flight engineer, reported that a cannon shell had taken a chunk out of the vertical stabilizer at the rear of *Hellfire and Brimstone.* As Lance discussed with him the possible implications of that for the plane's performance, hoping the German opposition might be tolerable at least until the target, a new onslaught of a fury beyond anything he had ever witnessed or heard began.

"Good Lord," Palmer gasped after just a couple of minutes of it.

Despite a cockpit temperature of thirty-five degrees below zero, Lance was pouring out such sweat he did something he had never before done—he unplugged the electric cords heating his clothing.

German fighters of every stripe and color swarmed over, through, and around them. The fearsome FW-190s and ME-109s led the storm, screaming at the bomber fleet in phalanxes of up to a dozen planes abreast, wing-to-wing.

"How the—how do they do that!" Remington shouted from down in the nose, as he commenced firing his .50-caliber gun, which Maier would take when they reached the IP.

If *we reach the IP.*

The thought contained more anger than fear. The Germans had killed Sarah and he would be disgusted beyond words, even cursing ones, if they got him before he could wreak havoc such as he had never in his life unleashed.

In the gathering darkness of a spectacle comprised of over two-hundred-twenty American bombers and more than three hundred German fighters, and ranging across fifty miles of sky, the gun- and cannon-mounted wing fronts of the FWs and 109s looked to him like strings of fireworks bursting on the Fourth of July at the Stephen County Fairgrounds in Duncan as they blasted away. The action before him now evolved into something akin to how he imagined Dante's ninth circle of hell might appear. He saw a Fort in the squadron below, two engines on fire. An FW roared to within a hundred feet of its nose, cannon blazing, then rolled belly-up—the hail of bullets the Fort's gunners loosed on it bounced right off the reinforced armor of its undercarriage—and dove away, just in time to miss the Fort's final explosion.

The Germans hurtled in from head on, above and below, clear across "the beam" from three to nine o'clock, charging the tail in single-file echelon—all the while flying with impunity right through the American formations, wings blazing, aglitter, twinkling orange death. The fury of the assault surpassed any Lance had witnessed in his life.

The Germans are giving everything they have, including their lives, to protect their people.

The piercing thought gave way to a communion stronger than any in his life with these nameless men he was growing to hate who were striving to kill him with an effort no one back home could likely begin to fathom.

I wonder—am I related to any of them?

A dismembered, blood-oozing leg smashed against his windshield and terminated the sentiment.

He squinted through his goggles, the billowing exhaust contrails from the bombers ahead and smoke from flaming and exploding planes conspiring to darken the sky. For the first time, true fear stabbed his inner parts.

I can't hardly see where to go, and with these losses, I need to shift and adjust the formation, need to lead it!

He cursed profanely, then fog began to cloud his goggles. He rubbed the sheen off the outside of them, but some remained inside. He blinked and stared in amazement at—

The parachutes.

They had sprouted for more than an hour, but now so many filled the sky it looked like an assault on Schweinfurt with paratroopers, not bombers. Everywhere, at every altitude, they soared toward the earth, some Germans and many Americans.

Two falling Fort crewmen collided just before their chutes caught on the wing of a passing JU-88, which yanked their flailing bodies behind it through the air. A German dropped into the whirring prop of a Fort, which churned him into a pulpy crimson mist. An American from a higher and more forward squadron sailed in front of a nearby Fort's top gunner, whose .50-caliber chewed him up as it was shooting down an ME-109 careening past.

"Navigator to pilot, Schweinfurt straight ahead, sir," Remington said from the nose.

"Sir," Palmer said, "There's some cross-wind, plus a lot of smoke over the target, sir. The secondary is clear, though."

He looked ahead and down, best as he could through the smoke and debris. Another Fort spiraled downward, one wing flaming.

Three chutes, four, *five—*

Then the big Boeing exploded.

Oh! Goodness, all the smoke goin' down from up here looks like it's meetin' the smoke comin' up from down there. Lord, ye can't tell where the one ends and the other starts.

A verse from Alfred Lord Tennyson, dredged from the recesses of childhood presented itself.

> *Half a league, half a league,*
> *Half a league onward,*
> *Into the Valley of Death*
> *Rode the six-hundred*

"No dice," he told Palmer, determined, despite all, not to be moved from what might become the most important mission he had ever flown. "We'll hit the primary. Pilot to bombardier, center the PDI."

"*PDI centered, sir,*" Remington said.

"All right, pilot to bombardier, you flyin' her now, Remmy, she's all yours."

"*Charlie Group leader to Charlie squadron leaders,*" Patton said over the liaison line, "*looks like the forward groups plastered the target good. It's smokin' like the lake o fire. Choose ya another target o opportunity.*"

As he pondered that, the plane jerked and Ripkowski shouted a profanity from the ball turret.

"*Pilot to ball, you good, Rip?*"

"*Yes, sir,*" Ripkowski said. "*But we just took a load of shrapnel just aft of my position. And sir? That town just ahead, they're jackin' everything but the kitchen sink up at us.*"

"Awright, thanks, Rip," he said. "Remmy, ye got that?"

"*Got it, sir,*" Remington said.

"*Ball to pilot—er, ball to navigator, wait a minute, sir.*"

"*Bombs away,*" Remington announced as he loosed the payload and the lightened plane jumped.

"Pilot to ball," he replied, "what is it, Rip?"

After a pause, Ripkowski said, "*Well, it's, uh, I think we dropped on the wrong town, sir, or, I told you the wrong town.*"

"What're ye talkin' about?" he asked, alarmed and angry.

"*Well, it's just I don't think we dropped anywhere near the town I was talking about, sir,*" Ripkowski said.

"*Bombadier to pilot, we dropped on the target that was just ahead, like Ripkowski said, sir,*" Remington said.

"*No, the heck we did, sir,*" Ripkowski said.

"*Uh, bombardier to pilot, sir.*" Remington shifted the conversation. "*I think that smoke's coming from the Germans, not us, sir.*"

"What?" He looked down, his stomach panging. "Smoke pots?"

"Yes, sir," Remington said. *"All across the town and all around it. They're filling the air with their own smoke to conceal the target."*

"Good Lord A'mighty," he mumbled aloud without realizing it, nauseous as he peered down through binoculars.

Them ball bearing factories look like they hardly been touched.

Palmer stared at him, holding his own binoculars in his gloved hands. He switched to the liaison channel, inaccessible to the rest of the crew, and asked, "What is it?"

The copilot's face took on a stricken pallor.

Another thought struck him. "Whadduya think we hit?"

"I—" Palmer said, his face pale. "It had a church and, apparently—a school, sir."

He stared at him, unable to process it all. He wanted to give him the plane for a while, but Palmer appeared on the verge of collapse. He whipped his head toward the front.

"Pilot to crew, let's git out o this cesspool." He gazed down at Schweinfurt. The only definite fire he saw in the town came from a B-17 that had crashed flaming.

Flak pursued them their entire turn toward home. Everyone in his crew reported in okay except for O'Connor, whom Jackson found at his station near death of asphyxiation from a disconnected oxygen bottle.

"I'll take the tail," Palmer said. When he saw his concerned look, he added, "At least until O'Connor can take it back."

"Careful with your ammo," he said to his crew through the interphone. "We still got a long way to go. Short bursts. Don't waste rounds."

Less than ten minutes out of Schewinfurt, the fighters returned—as well as Palmer, thank goodness—with the same fury as before and even more tricks up their sleeve. The FW-190s and ME-109s, as usual, delivered the lion's share of the pain. Once again, multiple American gunners would claim kills of the same fighter, which could mean five, ten or twenty planes tallied as kills when only one actually was.

"Got that cowboy!" Jackson hollered from his waist position. *"Right waist gunner to pilot, got me a' ME-110!"*

"Top turret to pilot," Utah said, *"that's affirmative, sir, I saw him hit it and I saw it go down. Clean kill and Jackson was the only gun on it."*

"Speaking of 110s, sir," Palmer said, nodding upward through their top glass. Up above, an ME-110 dragged a metal cable behind it, with a medium-sized bomb attached to the end.

What the—

A Fort flew into the cable, yanking the bomb against its fuselage, whereupon the ordnance exploded and blew the plane to pieces. He had no time to dwell on the episode, as Trigger's familiar voice sounded over the liaison channel.

"Charlie Four to Charlie One," Trigger said. *"Got us a Dornier-217 at three o'clock level lobbin' rockets at us, but settin' jist out o range."*

He looked just in time to see the medium bomber launch a direct hit on the cockpit of a Fort in Trigger's squadron.

Trigger hollered, *"Jackleg jist took out* Tallahassee Lassie.*"*

"Charlie Leader to Charlie Four," Patton said, intuitively, *"you keep your combat box tight and we fight as a team."*

"Charlie Four to Charlie Leader," Trigger responded. *"That sack o—he's tearin' us up—Bob. Somebody needs to go git him."*

"Wing Leader to all groups," Brigadier General Williams, commander of the wing and the mission, said from the front of the bomber stream. *"Large formations of FW-190s and ME-109s circling forward to twelve o'clock level for more head-on attacks en masse."*

"Charlie Leader to Charlie Four," Patton said to Trigger, barely suppressing his anger, *"you know better'n that. We got a whole bunch of us to git home and we're all gonna haf to work together to git there."*

Utah hollered from the top turret, in the most excited voice he had ever heard from him.

"Pilot to top gunner. What is it, Utah?"

"—an ME-210 jest tried to drop a bomb on us from above, Skipper! Don't know how he missed us, sir. That bomb passed by not ten feet from my turret."

No sign of the ME-210 or its bomb in any direction.

We seen jist about everthang but that cursed Black Knight today.

The FWs and 109s blazed in on them again. For almost two hours, the fight raged nearly constantly, smoke and flame roiled, and parachutes again speckled the skies. So much debris smeared *Hellfire and Brimstone*'s windshield, he could barely see through it. He was flying by instruments as much as possible, but in aerial combat, instruments were no help.

This time, when the Thunderbolts met them in Belgium, the Germans did not turn back.

Why, they flyin' till they run out o gas, then landin' at the nearest base, refuelin', and comin' after us again. Good gravy—they chasin' us all the way 'crost Europe! But I won't admire 'em, I won't. I hate 'em and I'm gunna do whatever I can to kill as many of em as I can. Oh, God, curse their wretched souls! Send 'em to utter, lowest perdition!

Elation filled him when a Thunderbolt outmaneuvered an ME-110 and knocked it out of the sky, then his heart sank as another 110, craftily lurking out of range against its superior opponent, shot a rocket that destroyed the Thunderbolt, the weapon's zig-zag smoke trail tarrying, baleful and dirgelike.

All the while, the stench of gasoline, cordite, and smoke persisted. There was, no longer, any cold to fear, nor even to notice. Sometime during it all, he wasn't sure when, he realized how remarkable were these roughhewn American fliers.

No way a normal man could even see what in tarnation's happenin' out here, much less react anywhere near quick enough to keep from gittin' his head blowed off.

The Germans, finally, headed home.

Relative calm followed for some seconds. Then Utah's wry voice broke the peace like a sledge hammer through stained glass. *"Top gunner to pilot. Two squadrons o FWs climbing at twelve o'clock, Captain."*

"I see 'em," he said, his stomach knotting.

Insolent so-and-so's, comin' on even with fresh P-47s loaded with fuel attackin 'em while us bombers keep blastin' away at 'em.

"Wing commander to all force leaders," Williams' voice sounded again. *"Looks like FWs massing for a final encore."*

"It's them yella-nose, JAG-26 hombres," Utah, his eyes as keen as Lance's, announced. *"Galland's old unit."*

Every airman in the Eighth Air Force knew who they were.

"Charlie Two to all force leaders," he spoke over the liaison channel, *"ME-109s comin' round from one, looks like they gunna give them FWs some cover."*

"Charlie Three to Charlie Two," Waddy said. *"Heckuva'n eye there, Pard."*

The Thunderbolts saw the gathering wave, too, and converged on it. Just as he suggested, the 109s took them on, while the Focke-Wulfs bore in on the bomber fleet, refusing to allow the P-47s or the mounting fire from the Forts to deter them, even when one, then another were hit.

His eyes widened at the audacious charge coming straight at him by twenty-four of the top aviators of one of the great fighting machines in the history of war. Then his weary eyes twinkled as a smile spread across his masked face. "Well, awright then, come on, ye sons-o-hell!"

"The Fightin' Parson!" O'Connor said.

"... tu madre!" Rodriguez said.

"I'm ready to kill," Jackson said.

The sky exploded into fire as the FWs plunged into the bombers, close enough he could make out the facial features of the enemy pilots. He focused on keeping his plane steady as the crew barked fighter positions to one another over the interphone and *Hellfire and Brimstone* shook from the firing of every gun on the ship. Another FW spiraled out of control, one of its wings disintegrating. One fighter flew straight toward a Fort in a nearby squadron, both aircraft blasting away until they smashed head on into one another and exploded into a scarlet fireball.

Another FW unleashed a trail of fire the entire length of a bomber flying just forward of his squadron. One of the Fort's engines burst into flames and its nose dipped, the plane heading downward in the dreaded, gradual, circular "flat spin" that ruined B-17s often took while descending toward earth. Three men in chutes emerged from it, the third on fire from head to foot. The same FW headed straight for *Hellfire and Brimstone*, cannon and machine guns roaring. Every gun in the squadron that could draw a bead on the German opened up on him.

"You bastige!" Remington shouted at the oncoming foe as he threw everything at him he could from his nose .50.

The same sentiment filled Lance. For a moment, he thought the German would fly right into him.

So be it, ain't turnin' away from any o these cockadoos.

At the last second, so close to *Hellfire and Brimstone* that he felt its wake sucking on the plane and saw the pilot's determined face, his canopy pulled back and his yellow scarf flying in the wind, the FW loosed a harrowing burst of fire that shook the bomber, then swooped upward. With no forethought, Lance pulled back the yoke to rise with the German and ram him. He didn't, but Utah blew the plane's cowling and propeller off from point-blank range, and the FW swirled out of control, smoke pouring out, nearly broadsided another Fort, then burst into pieces like a giant firecracker.

"Sweet Mary, you tore that schmuck wide open, Utah!" O'Connor said from the tail.

"Sir, he hit our Number Three," Palmer said.

He knew the plane so well he could feel it was in mortal peril without a glance at the now—

Oh Lord Jesus, we gunna blow up.

—smoking engine.

"Pilot to crew," he said over the interphone. "Got us a problem with our Number Three engine. We almost to the channel and I'll git us there. What're the Jerries doin', boys?"

"Top gun to pilot, most of'em are lightin' out for home, sir," Utah said.

"Tail gun to pilot, but a little pack of'em are circling around at six o'clock high," said O'Connor. *"109s, sir."*

He chewed his lip.

Gotta try and cool that engine down er she'll blow this plane to smithereens. Gotta keep her level and not drop out, er them 109s'll hang around to git'em one more notch fer their belts.

But the danged altimeter refused to cooperate—the plane was descending.

"Pilot to crew, boys keep me posted on them 109s, we gunna be slidin'." Worry filled Palmer's brown eyes. "Til we hit the Channel."

But there was lots else to do, and quick.

"Pilot to radio, Blevins, key the Brits' Air Sea Rescue Service an SOS and our position. Pilot to navigator, key in wind, headings, airspeeds into your EB6 and gimme a reading on how far we gunna make it." The familiar sight of the city of Bruges caught his eye below. "Never mind, Maier, we almost to the Channel now." His mind whirling, he said, "Pilot to crew, sorry everbody, grab ye chest chutes case we wind up bailin'. And chunk everthang outa here 'cept whatever ammo ye got left. I mean it—clothin', radio gear, oxygen—and condoms, O'Connor."

"Uh, Tailgun Charlie to pilot," O'Connor replied in a deadpan over the interphone, *"that's asking too much, even for you and my country. Parson. Sir."*

He smiled in his mind, if not his face. A faint, distant shriek sounded, but not over the interphone. He and Palmer looked at each other.

"Sir!" Rodriguez said in a near panic shout, more screams sounding in the background. *"Left waist to pilot, Jackson's, uh, he's hurt bad, sir."*

"Well what is it, Rodriguez?" he asked.

"Sir, I told him to use a condom, but he opened the chaff chute and started peeing through it, then his—his—"

"His puny little —?" O'Connor said over the interphone. *"He caught the—"*

"Shut up, O'Connor," he said. "His privates are frostbit, Rod?"

"Sir, yes, sir," Rodriguez said, barely audible now over Jackson's screaming. *"And—and he got stuck to the side of the opening and when he pulled back, he lost half his—"*

That silenced the interphone traffic for a moment.

"Well gosh, Rod." Horror filled him as he noticed the plane's plunging altitude, "then bandage him up best ye can and pop some morphine into him. And everybody start chunkin'—" Palmer blinked at the vulgarities which followed, then commenced to doing so.

Shutting off Number Three engine had at least staunched its burgeoning fire.

"Top gun to crew, three ME-109s six o'clock high, comin' this way," Utah announced over the interphone.

The French beach lay perhaps two miles ahead, and the Channel glittered in the late afternoon sun beyond that.

We maybe a thousand feet up and droppin' fast.

"Pilot to crew, fellas, grab your life jackets, we fixin' to be in the drink," he said. "Remmy, Maier, Blevins, y'all git to the radio room, git against the bulkhead like they trained us, and brace yourselves."

Oh, Lord, git us to the water, please.

"Tail to crew, those 109s are dropping to level and coming in single file from six o'clock," O'Connor called. *"Where'd the lousy Jugs go?"*

He could only assume all the Thunderbolts had engaged other German fighters. Both his shingles and his runs recommenced as he used all his strength to keep the plane, now cascading down to a couple hundred feet above ground, airborne til they reached the Channel, still half a mile ahead. It shook and rocked as O'Connor, Utah, and Ripkowski tore into the first 109, which was firing everything it had and heading straight for O'Connor. The 109 blistered the Fort's vertical stabilizer and blasted out the tail glass just before O'Connor and Ripkowski poured a hail of lead into its engine cowling and blew the fighter out of the air. The second 109's guns appeared to jam as it approached, and it veered away.

Hellfire and Brimstone dropped to a hundred feet, then fifty as it neared the beach. He leaned every ounce of his being into the yoke to keep it aloft.

Oh God, we not gunna make it. Just a few more yards, please.

The plane resumed tremoring from the gunners' firing, as well as from its mechanical struggles, as curses filled the interphone.

"I'm outa ammo!" Utah said.

"Look!" Ripkowski shouted.

"It's that black 109 son of a —"

The Black Knight? I don't believe it.

Then the harsh barking of machine gun fire sounded, the bomber jerked, and the fighter zoomed overhead and rolled onto its top out ahead of the plane as his gunners continued firing at it. Elation filled him when smoke belched from its tail and the plane careened for the water. Mere feet above it, the fighter suddenly whirled in a different direction, up, and away, and the smoking, which stemmed from a common 109 engine reaction to rolling and diving, ceased.

Oh my God—he's got rocket tubes under his wings! Surely, this far out, he's already fired 'em?

He could not conjure even the thoughts to express his hatred of the plane and its pilot as *Hellfire and Brimstone* reached the beach and dove to twenty feet.

"Tail to pilot," O'Connor breathed over the interphone. *"That's the luckiest son of a gun I ever seen, Parson."*

Such fury coursed through him, he felt he might explode out of his skin as his own plane reached the surf.

Too shallow.

He closed his eyes and committed himself to God's mercy, and that of the Germans he knew would soon be his captors, if he survived the crashing ditch. But the Fort kept going, sputtering and shaking, then shuddering again from the gunners' fire. He opened his eyes.

Goodness, we jist glidin' over the water.

The Number Two engine on his inside left had died, too.

Glidin' indeed.

"What the Sam heck?" Looking around, he could barely see the now-distant French coast.

We at least a couple miles out. How can that be?

Onward the plane continued, even as the Number One engine coughed and died, until the coast was out of sight and he was at least five miles out in the Channel. He realized Blevins hadn't appeared from the nose.

"Copilot to pilot," Palmer said softly. "Sir, he hit Number Two."

He saw it was not only hit and dead, but beginning to smoke—and flames licked out the front of the cowling.

"Top gun to tail," Utah said over the interphone, *"jackass is ignorin' me and comin' up our tail pipe at six o'clock level again instead. Him of all people knows I'm empty. Why's he—get him, O'Connor!"*

He just steered, knowing his exertions had no effect on the plane's altitude, his mind numb from the onslaught and rapidity of events. O'Connor's gun continued to hammer away.

I need to go ahead and ditch into the Channel.

A deafening crack shook him, and the plane seemed to coil back and hang for an instant in midair.

"Top to pilot," Utah said, "he shot off our tail—"

They collided with a wave, like crashing into a concrete wall going full speed in his old Ford pickup. Water cascaded over the plane, dousing any and all fires. "Pilot to crew, abandon ship, everbody out!" he shouted, but the interphone and all the plane's electronics were dead.

He unbuckled from his seat and turned for the passageway down into the nose where he could exit through the front escape hatch, but water had already filled the nose and was coming toward him.

But Remington and Maier—

"Sir, this way!" Palmer said. The copilot had smashed open the window above them with a fire extinguisher and motioned to him to let him boost him up through it.

He hesitated, glancing toward the rear of the plane. "The crew—"

"We've got to go, sir!" Palmer said, shouting to be heared. He felt the plane list toward the back and water surged toward the cockpit from the flight deck. Within seconds, he and Palmer were on the roof of the sinking bomber. Utah had climbed out of the top turret.

He turned. Nearly the rear half of the plane was already submerged.

But—that can't be—

A jolt of unexpected loss pierced him.

She's—truly gone.

He could not have enunciated his feelings regarding a craft that had carried him through so much, protected him, and finally brought him to the brink of deliverance as its own destruction occurred.

Utah saw his expression. "She was a whale of a plane. B-24'd never o made it to the Channel, and if it did, it'd already be hundred feet under. Joker took off our whole tail with a rocket." Something in Lance's expression caused him to add, "O'Connor unloaded on him till the rocket hit. Think he shot it while he was still outa range of our guns. Smart sucker, too." His face had all the expression of one of the Monument Valley rock outcroppings he had grown up amongst. "But he went right at the one gun we still had firing."

"But—" he began, noticing that only the top couple of feet of the plane remained above water.

"Rodriguez was already dead," Utah said. "Rip in the radio room, Jackson—"

He tried to take it all in. "Who's left 'sides us?"

Splashing sounded nearby. He turned to see Ripkowski pulling a delirious Jackson through the water alongside the fuselage, both of them buoyed by their inflated Mae West life jackets. Blevins trailed sputtering behind them, holding onto Jackson's Mae West.

"Your buddy McCurdy and his—cartel," Blevins said, accusingly.

"What're ye talkin' about?" he asked.

"My Mae West's worthless, and so was O'Connor's, if he'd needed it," Blevins said, "'cause those cretins stole the CO_2 cartridges that held the gas to blow'em up, from them and a lot of others to sell on their little black market."

Before he could think how to respond, the grumble of an approaching fighter interrupted them. The black ME-109 was diving down out of the sun for a final pass.

"You sorry cur," he said growling, standing to his feet as the water started to lap around them and pulling his stainless steel officer-issue Colt .45 from its holster.

"What the—" Utah said as the Black Knight roared down from twelve o'clock, headed straight for them, and the other crewmen ducked for such cover as they could manage.

He reckoned his only chance was squeezing off a lucky shot before the 109's guns found the range. He jerked off all his gloves except the thin silk ones. Pulling back the slide of the pistol with his left hand, he aimed with both hands to steady his bead and squeezed the trigger, again and again, resighting it quickly each time it jacked, until the clip, smoking, clattered out. He and his mates heard at least two .45 slugs ring off the Messerschmitt's metal body.

No fire was coming from the fighter.

Did I hit him?

As it roared right over, gleaming like onyx in the late-afternoon sun, he saw that it had no kill insignias on its tail rudder. The pilot, his canopy open and cream scarf flying, leaned back up from where he had ducked in the face of Lance's fusillade. Respect and dignity covered the German's handsome, square-jawed face as he saluted the Oklahoman, then disappeared toward France.

FOURTEEN

He slogged through the next two weeks at the Beccles station as a "happy warrior", an airman who had completed all of his missions. He visited Sarah's grave two or three times, and that of her mother, who had died heartbroken three weeks after Sarah. He led some replacement flyers on practice missions.

Most o these boys won't last five missions.

He also wrote a ten-page letter of condolence to Trigger's parents in Cyril, Oklahoma, a dusty crossroads town of a thousand souls between Corning and Duncan in the shortgrass country.

Trigger had flown his shrapnel- and bullet-riddled Fort and crewmen all the way back from Schweinfurt to Beccles, made a smooth landing on instruments in thick fog, announced to his copilot that "I feel like I been shot at and missed, and puked at and hit," and died. Only then, did the copilot notice that the back of Trigger's head, including a large section of his brain, had been blown off by a chunk of scalding hot flak.

Stories of Trigger littered the conversation as Lance, Waddy, and a couple others, working on three- and four-day beard stubbles, puffed on cheap cigars, sipped cheap whiskey, and played five card stud in the OC the night before Lance shipped out. Rain sprinkles pattered against the structure's tin roof and the radio standing against the far wall filled the gloomy room with Vera Lynn's melancholy *White Cliffs of Dover*. Patton sat at the table drinking milk and wincing periodically from his bleeding ulcer. Like Waddy, his final mission was scheduled the next day, thankfully a milk run on some sort of Nazi research site in Holland.

"So, we lost us sixty bombers, more'n twicest as many planes as any other mission, close to another hunnerd got the stuffin kicked out of'em, and at least five hunnerd and fi'ty boys killed, and a bunch o' others captured," Waddy said, shuffling, dealing and puffing. "Bobby here tells us his intel buds say our real tally o Jerry fighters ain't nearly three hunnerd like we claimed, but more like twenty-seven. And after all that, moron Tavington has the sand to tell us all the bombs we pasted them ball bearing factories with prolly won't affect the Krauts' aircraft production a lick?"

But we did wipe out most of a village a few miles away.

His mood acrid, he sipped down whiskey, which he'd taken up over the past few nights, courtesy of Trigger's delivery of two cases of Irish whiskey to his hut the morning of the Regensburg-Schweinfurt raids. Like swallowing liquid fire the first evening, it got easier and tastier every night.

"That boy musta had him a premonition," Waddy had said of his Sigma Chi brother's epic valedictory. "Left a note how he wanted it parceled out, and all of it free."

When Cappuccio adjusted the radio dial and the real Lord Haw Haw came on over a German-run French station, everyone in the OC stopped what he was doing. The last time "Lord Haw Haw" held forth, it was Trigger's far more winsome, only slightly less inebriated, version. Patton cocked back his arm, half-full milk glass in hand, then winged it forty feet across the room, where it smashed dead center into the radio, breaking the bulb-lit frequency glass, jerking the dial to another station, and splattering the cursing Cappuccio. As if on cue, a clap of thunder crashed overhead, the lights flickered, and the rain started pounding the roof. As robust an applause as the despairing crowd could muster rippled across the room in Patton's honor as Cappuccio shot him a one-finger salute.

"Shee-zee," Waddy said, cigar jutting from the side of his mouth as he shoved one-cent chips toward the center of the table. "Krauts tick off Bobby here, that gits God right in the middle o thangs, and they hineys is toast."

"And now, live, by special arrangement with the Mutual Broadcasting System, the United States Armed Forces Radio Network is proud to present one of the most popular and glamorous stars of this generation, as well as perhaps our greatest band," an excited broadcaster with a distinct if somewhat nasal Northeastern voice announced from the radio's new frequency. *"From the Stork Club here in New York City, I have the honor to present to our brave men, near and far, in an exclusive performance tonight with the Glenn Miller Orchestra, the Golden Girl with the Golden Voice—Miss Mary Katherine Murchison."*

As the Stork Club audience roared its approval, Waddy's cigar fell out of his mouth. Patton snapped forward in his seat, his eyes wide.

Lance nearly dropped the fresh half-glass of Trigger's whiskey he had raised to his mouth. A knot formed in his throat as the melodic voice from long ago wove its way into the room.

"I want to send this song to all the boys out there, so very far away from home, who are giving everything they have to defend and protect us," she said, her voice sweet as maple syrup, gentle as snow falling soft on shortgrass fields. He recognized with a flicker of emotion the nearly-imperceptible hoarseness to it that told him her throat was tight and her heart full. *"Especially, I want to dedicate it to a tall, sweet boy I went to college with, so long ago it seems now, back home in Oklahoma. I have no idea where he is, only that he joined the Army Air Forces. You see, this boy gave up more than almost anyone to stand up for you and me. So, Lance, wherever you are, this song is dedicated to you, honey."*

"Well, I be go to blazes," Waddy said, as Miller's horns swung into action across the world.

"Jesus, Mary, and my mother," Cappuccio, now at a nearby table, stammered, his mouth open. "So, it *is* true." He turned to the other fliers at his table and he heard him say, amidst an inspired flourish of vulgarities, "Them dumb Okies always said him and that—that *Goddess*—were the item at Okiehomo University, then they almost got married, but the Parson over there, why he give her the Houdini act. You believin this pile?" Eyes wide, he turned back toward Lance's table as the voice the music critics hailed as a sweeter version of Judy Garland's launched into one of the greatest songs of the era.

As the words to "Heart and Soul" flowed out, he knew who had chosen the song because it was not one of Miller's normal selections—and because it, at long last, fulfilled a request from a cold November night in Norman way back in 1938 when all seemed right in the world. When Mary Katherine, whom he had never formally met, appeared at the packed, triumphant Mont to apologize for hatefully throwing paint over his head the day before, after his borrowed horse had made a mess in front of her Kappa sorority house. A time when the two of them had walked through nighttime Norman and across the OU campus and shared the stories of their vastly different lives with one another. When he carried her, forlorn and heartbroken from a lifetime of paternal indifference, through that cold night to her house, tearing open a serious injury he had suffered in the day's dramatic, first-ever conference championship win, against the famed Nebraska Cornhuskers. It was an injury which would sideline him from the Sooners' first post-season football game ever and a possible national crown. Even his bodily pains only magnified the Homeric scale of his deeds that golden day.

Waddy whirled around so fast he nearly flew out of his chair with a grin the size of Texas, but Lance had vanished from the room. He sat on the soggy ground outside, under one of the two windows in the OC, where he could still hear her voice, even though a blackout curtain hung over the window from inside. As the rain grew into a downpour, he puffed his cigar until the deluge put it out. Then he just chewed on it as the rain mooshed his crush cap even farther down over his eyes than it already was. He didn't want to see anything, and he didn't care to see anybody, other than what he saw when he looked back. So many things he had long ago put to rest, especially how she had given her whole heart to him.

Cappuccio, who had also completed his twenty-fifth mission, appeared from around the corner of the building and stepped to within a couple of feet. He gripped the fifth of Irish whiskey Trigger had bequeathed to him, along with the epic "girly pics" collection—some of it reputedly custom-posed for Trigger—that had graced the walls of his half of the room he shared with Patton. He hesitated and then offered the bottle to Lance, who looked up at him. Lightning flashed, revealing the scars on the Jerseyite's face. An FW cannon shell had torn through Cappuccio's Fort's windshield heading into Schweinfurt, exploded in the cockpit, and killed his copilot and nearly him.

Around the same time that a Japanese Zero strafing a New Guinea airfield had killed his brother.

Lance grabbed the bottle, unscrewed the cap, and took a good belt. It slashed his mouth, his throat, and his insides, but it felt really good. He handed it back up to Cappuccio with a small nod.

"Listen, Parson," Cappuccio said, looking down at him. "I'm God—that is to say, I'm really sorry about your wife." *Heart and Soul* ended inside, and Mary Katherine and the band began another song.

He looked out into the darkness. A moment later, he said, "Sarah."

"What's that, Parson?" Cappuccio asked, lifting the bottle and taking a snort.

"Her name was Sarah," he said woodenly. "Folks need to know that. She was a real person and a wonderful girl and she helped them that couldn't help theirselves and she—she deserves to be remembered as much er more'n any of us."

Cappuccio thought about that for a moment. "You know, Parson," he said. "I think I was all wrong about you."

He looked up at him, climbed to his feet in the muck, then stuck out his hand and they shook. They looked at each other and gave the semblance of nods.

"I'm sorry about Trigger, too."

"And I'm sorry about Cochran."

"Yeah, little firecracker took a lot of killin'," Cappuccio said, looking down.

"Which one?"

Cappuccio looked back up and smiled. "Yeah, no kiddin'. Tavington's adjutant told me on the QT the division is recommending McCurdy for the Medal of Honor. He's a cinch for it."

He nodded his agreement. "Let's send them Huns all to the lake o fire."

"Let's go home," Cappuccio said, his voice much softer than Lance's.

—

The next night he sat alone in his little hotel room near Mayfair. He declined to stay at the Savoy or other nice lodgings where fliers from the 299th had rooms, because he had no interest in socializing. He had darned sure learned not to make Air Corps friends outside those he already had. He had lost enough comrades already. He had no desire to lose more.

Assuming successful completion of the day's milk run to Holland, Waddy and Patton—who was leading the entire 299th Group—planned to join him the next morning, and the three would ship out for the States the following day. Patton had told him about a revival taking place in the evenings a couple of miles away across the Thames River at the famed Metropolitan Baptist Tabernacle, where Charles Spurgeon had preached. He thought it over, while nursing a scotch and soda. Scotch tasted a bit less bracing to the tongue, throat, and stomach than bourbon. He decided he preferred bourbon.

A rap sounded at the door. The manager said he had a telephone call at the hotel desk. When he picked up the receiver, Waddy sighed before he spoke. "Got some tough news, Podnah," his buddy said, his voice tight as Lance's stomach suddenly was. After a tortuous pause, he got out, "Bobby—he didn't make it."

"What?" he said into the receiver he held, as though it were the cosmic culprit responsible for such a travesty. "Whadduya mean? It was a milk run!"

Waddy sighed again. "I know. Some FWs musta followed the formation back, circled round, and come at 'em from out o the sun like they was Run-

Away-Fast Spits or something." He sighed, employing the American airmen's derivative for Focke Wulf. "Most o our boys already had their guns folded up and put away. Group and wing commanders thought so much of him, he had him a regular copilot and no general ner cunnel ridin' shotgun like the group leader usually does. Tavington—already put through a request to promote him to major before that mission."

His head was on fire. "Why did'ja say, come at 'them'?"

"I didn't git to go today, piddlin' ground personnel wouldn't clear our bird," Waddy said bitterly. "Had over two hunnerd holes in her from cursed Schweinsuck, and a chunk o one engine gone. Think they gunna Category E-her. Still got one mission to go and met boys say they's a front blowin' in over France and Germany likely keep us grounded a week er more. Don't know when I'll git up again—er git home."

"But—Bobby—he was the best of us, he helped us all, no matter how we— slid," he argued, as though he could persuade Waddy to bring Patton back. "All this insanity, he was the only one it never really—shook. What the *hell?*"

Waddy sighed some more. "Sorry, lowdown—woof launched one o them rockets, bullseyed his—" his voice started to crack, and he seemed to get tongue-tied. "—his cockpit. Burnt it, uh, burnt it up—"

"Whadduya mean?"

A small gasp escaped Waddy louder than the Tannoy blasting through the Grand Canyon and telling him more than he ever in a million years wanted to know.

Bobby burnt alive strapped into his pilot's chair.

For the first time in his life, his spirit pulled loose from a God who could create the fragrance of lilies and honeysuckle and puff the wind up from empty space and hang the stars twinkling in their places in the skies, but could not keep Trigger's brain from getting blown off nor Bobby's face and eyes and genitals from slow incineration nor his Sarah and her—

—*Our*—

—baby from getting torn to shreds by a *Luftwaffe* bomb.

Or wouldn't.

Waddy was talking again. "Thousands and thousands of our boys gone, and fer what? Tavington hisself's three sheets to the wind earlier and told me we bein' used half as bait to git the *Luftwaffe* after us to wear theyselves down through attrition, and half jist to keep a'pokin' 'round till we find the important targets, even though we don't know our backsides from a hole in the wall."

Waddy screamed a profanity.

After they hung up, he headed over to the Savoy for a drink and a meal with some of the other 299th happy warriors. Cappuccio and two others were there, also headed back to the States. One of the latter sported the three-piece suit he had worn all day, including while flying to Holland and back, and with which he intended to impress a certain well-known English stage actress later in the evening.

Memphis Belle commander Morgan, famous now for commanding the second USAAF crew to successfully complete its required twenty-five missions—the first without a casualty—sat at the table with them. His and his crew's morale- and bond-raising tour across America had proven so successful, the government had sent him back to England, ostensibly as a consultant to various wing and group commanders, but secretly to buck up spirits. The respect for him from every battle-hardened aviator around the table was palpable.

When Cappuccio offered him a Camel from the pack, Morgan's face brightened as he pulled one out. "How the Sam Hill'd you git these over here?"

"Ole Trigger McCurdy got them for me, special order." Cappuccio glanced at Lance, his brown eyes wistful. "I saw a full-page ad for'em in *Life* with John Wayne, right across from the spread they did on you boys and the *Memphis Belle.*" Beaming, he offered Camels to everyone at the table, but his attention remained on Morgan, so that he didn't seem to notice when the pack got to Lance, whom Cappuccio knew did not smoke.

He stared at it for a moment.

John Wayne and Bob Morgan. Reckon that's good 'nough fer me.

He pulled out a stick, took a light, and carefully dragged on it. Fortunately, the waitress arrived just then with food, which distracted the table from his deep but stifled coughs, as well as his ashen face.

I ain't givin' up on this. He continued to puff.

As the waitress handed Morgan a plate of fried eggs and two double Scotches, Cappuccio asked him, "That your supper, Major?"

Taking a belt of Scotch, Morgan said in his soft North Carolina drawl, "Had it for breakfast, lunch, and supper all today."

Lance decided he would go with just the Scotch.

Then a wave of young English women descended on the table and the fliers' attitudes soared, except his. He was as committed to Sarah as when she was alive. A couple of the girls, though, looked stunning enough to hold their own on the silver screen with Greer Garson, and one of them, crowned with a welter of scarlet tresses, all but crawled inside his tunic.

Ambivalent feelings, and urges, now clashed within him—whether to converse pleasantly, run for his life—or fufill the familiar urge besetting him. Now the scarlet-haired beauty crowded against him, with her softness, her silver eyes—

—*Like Mary Katherine's*—

—her intoxicating perfume. He took a healthy belt and shook his head.

Morgan, he's engaged to be married, to the real Memphis Belle. *It was in* Stars and Stripes. *I'll peel off with him, er leastways stick close to him, as the other fellas pair off with these girls. Maybe I can talk to him 'bout what it's like to go back to livin' in the States.*

A thought that had lately germinated in his mind recurred.

Maybe not, though. Reckon I ain't finished with these Nazi curs.

He scarcely noticed the beautiful girl's hand advancing up his thigh.

How blessed—and short—had been the security and joy of Sarah as his cistern to drink from, as the church taught. He continued to find pleasure as he remembered and imagined her. Was that a sin? He took another drink, thinking. Yes, no doubt—such pleasure should be shared with your wife, not hoarded to yourself.

Wait, though, what if one's wife just—died? Besides—

His face swung upward, bitter with despair—

—*it wadn't my doin' what happened to her. If I's Awmighty God, no way I'd o let that happen to her.*

The first obscene remarks he had ever directed toward the Lord wreathed his thoughts as the girl's hand grew more assertive, her eyes glittered up at him, and her other arm coiled around him.

What the heck.

Startled, he nearly said it aloud when the other English beauty engaged in a full lip-lock with Morgan. The famed flier rose to his feet with the airborne girl in his arms, her own wrapped around his neck.

"Congratulations on gittin' home, boys," he said to the table. "Y'all have ya a good rest o the war and keep your sad carcasses down." As all at the table hallooed him and his jocular crudities and he carted off the giggling girl like a trophy of war, Lance felt suddenly vulnerable, more alone than ever in his life, uncertain as to what he should do, or wanted to do.

"I'm Patrice and you don't say much," his new companion purred into his ear in a bewitching Cockney brogue, nibbling at it. "But I have a few things I want to say to you." Then, grabbing him inappropriately, "And a few things I want to do to you."

A surge bolted through his body. He looked her in the eye and his own filled with tears. He was leaving his new home in the morning to return to a, now, strange and foreign land, and with a God he was pretty sure he didn't know as well as he thought he did. He offered a silent, heartsick apology to Sarah, but he really had nothing to say on the matter to God. He reckoned if anything, God owed him some explanations.

For just a moment, as his lips first engaged Patrice's, a sentimental old Irish ballad, "The Rose of Tralee," came to mind. Sarah had sung it during the long hours she tended her mother and while she nursed the numberless frightened and suffering children in Lowestoft. Her father had sung the same song to her mother.

The words echoed through his head in Sarah's sweet voice and the closing lines came—

But the chill hand of death has now rent us asunder.
I'm lonely tonight for the Rose of Tralee.

An instant later, long before he experienced the empty pleasures of Patrice's room and body, the old ballad vanished from his thoughts.

PART II

DRESDEN

"My son, hear the instruction of thy father, and forsake not the law of thy mother."

—*Proverbs 1:8*

FIFTEEN

DECEMBER, 1943
UNITED STATES OF AMERICA

It seemed he was proceeding in two alternate realities. One felt comfortable and familiar. In that one, as he made his way about, first in New York City, next on the cross-country train, and then back in Norman, he performed normal functions and duties, returned friendly, admiring greetings from strangers with his old ease, and acted graciously toward all. He did notice the glances of attractive women young and older in a way he had not earlier in life, but he went on about his business, even whistling and chewing gum.

The other reality had begun to appear about the time he returned to the States, but only periodically, and in thankfully short doses. It presented itself one evening in New York as he ate alone at a café counter and smoked a Camel from the pack he had swiped from a hardcase M.P.'s locker on the ship home. An exhausted little boy backtalked his mother about eating his vegetables and his daddy being deployed in the States then the Pacific the past eighteen months.

The child threw his food and then wailed loud enough to stop everything in the place when he did not get what he wanted. His head scalding with rage, he started to rise and give the mom some needed help, but a governor within checked him and he stayed where he was, trembling, unclenching his fists.

At the slatternly waitress's suggestion, he ordered the house special of hot apple pie and ice cream—available only to men in uniform. He no more savored or even noticed the taste than if he had been munching on his napkin.

The next episode occurred in his passenger train sleeping berth when he awoke at three o'clock one morning as the train lumbered through Missouri. Across the shadowy compartment from him sat Sarah, beautiful and demure, cross-legged, hands on her knees under the cherry tree behind the Stradbroke graveyard, as she had been following their first round of lovemaking on their wedding day. He rose up on one elbow, gleeful, shouting hosannas to God that *this,* not that other reality, was true, this shining temple of virtue and beauty, the faithful mother and wife God had promised him his whole life he would have if he was good and brave and followed Jesus, not the vale of darkness through which he had staggered for half a year.

And so, she smiled to him, as she had at the cherry blossoms, her sweet spirit that had so much to give and so much to live for. Then she heard something behind her, stirring, and he looked and saw something in the shadows… amongst the graves. She was shaking her head no, calling out against it… them, then turning to him, pleading for him not to let them reach her, tears streaming down her angelic face, but then the tears began to steam, to boil, to broil her skin as she began to scream, and she wept harder and more tears came. Then her soft body, his body, in full fair flower of young womanhood, was aflame, sizzling and popping and peeling and melting, those portions of it that were not petrifying, then flaking into ashes.

Her last agonized expression as he rushed to her, when only her luminous gray-green eyes remained, was a questioning one, a bewildered one, and he could hear it clear as the third point of a Sunday sermon even though the mouth that would have spoken it was a runny goo sliding down her blackened, hollowed-out torso.

"Why?" she asked him. "Why?"

He heard a commotion behind her and saw German soldiers, submariners, and especially airmen staring at him. They were bloodied and maimed and some had one arm or one leg, some had gashed heads, and some had no heads. Amidst them were some Japs who were in as bad a shape as the Germans. He moved toward them to finish them all, for now he gripped the .45 in his hand he had lied about to keep, but just before he began to fire he saw behind them all, Hitler and Tojo. Sarah was now a pile of smoking soot at his feet.

Slinging aside the Colt to pile into them by hand, he was caught by the train's Negro night porter and another airman wearing his skivvies.

"No wait!" he bellowed at them, for he saw two more figures, behind all the others, sober but determined, staring at him. He knew what they were thinking, even though they said nothing.

She does not belong to you, she is ours.

And it was as though Churchill and Roosevelt had spoken in unison.

It took the porter, the airman in skivvies, and an MP who happened to be birthed nearby to get the .45 away from him this time.

JANUARY, 1944
NORMAN, OKLAHOMA

"Jeez, buddy," Waddy said when he told him about the train scene. "Had me some nightmares, too, but nothin' like that."

He told him as they sat alone in the Blue Room of the two-thirds-empty Mont, sipping Jack Roses, lemonade courtesy of the house, applejack courtesy of a lady who had befriended him for the night in Manhattan. The old Wurlitzer was broken and unplugged.

"Think ye need to throw on your pinks and git out and shake a leg somewheres," Waddy said, scooting on his rear to exit, around the carpeted raised flooring that served as round booth seating under the table.

Whenever he knocked back at least a couple of drinks prior to retiring, he didn't have nightmares—or at least serious ones.

"Anyhow," Waddy said, "Gotta pick up Maggie at the train station. She gits in from Dallas tonight. Was doin some sort o fashion shoot there. We headin' up to Cushing and Ponca fer couple weeks to see all the folks 'fore I head out fer Basic, er whatever the blazes they gunna give a guy got his tail shot off fer eight months over Europe."

Just as he was about to stand up at the opening to the room, he stopped. "Say, you hear what we did on that second run to your old stompin' grounds o Schweinfudge?"

"You mean what they did to us?" He took a rather larger swallow than before.

Waddy paused. "Yeah, right." He glanced around, then leaned forward and, lowering his voice, said, "We lost seventy-seven birds, Pard. *Seventy-seven.* Six hundred and ten men gone in one mother lovin' mission." A hood came over Lance's eyes and he sipped his drink without expression. Waddy looked around some more. "Heard our genius generals finally throwed in the towel, said no more missions our little friends can't escort the whole way. Heard it cost Eaker his job."

Lance didn't even hear him, because he was looking up at where his Big Six Conference Champion teammates, Long John Starr and Cactus Face Taggart, had slouched the night of the '38 Nebraska game with their flasks. Over to where he and Waddy had danced, wearing their helmets Trigger brought them, while the Delts and Kappas sang "Don't Send My Boy to Texas"—at the table he nearly knocked Mary Katherine over the night they really met, when he and his cousin Clint, despite being the golden boy of U.S. Naval Intelligence, even if despairing of the Roosevelt Administration's covert pre-Pearl Harbor machinations toward war, tore up half the Mont, wrestling each other.

"See here, Podnah, you gunna come with me and gitchee a squadron o these B-29 mutha lovers? Lance?" Waddy asked, his voice rising.

"Huh?" He returned the glance of a shapely waitress who had peered at him while serving one of the few occupied tables, halfway across the room. "Nah, reckon I'm gunna git me one o them shiny new P-51 Mustangs and kill me some o them yahoos kilt all our buddies."

"So, what the heck ya think ye gunna be doin' in a B-29, bub—droppin' recipes fer ye Mama's fried rattlesnake on their heads? You know everbody from Mr. Murchison to Curtis LeMay's plugged us fer our own commands," Waddy said.

He gave a quick chuckle without smiling then reached his hand across the table to shake Waddy's. "You git the Japs, I'll git the Jerries. And we'll all have us a Merry Christmas."

"We jist had Christmas, jughead." Waddy stood. "Say, you ain't much of a 'Parson' no more, butchu one tailkickin' warrior, buddy. DFC, dang. Heard about'cha bustin' a whole clip on the Black Knight, ya idjut!"

"Yeah," he said, staring into his drink. "Well, bein' a 'Parson' didn't exactly help ole Bobby much, did it?"

"Hmm," Waddy said. "Well, all right then, podnah."

They gave each other a quick, knowing nod, then Waddy was gone.

The shapely waitress appeared at his table. She looked even shapelier up close.

"I'm your new... girl... *server* girl," she announced in a come-hither fashion, eyeing his uniform and rows of ribbons, her brown eyes glinting, even in the musky light. "Whadduya need?" He just stared at her. "Ya got a girl?" He stared some more, sipping his Jack Rose. "Well, ya didn't say, yes," she said, handing him a small piece of note pad paper with a phone number on it.

He didn't even look at it. "I need me some more lemonade," he said, sliding his ration book toward her. As she picked up that one, he pushed another across the polished pine table. "Y'all still got any Camels 'round here?"

She looked at him like he had two heads. "Camels? Darlin', we lucky we got Picayunes." She eyed the little cigarette book. "Ya only got one stamp left, anyhows. Don't waste it on them. I got a extra pack in my purse I give ya."

He eyed her as she shoved the booklet back to him.

"And I'll be at the Sigma Chi house in a little while," he said.

"I don't git off till ten."

"I'll still be there then."

He thought she might either melt into a puddle on the floor like Sarah had in his dream or whatever it was, or fall into his arms right then, and either would have suited him fine. Instead, she bit her lip like Sadie had the day he met her when her Marlow boys knocked part of one of his teeth out on the football field. She picked up his glass and turned to head for the kitchen.

"It's empty," he said. When she looked back—

—*Like a nervous scairt little beautiful girl, like Mary Katherine looked at me on that same spot the night we beat Nebraska, but ain't a hunnerd o her could make one Mary Katherine—*

—he added, "The house. Ain't nobody there but me till the boys—what boys they's left—git back next Saturday. Door'll be unlocked. I'm in Room Zero."

Lips parted, a twist of dark brown hair hanging down into one eye, she nodded and went to fetch his lemonade.

—

He didn't have a car, and when he got to the Sigma Chi house, his watch indicated it wasn't even nine yet, so he just kept walking. The waitress had poured his last Jack Rose into a roady cup for him and he sipped it as he walked, slashing it with more applejack every few blocks. His insides felt as warm as the air was cold in the January darkness.

He passed McFarlin Methodist to his right, looming high over him like a stone castle, like the most magnificent church building in Oklahoma, which he had heard it was. Then he passed First Baptist, to his left, sitting quiet and solid, like the church with the prayingest and preachingest pastor in Oklahoma, which he had heard E. F. "Preacher" Hallock was.

He heard, all through college, that Preacher would pray for hours on end like the mighty prophets of Old Testament times. That he would often do so through the night, on his knees, in his church office with a lone amber lamp alight and his Bible on a chair before him.

That amber lamp....

He saw the faint glow through a small window he knew to be Hallock's, because on another night, near the end of his senior year, he had walked across Norman—along this very street—seeking God's will about his future, flying, the Comanches, about Mary Katherine and even Sadie....

He already knew Hallock because of the man's pioneering work in establishing Christian ministries on the OU campus itself but had never spoken at length with him. That night, that 3:00 a.m. morning, he knocked on Preacher's door. The gentle, soft-spoken man answered and, despite clear exhaustion, bloodshot eyes, and stooped shoulders, spent more than an hour with him. It remained the singular event of his life where he felt he had come closest to entering into the presence of God on earth.

"God said to Israel," Preacher said, "'I know the plans I have for you, plans for welfare and not for evil, to give you a future and a hope.' This is true of all God's children, including you, Lance Roark. No true Christian need ever to walk in darkness, astray from the path. Some do, but they choose to do so, or they use none of God's means to find the way, instead depending on their own understanding."

Walk in darkness—

He looked toward the sky, but he could not see the stars for the overcast. He opened his mouth to speak, as so often he had, but no words came. He turned back toward the lamplit little window. He wanted so badly to go knock on that door again that a sob nearly choked out of him.

Oh, Preacher—

He shook his head with rue, hopelessness filling him.

They might as well be metal bars over that door like a prison cell in the McAlester Penitentiary.

His head drooped, and he trudged on, pressing the cup to his lips. Soon he turned onto Main Street.

They's the Sooner Theater, where Mary Kat and me went to see Gone With the Wind *and* Stagecoach *and* The Wizard of Oz *and she sounded jist like a sweeter version o Judy Garland when she sung.*

He passed the old eatery, simply called The Diner, the banks, and the stores, then the tracks and the Interurban Station and, across from it, Denco Bus Line.

Hold on—they got'em a café now? Denco Café? Bet that place make ye gag.

He remembered Long John and him sitting in the little waiting room one midnight with Cactus Face as the latter waited on the bus that would take him home to Arkansas, where his daddy had died under a tireless tractor that wouldn't run anymore in a field that wouldn't grow cotton anymore.

Mournfulness again spread through him as he stared at the new Denco Café sign and the garish red neon light in the window that said, *"Open 24 Hours."*

Seems like everwhere I go in Oklahoma I see places where folks was but ain't, and sometimes I almost think I see the ghosts theirselves.

He dropped the empty applejack bottle in a trash can brimming over with used food and gasoline ration books. He didn't know if he could muster what he needed for the waitress, but he reckoned he would try.

Then I'm gunna git the heck outa Dodge and go see Mama and Daddy in California.

SIXTEEN

"But Mama," he said, shaking his head at the sight of her hands, faint traces of cuts, slashes, and callouses remaining from the cotton-picking season that ended months before. "Everbody said...."

Everybody said it was the land of milk and honey in California. Oranges big as softballs, land enough everybody could have his own again, rain and fertile soil such that you could build your own plantations in the San Joaquin Valley. Turned out amidst all that paradise, Daddy had endured ridicule at the plant in Bakersfield from local workers who didn't cotton to "Okies," especially when they learned of his pious, pacifist, teetotaling ways.

"Makin' fun o how he talked, what he believed, how he dressed, bein a coward, so-called, added to him bein sad bein away from his own country. Why, after while guess the Irish side of him went off, and he walloped couple them boys good," Mama said at the cheap, scuffed, linoleum kitchen table one night. She sipped water. He sipped hot apple cider she brewed for him, and Daddy slept in the little bedroom on the opposite side of the one other room in the little apartment besides the little bathroom, the little living room.

"So... he didn't start back to drankin' 'til after all that happened?" he asked, tense and feeling like he needed to start back to drinking himself.

"No, son, no," she said. "Wadn't till after he lost his second job, when we moved down to Inglewood, factory town outside Los Angeles. Well, around that time, anyhows."

Good ole Mama, always defendin' the good in others, 'specially Daddy.

But it was like a knife was stabbing him through the lungs and he didn't know what to say next.

"But, Mama, you shouldn't be pickin' cotton... now."

She sipped more water.

"Aw, prolly done with that now," she said. 'Sides, got us back here to the Valley, amongst more of our own folk. Like I toldja, got us a little church not far away. Few folks from home there, few more new ones from out here. Why, even met couple boys from back around Hydra doin' CO work as firemen in the hills north o here. All in all, ain't a bad place, if we can't be at home."

"CO work." Wonder whuther Hitler and Tojo offerin' their more sensitive boys Conscientious Objector jobs.

"Tell her she's too old to be workin' on a blamed factory assembly line, too," Daddy's voice piped up from the bedroom.

When no one said anything further, Lance asked, "What's he mean, Mama?"

She shook her head. "They happy's pigs in slop to put a woman to work with all you boys off to fightin'. Reckon ole Fancy Pants Franklin got him his war he wanted," she said, nodding and looking at the wall that had no window and no land to see if it had. "Jist like the Senator said in our own livin' room back home, though, it's a trick pony, ain't no real fix," she concluded dryly, grabbing a ration book off the table and brandishing it. "Else why we got these, son?"

He stayed a week, sleeping a lot, going to work with Mama a couple of times, doing lots of pushups, and running along the roads out into the Valley. He managed to head out for one such run in plenty of time to miss his parents' departure for church on Sunday morning. Each day, he ran farther and faster, savoring the cool, clear air. It filled his lungs and filled his mind with something he had lacked since before Sarah's death—plans.

Oh, I am gunna learn to fly that P-51 like ain't no one else never did.

He passed raisin fields plowed and ready for spring planting.

Fer everone o our boys them Huns laid low, I am gunna take ten o them out.

The prospect thrilling him, he looked up into the azure sky. *Congratulations, Sir. You made me. You put all this into me, and ain't no one alive gunna be able to stop me. And if You try to—well then—*

He shot an obscene gesture toward the sky.

You. You the author o this unending parade o misery, anyhow, so I don't reckon You got any reason to quibble. Fact, You made me. You made the men made this war, You arranged it so's we could bomb and burn cities full o women and children, and You let jist a whole boatload o us git sliced, diced, gutted, and scalded to shreds, so why wouldn't You be happier'n a ruttin' hog if I shoot a thousand murderin' Krauts outa the sky?

His excitement grew so that, after already running five miles, he churned at a near sprint up a thousand-foot hill, dancing and punching the air when he got to the top and wishing he did have someone to box.

"I *am!*" he said in a shout across the quiet Valley, "Captain America!"

On his next-to-last day, he did something else he had never before done. He went to a bar to drink whiskey with his father.

Except for Daddy saying, "Good to see ya again, son. You take care yourself and git back in one piece, hear?" and "Don't go signin' up fer no more tours, neither," the two of them said hardly a word as they knocked back three drinks apiece.

"Like father, like son, they say," Mama said that night at supper.

Yet withal, despite all their troubles and sorrows, most of the week went well. They played Monopoly, Parcheesi, and Scrabble. They caught up on people and things, though he spoke little compared to what his parents did. He uttered nothing of the existence of Sarah Johnston Roark, nor had he ever to them. He had hoped to surprise them when he brought her home from the war. Something kept him from mentioning her to them before then. Now he was thankful he hadn't.

The night before he left, he noticed a *Life* magazine on the end table next to the couch, opened to a big article entitled "Saint Dorothy." A photo of an attractive, clear-eyed, middle aged woman handing mugs of steaming coffee to a couple of down-and-out men appeared under the header.

"Hey, Mama," he said, when she entered the room. "This here 'Saint Dorothy' Catholic?"

"Why, yes, she is," Mama said.

He chuckled. "So why you readin' 'bout her?"

She stopped. "Cause she's the most like Jesus o any woman I ever saw."

He stared at her. "But Mama, I don't know as I grew up ever thinkin' a person could be a Catholic and a Christian both."

She sat down. "Well, I'm sorry if I left such an impression, son, though from what that there article says, I don't reckon some o' the leaders o' the Roman Church fancy as high a view o' Miss Day as I do."

"So, what's so all-fired special 'bout this Dorothy Day, Mama?"

She eyed him, and sadness flickered across her face as she stood and crossed to her little bedroom. "Read Matthew Five and ye'll see, son," she said, shutting the door softly behind her.

He snickered silently and turned instead to the full-page photo of pin-up girl and movie queen, Betty Grable, her legs, and her new swimsuit.

—

"So that army's gone and taught'chu all the sorts o thangs we spected they would, ain't they, son?" Mama said at the Greyhound station the next day, spying the half pint flask silhouetted in his hip pocket, then looking him in the eye. The bus would arrive in minutes to take him to Norman for a few more days before he headed to P-51 Primary training in Lafayette, Louisiana.

When he said nothing, she went on. "Most amazin' thang, and I member my Daddy preachin' it from time I's a little girl. More'n half a century o life's taught me they's a strange mystical truth endures generation to generation.

More powerful and sure than what we say, teach, applaud, even believe. Why, even what we do. It is who we are. And you jist like your father. A man o heart and passion, a man o courage, a man o' arms, a wine bibber, a man who wants to change the world. But if you never member even one other thang I tell you, Lance Roark, you member this—You keep tryin' to change the world your own way and not God's, it'll break ya jist like it's broke ye daddy."

As the bus pulled away a few minutes later and he watched her through the window, smiling and waving at him, he said aloud, softly, "Mama, you the best they ever was." He wished he'd said it to her face.

But she knows I believe it. She prolly gunna outlive me. Anyhow, we gunna kick us some big-time tail and git this war over, then I'll come back and make it better for 'em—fer her.

He grabbed a sandwich from the basket she had stuffed with food for him.

Daddy, though, dunno if I'm even gunna see him again. He's goin' downhill fast.

MARCH, 1944
NORMAN, OKLAHOMA

With school in session at OU, the Sigma Chi house was not empty when he returned from California, though it was half-empty with so many boys off at war. An older couple he knew, who had been fans of his during his Sooner football days, and a 4-F former teammate both offered him a free place to stay, but since the waitress had proven even more attentive and far more shapely, in an intimate environment than she had at the Mont, he took her up on her own offer of lodging.

With enough liquor—which he bought through Cactus Face's old bootlegger, since Oklahoma, unlike the rest of the U.S., still prohibited the sale of it—he could block out Sarah's memory during the initial stages of intimacy and then imagine Sadie's face and body and voice when he really got down to business.

He smiled wryly one cold overcast late morning as he left the waitress's tiny flat to go work out over at the OU football stadium.

That little gal'll never know how much pleasure she owes to Sadie.

His mood foul, at the stadium, after striking out on booze even with the bootlegger because the government had ordered distilleries to ramp up industrial alcohol production, he noticed a couple of fellows boxing in a make shift ring near the weight room. One of them, Hankins, a former football player a few years younger than him, whom he vaguely remembered, had a heart murmur that had kept him out of the war. It didn't keep him from growing into a hulking physical specimen. Admiration filled his eyes, though, when he recognized Lance, and he accepted his request for some boxing lessons.

He dedicated himself to learning a significant amount of boxing style and strategy over the next week. Already in rugged physical shape, despite his growing intake of liquor and cigarettes, he could protect himself well from his teacher and even land an occasional punch. He decked three other opponents, all of whom had been boxing semi-regularly for at least a year.

"Man, you dang sight bigger'n you was when you played here, ain'tcha?" one opponent, a heavyweight on the wrestling team said, spitting blood from his cut lip. "It ain't table fat, neither."

It was his last night before heading to Mustang flight school, so he agreed to accompany Hankins, the heavyweight, and a stocky little acne-faced OU wrestler to a bar in Capitol Hill, the south side—the rough side—of Oklahoma City. One of the area's more popular sobriquets was Little Dixie.

Norman may have ranked as the "most redneck college town you'll ever see," as Hankins declared with pride, but its lawmen kept the town as free of liquor bars as they did Negroes after dark. Oklahoma City's Police Department preferred to look the other way from Capitol Hill's handful of such establishments rather than deal with the wrath it would otherwise face from the tough customers of Little Dixie.

He and his new acquaintances slammed down a couple beers apiece before leaving Norman and a couple more en route to the city. He also shared from the pint of Jameson the husband of the older couple, who had offered him lodging, had given him. The group felt large enough when they reached the city that Hankins, who was driving, opined they should "swing through the Deuce"—business and cultural hub of the segregated city's negro section—en route to the south side.

"You boys ain't bad," he said, "haulin' me through the two toughest parts o' the whole city, Capitol Hill and the Deep Deuce, fer nothin' more'n a few slashes o' whiskey."

"The Deuce" housed clubs, saloons, and other establishments of revelry that apparently lay beyond the arm, or interest, of white law in the capital city. It boasted a musical legacy that included Count Basie, the Blue Devils, Charlie Christian, Jimmie Rushing, and others.

With Lance riding shotgun, Hankins purred his late model Buick coupe down the bustling Thursday night Second Street that was the spine of the Deuce and the whole black section of Oklahoma City. Despite the brutal toll of war, it pulsed with energy and light. Jazz, swing, and rumba music wafted out of the clubs through doors that were open despite the early March chill. Throngs of people moved about, most dressed to the nines in suits and ties, stylish dresses, and freshly-styled, often "white-styled" hair.

"Pull yo head out, boy!" a lanky man of thirty-five or so hollered at an acquaintance out front of Ruby's Grill, whose reputation for music and famous negro bands, even Lance knew. "Benny Goodman'd never been nuffin' thout Charlie Christian! Wrote his best songs, give his band beat that set 'em apart. He *is* man invented electric guitar, foo. Why, if he ain't die so young—"

"Hey!" the wrestling heavyweight said from the back seat. "Ain't that—you know, that politician?"

He saw, next to another hopping night club, a husky white man wearing a homburg and expensive overcoat. He took a brown-paper sack creased in the familiar shape of a fifth-gallon bottle from a black man in a coat and tie, shook his hand, and flashed a winning smile.

"Yeah," Hankins said, nodding and smiling, "the famous tee-totalin' leader of our state."

And so, it is!

The self-assured smirks he and his new friends gave to the blacks who surrounded them drew a multitude of suspicious looks, but apparently the whites' size, something in their expressions, and the various nicks and bruises on their faces and necks, discouraged anyone from threatening them. At one point, as Hankins passed the car within a few feet of a cluster of black men about Lance's age, one of them, gripping a paper sack that sported the outline of a liquor bottle, gave him such an insolent sneer that when he started to step toward the car, Lance, wearing his fleece-lined leather aviator's jacket, grabbed the door handle to jump out and oblige him. He had taken to carrying his old hunting knife on a small holster in the back of his belt, after hearing that the grim, aloof, Captain Clarke did the same with a switchblade following a dust-up in London with some English soldiers. Clarke had absconded with the fiancée of one of the men.

Just as he started to open the door, he saw a handsome negro soldier with a square-jawed, world-weary face standing near the angry man. There was such an inscrutable but clear expression of mutual respect between him and the soldier that the other man stopped his move toward the car. When he saw that, he relaxed. By then, a hooting Hankins had moved the car past.

"Lookee at that, they got 'em their own pitcher show, fer coloreds," the heavyweight chortled as they passed the Aldridge Theater.

"How else they gonna go to the pitcher show?" Hankins asked. "They can't git in ours."

Next, a tall, willowy woman, alone in the milling crowd, passed in front of the car in the middle of the street. The beauty of her face and form electrified all four men.

"Sha-zam," the heavyweight said. Hankins nearly rolled into her, the car's lights causing her to whirl toward them. Lance caught his breath as he saw a face as beautiful as any he had ever seen of any color. So bedazzled was he that for a moment he didn't decipher the banter from the other guys in the car. When he did, it was the heavyweight assuring them he would happily pursue any sort of relations with the woman she would allow.

Sipping his beer, Hankins cheerfully responded how lacking the heavy-weight was for such a task.

"Oh, I want her," Acne Face said.

The woman glared at them, then hurried on. Confusion gave way to stir-rings of desire for her. Lance recalled seeing bare breasted black African women in *National Geographic* magazine.

They'd never show white girls naked like that. It'd be obscene. They'd git shut down. He scolded himself. *Dang, son, you wouldn't lust for one o' them naked zebras er chimpanzees in the other pitchers, wouldja?*

"So would'ja, Lance?" Hankins was asking him with jocular obscenity wheth-er he would pursue relations with the woman.

"Not even with the help of Dopey, Grumpy, Sneezy, and Sleepy," he lied as he took a nip from the Jameson to settle himself, reciting the line Trigger sprang on Cappuccio regarding a homely and very drunk English lass in the Beccles pub they frequented. The heavyweight laughed so hard at that, he fell into his door and nearly out of the moving Buick.

He saw folks streaming out of the stately, red-bricked Calvary Baptist Church. *They look happier'n the revelers we jist passed.*

Sadness and shame pierced him. He hadn't set foot in a church or chapel since Trigger died. He took a pull from the Jameson and forlornly saw a young man and woman amongst the church folk talking and laughing with each other.

Look out, er life'll crush y'all, too.

Hankins turned south toward Capitol Hill. The church and the happy young couple receded from view.

Crossing over the North Canadian River, he saw a white sign with ma-roon lettering. *"Welcome to Capitol Hill, CHHS Redskins Large School State Football Champions 1927, 1930, 1933, 1935, 1937, 1938."* Another smaller one behind it read, *"Negroes leave by sunset."*

"Dang, boys play some football 'round here," the heavyweight said.

Acne Face piped up bravely with, "Forget them boys, I jist want me a woman!"

"Played with two er three of 'em at OU," Lance said, ignoring Acne Face. "Tougher men I never knew."

"Sons o' bucks knocked two my front teeth out when we played'em in high school," Hankins said.

He smiled a little when they passed Robert E. Lee Elementary and Stonewall Jackson Junior High within a few blocks of each other. He tipped his pint toward the latter in salute.

Daddy always loved that man, I could tell, no matter how he covered it up 'round Mama, and Great-Great-Grandpa Patrick did, too. He was a Christian, too, fightin' fer his country and the glory o' God, Daddy always said, when Mama wadn't around. Jist shows it's possible.

One of the Forts in his group had carried the name *Old Jack* and featured nose art of Jackson's stern likeness.

By the time they arrived at The Hill Club, everyone in the car was ready for more booze and more excitement. He smiled again when he heard the strains of Bob Wills and the Texas Playboys on the juke box inside the smoky bar. He scanned the tough-looking bunch around the room.

This could be Duncan sure as it's Oklahoma City.

One fellow sat by himself on a stool at the bar who looked enough like O'Connor to be his twin. He even had red hair.

Sinking guilt crawled over him again. He had gotten himself home but not the men who depended on him.

The men I was responsible for.

Not even the loss of Trigger and Patton bothered him more than O'Connor. Sarah's death scarcely did. His mood turned grim and hard.

"Ain't seen y'all 'round here before," a pretty young waitress said as she came to their table. She turned her gaze to him, just as he crammed a lump of snuff into his mouth from Hankins' offered can. "I sure ain't seen you before."

Just as he started to take notice of her, a menacing voice said, "Well I shore have."

Across the table, his high school nemesis Ernest Porter, wearing a beribboned army uniform. glowered at him. Ernest carried as much weight as before, but more muscularly-defined. His brother Elbert stood between them, to his left. Like Ernest, he wore sergeant's chevrons and his chest and shoulders filled his uniform like a slab of concrete. The two were raised in a Ku Klux Klan home that hated German and Irish heritage with equal passion. They had bedeviled him throughout his pacifist childhood and youth in Duncan, mocking him verbally in front of fellow students on countless occasions, stealing some of his belongings, urinating on others, flattening his truck tires. They had roughed him up physically more than once, including during a broomcorn cutting when they broke his nose, but unwittingly kindled Sadie's feelings for him.

"And lookee, Elb, he playin' dress up like one o them Fancy Dan flyboys," Ernest said.

He spit into a glass as his heart pounded and the instinctual calm flowed through him pursuant to not responding to a provocation. Even as it did, however, his blood, already heated, turned to fire. He had turned his last cheek for the Porters.

"Hey, buddy," the heavyweight started, rising from his seat just in time for Ernest to grab his shoulders and sling him aside. He crashed into a nearby table of folks and onto the floor like a bale of hay.

"Hey!" Hankins said in a shout while standing. Elbert grabbed him by the collar of his letter jacket, kneed him crushingly in the genitals, and flung him into another table, chairs and glass crashing. The Porters stepped to Lance, one on either side, as Acne Face looked on, wide-eyed.

"You had this comin' a long time, and what're the chances we'd find you here after all these years," Ernest said in a growl.

He noticed an indented scar along one side of Ernest's neck.

A bullet crease.

The brothers stared down at him as he enjoyed his dip, his face impassive.

"You ain't gittin' out of it this time jest settin' there, Bible thumper," Elbert said, murder in his voice. "You might's well fight, cuz we gonna kick the stuffin' out o you one way or t'other."

When he continued to sit there lazily eyeing them as though he were daydreaming on the front porch of a summer evening back at the old home place, they huffed up. He grabbed the glass and spit more snuff juice into it, but Ernest grabbed it and slung the refuse into his face.

When Elbert, stinking of alcohol, cigarettes, and sweat, pulled him up out of his seat by his sheepskin collar and sneered obscenely that they would "gut-chu," then rape "your whore wife," he exploded forward, slamming the heels of his hands into the hulking giant's chest, knocking him back into a chair. Off balance, Elbert swung at him. Despite his own whiskey and beer intake, Lance ducked under the roundhouse and in the same motion, as he'd learned in boxing, moved in close and popped him two cracking left jabs under the chin, then a lightning right haymaker that froze him on his feet. He stood there for a moment, confused, then dropped to the floor like a sack of feed.

Just as he did, a crushing pain struck the back of Lance's head as Ernest smashed a chair across it. He stumbled a couple of steps away, his mind beseeching God and commanding himself back to action. He shook the fog from his head, then, feeling Ernest before the black inside his eyes was even cleared to see him, caught his old enemy as he piled into him. Hand-to-hand, chest-to-chest, wrestling on their feet, they jockeyed with all their might for position. He carried the most weight of his life, 220 pounds, and he carried the most muscle he'd ever had with it, but Ernest had a good twenty-five country- and infantry-strong pounds on him. Sweat beaded from the huge man's forehead as he grimaced and grunted. Lance felt his ancient scrotum wound tear open.

Ernest sputtered and cursed, spittle streaming and spurting from his mouth like cottage cheese. The soldier's head lunged forward, and he bit his ear, but Lance jerked his own head away and lost just the tip of the lobe to Ernest's gnawing teeth. Fury boiled up and he channeled its power into his upper body, girding himself and gaining the advantage on Ernest, who now heaved for air. He shoved Ernest's left arm and shoulder away, clamped his right hand around the man's throat, and began to squeeze, still holding Ernest's right arm at bay.

Ernest's eyes widened in surprise and rage and he clawed at his grip with his left hand. He tried to free his right hand to do the same but couldn't. Lance poured every shred of strength he possessed into his right hand, which barely fit all the way around Ernest's trunk-like throat. Fire burned in his right wrist, forearm, bicep, tricep, shoulder, even his pectorals.

Ernest gasped in frustration and pain, unable to shake his tightening squeeze. He tried to drop to his knees to elude it or maneuver an improvement in position, but that just increased Lance's advantage and leverage. Now he threw more of his body strength and weight into his grip. Adrenaline streamed through him as he felt Ernest's resistance fade. He kept squeezing, no longer able to feel anything from his right shoulder down, willing his grip to continue.

Ernest coughed and wheezed, drool streaming out of the corner of his mouth, as his eyes fluttered, lost their focus, then rolled halfway back in his head. When his arms dropped to his side, Lance squeezed for a few more seconds. He started to let Ernest drop and leave. Then remembrance of Sarah and what Ernest had said about her—

—*Or was it Elbert? Did he see the wedding ring I'm still wearin?*

It recharged his fury. *I'm gunna finish you, scum.*

It was no worse than what he and his crew had done to a lot better folks than the Porters.

Excited now, as though released from a long captivity, he grabbed the back collar of Ernest's uniform and began to drag the heavy, unconscious load across the wood floor toward the exit. Halfway there, the sharp cold sensation of ice tore through his side. He jerked away. Elbert had revived and rammed a knife into him that skittered along his rib cage before he got loose.

He released Ernest and turned toward his brother just as Elbert, his nose mashed to the side and streaming blood, lunged at him again with the knife. All he had time to do was try and parry it with his left hand, which Elbert sliced open. He backed away a step, saw the huge form coming at him again, spotted a half-full bottle of Falstaff on a table next to him, grabbed it with his right hand, with a lightning flick of his wrist smashed it on the side of the table, then with another slashed Elbert's knife-wielding hand with the jagged bottle as he plunged it again.

"Oww!" Elbert screeched. "You *mother—*"

Blood dripping from his hand, he flashed the knife at him in x-shaped thrusts. He tried to use the bottle as a neutralizer, but he was cramped for space as he backed into tables, their occupants flying out of chairs and away, more glass breaking behind and around him. And Elbert was enormous and coming on like a man possessed, backing him onto his heels and cutting off space for him to maneuver or evade.

Bleeding from his scrotum, ribs, head, ear, and hand, his strength ebbed. He didn't know if Elb saw him sag, but he sagged inside.

Oh, God, that knife.

Panic edged closer as he wondered whether he could keep it out of him.

"'Not by might nor by power, but by My Spirit,' saith the Lord of hosts."

He remembered it from long ago. As Elbert came on and he stepped back again and again, he summoned what strength he still had for one desperate final attack. Eyeing Elbert's rhythm of movement with the knife, he timed his left hand to grab the other man's knife hand when he thrust again, but the knife pierced his palm, sending a shock wave of pain through him. He grabbed Elbert's wrist anyway, squeezed, and whipsawed the bottle across his face, gouging one of his eyeballs.

Elbert screamed and grabbed for his eye. He threw himself into him and drove him over a table covered with pitchers and bottles. The table collapsed beneath them, debris and chairs flying in every direction as they crashed to the floor, Lance landing with all his weight atop Elbert.

Jamming his left forearm into Elbert's larynx, he pulled his own hunting knife out of its holster behind him. He shoved Elbert's head back enough to expose his fleshy jugular. He put the knife to it just as he heard Mama's voice say, "No, son."

He froze, the enormous blade against the bulging vein. For a moment every power that had ever animated him and others new to him urged the knife forward. Then the wake of the gentle voice vanquished them like dogwood blossoms swept before a spring shortgrass twister. He shifted the blade up to angle it against Elbert's cheekbone and flayed a modest strip of flesh off his face. Overwhelmed into a state of shock, Elbert gasped, his mouth and eyes—eye—wide open. He leaned to within a couple inches of his face.

"I ever see you er your brother again, I'll finish the job."

Elbert let loose a short whimpering moan, then passed out. He wiped the flesh and blood off his knife on Elbert's tunic, dragging it across the lines of ribbons, then struggled to his feet, wincing and gasping at the pain screaming from his multiple wounds.

It was a bad fight even by The Hill standards and the cowboy-booted manager, who looked rough as a cob himself, left his club on the bar when he approached him. "That's some hellacious bad blood ye boys got."

Lance stopped and eyed him. He made sure of his grip on the hunting knife still in his hand.

"Ain't my bidness, but my place is wrecked, and that *is,*" the manager said.

He relaxed just a shade and glanced around. Half the tables were tumbled or wrecked, and most of the sixty or so patrons and employees, many of whom looked plenty capable of handling themselves in rough situations, stood warily around the margins of the room, with no interest in butting into this exchange.

"Sorry, I didn't want it."

"I know ye didn't," the manager said. "Them's some rough boys. But these is hard days—it's still the cursed Depression roundchere—what with shortages, rationin', and all, and they—well they pipeline me red-eye, and at prices I can make good on sellin' to folks."

A searing jolt tore through his head from whatever the chair did. He wobbled for a second, felt a hot wave cascade through his brain, and thought he might faint. Composing himself, he noticed the manager had reached out an arm to steady him.

"Sorry, sir. Monday mornin? Call Murchison Oil, downtown?"

"Yeah, sure, I heard of it."

"Ask for Mr. Murchison's office," he said, looking him straight in the eye. "Tell Helen that Mr. Murchison's favorite flyboy asked him could he help out here."

"Whadduye fly?" The manager eyed his leather jacket. "Er—fly *in?*"

"B-17s till August past," he said. "Fixin' to start P-51s."

The other man started to say something, then looked him over closer as blood stained his crotch and side, and dripped from his hand, head, and ear. The man nodded.

"Sure, bub," he said. "But if they gimme the high hat..."

"They won't," he said.

The manager nodded again. "I believe ye, bub. And I don't believe much."

He nodded back and walked toward the door where his friends waited, a Confederate battle flag flanking them on the wall. Hankins crouched and grimaced, holding his privates. The heavyweight, his face bleeding, pulled his arm into a sling made from someone's scarf.

"Tear them Japs to pieces," the manager called after him.

"Jerries," he said softly as he neared Ernest, who was muttering curses and pulling himself to one knee. He reared back and with one final marshaling of force kicked the big man's face as hard as he could with the toe of his calfskin boot. Ernest's chin and buck teeth crunched as the enormous body whirled over and thudded face down on shards of broken glass.

He walked slowly past his friends. A lamp outside the front entrance caught him full in the face just as a trail of blood from his busted head trickled into one eye. Dazed and blinking, he saw Sadie standing under the lamp, her face sad like the last time he saw her, the day Will Rogers and Wiley Post died. The day she told him she would marry another since she—since her *father,* who was in financial ruin because neither the Depression nor the drought would quit no matter what the government tried—disapproved of his Mennonite ways.

"What?" he said, trying to clear his eye but smearing more blood into it with his bleeding hand. "Sadie?" She was gone. He hurried toward her, but she was gone. "Sadie?" He looked around. "Sadie!"

"Who the heck is Sadie?" he heard Acne Face mumbling from somewhere.

He staggered to Hankins' car, opened the door just as his knees buckled under him, and collapsed onto his seat. "Oh, Sadie."

SEVENTEEN

Waddy's wife Maggie loaned him her robin's egg blue Cadillac LaSalle V-8 convertible to drive out to his uncle's funeral a few miles south of Corning. His injuries from the Porter fight and the nearly two hundred stitches they required had hospitalized him for a week and postponed Mustang training for at least a couple of months. Aching again down low, he took a different route back to Norman from the funeral, State Highway 9.

Heading east out of Chickasha as luminous late afternoon rays of spring sunshine bathed the greening Washita River Valley, he spotted the old Grady County Fairgrounds up ahead on the right and the football stadium where he and Patton had staged their epic high school duel.

Dang, that's been ten years now.

It was a bewildering realization.

Bobby...

He stuffed the emotion that threatened to overcome him. He had vowed, during those painful days in the hospital, never again to cry about anything so long as he lived.

He began to ruminate anew on what all the Germans had done to him and to those he cared for. The list had grown in the hospital and through the week since. It had grown so unwieldy he marveled he could remember everything on it. But he did, because he thought about it every day, sometimes every hour—sometimes minute upon minute.

He wasn't forgetting the Japanese, either. Since coming back to Oklahoma, he had heard of two more friends killed in the Pacific Theater of the war, another imprisoned by the Japanese in one of their jungle torture dens, and another whose whereabouts had been unknown since the Bataan Death March two years before. The mass murder and other barbarism committed against unarmed American prisoners during that nightmare, revealed to the U.S. public only a couple of months before, tipped the scales for Waddy to choose the Pacific rather than return to Europe—or to Maggie, as she had begged and nearly persuaded him to do, until he learned the truth of Bataan.

He thought of Pearl Harbor, Wake Island, what the Japs had done at Shanghai and Nanking and Seoul, and everywhere else they had inserted their brutal, demonic bootprint.

I hope you bury the lot of them ten feet under Sheol with your new B-29, Wad.

He knew now that Roosevelt had provoked, bullied, and damaged both those Axis countries for years prior to Pearl Harbor.

He hoped they would attack us so's he could git into war with 'em and save his wretched economy and presidency. And I hate him. But Roosevelt, er no Roosevelt, if they'd o' stayed the heck home like they shoulda, none o' this would o' ever happened.

A new thought perked him up.

I am gunna head to Louisiana early and git started with them Mustangs.

Up ahead on the right was one of the German POWs the army had transported across the world to the Grady County Fairgrounds and dozens of other towns around Oklahoma. He couldn't believe it when he heard it and he couldn't believe it now. The soldier, wearing his dark gray Wehrmacht tunic sans insignias, his uniform trousers, and boots, walked toward him along the side of the road. A cold hollow sensation filled him.

Him and hunnerds others in there, they git to breathe our air, drank our water, use our toilets, go into town like that cur is right now fer groceries, maybe flirt with our girls in the Piggly Wiggly, er IGA—whilst Trigger and Bobby and O'Connor and all the others—whilst Sarah—lie molderin' in their graves er at the bottom o' the sea er scattered to the four winds.

It seemed the most natural thing in the world to press the pedal, nudge the wheel a bit to the right, and barrel into the German—

—He's young, oh well—

—knocking him into the air and clear of the car.

Nice. And no one comin' from either direction—*oh crud.*

The yellow-haired young girl sat alone at the opposite edge of the road.

She saw the whole blamed thing. She saw me. Oh Lord. Maybe I better go back and "help" that Jerry, and tell the girl I's so weak and tired from all I been through, I jist went to sleep at the wheel fer a minute.

Disappointment filled him when he looked through the rearview mirror.

Shoot, the little cull's gittin' back on his feet like I tackled him ruther'n run over him with a motor car!

There was that poster which was appearing everywhere, including on the wall at the Monterrey, the one with the large sketch of the Jap soldier bayoneting the unarmed American prisoner on Bataan as others suffered in the background, and the caption: *"What are YOU going to do about it? Stay on the job until every MURDERING JAP is wiped out!"*

Obscenities of every stripe streamed through his mind and out his lips before he smiled.

Hah, most the folks 'round here prolly gimme a medal fer doin' it.

Fear gave way to amused satisfaction as he gunned Maggie's Caddy toward Norman. He never saw the little girl across the road's surprised expression blossom into one of the first smiles that had graced her pretty freckled face since her daddy, whom they said was the greatest football player ever to wear the purple and gold of Chickasha High, was killed by the Germans on his final flying mission before coming home to her.

APRIL, 1944
OKLAHOMA CITY, OKLAHOMA

Murchison did more than cover his tab at the Hill Club. Once he learned he was in Oklahoma but headed for flight training in Louisiana, he pulled strings to get him assigned to a P-51 Mustang fighter group based at the colossal new Tinker Air Field located just southeast of Oklahoma City. The base was named for one-eighth-Osage Oklahoma General Clarence Tinker, the first American general to die in the war, shot down while personally leading a squadron of B-24 Liberators into action at Midway.

He affected interest in Murchison's crowing over the reassignment, but his mind was on the shapely waitress at the Mont and could he hang on to Maggie's Caddy long enough to get back down there and see her.

I'll offer to Simonize it for her, then make a beeline to Norman.

He had already smoothed out the dent left from his German victim.

"This P-51 Mustang you're going to be flying, Lance," Murchison said, more serious than he had ever seen him and even more profane, "some of us believe the outcome of the whole war may hinge on getting masses of these beasts into action. If we can't get the *Luftwaffe* out of the sky, we can't succeed in a northern European invasion. They'll massacre us. I guess you know, rough as it was for you fellows over there last year, it only got worse after you left. The Krauts just shot our boys to pieces. I had one of the three highest ranking generals in the Army Air Forces sit right where you are on Thanksgiving Day—actually, he was standing and cussing me like a junkyard dog—and tell me if we couldn't mass produce a fire-breathing escort fighter that could go from England to Germany and back with the bombers and out-fight the 109s and FWs, we were going to have to suspend daylight bombing operations over Germany—meaning we might lose this war. Uh, those were his words, not mine."

A steady seething rage increasingly simmered just beneath his own surface, or sometimes not beneath it. Some sort of internal governor prevented it from erupting, other than when external circumstances beyond his control intervened. Now, the governor checked his fury at this report of new Hun actions and revisiting of old ones. He detached from the conversation and responded with an idle half-nod. Murchison seemed perplexed for an instant but shifted into the mode that had helped him rise to the top of the petroleum and, now, aviation industries, not to mention the behind-the-curtain world of political kingmaking.

"Never seen anything like 'em, Lance," he said. "First ones started wreaking havoc in combat over Europe just before Christmas. We've got several groups in the air now, and more on the way. You are going to revel in flying this magnificent warship—and by the way, you are headed straight for a P-51, no Thunderbolts or Lightnings for you, son. Only the best for the best."

As Murchison rambled on, he mused at how the man seemed to speak with the authority of a Caesar or at least commander of a military branch. "This Rolls Merlin—Packard's building 'em here in the States," Murchison said, "is not only the most dependable aircraft engine I've ever heard of—and Lindbergh backs me on that—it's got a two-stage, two-speed supercharger for—yes, boy, I see you know what that means—"

"It means it'll knock them FWs out o the sky like ten pins at high altitude, and with six fi'ty-cal machine guns, it won't matter how much armor the Jerries strap on 'em," he said, now spellbound at the prospect of it, in spite of himself.

Murchison blanched at a subsequent vulgarity, the first he had ever heard from Lance, which spiced his continued, elated musing. The oil baron cleared his throat and continued. "Yes, and at nearly four-hundred and fifty miles an hour, even at high altitude—watch for that number to rise close to five hundred with subsequent models, thanks to Boots Adams and his science boys' work on high octane aviation fuel over at Phillips Petroleum—yet with superior maneuverability, the Jerries can't even run from it," he said, picking up steam again.

"And whereas the Spits, 109s, all of 'em, might stay aloft for two or maybe three hours, you put a set of long range drop tanks on this Mustang and she'll go eight hours!"

Jeez, that sure is long enough to go from East Anglia to Germany and back.

He had heard such but didn't really believe it until now.

Glory hallelujah, I am gunna wreak me some havoc.

He barely heard Murchison say, "Then when you finally track down the vermin, you've got the most sophisticated and effective gunsight in the world, a gyroscope, to guarantee that a crack shot like you won't miss what you aim at. It calculates target lead, bullet drop, even enemy wingspan and distance for you, then lines up the crosshairs for you for some delightful deflection shooting. Heavens, an eagle eye like you may tell your armorers to shove the tracers up their tailpipes!"

But he was already picturing catching 109s and 190s.

And maybe, oh if there is still a God o some sort up there, that—

He could scarcely bring himself to utter the name even silently.

— that "Black Knight." Oh, if I could bag that spawn o' Satan I might even consider forgivin' You fer all Ye done and let happen—I might.

He began to visualize catching them just before they dove into a vulnerable group of Forts with those paper-thin fuselages, their inability to take even the least of evasive actions. He could see those exhausted boys with feces filling their uniforms, their... appendages... freezing and breaking off like icicles when they just wanted to relieve themselves after eight hours of horror. He saw their oxygen disconnecting without them knowing 'til they were dead on the cold, spent cartridge casing-covered floor, not to mention the fighters, the cussed flak from them cursed .88s....

When Murchison noticed he wasn't even listening, he cleared his throat and said, "See here, Lance, Mary Katherine's done a remarkable job and I'm mighty proud of her, we all are, but I don't like what I hear about her off-stage activities. If I can get her back in town for a few days to visit, well, compared to the parade of derelicts and—well, I know you've got strong religious convictions, compared to them, you're a shining light from the fields of Elysium, son. If it ain't a slimy, opium-snorting, Jew, movie producer, it's this piddly ant Wop manager she keeps around for Lord-knows-why. Bunch of renegades and, reprobates if you ask me." He leaned forward a shade and his expression indicated the most interest Lance had ever seen him display for the words of anyone beside himself. "Guess what I'm asking, son, is, well, I know you two had some feelings for one another at one time. Do you still have any for her? Could you?"

He stared at him, curious now, if still not interested. "She'd be a good, uh— fling—to finally have" is what he wanted to say, but what he said was, "She's a special lady, Mr. Murchison, but I don't reckon she'd have any interest in me."

"Oh, now, there's where you're wrong, son," Murchison said, leaning way forward now. "I wasn't going to say anything—fact, I'm bound to her not to say anything—but well, what the heck, with wartime conditions and all, young people, the good sort of young people, you can't necessarily be as conventional about matters as in normal times. But Lance, my daughter sat and wept like a baby in my arms about you a year or so ago. Why, she hadn't even been in my arms since junior high school days, probably. Too independent, too proud, all that horse hockey that fills the young people these days."

His eyes grew distant, rheumy, and he drew back and turned a bit. For the first time, Lance focused on him closely enough to notice the man looked much older than when he last saw him. A decade older at least, rather than three years or less.

"All this money, all this... *fame*," Murchison continued. He swung his gaze back to him. "Why, I don't believe it's done her a whit o good, Lance. You two should've got yourselves married that Easter down in the Wichitas." He blinked in surprise. "Aw, for cryin out loud, she told me about that, too. Said it was the biggest mistake she ever made, chasing after fame and fortune and leaving you."

He chewed on that some and wondered why Murchison was telling him any of this. "Why sure, Mr. Murchison. I'd be proud to see Mary Kat—Mary Katherine—again, if she'll see me, sir."

"Oh, criminy, yes, she'll see you," Murchison blurted before catching himself as he rose from behind his desk, walked around it—he noticed one leg seemed almost to drag—and extended his hand to shake. "I'll have Helen call you once the arrangements are made."

A moment later, he stopped as they reached the door. "I do have one question for you, Mr. Murchison."

"Sure, boy, anything you want," Murchison said.

"So, you've heard from Colonel Lindbergh?"

A wry smile spread across Murchison's lined, wan face. "Indeed, I have, son," he said, placing a hand on his shoulder. "I know I can trust you to keep a confidence, eh, son? Well, General MacArthur recently got word to me that Slim's been out there in the Pacific with his boys for a while. Did you know that philandering blackguard in the White House never even let him enlist? So, after helping design and perfect the B-17 and correct the deficiencies of the B-24, he's now taught Mac's boys how to double the bomb load of their Corsairs and get nearly twice the distance on the same fuel in their P-38s, while managing to fly a few dozen combat missions with a Lightning Mac gave him, strafe Jap garrisons, bomb trains and barges, and shoot down a Nip plane piloted by a group commander in a one-on-one dogfight. All while forty-two years of age and not even a member of our armed forces!"

He could only smile and shake his head slowly. Lindbergh was like a bright light flickering in the darkness that had enfolded him and the nightmares that had returned.

Later, he drove the baby blue Caddy south out of downtown Oklahoma City and down Highway 77 toward Norman, its tank stocked with gas from Murchison's private, non-rationed pumps.

Hope I git to see the Cunnel again sometime. Think I might even ruther see him then Mary Kat but guess if she still wants to... do what she wanted last few times I seen her, well, that'd sweeten the pot some. Golly, I missed the boat on that back in Dee-troit. What a sap I was.

What a sap I always been.

MAY, 1944
MIDWEST CITY, OKLAHOMA

Cousin Clint was waiting for Lance in the Officers Club when Maggie dropped him off at Tinker a month or so later. With the country and world engulfed in blood to an extent never before seen in history, alcohol, too, was now rationed to the bone, including in Officers Clubs. Clint, though, had him an unopened fifth of Black Jack, courtesy of his Naval Intelligence office in Washington. They sat and sipped, Frank Sinatra's *I'll Be Seeing You* wafting through the large room from a Victrola radio.

He looks tanned and sad. Not angry like before, jist sad.

"So, I heard right you changed your persuasion regardin' the demon rum," Clint said, eyeing him.

He said nothing and stared stone-faced at him. After a moment, Clint broke off his eye contact, sipped more Jack, and looked away, the most forlorn and aged countenance he had ever seen painted on his cousin's face spreading across it. He added, in barely more than a whisper, "Guess a stint over the friendly skies o the Third Reich'll do it for ya."

"Somethin' eatin' at you, Cuz?"

Clint wouldn't talk about it in the Tinker Club, so Lance requisitioned a Jeep and they drove south through open country carpeted with young cotton, alfalfa, and maize. The road ended as a dirt path overlooking the wide ruddy bed and thin stream that was the South Canadian River, which he used to ride along on horseback in college. They walked down to the edge of such water as there was and sat, sipping straight Jack from the Tinker glasses they had appropriated. A light spring breeze carried the sweet fragrance of unseen greening fields and blossoming flowers across the river from the south.

They lit up Camels from a pack Clint had and puffed away. He realized his cousin was carting along the best of everything these days in a ration-depleted society. They sat for five minutes listening to the chatter, clicking, and singing of red-winged black birds before Clint said gently, "They's so much I'm trusted with only a few fellas know and it don't appear to bother them, but I can't hardly git past it any more." He waited a full minute, before adding in hardly more than a murmur, "Turns out we knew the Japs were comin' 'fore ever they hit us at Pearl."

He nodded. "Yeah, I heard we knew somethin' was up."

"No, you didn't," Clint said, drawing his full attention. "I mean we knew they's comin' to Pearl, and when."

"What're you talkin' about?"

After another long pause, this time Lance watching a hawk sailing through the blue sky to the south, Clint said, "I been, uh, purty neck-deep in our cryptographic operations out in the Pacific. Breakin' the Jap codes. Our Pacific communication intel ops are primarily naval ops. We had twenty-one radio intercept stations, rangin' on the North American coastline from Alaska to Panama and in the Pacific from Oahu to the Philippines. When we intercepted a Jap message, it was sent to one of three regional control centers, decoded, then sent to our naval intel headquarters in Washington. That's where I worked—er, work," he corrected himself, eyeing his cousin. "Anyhow, had me a visit with Admiral Richardson, former commander of our Pacific fleet. Knew him fer couple years through my work with naval intel. Good man. Told me we busted all their codes, but the President and Secretary o War Stimson, whole motley gang of 'em, wanted Japs to fire on us first to git us in the war—against the Germans."

He stared at him like he just turned into the man in the moon. "But somebody told me Richardson wadn't even in charge o that fleet anymore."

"Yeah, and why ya think not?" Clint said. "'Cuz he wouldn't play ball with the President, who wanted him to dangle the fleet front o the Japs like Catfish Charlie, which is exactly what Roosevelt had his replacement do after he fired Richardson 'cuz he wouldn't. The poor loyal sap in charge o the Navy in Hawaii and his army counterpart, doin' as they were told, are gittin' hung out to dry. Their names gunna be blacker'n a blue norther in February in the history books."

Now, the story was beyond just Clint and it was disturbing. He poured himself four fingers more.

"Anyhow, back when their imperial sun started rising over there in the Pacific, we recommenced to sellin' 'em rubber and iron and fuel," Clint said. "But jist enough to encourage 'em on. Then at jist the right moment we embargoed everthang, froze all their money in our banks, and forced 'em to start a war we made certain they had to fight but couldn't finish. We planned it down to the month how much they'd have, and that month's done passed. Fer all the Japs' capabilities, they're an arrogant bunch o stupid jackasses er they'd o knowed we'd kick their everlovin' hides, which we in the process o doin now, case ye ain't heard."

"So, Richardson told you all that?" he asked.

"Some of it come from the Senator, when I went to see him," Clint said. "He's sick unto death over it. Bein' in Washington, he still knows everbody, though he's broker and less popular than ever cause he's devotin his life tryin to help the Indians round these parts, git at least somethin' that was stole from 'em."

"But... why would they tell you all this but keep it a secret from the world?" he asked. "Over two-thousand of our people died in that attack and a pile more since."

"Both said they can't do nothin' might hurt our boys' morale now," Clint said, looking down at his glass which still held Jack, but not drinking. "Er give the enemy any fodder fer their propaganda machines."

They sat in silence and lit up new Camels as the sun dipped down under where the South Canadian wound away to the west.

"Shoot, maybe it's all fer the best," Clint concluded. "Maybe the Nips and Krauts were aimin to jist keep a'goin'. The Limeys and Reds sure couldn't put a lid on 'em."

Lance slurped more whiskey, clicked his tongue, and gave a quick sideways jerk of his head. "Maybe once we finish guttin' the Japs and Jerries, we oughta go after Roosevelt."

Clint turned and stared at him. "Ever guy I know in combat's tryin' to finish his tour and git home," he said softly, but without mirth. "You? You goin' back fer more, and open fer more still after that."

He licked his lips and stared out across the river. "What the heck reason do I have to go home? What home?"

Clint blew a smoke ring up into the now-still air, then sat for a moment, staring sadly down into his glass but still not drinking. A mosquito catcher jumped down into the Jack, shuddered, then fell into it and floated, dead. "Hate seein how ye changed, Cuz," he said, hardly louder than a whisper. "You the one always kept your good heart when everone else lost theirs; when I lost mine."

Neither man spoke for a couple more minutes. As the shadows deepened around them and the water darkened, he tossed another cigarette stub down onto the pile they had formed during their talk and said, "Yeah, and that's why I ain't quittin' till ever Nazi cur on two legs is pushin' up daisies. They ain't much I had they didn't take."

Another minute passed before Clint, his face despairing as the grave, said, so soft he had to lean closer to hear, "Shucks, all these leaders, of all these countries, they the ones deserve gittin' lit up like Roman candles. Reckon they all the same, doin' what it takes to git there. Even wantin' to git there makes 'em guilty in my eyes. One thing they all got in common though, none of 'em coulda got where they are without us, the people, puttin' an amen to it."

He could not have agreed more. And whatever Jerries had the misfortune to cross his path in the days ahead were going to pay for this and everything else that had conspired to steal the light that had always before illumined his path through this long, dark vale of tears.

EIGHTEEN

It was hard for him to figure out whether flying his own Mustang or Sara Lee Cantrell, the glamorous Theta from college days, provided the greater thrill the next couple of months. It was now Sara Lee Carpenter, and her husband held a lofty army intelligence operations command in the Twentieth Air Force, the dominant American air presence in the Pacific Theater. He had returned there a couple weeks before, after a thirty-day furlough in his native Oklahoma City, where his father reigned as one of the elite trial attorneys in the state, and had just built the greatest mansion in Nichols Hills, perhaps the most fashionable neighborhood in the state.

Sara Lee, feeling lonely and neglected to the point of collapse, had sweet-talked one of Carpenter's Tinker buddies into accompanying her to lunch at the most prestigious golf and country club in Oklahoma City, where her father headed the Board of Trustees. Lance raced up at the end of a five-mile run just as she dropped the buddy back at Tinker.

She took him to supper that evening, at the club, and a lot more later that night. She spotted the changes in him and could not restrain her passions over his retaining what she had always desired most about him, while jettisoning his least necessary attributes, such as sobriety, gentlemanliness, and piety.

The Mustang, meanwhile, proved more than he could ever have imagined. The cockpit crammed him in like a sardine and had disqualified Waddy from flying the plane due to his size. Murchison prevented the same fate from befalling him. But its compactness contributed to the sleekest streamlined exterior he'd ever seen, gleaming silver in the sun. It coupled with a powerhouse Rolls-Royce Merlin engine to render the experience of piloting it as joyous as his old Fort had finally been dreadful. His instructors warned that its efficient new liquid-cooled engine left it vulnerable to flak and even small arms fire due to the requisite tubing. He didn't intend to give anyone the opportunity to prove that axiom.

When he had first opened the throttle, ignoring his trainer's shouts, the speed sucked the breath from his lungs. More thrilling still, was how it handled smoothly and with precision, anything and everything he asked it to do, despite its muscle. Provided just a few degrees of horizontal angle, it not only got to high altitudes faster than anything else powered by propellers, it performed as well—

—*if not better!*—

—once it got there.

When he wing-rolled to dive to the deck, a whole nother universe of elation took hold. After only a couple of days, he was taking his plane to within yards of the ground, at nearly full speed. The classes taught him that he would fly in basic four-man sets called "flights" which formed sixteen-plane squadrons. Versatility would be the hallmark of his work. Dive bombing fighters on the ground, strafing barges, trains, fuel depots, and any other targets of opportunity, and hunting German fighters on area sweeps would be routine. Even the bomber escort duty now gave precedence to stalking enemy formations before rather than after they could get at the bombers.

His excitement mounted, and he grew restive to the point of insubordination to ship out. America and its allies stormed the French beaches at Normandy in

June, then slugged their way across northern Europe, while taking the Marianas Islands in the Pacific from which they could bomb the Japanese mainland. He grew fearful, nearly frantic, that the war, at least against Germany, might end before he got back into it. He pulled every string he could, including with Murchison, to accelerate his departure. He even began praying to God again for this particular desire.

He was ready. He breezed through the phalanx of classes; weapons, meteorology, aircraft recognition and characteristics, fighter interception and engagement, instruments, hydraulics, fuel, and electrical systems of the Mustang. He had an enormous advantage over the other trainees due to his B-17 training and experience, as well as his pre-war flying. He, nonetheless, poured himself into the exercises, working harder than anyone, and churning ahead in the lessons, hoping it would clear him sooner for graduation back to Europe.

Gradually, Lance realized that the responsibility for the delay rested in one place, the commanding officer, Major Grider. He had flown over fifty missions against the Japanese with the Flying Tigers in China and had a scar traversing his left cheek to show for it, as well as a chest full of decorations and the rank of full colonel at thirty-two years of age. Even other instructors told him they had no reason to keep him at Tinker.

Grider determined that the men under his charge would emerge as not only the sharpest flyers mentally in the USAAF, but the most physically rugged. In addition to rifle and marching drills, he and his fellows endured a vast assortment of physical workouts, including some he had seen neither at OU, nor during bomber training. They ran sprints and distance, tackled ropes and other obstacle course exercises, and did pushups, situps, pullups, and crunches by the hundreds. Grider pushed, provoked, even bullied them. He pitted them against one another to bring out their best, as well as to coach them on keeping their cool while exerting maximum effort under duress. Most amazingly, he led them through most of it himself.

They wrestled, fenced, did the old bull in the ring with a football, and boxed. He had added more muscle since his boxing sessions at OU, and he thought himself a shade quicker. He knew his killer instinct had blossomed beyond all else. After a few weeks, few of his comrades dared set foot in the ring with him. When no one would, he pounded the bag until he couldn't lift his arms.

In a few more weeks, he was outflying everyone at Tinker, including his instructors. Grider, meanwhile, never missed an opportunity to chide an instructor when he excelled them in a drill or contest, for missteps real and imagined, and both, in front of as large an audience as possible, when he disdained the instructor's orders.

Halfway through his fourth month at Tinker, on a broiling mid-August afternoon, Grider inserted himself into the simulated combat exercise lineup against him. The pairing set the whole base buzzing. The general feelings of the Tinker population for both men meshed grudging admiration, even awe, with jealousy and dislike. On the runway just before takeoff, accustomed to scanning the sky in Europe like he had at the farm back home all the way to childhood, he spotted a bank of cumulus clouds drifting onto the horizon several miles to the southeast, away from the Oklahoma City metropolitan area. He squinted his eyes and stared.

Unusual from that direction, but I believe them clouds are headed thisaway.

Grider explained the ground rules. The two would fly together to 12,000 feet, then Grider would turn right, Lance left, and the contest was on.

"Can I turn right, sir?" he asked.

Grider eyed him and said with a rough epithet, "What for? That'll give me the sun behind me. You don't want to put yourself at any worse disadvantage than you already are, do you?"

"I can trade planes with ya, too, sir," he said, a steely smile chipping a corner off Grider's hard self-assurance. Grider had grown fond of the P-47 Thunderbolt since returning from Asia. It far excelled the often-cannibalized Curtiss P-40 Warhawks he had flown in combat. Despite the ascent of the P-51, in which all new fighter pilots trained, he continued flying one of the few remaining operational Thunderbolts at Tinker in combat exercises with the trainees, though beginning next week the last P-47s would leave the base.

"Dumb Okie." Grider shook his head, his scar gleaming in the scalding sunlight, and turning toward his plane.

Yeah, I know his game. Choosin' that big ole honkin' Thunderbolt fer hisself and givin' me the faster, more-maneuverable Mustang will help him put a exclamation point on bestin' wise guy me. Or so he thinks.

"Go ahead and turn right, but keep the Mustang," Grider said over his shoulder as he climbed up into the Thunderbolt.

When they made their break at 12,000 feet, the cumulus bank was waiting a half-mile ahead of him, just where he had anticipated. Utilizing it to veil his moves, he immediately steered the Mustang up into as steep and fast a climb into the clouds as he could without stalling. A couple thousand feet up, just before the cover ended, he wing-rolled into a free fall back down through the formation. He knew Grider wouldn't risk entering it for fear of colliding with a trainee, so, his still-sensitive skull wound from the Hill bar fight pounding him, he screamed down at nearly 500 miles per hour with the aid of the sixth sense he seemed to have when flying, for the spot he had judged would place him just behind his foe, based on his close observations the past many days of the man's flying tendencies. When he blazed forth out of the clouds and into the sunsparked sky, he was a thousand feet above and directly behind Grider.

One thing that Jug can do is dive faster'n a Mustang, so I gotta git to him 'fore he sees me.

Adrenaline surging, he pushed the control stick to the firewall to plunge downward, rammed the toggle handle through the safety wired gate to full war emergency power, in defiance of base regulations, for maximum speed, and tore after Grider. Less than thirty seconds later, he was on his tail and "firing" the wing-mounted gun camera that chronicled his "kill."

Grider never even saw him until he buzzed over, feigned evasive maneuvers, and let him have what he thought was his own kill. The colonel waggled his wings to signal the end of the exercise and they both headed back to Tinker.

He wasn't sure he could remember a greater feeling of exhilaration as he headed down. He let Grider lead the way. Sure enough, when they got to the ground, the colonel sprung from his fighter and strutted toward the hundreds-strong throng that had gathered for the showdown between the hardcase veteran commander and the cocksure bomber jockey. To Grider's everlasting shock, the throng surged right past him and toward Lance as he pulled up in his Mustang.

Observing the applause and congratulations heaped upon him, Grider barked, "What is going on here? Why is everyone back-slapping this overrated showoff after he overshoots me, panics, and gets his wings clipped in front of God and creation?"

It's just too perfect.

He could scarcely control the urge to belly laugh.

"Grider, tell me you saw him lightin' up your panties from behind," one of the most respected instructors on the base, himself a major and P-38 Lightning veteran in the European Theater, said in surprise.

Grider thought he was joking until he detected the titters and stifled laughter rippling through the crowd. He thought back for a moment, then clenched his jaw tight. "You must think you're some kinda hot stuff, Roark."

Lance was through playing. "They's a reason they call it 'The Big Show,' jackass," he said without mirth, referring to the common moniker for the brutal, colossal air war in Europe. Eyes narrowing, he paused a beat for effect as murmurs filled the crowd and Grider blanched.

"Hey," the major objected to the insubordinate chide, stepping toward them.

"No." Grider waved him off. He glared at Lance. His next words dripped with venom. "And why's that?"

"It's 'cause we flyin' against the bloody varsity."

For a moment, he and Grider locked eyes in a burning stare-down. Just when it occurred to Lance he would as soon snap the arrogant jerk's neck like a chicken's, here and now, and devil take the consequences, something in his expression caused Grider to break off the stare, wheel, and stalk away cursing.

"Well, not sure what I think of all that," the P-38 major said as he approached him. "But you are one butt-kickin' hellion." There were no more cheers, but the throng parted for him like the Red Sea had for Moses.

The next day, he had the base artist paint *"Captain America"* on both sides of the forward fuselage of his Mustang and he told Grider if they didn't graduate him by Labor Day he would get a plane from Murchison and fly himself back to England, "And screw you inbred Nancy boys if ye don't like it."

—

As long as Sara Lee kept him supplied with Wild Turkey bourbon, a brand he first heard of when Trigger provided it and which he now drank in honor of his departed buddy, he would listen to her petulant, self-absorbed ramblings as they lounged about her mansion. His Captain's rank usually allowed him to sleep off the base. That way, too, he never had to say much. His presence and lovemaking filled the needs in both her life and body—*Least till the next sucker stumbles along*—and provided him free booze and a beautiful woman for pleasure. He needed both with the return in early August of his nightmares, escalating in clarity and horror. Strangely, Sarah's face no longer appeared in them. None of his crutches, however, solved the persistent shingles that now numbed part of his right hand and the top of the right side of his back, though they helped some. His skull wound continued to ache along the part of his hair during and after his more audacious flights.

The most he said to her at one time was the evening she realized he never said anything to her and pressed him on it. "Well," he said, leaving the Wild Turkey alone for a moment and looking her in the eye, "love that Mustang, but strangest thing, darlin'. Moment I saw it in person fer the first time, I thought, 'What the heck, paint that sucker green or gray... or black... and it's a bloody 109.'"

She stared at him like he had just spoken in Swahili, cupped his chin in the palm of her manicured, beringed hand, and for a moment, honesty, perhaps even sympathy for another person, crept into her eyes. "Why, Lance, this war *has* changed you, hasn't it?" For a brief moment, they stared deep into one another's eyes, before he looked away. She blinked, her eyes detached from him, and her focus returned to her own interests. She drank her wine, brightened, and said in a bright chirping voice, "Gimme jest a minute, sugar. I got the most scandalous nightie to show ya. Ordered it all the way from New York City. Can't exactly git anything from Paris these days."

Two days after his exploits with Grider, orders arrived for him to head back to England the next day. He scarcely noticed the devastation wrought on Sara Lee's face. He had noticed that lovemaking was the one activity guaranteed to stopper her drinking in the evening. She would kiss him, roll contentedly—and independently—over, and be breathing deeply within a minute or two. After lovemaking, she did not even need sleeping pills. Tonight, however, she put on a robe, longer and less sheer than her norm, lit a Lucky, and poured herself brandy. She sat on a small couch across her bedroom from the bed and puffed her cigarette like a chimney.

"Ain'tchu goin' to sleep?" he asked, contentedly fatigued from head to toe. His day had included classes, formation flying to Muskogee and back with seven other pilots, dinner with her at the Beacon Club, and the frenzied, physical lovemaking standard for Sara Lee, especially a tipsy Sara Lee.

"I don't feel much like sleepin', right now," she said, puffing and sipping brandy, her shapely tanned legs crossed under her.

He thought about making himself something from one of the three well-stocked bars in her house, but he already felt relaxed and tranquil enough that he couldn't justify the effort to walk the few feet to do so. He did fire up his own Lucky and sat back against the headboard of the bed, atop the covers.

"So, what's eatin' you?" he asked, after five minutes of silence. After five more, he wanted to ignore her, go to another room, and go to sleep. "Come on, I can't sleep with ye like this. What is it?"

Tense with emotion and lighting another cigarette, she replied, "My dear hubby. I'm not sure how dear he is any more."

"Why?" he said, surrendering to pour Wild Turkey over ice. "What'd he say?"

"That's jest it," she said. "He said barely a thing. I couldn't git squat out of him. Fer all his many faults, he always told me whatever I wanted to know about anything. We never had problems findin' conversation. The only clue I squeezed out of him this time was those monstrous Japs, those animals, are apparently torturin' all our boys they capture, in their prison camps all over the Pacific. Torturin' many of 'em to death."

"He told you that?" Similar rumors had reached him even in England.

"Well, he told me part in his sleep, durin' the worst nightmare I've ever seen anyone have in my life. I got the rest of it out of him when he woke up." She puffed faster and drank more. "Then he started cryin' and couldn't stop for a whole *hour.*"

"I'll never cry again." His words were hard, hollow, and final like stones plunking into a deep stock tank.

She stared at him, her eyes flickering for an instant, as so often they had at the sight of his broad shoulders, well-formed chest, and lean, hard torso. She said, "One o the boys I went to high school with at Classen? He was like the brother I never had since we were six years old? I wrote letters to him while he was over there in the Pacific, just so he would have somethin' to look forward to? Well, he's in one o their prisons now."

He stared at her, unsettled by where this was going, or more so, his ignorance of where.

"You don't give a flyin' fig about me, do you?" Her whole demeanor changed. He just looked at her, feeling nothing. "Hey buster, I'm not some cutthroat climber like that princess Mary Katherine Murchison of yours, the famous Mary Katherine, the 'Golden Girl with the Golden Vicious Voice!' That arrogant—"

"Hey!"

"She was good enough for you, but I'm not?" she continued to shout, standing and stalking toward him. "Why, I know all about that social-climbin' shrew, and her abortion in New York."

"You shut'cher mouth right now er I'll shut it for ya!" he said, leaping to his feet, his fists clenched.

"Oh, really?" she replied screaming. "Well go ahead and shut it, see if I care, you stupid redneck oaf!" She stood toe-to-toe with him, on her own tiptoes, leering and shouting up at him, close enough he could sniff the motley mix comprising her breath. "Everything! I'm giving you everything I have! Everything I am! Oh!" she said, crying, shaking, slugging at his bare stomach, chest, and face as he stood there, then falling to her knees sobbing when he did not react. "Oh, curse you, Lance Roark, curse you to hell," she wept mournfully as he looked down at her, amazed but unmoved. "You and your precious Mary Katherine."

He pulled her up by her hair, jerked her back onto her tiptoes, and looked her in the face, inches away. "You stupid spoiled brat," he said, his blood up for a fight more than in anger. "If you so much as breathe her name again in my presence, I'll squash that purty little head o yours like a ripe grape."

Something in his words, his voice, his countenance, his glinting green eyes took all the anger out of her. Took the very life out of her. She hung like a limp puppet, his fist still gripping her lustrous chocolate hair. When he released her, she collapsed to the floor in silent, heaving wails.

"Oh," she said, on all fours as he grabbed his kit and left, his mouth bleeding, "oh, it's all gone, everthang is gone. There's nothin' left."

NINETEEN

TOFT MONKS, ENGLAND
SEPTEMBER, 1944

Of all the American airmen in the world, who but Clarke from their 299th Fort days greeted him as his Group Operations Officer, second in command to the Group Commander, when he arrived at the USAAF's fighter station just outside the quiet village of Toft Monks, a few miles up the road toward seaside Great Yarmouth from Beccles.

"Welcome to the 77th Group, Captain Roark," Clarke hailed him cheerfully when he arrived under the familiar downpour of English rain.

Sly yahoo seems lot friendlier'n before.

Clarke's affable manner continued that evening in the officers' mess.

"Remember how we used to be sittin' ducks, just waiting for the Jerries to wale into us whenever they chose?" Clarke asked him. "Well, with the Mustang, we've turned the tables on them—we break loose from the bomber stream and go bounce them while they're still on their way up to find us. Man, you're gonna love it, Parson."

He nodded, but said nothing.

"So how do you feel, Roark?" Clarke asked him.

"Glad to finally be here," he said, his mouth full of B-Ration meat and beans.

"Most people are tearing the pages of their calendars out to get home as soon as they can," Clarke said with delight, "but you're like me."

That caught his attention as he shoveled powdered mashed potatoes into his mouth. "Oh? How'zat?"

"You're running right back to it," Clarke said, with a smile that seemed somehow not that different from the icy frowns he used to give him.

—

Fall rains prevented him flying his first fighter mission until near the end of September. By then, he not only had *Captain America* painted on his fuselage, he had him punching Hitler, as on the comic book cover. Once he got going on his missions, he advanced from two-plane element leader to four-plane flight leader after a half-dozen missions while barely seeing a German plane. From there, he moved up to eight-plane section leader after another ten missions, with only Clarke, the squadron commander superseding him in authority. Clarke excelled him in something else as well—the twelve black Maltese Crosses garnishing the fuselage of his Mustang, just under the canopy.

"They's less'n ten flyers in the whole Eighth got more'n that cocky son of a gun," Ben Posey, Texan chief of Lance's three-man ground crew, said, spitting Red Man. "I reckon he's determined to pass 'em all 'fore he gits out o here."

It was November by then, and the flying was as exhilarating as it was awful during the final *Hellfire and Brimstone* missions. Life on the ground was fine, for the most part, as he continued to bully his body into the best shape of his life. Every few days, though, the absence of all he had come to have, then lose, at Beccles enveloped him like a much darker version of the pervasive English fog.

His Bible might as well have been printed in Sanskrit for all the good it was to him. The married Protestant base chaplain had heard Clarke call him Parson and asked if he was a minister. He reckoned it didn't much matter what impression he made on the man, because he was a "progressive" Methodist who seemed to enjoy the same recreational pursuits the fighter pilots did, including having an English girlfriend. The single exception being that he was more discreet about the last part, which Lance didn't count to his credit.

On the other hand, the enhanced freedom of his rank usually allowed him evening liberty off the base when he desired it, which he particularly took advantage of when the black fog came. Leveraging the experiences of nearly a year in East Anglia during his first tour, he soon established a friendship with an enterprising pub owner in nearby Toft Monks. The man provided him his own supply of whiskey that was, even if of an inferior sort, unattainable at the base, at least in such volume.

One dank evening that featured an unusually fierce downpour even for North Sea-encompassed East Anglia, he made do at the OC rather than biking or Jeeping to the pub. The large room featured a fireplace, before which he perched himself in a scuffed wooden chair to drink and smoke alone, or at least as alone as he could manage within the setting. After a couple minutes, Johnny DeLozier, a darkly handsome young pilot in his squadron and probably its best-liked flyer, plopped himself down in another chair a few feet away. He had a wad of snuff stuffed inside his upper lip—he was "resting" his well-worn lower lip—and a beer in his hand.

"Captain Ro-ark, that was a heckuva move you put on that fella today, sir," DeLozier announced in guileless admiration.

"Aw, whatever."

"Nah, really, he had'ju bounced when we hit that airdrome."

"Well, if I's a JU-88, I wouldn't jack with a Mustang from any direction." DeLozier just smiled in appreciation.

"So, where you from, DeLozier?" he asked. It was the first question he had asked anyone since his return to England.

"Well, Visalia, California, now," DeLozier said, almost apologetically. Then he brightened and added, "But I'm from Chelsea, Oklahoma, till my folks headed west when I's fifteen."

"I thought'chu might be an Oklahoma boy," he said with a proud smile.

"Shoot yow," DeLozier said, nodding. "And I ain't no 'Okie' neither, and I'm goin' right back to Chelsea soon's this war's over. My girlfriend since third grade's still there and we finally gunna git hitched."

"Dang straight ya are," he said, as though amening a pastor's climactic sermon point.

DeLozier's face grew focused. "Say Cap'n, didn'tchu used to fly and play ball with Waddy Young?"

"Sure did," he replied. "My best friend in the world."

DeLozier's face beamed as he straightened in his chair and announced, "Well, my daddy'n his cowboy'd together fer the Millers at the ole 101 Ranch."

"No foolin?" He glanced around to make sure no one else was in ear shot, then lowered his voice a shade and said, "My folks, they live in Visalia now, too."

"No kiddin!" DeLozier said. "Me and you over here, and them over there. Hey, we need to git 'em together. Us Oklahoma folks need to stick tight—everone else thinks we the way that Steinbeck four-flusher painted us. Uh—if that's okay, sir."

"Heck yeah, it's okay," he said, surprising himself at reaching across and slapping the boy on the arm. "The whole bunch of us'll git together—when we git back." It was the first thought he had given in a long time to any further life in America. A jolt of emotion pricked him as, for a moment, DeLozier reminded him of a young Trigger, as he was when he first met him at the OU Sigma Chi house and they were both, literally, just off the farm.

"There's the man who always finds a way to score a touchdown," Clarke said as he walked up.

He gave him a half nod.

"Major Clarke, you don't never drink, do ye?" DeLozier asked quizzically. "Ner smoke ner chew ner even cuss, sir."

"Don't need to," Clarke said, handing Lance a *Time* magazine.

"You got religion?" DeLozier asked.

"Don't need that, either," Clarke said.

"I'll be switched," he exclaimed, staring at the cover of the magazine and its dramatic headline, *"First Back from Japan."* A remarkable photo spread across the page. It featured a shirtless Waddy pulling a wagon atop which perched his crew, aiming peashooters, watching for enemy aircraft through telescopes, and in other poses. Behind them stood a silver B-29 bomber aircraft, the name *Waddy's Wagon* painted on it under a cartoon of Waddy, his wagon, and the crew in a like pose.

"So, the big shots picked Bob *'Memphis Belle'* Morgan to command this first B-29 squadron," Clarke said, "and Morgan handpicked all the captains, including Waddy. They flew the first bombing mission over Japan since the Doolittle Raid. Apparently, a crowd of press waited back on Saipan to mob the first crew to return. So Waddy has his crew throw everything but their jock straps off their plane to lighten it, see? And they beat Morgan back to base! Now they're more famous than he is."

He whistled. "From what I remember o Bob Morgan, I ain't sure how he'd cotton to that."

"There's another article in there mentions the Black Knight getting his two hundredth kill," Clarke added. "Says his name's Christian Schroeder and he's from Dresden. Apparently, he was becoming one of Germany's greatest soccer players when Adolf and the *Luftwaffe* intervened."

He found the article. It didn't take long to recognize it as a typical anti-Nazi or anti–Jap propaganda piece, mostly featuring the revelations of a different German fighter ace. This one, however, learned the Gestapo had executed his parents and thrown his wife into a concentration camp—where she soon perished through disease and exposure—for their involvement in the devout, Nazi-persecuted Confessing Church of Bonhoeffer, Niemoller, the martyred Paul Schneider, and thousands of others. He thereupon flew his FW-190—rockets and all—to Allied-liberated France and surrendered it and himself to the Ninth Air Force.

A treasure trove of information for his erstwhile enemies, he described for the magazine article the uneasy truce between the Nazi Party and the *Luftwaffe*, most of whose pilots ignored or outright disdained it. He explained that many *Luftwaffe* squadron commanders conducted casual and unauthorized interviews with new and prospective pilots to uncover Nazi Party allegiances. "They marginalize, seek transfer, or sometimes just neglect to assign missions to those men who do possess Nazi credentials or even membership." At one point, he claimed, only Hitler's personal intervention prevented *Luftwaffe* chief Goering from executing the anti-Nazi Adolf Galland, commander of the *Luftwaffe* fighter force and himself one of the greatest aces of the war.

The refugee pilot clearly harbored no love for Germany's actions under Hitler, and he catalogued a slew of its crimes in the article, including the apparent mass-internment, slave labor, and "disappearance" of Jews, including children and babies, from across Europe. Yet near the end of the piece, he declared, "Whoever christened Schroeder the Black Knight hit upon more truth than he realized. Schroeder considers himself a direct heir to the Knights Templar—whose Maltese Cross insignia graces German aircraft, tanks, and other armaments—and their mantle to protect and defend Western Christian civilization. He is a devout Catholic who has been lobbied by high Church officials to take up the priesthood after the war."

His eyes shot upward, marveling.

Is anything beyond the pale o decency in this twisted world?

"Like the original knights, he realizes he fights for an imperfect realm," the refugee continued, "but believes that, only by its sustainment, can improvement be made to it, and only through that realm, its principles, and influence, can the world find blessing and ultimate peace." He revealed that Schroeder refused victory insignias on his plane because "he considers them neither kills nor victories, and certainly no cause for celebration or pride. He also knows he has numerous relatives in America. He chastened me when I took issue with his notion that every man against whom we fly is a human being of infinite dignity made in the image of God Himself and worthy of commensurate respect."

He shook his head, incredulity and disgust filling him. He quashed his uneasiness over Schroeder's supposed humility, "relatives in America," and God.

"Christian Dietl Schroeder is a dangerous and misguided man and he is doing untold damage to the true defenders of freedom and liberty," the pilot concluded. "But he is also the greatest and noblest man I have ever personally encountered and utterly worthy of his sobriquet 'The Black Knight.'"

His face turned crimson as he slung the magazine, *Waddy's Wagon* and all, into the fire, then swung his burning gaze onto Clarke. "'Black heart,' you mean," he said fairly spitting in rage.

Even Clarke paused at the subsequent eruption of vulgarity.

"You... come across the Black Knight?" DeLozier asked.

Schroeder—Lord God, or whatever you are—Mama's family the Schroeders come originally from Dresden and all our cousins on her side are still there.

One of Mama's letters said the Kansas Schroeders told her his cousin Kati nursed babies in the Johannstadt Frauenklinik, the largest maternity hospital in Dresden, that she faced constant peril from the Nazis as a member of the same outlawed and suffering Confessing Church as the refugee pilot's family, and that everyone called her "the angel of mercy." Her oldest daughter Liselotte was now eighteen, beautiful, brilliant, a potential Olympic runner, and six feet tall, with flaming scarlet hair that curled clear to her waist. *Good grief, poor Mama 'bout give up. She tryin' matchmake me with a cousin in Germany!*

He had also never seen an American pilot fail to placard his fighter with a Maltese Cross for every "bandit" he downed, no matter how many. The Black Knight had ten times as many as the best of them, but still not one kill insignia on his ME-109, a recent photo of which the refugee had apparently provided to *Time*.

"Come across him?" Clarke said with a chuckle, speaking to DeLozier but eyeing him, then patting his shoulder. "This brave young bomber boy tried to bring down the Black Knight with a .38 Special."

"It was a .45," he said softly, still staring into the fire.

DeLozier gawked at him, speechless for many seconds. "Before this is over, Captain Ro-ark, I aim to be jist like you."

He winced at that and kept staring at the fire.

"You might give that one a little more thought, Johnny D.," Calhoun, a Bible-thumping Mustang pilot who reminded him of an unlikable, high-strung version of Patton, said earnestly as he passed by.

"And in this one," Clarke continued merrily, tossing him a recent copy of *Movie Stars Parade* magazine, "is good news for you."

He scanned the provocative cover photo of Dorothy Lamour and a story titled *"Gene Tierney Turns to Sex."* He had met Lamour in New York before the war at the same Stork Club table as Bing Crosby and the former Ambassador to England's charismatic young son Jack Kennedy. It was the night his and a now-famous—but very drunk—Mary Katherine's hopes for a future evaporated. "What?" he said.

"Look at page five," Clarke said.

He opened the magazine. Soon as he saw her picture, his lungs hollow, there was no need to read the story.

Even though she's smilin', lookee at them furrows and that dimple, which only shows when she's sad, not happy. Nobody else prolly can't see em—but I can. No wonder her daddy made such a fuss over gittin' me with her. Maybe even he's finally worried 'bout her.

"Looks like your old flame just became available," Clarke said with the faintest trace of smugness. "Again."

"What is it?" DeLozier asked.

"I'm sure you've heard of the Golden Girl with—" Clarke said before DeLozier cut him off.

"The Golden Voice? Mary Katherine Murchison?"

Clarke laughed. "Yeah, the one and only. Well, your idol Captain Roark here had that for years back at Okie-homa U. and after."

"What?" DeLozier gasped in awe.

He sighed and shook his head as he threw that magazine in the fire, too. "I didn't ever *have* that," he said snarling at Clarke with an insubordinate sneer. "We dated is all. She was... a swell girl...."

Clarke, enjoying the conversation, said, "Well, according to that stellar journal of silver screen personalities and events you just destroyed, her second divorce is now final and she is continuing to prosper with a new-found lifestyle of health on an extended vacation in Malibu, California—which just happens to be the location of the largest celebrity alcohol dry-out center in the country."

But he was seeing the icicles of her silver eyes glittering up at him happy and without guile at the front door of the Kappa house, with the fragrance of magnolias and hydrangeas filling the still evening air, and hearing her open her heart wide to him as her beautiful smile spread across her flawless face. *"Thank you for one of the most wonderful days of my life. Maybe* the *most wonderful day of my life."*

He stood and stalked out of the Officers' Club, so he could drink alone outside, thundering storm be cursed.

—

Despite the teeth-chattering winter cold, it was good getting back in the air. It grew clearer with each passing day that his efforts in the B-17 and now the Mustangs were all helping gradually wipe the *Luftwaffe* from the skies of Europe. This, in turn, had enabled General George "Blood and Guts" Patton and allied ground forces to slowly gouge their way step by blood-drenched step across France and the Low Countries.

Roosevelt oughta build statues to Trigger, Bobby, and all the rest of 'em fer doin' his dirty work. They got nothin' out o' this war—Bobby didn't even git him a pine box.

Bitterness and curses slathered his thoughts.

When he commanded his Fort, he had no fighter escorts into Germany. For over a year the *Luftwaffe*—while simultaneously battling the British Empire and the U.S. in North Africa and making mincemeat of the world's largest air force, the Russians, on the Eastern Front—had beaten the daylights out of America's European bomber fleets. He still couldn't figure out how the Germans, with only half the population and a fraction of the natural resources of the U.S. alone, could do it all. He hated them all the more for it.

When the Mustangs arrived shortly after his final B-17 mission, it took months to obtain enough of them to come close to shielding the bomber stream. Now they so filled the skies that he never saw a bomber on half or more of his missions, including today's dive bombing raid against the airdrome.

Seems like we see the Luftwaffe less'n that.

During his first tour, swarms of relentless German fighters bedeviled *Hellfire and Brimstone* and all the others. The enemy continued to churn out waves of fighters from its aviation assembly lines, but it no longer had the capable pilots nor the fuel to get them off the ground much of the time.

Now, as he and the rest of the 77th fighter group raced toward a German airfield near Bremen that had long dispatched some of the deadliest fighter armadas of the war against the bomber boys, including him and his friends, thoughts of Mary Katherine cascaded into his mind, as they frequently had in recent days.

Oh, what would I do with her now!

Clarke's announcement over the fighter group radio channel that his oil pressure was low and he had to return to England, accompanied by his wingman, immediately cleared his mind of Mary Katherine.

Dang, he'll be lucky to make it far enough back fer our boys er the Limeys to fish him out o the sea, much less to England.

"You've got the squadron, Blue 1," Clarke said to him. He hadn't even realized that, and it was the first time he was in command of an entire squadron. His adrenalin churned.

He spotted the airdrome a few miles ahead from several thousand feet aloft, lined up on it, winged over into a steep dive, sailing toward the earth upside down, then, right side up again, opened his butterfly flaps to slow his descent as he approached the field, the other thirteen Mustangs following in trail formation. He spotted the flak emplacement he'd seen in the group briefing photos, but the row of parked ME-109s that came into view beyond it looked much more attractive. He peered through the Gyro gunsight in front of him, lined up the reticles, and took aim as flak began to explode around him. He ignored that, and the burgeoning rifle and machine gun ground fire, too, his finger against the bomb switch, his mental faculties locked in like a vice on the 109s. At just the right instant, already over the field, he let go the Mustang's two 1,000-pound bombs.

He zoomed over the airdrome, pulled up at 1,500 feet, and rolled away from the field as his and the others' bombs began to demolish the target. Peering down, his mouth dropped in awe.

An entire row of 109s burned and exploded.

Gee, if only the ole Fort coulda sported such accuracy.

Banking around for another pass, he caught a glance of DeLozier, leading an element for the first time. The kid had spotted a fast-reacting German pilot who had already managed to get in a 109 and was tearing down a runway to get into the air and fight, DeLozier a good thousand feet behind him. *Lookee at that little son of a gun.*

To his delight, the boy raced through blazing fires, exploding bombs, and small arms ground fire spraying in every direction.

Dang, sucker's too far out front, he's off the ground now, and he's gunna git up and into them trees over there and raise Cain with us.

His concern mounted, since the 109s were particularly deadly at low altitudes. Just then, DeLozier unleashed a volley of fire at the plane.

Too far away, buddy.

He headed upward to line up for another pass. He took one last look at the 109. Chunks of its fuselage and cowling were splintering off, then its engine exploded, and the plane blew into a blizzard of flaming, smoking debris.

Hot dog, what a shot!

It was one of the best kills he had seen the entire war.

The 77th destroyed over a dozen 109s and ME-110s on the ground and virtually everything else in sight as well. DeLozier even spotted a shiny Mercedes convertible speeding for the woods, carrying what looked to be the commanders of the installation. There was barely enough of the vehicle and its passengers remaining after he unleashed his .50-cals on them for the car to crash into an ancient pine tree, explode, and burn.

Growing warier and in ways wiser as he lived through the tumult of the war, he wondered on the trip home what Clarke's reaction would be to the utter destruction of the base, which he and the other flight leaders had captured on their mounted 16-mm gun cameras, assuming the man made it back to England.

Surprisingly, he did make it back, and his reaction exhibited just the sort of ambivalence Lance had suspected.

Scheming sack's smilin' like a friend on the outside, but they's murder in his eyes—and not toward the Jerries. He could barely suppress a smile. *He ain't no friend o mine, nor any fighter jockey in this squadron worth his salt.*

By the time he got to the Officers' Club that evening, the whole squadron was toasting DeLozier and buying him drinks. Eyeing the unusual abundance of alcohol flowing in an Officers' Club, he wondered whether Trigger's cartel yet lived. When the other flyers saw him, they roared their lewd approval.

"You're an ace after one afternoon's work, Captain America!" DeLozier, already well in his cups, said as beer sloshed from the soup tureen serving as his mug. "You got credit fer five o them 109 mother lovers!"

Lance smiled, putting an arm around his shoulder as someone handed him a beer. "But this good Oklahoma boy right here made the dad-blamedest best shot I seen the whole sorry war on that airborne 109!"

Some of the gathered flyers saw it and the rest had already heard about it, but they shouted their appreciation anew. It was already DeLozier's third air-to-air kill.

Two more and he, too, would be an ace.

"Those doe-eyed bomber boys ought to thank their lucky stars they have their massive planes and all their guns and us to cover their snooty halos!" another of the hot shot young pilots shouted as he poured bourbon into his beer.

His smile vanished. "Why, you little twig."

"Aw, stick 'em." The hot shot laughed and lifted his glass.

In an instant, he slapped the youngster's drink out of his hand and moved nearly nose to nose with him as the glass shattered on the floor. It silenced the gathering. The pilot glared in shocked fury at him. "What the heck—"

He stared into his eyes, his expression inviting action. When none came, he said in an even tone, "You ever speak in such a manner again 'bout the bomber boys and you'll think heck. They been through a steamin' pile o' dung you wouldn't last a ten-count in." He let that sink in. "Jackass."

"Thanks, Captain Roark," Clarke declared as he stepped into the Officers' Club. "You just picked out my plane for me." He slapped Lance on the back, his gaze boring in on the hot shot. "Mine won't be ready tomorrow and I need another, so you'll sit out our bomber escort run and your plane'll have its most productive day of the war." His gaze swept the sombered crowd. "This party's over. Hit the sack."

TWENTY

When the sun rose on a rare clear winter sky the next morning, he laughed wryly. *Well, that guarantees we won't fly today.*

He was right, as he had been before on the same topic. Cloud cover returned the following day and the 77th was in the air at midmorning with the rest of the Wing. Clarke commanded the entire group for the first time—minus the pilot he cuffed, whom the major had already ordered transferred—leading them toward Berlin to catch the bomber boys on their return trip from another of their myriad strikes on Germany's bleeding capital.

He had a headache, which he suspected came from *not* drinking the night before, and he was spoiling for a fight. The farther east they flew, the thicker the cloud cover grew. He feared that any minute the order would come to return to base. It never did, and a hundred miles from Berlin, he noticed his wingman crowding him. When he turned he saw it wasn't his wingman, who was on the other side of him, it was a 109, close enough for him to see a pilot so young he could scarcely believe he was old enough to fly the plane. The youngster looked at him and smiled, as if relieved.

Good Lord, the kid's lost and blinded and is thankin' his lucky stars he found a friendly face. He's the spittin' image o my cousin Dirk near Wichita. Is there anything too crazy to happen in this jacked up war?

When he pointed down and back at his USAAF insignia and the kid realized his mistake, he thought the poor fellow might faint. He couldn't stifle a belly laugh, which seemed to relieve the boy again. He motioned him to leave, shouting "Git the heck out o here!" as if the kid could hear him. When the young German looked around and saw other Mustangs appear in the haze, he nodded, mouthed, *"Danke shoen,"* and zoomed off. Unfortunately for him, DeLozier riddled his cockpit with an ammo box-full of .50-caliber cartridges seconds later. Lance stared at the smoking, nosediving plane and was unable to process a reaction.

"All right boys, Liberty squadron maintain escort, Rodeo and Hammer squadrons, let's go kill us some supper," Clarke announced in his fresh California way.

He ain't got any intention o waitin' for the bandits, as the fighter jockeys call 'em, to bring the party to us. Guess that's one reason he's got him fourteen kills now.

They found the Germans right where he expected, coming up from near Dummer Lake, northwest of Berlin. All the home team could muster was one squadron, and they split-essed for the deck soon as they saw twice that many Mustangs screaming down at them from above, the sun behind them.

Shucks, don't think most o the Jerries' first team is still in the game.

Disappointed, he jettisoned his nearly-empty babies to lighten the plane's load for maximum speed. Through the months, he had noticed that one after another of the Reich's top aces—men with awe-inspiring kill totals of 100, 150, 200, even more—had fallen, some of them after flying more than a thousand missions, against every opposing nation in the European Theater.

At least one of 'em ain't gone down yet, least last I heard....

The gleaming black 109 with no kill insignias.

Then he was wing rolling his Mustang down into roiling cloud cover after the Germans and the thrill of the chase replaced his grumpiness. When he emerged, at about 10,000 feet, he saw Clarke ahead, leveled off and catching a line of ME-410s, his wingman Travis—who had ten kills and two probables himself—on his elbow.

Sheesh, Huns gittin' desperate if they flyin' them boats in daylight now.

Suddenly, Clarke opened up on the rear 410, and tracer fire poured into the plane's tail. It shuddered, then the tail fell off whole, splitting into two, each with a vertical stabilizer, both smoking pieces spinning down, followed by the front section, even as Clarke hopped over it, debris splatting his windshield and wings, as he shredded the cockpit of the next 410. Then he caught the lead plane, the latter likely never seeing him, as he loosed a trail of fire the length of its fuselage.

Dang, that's a hat trick fer Clarke right there, sumbuck is good. Time to quit spectatin'.

He heard Clarke singing "Rhythm is Our Business" over the group radio channel in merry imitation of the negro Big Band hit by Jimmie Lunceford and his Orchestra.

...and "our work" is definitely going well.

He saw a couple of 109s at ten o'clock, just turning to dive for the deck. He noticed they were headed southwest, back to their base. He cut inside on them and, with the element of surprise and a 50-mile-an-hour speed advantage, he had them bounced within a minute.

Don't think this fella sees me, either.

He flew into the accelerating 109's exhaust trail. He started to weave out of it, then decided to use it as additional cover in case the pilot did happen to look back for him. He couldn't see the German plane to line up the Gyro on him, so he just stayed centered in the contrail and opened up his six machine guns when he sensed he was within good range.

After finishing off that 109, he spotted another far in the distance. That one led him to the German base, which DeLozier and others were lighting up. "Fixin' to join you boys, Johnny," he said brightly, angling down to pile in.

"Oh, hey, sir," DeLozier said, excited. *"Think I'm hosed, dang Mustang engine cuttin' out on me again."*

"Take it easy," he said, sobered. "Just stay cool and give er some gas. You'll fly yourself right out of it."

"*God!*" DeLozier hollered. "*She's chokin' on me.*"

"Push it to the firewall!" He smiled with relief as he saw the Mustang start to rise. "Atta boy—"

With his dexterity, instincts, and nerve, DeLozier corrected his problem, but just as he rose, his wing clipped a smoke-concealed power line with multiple thick wires. It tipped the Mustang off its trajectory and velocity and toward its right side. The plane stalled anew.

"*There it goes again!*" DeLozier hollered.

"Johnny!"

The Mustang seemed to drop out of the air, the right side of the engine cowling crashing to earth first, exploding on impact, a giant orange fireball engulfing it.

"No!" he said, his scream a stab of pain piercing his heart.

Dazed, he turned toward home as someone said, "Hey, DeLozier crashed!"

"*Let's take it to the house,*" Clarke said. "*You guys did great. DeLozier did, too, but we've got to go now.*"

He looked toward the squadron commander's plane, a half-mile ahead and a thousand feet above him. *You selfish son of a... Same old Clarke, just more dangerous and rotten with success.*

Loathing for the man filled him as he gave one last look back to the ground, where DeLozier's plane flamed. He realized he should be crying, but not a tear came. "Don't worry, Johnny," he said aloud, the microphone off. "Somebody'll pay fer that. A whole bunch o' somebodies."

He started to pray that God would deliver them soon and numerously, then he decided he didn't need or want God's help with the task. As if on cue, he saw something streak across the sky from the opposite direction, far off to his left.

"What *was that?*" someone radioed.

"*Fastest thing I've ever seen,*" someone else said as the epithets multiplied.

Still a bearcat for aircraft study, he recognized the plane. A Messerschmitt

262 jet fighter—and that it could fly faster than anything else made by man, a hundred miles an hour faster than even a Mustang at full tilt, but it gulped fuel like a skid row lush gulping rotgut and could only stay aloft for twenty-five or thirty minutes.

Peckerwood's gotta be fixin' to light down at that same base we jist come from. Sweet...

"Look, Dickinson's going after him!"

His heart sank as he watched Dickinson, an ace with fourteen air-to-air kills, four more on the ground, enough railroad locomotives and cars to supply an entire army, and the best fighter pilot in the Hammer squadron, intercept the jet. He liked the quiet Indianan, small and wiry like so many American pilots, who assisted the station's Catholic chaplain with Mass. He was no longer sure there was anyone present—spiritually, physically or otherwise—during this or the Protestant chaplain's communions, but he respected Dickinson for believing there was.

"The ME's faster, but Dick'll outmaneuver," Clarke assured them.

But the jet skidded away from the ambush like a vanishing genie, then high-G barrel-rolled back around and onto Dickinson's tail.

Someone shouted an alarmed profanity. As he said it, the jet fired a rocket that blew Dickinson's Mustang into a flaming cloud of debris.

Lance clenched his jaw, saw his wingman Weinstein was nowhere in sight, found a clear lane, kicked rudder, and turned his plane around.

"Blue 1, get your tail back in the line!" Clarke shouted.

Instead, he wing-rolled and headed straight down to where, if he could get there in time, he'd be behind the jet as it made its approach on the lone runway he had noticed was still clear as he scanned the smoking field during the Mustangs' attack.

And he'll come in from the southwest, too, 'cause of the direction of the crosswind.

He recalled his wind gauge reading during the run.

He jammed the stick to the firewall, throttle to the maximum, and hurtled straight down. The plane shook like none he had ever been in and his vision turned to black. He didn't lose consciousness, though he feared he would and pleaded with God he wouldn't. Then it felt like the plane was coming apart. He realized with a shock, still blind, that he had no control over it. He eased the stick back, but it felt like a dancing puppet.

Dang thang's jerkin' all over the cockpit. Oh, God, please don't let her stall.

It was the closest to panic he could ever remember being in the air.

"Roark!" Clarke said, nearly shouting.

A fleeting remembrance struck him from one of his classes on the P-51 at Tinker, to which he always gave one hundred percent effort—*compressibility.*

They said the Mustang's so fast, when it gits a head o steam goin' downhill like this, it's near the speed o sound, the air rushin' against the forward surfaces o the plane compresses, and it sends a shock wave—feels like a lotta shock waves—through the plane. They said keep your cool, ride it out till ye get to lower altitude and thicker air, till ye can feel somethin' on the stick again. God help me, 'fore it's too late.

Every second seemed like minutes to him and he still couldn't see, as the plane threw him around. Finally, some torque returned to the stick. He eased it back and the plane responded.

Crud, though, I'm still in clouds and they're dark.

But he wouldn't know that if he couldn't see again! Confidence growing, he kept pulling back and the Mustang kept pulling up. Glimmers of light speckled the clouds, then shafts of sun shot through, then he was out in the blue again, just five hundred feet off the ground—and the 262 was no more than two or three degrees off being straight ahead of him, a quarter-mile at most, heading down for the runway.

Now, he heard that raspy sound in his plane's engine he'd heard on a couple of previous missions. It was the spark plugs taking on grime in a manner peculiar to the Mustang, and you could fly for a while with it, maybe a long while, but you might drop like a rock out of the sky in the next five minutes. A wise pilot turned immediately for home and tried to make it at least to the Channel. The only wisdom he knew was that the jet in his Gyro gunsight was a magnificent creation and the death knell of the piston-engine fighter plane, even the Mustang, but not his. For they told him in class the place to get an ME-262 was taking off or landing from its airfield. It had no speed advantage then.

"I'm your death knell, you son o Satan," he said aloud as he opened up all six fifties on the jet in deflection shooting when it was within a couple hundred feet of the ground. A piece of one wing splintered off and the jet engine on that side burst into flames. He hollered curses as debris spattered his teardrop canopy and he realized he was about to run into the jet. He eased the throttle, pulled the stick toward him, right-ruddered, S-turned, and backed off. Then the 262's nose rose and the plane headed straight up. "Lord!" he shouted. He tried to pursue, but the Mustang stalled, its Rolls Merlin engine nearly going out. A train of epithets churning through his mind, he veered away to set up an angle of ascent to get above the German again if he could, the raspy sound resuming in his engine.

I should head home right now.

He paused.

Home—where the heck is that? An empty farm in Oklahoma and a grave in Beccles, England.

He watched the jet out of the corner of his eye as he wheeled the Mustang into position to head upward at as steep an angle and with as much velocity as he could manage. He couldn't conjure sufficient expletives to express his fury toward the 262. *Shot to pieces and on fire and he's flyin' straight up! I am gunna bury that dog er die tryin'.*

Just then, the 262, still roaring straight up, stopped as if hitting an invisible wall. It hung in the air for a count, then began to slide back down, tail first. Just before it came apart, the pilot parachuted. He started to go after him, though he had never seen the Germans attack an American who parachuted, but his raspy engine regained his attention and he turned for England.

His stomach and chest felt like an ice block the whole way as he worried his engine would give out. The raspy sound disappeared once he got over the North Sea and a rare, cloudless, blue sky blossomed. The trip seemed endless. Maybe twenty miles from England, something caught his attention out of the corner of his left eye.

Good grief. That's one o them V-1 rockets. His jaw clenched. Thang's gunna come down on somebody's house like Sarah or her mama er the like.

He peered out at the arcing, blazing projectile. A big grin filled his face. "You little …" he said with a growl as he turned the Mustang toward it. When he pushed the throttle all the way forward, the raspy engine sound returned. He didn't care.

They say a Mustang can catch you and that's what I'm gunna do.

Glee filled him, but his gas tank was nearly empty. He hurtled toward the screaming rocket as land came into sight far ahead.

Dang, I'm catchin' him, but can I catch him in time?

He wanted to ram the V-1 and knock it off course, not just shoot at it, but he was still a couple hundred yards away as the shoreline spread out before him, and the raspy sound was louder than ever. He kept chasing it, crossing over land, glancing down at the ground a mile or so below.

If I can't ram it over open ground, I'll shoot it down.

All of a sudden, he was right on it and about to collide full blast. He hollered, veering out of the way. He wasn't ready to go up in smoke with it. He turned back toward the rocket, which was now in a gradual descent, chose his angle, caught it again, and flew alongside it for a moment, fascinated by the sight of it. He looked down, saw nothing but fields, then bumped the rocket with his wing, sending it spiraling down toward a wooded area. He followed it partway down from a safe distance, shifted his gun switch down to "sight and camera" and took pictures for proof as he had done with the day's other kills, then watched it crash and explode in a pond.

Two 109s…a 262 jet…a mother-lovin' V-1 rocket—what a day!

Elation filled him, not because of the laurels that would attach themselves to him, but because the mission's scorecard provided stark evidence of his great deeds toward eradicating the world of the Third Reich and anybody or anything aligned with it.

His joy lasted until he remembered DeLozier. He cursed God. No matter what feats he accomplished, a dark hopeless sinkhole lurked just beyond. Whiskey from his pub-owning friend tonight would solve the dilemma, at least for a spell, and the petite new girl with the sandy hair he had hired wouldn't hurt any, either.

After proceeding through the usual sequence of the briefing room, the ready room, the shower, and the officers' mess, he got back to his hut well after dark. Suddenly exhausted nearly to the point of collapse, he had not glanced at the pack of envelopes until he sprawled back onto his bed. He recognized Grandpa Schroeder's name and shaky handwriting.

God bless him, he ain't never quit on me, no matter how far I strayed. I reckon I'm the prodigal grandson in his life.

He shuffled through a mish-mash of USAAF correspondence, an OU alumni newspaper, and one with familiar handwriting from California.

That must be from Mama.

The last one had a Pacific postmark from Waddy. He was going to save it to read until last, but couldn't hold off reading it first. It contained more news than any letter he received during the war. Long John Starr was in a German prison camp. Waddy loved *"getting that arrogant so-and-so Bob Morgan's goat, though he's a heckuva drinker, flyer, and leader."* The B-29 was the most unbelievable machine of any sort Waddy had ever seen. *"We make mincemeat of any Nip flyers foolish enough to come near us."* He had been adopted by a local orphan boy named Skipper who insisted on being Waddy's butler, maid, and servant, in return for being allowed to play on Waddy's side in the base football games. A couple of the tougher bomber boys had separately started fistfights with the former USC football player and now world-famed actor known as The Duke, John Wayne, as he drank in the same bars they did while on location filming a movie entitled *The Fighting Seabees* about the war. Everyone had made a pact not to get captured alive by "the Japs, because you won't end up thataway with them anyhow, but it'll take a long time to get dead."

Indeed, stories of terror were spreading across the world through the U.S. armed forces about the unspeakable horrors visited upon American prisoners by their Japanese captors. *"Things you and I'd never even think of, even with our fertile imaginations,"* Waddy wrote, *"much less do. And I know it's true, because I* talked to a couple boys escaped from different Jap prison camps, and a couple other informers. One of them animals raped a pet duck our boys had—a duck, Parson! It killed the poor critter."

Hmm. Whatever the Germans are, however bad they treat the Jews and other Europeans, they treat our boys square for the most part.

The Stalags where the bomber and fighter boys went weren't country clubs, but they were decent enough, according to the several escaped POWs, Red Cross workers, and captured Germans he had spoken with over the past couple of years. He thanked God that Long John was in a German prison and not a Japanese one, and he prayed, grudgingly, that God would keep Waddy and his crew safe.

After all the others, saving the most important for last, he opened Mama's. *No wait—it's from Daddy.*

His heart skipped for joy, as it was the first he had ever received in England from him. Then he blinked, trying to make out Daddy's scrawl.

What is he trying to say, "Mama is gassed?" Or "Mama is massed"…"for the" no, "to the"…Wait a minute, that says… "Mama has… passed?" *Passed?*

He looked toward the ceiling, shaking his head and speaking aloud. "Passed?" As he read on, it grew clear what Daddy had written.

She is the greatest woman, the greatest human being I have ever known. She never complained so much as a word about having to live the way we do now and where we do, yet I know her better than I know myself and it was her heart, not mine, that broke getting exiled from Oklahoma. Her whole life was laid down in a sacrifice to three people—me, you, and our Lord. All you or me have done in a long time is bring her sorrow and heartache. That you have, I am sure is judged on my account as well. You just followed in the way of what I still deep down believed, even if I didn't say it or even know it. Well, I can't make you do right, son, but I can change my own ways. From this day forward, whatever time I have left, I aim to spend dedicated to her and the Lord she loved so true to the very end. I ain't never touching so much as one drop of liquor again. I'll put a bullet through my brain before I do. As for you, son, I promise to try and be a better Daddy to you than I been in a long time, really ever, and to pray every hour of every day that the Lord will bring you back to Hisself, because I know you are far from Him nowadays.

Your loving Daddy.

When his eyes remained dry and his heart grew hard as the limestone out-croppings west of the old place, he felt more confident than he ever had that he was, for sure, never going to cry again, just like he had hoped.

His shingles assaulted him inside and out, but whiskey did sound good, especially because the nocturnal horrors had returned. His new roommate, to whom he had barely spoken on the ground, had been killed in an explosion while taking off for a mission a couple of days ago when his plane ground looped into an oxygen trolley, but the night before that, he had roused him from a screaming nightmare. Lance had torn his own t-shirt to shreds and his bed was as wet from sweat as if a gullywasher had poured over it. Tonight, meanwhile, he had drunk up his private stash and was too tired even to go to the Officers' Club for whatever cheap limited quantity he could get there, much less to ride into Toft Monks to his friend's pub.

Instead, he walked to the toilet in the latrine hut near his own to relieve himself. As he sat, he gazed around the metal walls at the rich scenery that had garnered the moniker "The Porno Palace." His eyes widened as he gave the closest scrutiny to the most spectacular pinups he had ever seen, the fully unclothed ones not even the best of them, though he could not find Ginger Rogers. Oh well, he would feast his eyes on the sensational Rita Hayworth and her legs instead.

This stuff's better'n booze to gitcher mind off sad tidins.

He decided Rita might give him a reason to go back to the States after all. He would find her and make those legs shudder.

Shoot, I got as much goin' fer me as them girly boy movie stars she goes out with.

For now, he would peel down her dazzling likeness and take it to his empty room with him.

Then he saw a pair of legs that matched if not excelled Hayworth's. Good gosh in heaven, who the blazes is—

It was Mary Katherine. A welter of emotions assaulted him. Rising from the toilet, he jerked her poster off the wall to crumple and flush it. Something stopped him. He glanced around and saw no one. Her beautiful likeness was garbed in a fashionable, not immodest one-piece swimsuit, at least according to American society's wartime standards.

But Mama—

Well, you mine anyways, honey, I don't give a rip how many husbands you had, I know ye love me and I... well, I'd sure love to be with you tonight.

Climbing into his cot a minute later with the foldout and firing up his Zippo for light, he got as close to her as he could til he found *her* back in the States, too.

TWENTY-ONE

JANUARY, 1945

Hitler launched his electrifying Ardennes offensive, known to history as the Battle of the Bulge, in mid-December. Nearly the whole world had thought the Germans licked—except the Germans. The Soviet Russians, lopsidedly outnumbering them on the Eastern Front and bolstered by American supplies and arms, were shoving them back step by bloody step, and paying a gruesome toll for doing so. They reached the German frontier of East Prussia in late January.

He knew from briefings, *Stars and Stripes*, and Armed Forces Radio that the U.S., Britain, and their numerous Western Allies, meanwhile, had driven close to Germany from the west when the offensive began. A blanket of snow and clouds sidelined the USAAF for several days as the Nazi forces ambushed then churned through the American army, killing, wounding, and capturing scores of thousands of soldiers. When the skies finally cleared, he and his colleagues flew daily missions against the enemy supply, communication, and transportation lines. This, the Americans' gritty, blood-drenched ground defense, and depleted German fuel finally stalled the historic charge near the end of January.

When that happened, General George Patton's Third Army slammed into the exhausted German forces and drove them back toward their own country. "They couldn't have done any of it if we hadn't cleared most of the *Luftwaffe* out of the friendly skies over Europe," Clarke said as he and Lance played ping-pong in the base rec room. "If we hadn't spilled our guts the past how many years? While most of our brethren in the other services were dancing the jitterbug and chasing skirts. I just hope they remember it," he said with anger, slamming the winning shot skittering off Lance's swinging paddle.

"Let's go again." Lance fetched the ball from atop a pool table across the room. They competed against each other in everything from poker to predicting the winners of football games back in the States. From the time of DeLozier's death and Clarke's excited crowing about the legacy of honor the young Oklahoman had left the remainder of the squadron, his respect for the man's flying skills, battlefield cool, and determination to persevere grew in direct parallel to his dislike of him. He played games with him, not out of affection or enjoyment of his company, but because every single victory over the man, no matter how minor, brought as much delight to him as it did disgust to Clarke.

Clarke inaugurated a new sort of contest the last day of January as they returned from escorting B-24s on a bombing run to the Ruhr Valley. Not far from the Channel coast in France, he sent the rest of the squadron on, saying he and Lance had a modest reconnaissance sweep to run. It turned out to be a flying contest between the two.

"If you're like me, these Jerry third-stringers, even when they show up, have grown boring," Clarke said. "I've concluded we can create better challenges for ourselves by our own devices."

He didn't agree with either declaration. Though the *Luftwaffe* was not what it was, time and again, just when you counted them out or didn't expect them on the scene, an ME-109 or FW-190 would shriek in from nowhere and shoot one of your buddies out of the sky, including two of his wingmen in the past sixty days. The flak was worse than ever, because the Germans had hustled thousands of guns back into Germany that were previously placed in countries now reclaimed by the Allies. It seemed like every train or boat in the Third Reich had flak guns popping out to blast away at you. The weather and cloud cover stunk as bad as ever, particularly this winter. The abort rate on Mustangs was significantly higher than on Fortresses—and that was when your engine, fuel line, gas tank, instruments, or cartridge feeders fouled up when you were close enough to even get home.

But now Clarke was diving as close to trees as he could without hitting them, then pulling up to let him go. It was like a game of H.O.R.S.E. in basketball.

Except that, you git an "H" in this game and that's all she wrote.

Clarke swooped down at a building three or four stories high in a small coastal town.

Dang, them windows gotta be rattlin' from that.

Clarke chuckled as villagers scrambled in all directions for cover.

Next it was a hedgerow along a road with traffic, including a U.S. armored personnel carrier. Finally, Clarke dove for the ground itself, pulled up at the last instant, and skimmed along the snow-piled pasture until he approached a lone, spindly cow leaning against a fence not far from a barn. Rather than pulling up or veering away, he tore right through the beast, shredding it into a bloody spew.

"What the heck!" Lance said, shouting. "You crazy fool!"

Now, Clarke laughed in a manner that would have been considered controlled for most men but was as animated as he had ever heard his group commander.

"Uncle," was all Lance added as he turned toward England. It was the most bothered he had been since DeLozier went down, other than maybe Mama dying, but that seemed somehow remote. He felt no emotion over it. It was like a wall had risen between him and whatever it was that had happened with Mama. He could not even picture her face. Sometimes, like on the flight back across the frigid Channel and fog-shrouded East Anglia, he strained to remember if Daddy really had written that she—died?

By the time he landed at Toft Monks, yet again on instruments, he was in no mood to be trifled with. All he wanted was to get to his friend's pub, wolf some shepherd's pie, and chase it down with ale and whiskey. Then he learned, all leave was cancelled for the night. Anger boiled up within him.

"It's 'cause some jigaboo bomb transporting company that brought us ordnance today couldn't make it back to their base," Posey his crew chief told him.

"So, what the heck's that got to do with our leave?" he snapped.

"Well, the jigs' white officer asked could they bunk down here for the night, especially on account of the rain," Posey said, "but our CO said that wouldn't go with our boys, see? So, they got permission to park their trucks on the village common and sack. But I guess they got 'em permission to hit one of the village watering holes for a couple hours, too. One of our other Joes told me he heard there's been so many fights between our boys and the jungle bunnies on leaves all over East Anglia, the grand poobahs come up with a rule we have to rotate leave nights with 'em when we're in the same town or even if they want to drive in to the same town from somewhere else. Guess the 82nd Airborne hooked it up with a bunch of 'em one night over in Ipswich and a couple of folks wound up in the morgue, not the hospital."

He stood mute with rage as rain began again to thump down on his crush cap and sheepskin-lined leather jacket. A Jeep wheeled up from the main gate with four MPs on board, Flanagan the head MP on the base driving. He saw the man riding shotgun had a shoulder wound and one of the MPs in back was unconscious, a bloody bandage wrapped around his head.

"Great gosh amighty," the crew chief said.

"... spades in town," Flanagan, a strapping Montanan, growled. "They wouldn't leave when the pub closed. These fellas tried to arrest 'em and them black African baboons swarmed 'em."

"Which pub?" he asked.

"Your buddy's," Flanagan said. "Pick a dozen o the toughest men on the base and meet me back here in ten minutes. I'm depositing these boys at the infirmary and roundin' up the rest o the MPs." He shifted the Jeep's gear stick into low and gunned the engine. "And Roark? I don't want any shrinkin' violets for this errand."

The orders somewhat mollified his fury.

Fifteen minutes later, the rain slowing to a drizzle, Flanagan led a convoy of a half-dozen Jeeps into Toft Monks from one end of the little village and Magruder his second-in-command led another from the opposite end, a Browning Automatic slung across his lap. Lance, a Colt .45 holstered at his side, rode shotgun with Magruder. The drivers parked the Jeeps in the little village's main street, headlights illumining it from both ends. Four black soldiers strode out from behind a little building and walked toward Magruder's Jeep, brandishing rifles and frowns. Without a word, Magruder swung up the BAR and opened fire on them, knocking one flat. One of the other blacks loosed a rifle shot that shattered a Jeep windshield as he and his colleagues scrambled for cover.

Lance was already out of the Jeep and halfway to an alley behind a nearby row of residential bungalows, .45 in hand with the safety off and slide and hammer back. He heard more shots from the other end of the village. Footfalls sounded in various directions among the shadows and lamplight. Edging down the alley, he heard a hammer cock. He turned and saw, not ten feet away, a tall, broad-shouldered black airman pointing an M-1 at him from where he lurked at the back corner of a shop.

He could kill me before my next breath.

The man looked nervous, and he noticed the rifle shaking slightly in his hands.

He smiled and said, "You got a brother 'n Oklahoma?"

"No, why?" the man responded with nervousness and irritation.

"'Cause you the spittin' image of a fella I hauled hay with ever summer when I's in high school," he said.

"Yeah?" the man responded. "Well, I done plenty o' that down around Amarilla."

"No foolin'?" he said, maintaining a friendly demeanor. "My cousins worked the harvest out there, all through Borger and Pampa and Shamrock and what-all."

The man nodded. "Pampa, that's where I's from."

He gave an earnest nod back. "Shortgrass country like where I'm from. Good people out there'n the Panhannel."

"Yeah, they is."

"Look." He gave a serious sigh. "I don't wanna git shot, and I know you don't wanna get the boom lowered on ya fer shootin' me. What say we both git the heck home 'fore either of us gits in trouble?"

The man considered that and seemed to be sizing him up. Just then several gun shots sounded a couple blocks away, and what sounded like a short burst from a BAR. Nervousness filled his eyes. He nodded. "Yeah, but you jest head on that way and I'll go this."

He nodded and said, "Well, all right, then. And I hope you git back to Pampa sooner ruther'n later."

The black man nodded, then Lance ducked quickly into the shadows just in case the other fellow reconsidered their truce. He had sized him up, too, and reckoned, as the shooting got closer, that the man, already nervy, would head for a better perch. He had scanned what he could see of the area during their standoff and reckoned the man had only one way to head besides where he had gone—up the alley. Rather than following him, he circled around the block at a fast run to get ahead of him.

As he raced past the row of little bungalows, he saw a boy crouching in the bushes, shouldering an English cricket bat. He stopped. "What the heck you doin' out here, son? You folks know where ye are?"

"No." The boy glanced back at the flat behind him. "Me dad was at Singapore."

"Oh," he said. "Well, git back inside with ye mama. Now. I'm sure she's worried 'boutchu. 'Sides, we takin' care o' bidness out here. Now go on, git."

As the boy stood to go inside, he yanked the bat from him, said, "I'll bring it back in a few minutes," then ran on as a dozen more gunshots, and more BAR fire, sounded from various directions.

Reaching the corner of the row, he turned into the dim alley and saw the tall black soldier silhouetted next to a fence, creeping toward him. He waited and when the man neared, he said softly from the shadows, "Oh, hey, Pampa, fancy meetin' you again." He stepped carefully into the semi-light of the alley, smiling again and concealing the bat behind one leg.

The man halted with a jolt, nodded pensively. "Yeah."

"Well," he said, stepping closer and nodding, "I'll be on my way again—" As he finished the sentence, he swung the bat up in a blink and into the soldier's left cheekbone. It cracked like the sound of a small-caliber pistol and the man grunted, then fell straight to the ground. He pulled out his Zippo, flicked it on, knelt, and held it to the man's face. Blood trickled from a gash across his swelling cheekbone. He breathed normally but did not stir.

"One less uppity nigger'll steal my liberty from me." He looked upward. "'At's fer you, Trig." Disgusted, he tucked the bat under one arm, stood, glanced around, fired up the Zippo again, and held it down over the man's long legs. He put it away, stretched out the legs, then pulled out the bat, gripped it with both hands, and eyed one of the man's shinbones. He stopped himself when two shots sounded, closer than any of the others. He turned and headed back toward the street, but after a dozen steps nearly ran into two more black airmen, both an inch or two taller than himself. One carried a club and the other a rifle at his side. These men had hulking, powerful physiques. They looked ready to kill. The one gripped his club and the other pulled his rifle slowly up toward a position to fire, only a few feet from him.

His eyes narrowed, his jaw set, and he brought up the bat and slapped it against the palm of his other hand two or three times. "Here I am, boys," he said, not caring, his voice low and hard.

The eyes of the man with the rifle, spotting the .45 he blithely ignored, grew uncertain and he halted raising the weapon. He glanced at the other man, who wavered. He slapped his palm a couple more times with the club, his knees flexing just a bit as he prepared to spring into them. Before he could, the man with the club glanced at his colleague, nodded, and they stepped back, then away, and headed in the opposite direction.

By the time he returned the boy's bat to him, several more Jeeps full of white MPs were wheeling into town from nearby bases. They rounded up a dozen or so black soldiers and took them away, and they disarmed a few others. Numerous others had retreated to their trucks at the common. The MPs left them alone. The "battle" petered out.

"Day we let niggers into this man's army, day it all went to blazes," Magruder snarled to him as the other man shoved a wounded black airman into a Jeep.

After most of the MPs and other whites as well as the blacks had pulled out, an MP he didn't know said to him and Flanagan, "Why are they even here in England?" then stalked to his Jeep and wheeled away, a wounded MP in tow.

Flanagan turned to him and mumbled, "Why are they even in the army?" He paused and sighed. "Aw, geez, ask me, coloreds are dumb as telephone poles, but most the trouble we've had with 'em over here—and we've had a boatload—it's 'cause o our boys. They just don't wanna be around 'em."

Lance had jammed a chaw of Red Man into his cheek a minute before. He continued to position it with his tongue, spat, then grumbled, "Git me back to the base, Sergeant. These idjuts wasted 'nough my time fer one evenin'."

TWENTY-TWO

FEBRUARY, 1945

Cold rain and thick charcoal clouds grounded him and the rest of the 77th the first couple of days in February. After the days' ground assignments, he caught up on his time at the pub with his friend, his whiskey, and the fair-haired waitress. Then a mission got scrubbed just before take-off due to cloud cover over France and Germany, and he led the squadron on strafing practice up in the Wash, the marshy, sea-bounded northern reaches of Norfolk, the county running north from Toft Monks.

Strafing alternately thrilled and terrified him. A couple of missions had so stressed him, he had vomited before them. Yet, he was becoming disappointed when a mission did not allow for strafing opportunities. To his pleasure, the increasing number of missions where the Americans encountered little or even no *Luftwaffe* opposition allowed for more strafing. And with his Mustang's long-range capabilities, even after dogfights he could usually work some in.

Once a choice strafing run commenced, he could do things with his plane he could do at no other time, even when freelancing by himself on a practice run, because no matter how he tried when safe over England, he could not duplicate the adrenaline triggered by the speed and danger of strafing. The rush of blood to his head when diving to a target, even more the temporary visual blindness on a steep, fast one—the glee of buzzing buildings, tree tops, even vehicles and wagons without hitting them, though taking off the tops of trees could be fun—the unparalleled sensation when he neared the deck and the bullets and .20 or .30 mm flak came, especially knowing that "a boy with a rifle" could bring down *Captain America* with a lucky shot to that liquid-cooled fuel line—

It was the only sensation of his life that recaptured the elation and rightness, the sense of things being as they should be, of when he would chase down a speedy running back and plaster him to the ground, or take the football and gallop for a touchdown and no one could stop him. It was him taking the fight to the opponent, showing what he could do, what he had.

On a mission the day after the Wash strafing practice, he tried to take the squadron above the billowing cumulus over Holland. A sinking sensation crawled through him as he eyed the figures on his altimeter. *Criminy! Twenty-seven thousand feet and it's still 10/10 visibility?*

By the time he got clear of the cloud cover, he was over Germany and he had no idea where anyone was, nor could he reach anyone over the radio. His wingman had turned for home an hour before when he realized he wasn't drawing fuel from his 700-pound auxiliary gas tank.

Spewing curses, he was so disgusted, he could barely restrain himself from smashing his instrument panel with his gloved fist.

He cycled through his radio channels, hearing pithy chatter on the bomber frequency. It was the B-24 group he was supposed to escort on their run against the oil refineries near Stuttgart! Even better, as the sky cleared, he saw the lead box off to his starboard side, not more than a mile away. The bomber crews were unnerved that no fighter escorts had found them. The cloud cover that had reached this far east appeared to be drifting away to the southeast, which helped for bomb targeting but also for bomber targeting by flak guns.

He decided to mosey ahead on his own mini-sweep of the area toward Stuttgart, fifty miles away. He arced a bit further north to stay out of sight in case a fighter formation converged on the bomber stream. Within a couple of minutes, he spotted a forest of black specks far to the east, roughly level with him. He slid father north and up a couple thousand feet, and kept ascending. He cursed anew when he saw what and who it was.

"Three dozen FWs!" one of the bomber boys confirmed a moment later.

"Abbeville boys," another voice added, laconic but dread for its message.

The last two words sent a chill clean through him.

Is it?

His breath caught. He had gotten above and behind the fighters. He peered down, squinting but couldn't see any. Then—

Sure's heck.

The famed yellow noses at the front and vertical stabilizer rudder at the rear of several distant fighters gleamed in the sunlight. He edged nearer. They formed the entire front rank of nine planes.

Ain't enough 'em left to form near a full formation, but—

A friend in division intelligence had shared some disheartening news with him one night during a London pub crawl after finding out about one too many Jodys and knocking down one too many Scotch and Sodas. He said the Abbeville Boys of the Germans' Jag 26 fighter wing had shot down between twenty-five hundred and three *thousand* Allied fighters and bombers since the war began.

Calibrating his angle and rate of climb so that he could just keep the enemy fighters in sight and lessen his own danger of getting spotted, he glanced over the back three German ranks, the spots not taken by Abbeville Boys, then pondered how many such spots that replacement fighters and bombers filled in the Allied ranks.

Right around four times as many.

His stomach knotted up.

They linin' up in phalanxes to charge and ram our boys.

All this, coupled with the brave chatter laced with the fright he could detect so well from his own long months in *Hellfire and Brimstone* spurred dormant emotion to rise for the boys in the "Constipated Lumberers," as Consolidated Liberators were often derided. He was one against thirty-six, and at least a quarter of those were battled-hardened aces from four of the most elite squadrons in the history of air warfare.

That's one more'n none.

The thought wasn't actually quite that coherent. He was going to get between those fighters and his boys and raise Cain for as long as he could. He was very coherent about that.

The FWs were zooming straight for the Liberators, ranged across their front in four lines. For the Germans and their continued audacity, he felt equal measures of respect bordering on awe with hate beyond calculation or words. He was right where he wanted to be, a half-mile above the enemy planes and a quarter-mile behind.

Valhalla, here I come. He shrieked a Rebel Yell into his mike, pushed the stick to the hilt, and hurtled down into them.

For maximum disruption, he first unleashed on a plane on the left side of the second rank, his Mustang roaring and shaking. The 190 exploded, jolting the other FWs around it, as he dove at an Abbeville Boy in the center of the front rank, unleashing all six of his wing-mounted .50-caliber machine guns at it. The plane, at a complete disadvantage, started to spin away.

Boy's quick.

He kept firing until he was no more than fifty yards away, though, shredding the cockpit area and blowing off chunks of the fuselage around it. He roared right over the savaged plane—

—*Dang, that boy still got hisself out o there and into a chute*—

—and wing rolled down, giving the entire formation, and the front box of Liberators, an eyeful.

Three FWs peeled off from the right and took after him. He was glad to get them away from the bombers and he knew he could run rings around most FW pilots in a wide-open chase situation in *Captain America*, especially at this altitude, but he needed to get back and divert some others.

The lead FW was behind him at 5 o'clock level, the second in a wingman position to the first at 6 o'clock, the third out at 7 o'clock and slightly higher to help box him in. He yawed to the right and left, trying to disrupt the Germans' formation and maybe distract them a bit with staying out of each other's way. They stuck to their set like glue, though, and when tracers blazed past him from the lead plane just as the peaks of a towering range of stratocumulus appeared ahead, he decided to take leave of his pursuers and get back to the bomber stream and the planes without yellow noses.

He dove into the clouds, hurtled downward for a couple of seconds to build velocity, then pulled the stick to him, shoved the throttle forward, and kicked rudder right into a steep climbing turn, praying he would not collide with any of the FWs. He didn't, and when he emerged from the clouds again, they were nowhere to be seen. The rest of the group was all too apparent, assaulting the Liberators with reckless ferocity.

He circled the stream as it lumbered on, refusing to waver in the face of the withering assault. He knew it meant German guns from one side and American from the other, but he heard the bomber boys on the radio shouting around the word to watch out for him.

"Who is that crazy renegade!" someone asked in a yell, more respect dripping from his words than a thousand hosannas and hallelujahs.

"Look at him go!" another replied.

"Takin' on the Abbeville Boys and everbody else they got!"

"Come on boys, let's get em!" someone else said.

Yeah, that's what I want, fellas, and that's what'chu need—

"Kick some heathen butt and take some names, boys!" he said into his throat mike before he realized he wasn't thinking just to himself any more. A chorus of cheers and huzzahs erupted over the channel.

"Kill those bloody Krauts!" someone said in a roar, and a score more voices ranted their approval as he swooped between a charging FW and a Liberator, nearly ramming the German and knocking him off course, just as he saw a B-24 tail gunner blow apart the cowling of an oncoming 190, which spun away, then exploded. Beyond that, another bomber spiraled downward, pouring out smoke and a few parachuting crewmen.

The fighters came at him like sweating stallions swatting at stinging horseflies, with rage and frustration. He expected to die at any second, but he had never felt more alive, more filled with purpose and rightness. He spotted two FWs zooming up from below at the Liberators, who had no bottom guns like Forts.

Cheap-shottin' lowlife Huns—

He used the bombers as a shield from the two fighters, then, when the attackers were fully committed, wheeled and dove right at them from two o'clock. He sent a stream of .50 cals into the first when he had barely cleared the bombers, the tracers peppering one wing root and under the cockpit, flew through that plane's billowing smoke, and zeroed his aim in on the second 190's tail. He poured in so much fire, he shot off the entire vertical stabilizer. The broken plane spun towards earth.

As he careened up and down, back and forth, in and out of scudding clouds, but never veering far from the bombers, one particularly determined Abbeville Boy kept popping up. Once, the FW came out of a cloud himself and stitched a string of bullets diagonally down the rear section of his fuselage. *Captain America* bucked, but evidenced no further symptoms of the hits.

Gotta git that sucker.

As the minutes passed, the bombers knocked down a couple more fighters. A B-24 down below erupted into an orange-brown fireball, but, despite their numbers, the Germans were in disarray, both fighting the Liberators and distracted by his relentless maneuvers and attacks.

Charging up from below at a fighter headed for a B-24 in the more-vulnerable low squadron, he fixed his brand-new K-14, the most advanced deflection shooting gunsight on earth, on the plane and squeezed the fire button on his control stick yet again.

Gotcha, you sneaky devil, you.

His tracer fire seemed more sporadic, though, and the FW, though hit, kept on for the Liberator, poured a hail of fire into its fuselage, then swooped up and over and away.

What the heck!

Only two of his six guns were firing, and the determined Abbeville Boy who had stitched him screamed in again, blasting away.

He hollered curses, whirling away as a bullet shattered a rear corner of his teardrop canopy.

Fighting fatigue and tension and worried now about his fuel situation for the long flight home, he looped back around the front of the bomber force and disrupted a head-on attack by a different Abbeville Boy, then drew hot pursuit from two other FWs—fighters that otherwise would have been attacking bombers. Quickly surveying the scene around him, he climb-turned up and led them along the starboard side of the uppermost, twenty-seven-plane-strong group combat box of Libs.

"He's bringing 'em our way!" a bomber boy shouted over his channel.

The top, waist, and tail gunners unleashed a torrent of fire on the two pursuers. Wincing as tracer fire streamed past him, he heard an explosion behind him and the tracer fire disappeared. He nosed down, glanced over his shoulder and saw B-24 machine gun fire tear off a wing of the second pursuer, the first one already scattering like coal dust as it descended far below. Ahead, the lowermost Liberator, one engine dead, dropped behind the rest. He caught the glint of the sun off the green camouflage fuselage of an Abbeville Boy up above, commencing an attack on the struggling B-24.

I been in the Coffin Corner.

Passion that seemed only possible now for his brother warriors filled his heart. *I been the straggler set upon by them cruel tyrants that'd take a family's leader, a wife's husband, a child's father away from 'em ferever.*

He charged at the FW, seeing now the yellow nose, and he remembered words from a long time ago.

Oh God, be not far from me, return not my sword empty, sir.

He jammed forward the throttle, the Mustang eclipsing 450 mph, the Abbeville Boy's guns already twinkling like popping orange firecrackers as he got within 400 yards of the Liberator.

Git me there in time, Sir, please.

He didn't think he could make it, with his measly two guns firing on one of the most rugged fighter planes ever built.

I'll git between him and the boys.

He rudder pedaled a couple degrees toward the spot where he thought he could get just in time to collide with the FW before it got all the way in.

The fighter got bigger and bigger until it nearly filled his gunsight ring, then something burst from inside its cowling. His eyes widened as he prepared for impact, but the FW exploded, pelting his plane with debris, shaking it, and shattering the right half of his Plexiglas canopy. He swung up and the German spun away so that more debris hit.

Good Lord!

The persistent Abbeville Boy was just behind him.

That snake been chasin' me!

Before he had a chance to do anything but feel his heart drum, the FW veered up and away.

Had me dead to rights, but didn't fire a shot. Musta been out o ammo—er his guns jammed on him?

Dazed, he glanced upward toward heaven but processing so much so fast for so long had about short-circuited his brain. He had heard the American bombardiers taking control of their planes a minute before as they passed their IP, and now he saw all the Germans heading away, from what now seemed all points in the sky.

Gummed up your works, jackals.

He swung back around and saw the beleaguered B-24.

Constipated and lumberin'.

He was so proud of it and its crew, he was surprised tears didn't fill his eyes. Far behind, now, he saw the persistent Abbeville Boy, other FWs forming on him.

Squadron er group leader. Tough son of a gun. Never saw him that last run.

For a brief instant, he realized how vulnerable, how imperiled he had been, without having a clue. Then he got into position to make visual contact with the struggling bomber—silver-rimmed bullet holes polka-dotting its entire back half, waist guns flopping around without gunners—motion toward himself, then the Liberator, then England. To his great satisfaction, the pilot nodded and turned with him.

Blind leadin' the blind.

But he knew the bomber had a better chance with him if trouble came than on its own. Then that rough engine feel set in that turned a Mustang pilot's blood to ice. No matter how strong the urge to "try for home," he knew better. Trying to get out of Germany was all he could do, and that meant staying away from flak guns and flying high enough despite their reduced conditions that he and the Liberator crew could survive parachuting if they had to, and that he had maximum radio transmission range. It also meant flying west toward Allied-held France, not north through Nazi-held territory, all the way to the Channel, then England.

Thank God fer them G.I.s down there on the ground, sluggin' they way through France, else at best I'd be bailin' my keister out into a lynch mob o' Jerry farmers with pitchforks and axes.

His plane's engine cut out once, twice, and a third time. He began to wonder whether either plane would make it out of the Fatherland. With the slaughter of German women, children, and other civilians mounting into the many hundreds of thousands at the hands of British and American bombers, Hitler had decreed the immediate execution of any captured Allied "Terror Bombers." He didn't cotton to his chances as a fighter pilot, either. When he saw his coolant temperature nudge the red instrument peg and felt the engine lose power again, he flipped on his Identification Friend or Foe —IDFF—radio emergency switch to transmit a distress signal. Several minutes passed with no response but static. Finally, a Ninth Air Force base in eastern France responded, then proceeded to steer him and the Liberator in through a rain shower.

—

"All the bloody saints," the group crew chief, gnawing on a fat, unlit half-cigar and gripping a spanner wrench with one beefy, grease-stained hand, sputtered when he saw *Captain America*'s bullet-riddled hide.

"I ain't never seen a P-51 still movin' with that many holes in her—sir," a medic added after hopping out of his ambulance as lighting and thunder crashed and freezing rain poured. It took several days, but the crew chief and his men resuscitated *Captain America* for the return to England.

One of the local villagers, a willowy nineteen-year-old sprite named Claire, resuscitated him, though he noticed with perplexity by the final night that, despite the girl's beauty and charm, Mary Katherine's pinup poster would have been more satisfying. Not even a stash of local wine hidden from the Nazis during their occupation could improve matters.

He shook his head as a Jeep-driving airman took him to his plane.

What the blazes is wrong with me?

He had first approached Claire's older sister, but she seemed unnerved by him and vanished. He did not see her again during his stay in the village. The final night he was there, Claire divulged that one of their American G.I. liberators had raped her sister, and others had done the same to two girls in the next village. "The Germans were here for four years and no one experienced so much as an insult from them. A number of them had interest in my sister and I, but they were gentlemen, even as we—how you say—rebuffed them? I fear I understand very little of this war or of life itself."

TWENTY-THREE

Clarke gave him the option to sit out the Dresden raid and take a milk run since he lacked only two hours of mission flying to hit the three hundred that completed his tour, and he had relatives in the city.

"Of course, it sounds like everybody else from the eastern half of the Reich is there, too," he said, after finding him on his favorite bar stool at his friend's pub.

"Whaddaya mean?"

"You haven't heard?" Clarke asked. "The Reds aren't just beating the Nazi armies now, they're massacring all males eighteen and over—though it sounds like they've gradually lowered it to sixteen—they're burning down the towns and cities they 'liberate,' and they're raping and killing as many women as they can get their Commie hands on."

He let loose a half-chuckle. "Yeah, lotta that 'goin' 'round these days, I hear."

"Well this isn't what's goin' around'," Clarke said. "They're raping whole townfuls of females. Some captured Jerries told our intelligence boys, if they're good looking, they crucify 'em naked over barn doors and church entrances and such after as many of 'em have their way with 'em as can—until there's not much left to have their way with."

This didn't fit with his evolving political theology of good and evil and he stirred in his seat.

Clarke, perceptive as always, eyed him. "Tender sorts would condemn such behavior. But what are they doing the Huns haven't done to half the world?"

Lance just listened.

"Like General Patton says, though," Clarke said carefully, "we're going to have to lick the Commies as soon as we're finished with the Nazis, anyway, so it's good to know what we're dealing with. And I suspect tomorrow will be a preview of sorts, like in the picture house trailers, of what we'll do to them, too, if they ask for it."

He couldn't get his arms around all that, so he poured more whiskey into his glass from his pub owner friend's supply and tossed it back.

"Squadron and group commanders pre-briefing at nineteen hundred," Clarke said as he left.

He listened for a moment as Armed Forces Radio teed up Bing Crosby and the Andrews Sisters and "Don't Fence Me In," the number one song back in the States.

He gave a mocking, half-hearted "hmmph" at the hopeful ballad of land under starry skies, wide open country, and murmuring cottonwood trees as he heard one of the boys laugh and another shout a curse over a contested shot on the dart board across the room. A new *Saturday Evening Post* sat atop the bar several feet away. The cover feature read, *"An American Battleship That Wouldn't Quit."* He hoped maybe it would chronicle the extermination of some Japs, so he picked it up and read as he sipped his drink.

A few pages in, a sidebar appeared with a familiar image—the parked B-29 named *Waddy's Wagon* and Waddy pulling the wagon, fronting it with his crew aboard the wagon, emulating the massive ship's nose art. This story, however, paid reverential farewell to the Superfortress and all its crew. It chronicled how Waddy had them in the clear, beyond Japanese fighter planes, following a daring bombing run on Tokyo industrial plants. Another B-29 in the group, one engine dead and besieged by Mitsubishi Zero fighters, maydayed for help. Defying standard operating procedures, Waddy turned his craft around and went back to help his stricken comrades.

The story concluded that both planes went down slugging, likely taking a locker room full of Japs with them. Beyond his stunned disbelief at the staggering news, something in the piece—he couldn't pinpoint exactly what—sent a shudder through him and wrenched his focus from the overwhelming specter of loss.

He calculated, based on the story's information and his own knowledge of bombing protocol.

Boys may o' been less'n five miles from the Jap mainland, within sight of it. Japs may o' got 'em and hauled 'em off to their torture camps.

The specter seared away whatever modest alcohol-induced feeling of well-being he possessed. Somehow, enough information had squirmed out of the Japanese prison camps the past few years about the criminal, often unspeakable acts within them that most of the world was aware that whatever fantastic theories might be spun about the Imperial Japanese government and military's practices, they might be underestimating the true situation.

What is a people capable o' butt-rapin' the prisoners' pet duck to death not capable of?

Waddy's story about that had since been verified to him by a Red Cross friend who had personally interviewed American bomber boys imprisoned in the camp where the duck died.

He didn't know whether to hope for Waddy's imprisonment or death. The weight of hatred that the contemplation of either loaded onto him was not bearable. He slumped over where he sat, his face dropping to within a few inches of the bar. For minutes he remained in that position.

"Aye, Major," his friend, tending the bar, said. The promotion had come through the day before. He reckoned the timing was to help induce him to return for another combat tour. He needed no inducement. "Major Roark, you all right, chappy?"

He raised his ringing head.

Wad—dead? Poor Maggie—no, it ain't possible. He might be a prisoner, or he prolly got plumb away. But his body trembled with an unshakable chill. He slammed down the rest of his drink. *Whatever the case, I am gonna light up Dresden like one giant Fourth o July firecracker.*

FEBRUARY 13, 1945

"I guess you gentlemen have figured out by now that neither the Jerries nor the Japs evidence any intention of throwing in the towel while they've still got a man standing," Group Commander Shanklin opened the next morning's 0530 group briefing. "Well, there shouldn't be as many of them standing, at least in Dresden, Magdeburg, or Chemnitz, in a few hours."

In the day's Operation Thunderclap, nearly eight hundred Mustangs would escort nearly thirteen hundred Forts and Liberators in separate raids to the three cities. Over two *thousand* American combat aircraft would converge on the Saxon states of Germany on Ash Wednesday morning. The 77th would comprise a portion of the seven-hundred-fifty aircraft swarming Dresden. It was the fabled "Florence on the Elbe," due to its magnificent Gothic architecture, opera house where Wagner debuted his works, legendary three hundred-foot domed *Frauenkirche* where Luther preached, and his statue stood, and center of world porcelain mining and production.

"They say it's the most beautiful city in Europe, especially since no one's laid more than a glove on it in six years of war," the big, bluff Shanklin said. "It's also, next to Berlin, the key transportation nexus—both North-South and East-West—in all eastern Germany. Ditto as a communications center. Trainloads of Nazi soldiers pass through Dresden every day toward the Eastern Front—which, by the way, is now only about eighty miles away. Supplies, ordnance, weapons, the same. Meanwhile, as the Reds kick the smithereens out of the Eastern Reich, the folks living there are pouring into Dresden every day from the opposite direction, on foot, horse, donkey, by cart, wagon, and train."

He turned with his pointer toward the large situation map on the group briefing room wall. Thick blue lines indicated Allied advances from the west, in some places to the German frontier, as well as the colossal Soviet horde's positions along the eastern frontier. The familiar scarlet thread indicating the group's current mission ran from Toft Monks to Dresden.

"Our big friends are going to take out the railroad marshaling yards." Shanklin pointed at an illuminated overhead map of the city, "and bomb the stuffing out of its industrial plants, in these areas outside the old city center. The actual ground zero of the attack, though, is this little outhouse right here in the middle of a fashionable Nazi neighborhood in the built-up center of old Dresden." He paused and turned toward his audience, some of whom snickered. A few appeared concerned at the last comment, if not offended, to Lance's dismay.

"Now, as for the two British attacks that will follow us, striking at around 2200 hours tonight and 0100 hours tomorrow morning, well, let's just say I wouldn't want to get in a game o' chicken with Churchill and his boys. The party favors they're bringing include four hundred seventy-five tons of high explosives, much of them of the blockbuster variety, along with nearly three hundred tons worth of those charming little twenty-one-inch-long thermite incendiary sticks that will rattle around on the roof, the street, the ladies' vanities, and light up all the goodies our boys and the Brits' first attack open up for business." He looked to be suppressing a smile. "And 'scuse the misspeak, but of course by the time the incendiaries introduce their delighted little selves to Dresden, there won't be many roofs left, which is the point."

Tapping the pointer on the palm of his hand, he concluded, "Safe to say that 'Bomber' Harris and his boys intend to create out of the whole charming fairyland of Dresden a nightmare netherworld everyone from Uncle Joe Stalin to your baby sister back home will applaud. After all, their briefing instructions order them 'to show the Russians when they arrive what Bomber Command can do.' All fighter A groups will escort the bomber boys in and out. As for us, B groups get to add to the nightmare."

"Colonel," Calhoun, the bothersome Bible thumper, asked, "isn't that something along the order of a 60-40 ratio of incendiaries vs. explosives—er, the incendiaries being the sixty?"

"As a matter of fact, I believe it is," Shanklin said. "Fact, one of the Coke bottle-lensed boys in operations got on his adding machine last night. He estimated that between us and the Limeys, we'll drop around six hundred and fifty thousand of the little Fourth of July sparklers on this bunch of Jerries whom our intelligence sources say seem to think, since they have more pretty paintings and statues than the average Nazi city, we wouldn't dare bomb their square heads for real."

That brought a host of snickers and a couple of hoots.

Calhoun ignored the crowd noise. "Isn't that a formula more geared to burn *down* a city whose center is apparently our bulls eye, and all its civilian inhabitants—plus a couple hundred thousand homeless refugees fleeing the raping, murdering Reds—than gut Nazi war-making capacity on the Eastern Front?"

Lance felt like blurting, "And what the devil's your point?" across the room at Calhoun, but didn't. Shanklin's face turned scarlet. He noticed some of the flyers were stirring in their seats at the conversation, and a few actually appeared to share Calhoun's concern.

"Well, maybe we're finding the two work hand in hand," Shanklin said.

"Is that what Berlin taught us last week—sir?" Calhoun said, his own color rising, referring to the recent raid where for the first time the USAAF had blatantly bombed the civilian population to create terror and destroy morale.

Shanklin's eyes narrowed and he stepped toward Calhoun. "Lieutenant Calhoun, if helping end this gangster regime's twelve-year reign of terror is not something you consider worthy of your time and talents, just let me know and I'm sure we can fill the spot of your twaddling, court-martialed hide."

"Dang right we can." Lance's growl earned nods and a few claps.

"This is a mission orchestrated from the highest levels," Shanklin said, in a tone that quieted the room. "Above military personnel—way above. Now I'm leading the 77th on this mission myself, so I hope that addresses any more such questions as the Lieutenant here or anyone else might be contemplating."

He noticed that *"The Lieutenant"* appeared to be considering the merits of pounding Shanklin's face with his fists.

He could never remember feeling so thrilled before a mission. He delivered the squadron briefing for Clarke regarding formation, closing on the enemy, and evasive maneuvers with the zeal of a camp meeting evangelist and was buckled into *Captain America* before any other Mustang pilot even appeared on the fog-shrouded flight line. Then, the tower announced the mission was scrubbed due to bad weather over much of the seven hundred-mile distance between Toft Monks and Dresden. He slugged the top of the instrumental panel in front of him. It felt like his senior year at OU after they won their first conference championship, were 10-0 and Doc Merrill told him he was out for the Orange Bowl against Tennessee.

The mission was rescheduled for the next morning, now following on the heels of the two British missions, which flew as planned, after the skies cleared along the flight route. On his way from the ready room with his Mae West, parachute, and other gear to the Jeep that would take him to his plane, he spotted an animated discussion near a new blister hanger. Spoiling for activity and, if possible, trouble, he turned that way. It was Shanklin, Clarke, Clarke's wingman Travis, and a British airman, all suited up to fly.

"Cheerio, then, boys, be just like us," the Brit shouted at them as he stomped away from the group, "conquer, annex, civilize, conquer, annex, civilize—you can be the new empire!"

"What's eatin' him?" he asked the group that remained.

Clarke shook his head. "Whining because he doesn't like breaking a few eggs to get the omelette." He turned to him, a hint of mischief in his eyes. "That's what William Tecumseh Sherman said and it's good enough for me."

"Uh, believe Lincoln said that," Shanklin said.

"Well," Clarke said, affecting embarrassment and glancing again at him, "Sherman was still a great man."

"Shove Sherman and the horse he rode in on where the sun don't shine," Lance said, his jaw tight. "He burned down the South."

"Well, we're getting ready to burn down Dresden, Ace," Clarke replied with a chuckle.

"Huh? So, what sorta burr'd that Limey have under his saddle?"

The other three men looked at each other.

"He's already back from their second attack, and he says they've carried out their portion of Thunderclap in spades," Shanklin said.

"Says the whole city is on fire." Clarke's eyes were alight, "and he wasn't exaggerating, Lance—he swears the entire city is on fire! Over six hundred thousand people live there, and hundreds of thousands more Huns are refugeeing in from other Hun countries. This may be the greatest victory of the entire war."

"Let's hope they leave something for us," Shanklin said, starting for a Jeep that had pulled up for him. "Men...."

Clarke, Travis, and Lance stood there for a moment before he shook his head. "And here we still stand, a whole day later. Sheesh. So why is that Limey so ticked? Hitler'd have turned his country into a pile o' ashes by now if he coulda."

"Who knows," Clarke said. "Anyhow, I got dinner and drinks at the Rainbow Club says I clip more bandits today than you do. I still have more kills than you overall, but I'm on my second fighter tour. I'm keeping count between us based on what we both have since you got here. You on?"

"Dang straight, I'm on." He purposed to make up the now-six-kill overall differential—which he knew as well as Clarke—today if possible, as the squadron leader departed, laughing. He turned to the sullen Travis and said, "You look like you weaned on a dill pickle, boy."

"That Englishman said Dresden's got no flak guns, no fighters in the air," Travis said, troubled. "Said the Brits were sprayin' the whole city with flares and target markers and wasn't so much as a searchlight peeking at 'em. Said it's the least prepared bunch he's seen in five years of fightin' 'em. It's like they never thought we'd come there."

He nodded and turned to walk away. "Well, they shoulda thought it when they started wreakin' so much havoc."

"He said the Brits aren't even bombing the areas related to the war effort,"

Travis called after him, as he hustled away to his plane and waved a hand in the air without turning around. "They're scalding out the center of the—well, he got ticked and dropped his payload in a field out in the country!"

—

By the time he and six dozen other Mustangs rendezvoused with the Forts and Liberators near the Zuider Zee in Holland, he was spoiling for a fight like he could never remember. He was mad at everyone.

How in tarnation did we all get shanghaied into fightin' to save the British Empire? Still can't figure that out. And Clarke and Calhoun both say the dirty little secret of this mission is we're usin' Dresden to show the godless Bolsheviks what we can do, case they forget they don't own Europe after the war. And Roosevelt... if there was a God, He wouldn't o' let that lyin' demagogue git dang near everthang he ever went for. No matter who he shades, who he hurts, who he destroys, we jist keep electin' him, over and over. Four times! He'll never leave office alive and no one'll ever kill him.

Waddy came to mind and he felt his blood turn to ice.

But the Krauts and Japs.... No words, no thoughts could capture his hatred. *I ain't never gunna quit layin' 'em under while I got breath in me.*

That was the closest thing to a coherent notion he could muster.

As they crossed into Germany and began a slow descent in a towering cloak of strato-cumulus, the 77th arrayed behind the rear bomber combat boxes, he began to curse the 10/10 cloud cover the met boys said was now blanketing the continent.

Sheez, them bomber boys can fly and drop on instruments, but what the Sam Hill we gunna do? A nation full o trains, ammo dumps, oil depots, tanks, ground troops, fighters on the ground with no fuel, on and on, and I can't see diddly to strafe any of it!

His wingman, Rosenberg, radioed that his fuel selector wouldn't switch from his nearly-empty long-distance drop tanks to his inboard one, so he couldn't punch the externals.

"What do you think, sir?" The words squirmed out bitter as death to the handsome, nine-kill Brooklyn native.

He's got more kinfolk in Nazi concentration camps than I do. In his mind, ever aborted mission means more of 'em suffer, more of 'em die.

"I think you better gitcher rump home. You saw what happened to the two boys that didn't."

Twice in recent missions the same malady had struck other pilots in the group. One waited too long before giving up on correcting the problem and turning back, and he died of hypothermia after bailing into the North Sea. The other continued heading for the target and ran out of fuel, had to bail out over Germany, and was shot on sight by an SS officer. Citizens, from a nearby city the Americans had devastated in a firebombing two months before, took the still-breathing pilot to a doctor, who operated on him and saved his life. He was now in a *Luftwaffe* prison.

Rosenberg departed with a clipped one-word affirmation.

Geez, is that my imagination again, er is Captain America *runnin' a little rough?*

Nothing bested the Mustang in either fight or flight, but he had learned the IDFF emergency channel button and his parachute were both one heartbeat away any time you left the ground in the plane.

"Actually, they should be one o' our forward bases that's providin' support to the ground troops hunnerd miles or so back," he said to Rosenberg. "Sorry I ain't goin' back with ye."

"Showtime 1 to Rodeo 1," Clarke's voice came over the VHF interplane channel. Clarke was leading the second squadron, Lance the third. *"Switch over to your Detrola and find the Armed Forces Network."*

"What the heck?" he asked before clicking on his throat mike. "Yes, sir."

"Hammer 1 to Showtime 1," Shanklin's curt voice sounded at the breech of radio silence. *"What in the—"*

That was the last he heard. He reached to his right and turned on the UHF receiver knob, found the Armed Forces frequency, and heard Mary Katherine's voice, quite clear across the miles, singing Glenn Miller's classic, "I Know Why

(And So Do You)." He was in a fighting mood and he started to turn it off, but the on/off knob was loose and would not click off.

Good grief, dang ground crew.

Anger piled on anger.

As the haunting verses and voice cascaded over him, it seemed strangely as though she were there in the cramped cockpit with him, alone and uninterrupted by the world and all its problems. Just as she sang of the mysteries of robins warbling in midwinter, months before the advent of new life for another year, he saw a break in the clouds below him. A flock of birds winged past, far beneath, but discernible with his keen eyes, and higher than he had ever before seen such creatures, especially in northern Europe in mid-February. When she marveled at flowers emerging amidst wintry snowfall, bright blooms glowed across a wide expanse of the distant ground below.

But, that dudn't make sense. Ain't nothin' growin' this far north this early.

When she sang of the wind speaking her beloved's name, an air current whooshed against his canopy, softly creaking it. His mind cartwheeled as the sun burst through the cloud cover above and bathed him with its radiance just as she sang of its beams shining through a downpour and chasing away the overcast. For just a moment, he reared back his head, closed his eyes, and let the mystical "little" providences tide over him, as they had so often in the past. He could not conceive even the possibility of such a sequence. He opened his eyes again.

Providences.

He scoffed at the notion. He gazed out and saw the entire air division, hundreds and hundreds of Fortresses, Liberators, Thunderbolts, and Mustangs, ranged as far in every direction as the human eye could see, their countless contrails forming a new and massive cloud bank.

Them boys is my providence.

He felt the closest thing to emotion of which he was still capable and, as he passed south of Magdeburg, where a third of the division had peeled off to attack, he reckoned his tear ducts must be out of commission, or his cheeks would have been running wet.

You wild-eyed bunch o' renegades. 'Overpaid, oversexed, and over here,' them Limey soldiers say about us. Well, two out o three ain't bad. I love you boys, and all I got's yours today. You the only thang in this sorry world left that's worth a hoot in heck.

Actually, there was something else, as the clouds closed up on him again.

Glad I ain't in charge o' findin' this dang city.

He glanced for the first time at the three, old, wallet-sized photos he had taped to his front dash instrument panel before takeoff. Then Clarke interrupted, turning the group right.

We musta hit Torgau. And the Elbe.

Now it was seventy miles up the winding river and straight into Dresden.

Completing the turn south, he cursed the thickening, darkening, soupy air—*sorry clouds, sorry contrails, sorry Europe, can't see nobody*—and shot a quick look back at the photos while he had a moment. There was Sarah, between the altimeter and the bank-and-turn indicator, Sadie to the right, next to the rate-of-climb dial, and Mary Katherine to the right of her, under the coolant temp gauge.

He got a Jeep just before dark last night and drove to the Beccles cemetery to say farewell to Sarah. Her mom rested next to her, since her passing just three weeks after Sarah's. It pretty well summed up his views on life and "God" that such a sweet and selfless girl would be destroyed in terror so soon after happiness had come to her life. As he draped his Silver Star and Distinguished Flying Cross around her cross marker, he rested on the fact there was no God, for the alternative that there was and that He or it would allow, much less ordain, such innumerable horrors, was too awful to contemplate.

He spoke to her from his heart as the light faded

The medals are fer you, darlin', 'till I catch up to ya, which I 'spect'll be about another day.

After checking his gauges in the plane, his position, and the planes around him, he peeked for an instant at Sadie. That one was taken while she was still head cheerleader for the Marlow Outlaws, his own high school's arch rival, the wild black hair half down in her face, the black eyes challenging him, beckoning him, tormenting him.

Now, they were turning left, away from Leipzig and Chemnitz, which more hundreds of the division's planes were attacking, and heading the final fifty miles up the Elbe to the city of castles and fairy tales.

Finally, he looked down at Mary Katherine. It was an old picture, before Frank Sinatra and the Stork Club and Glenn Miller and "The Golden Girl with the Golden Voice." Grief and guilt flooded him.

Before me.

It looked just as she looked in the Mont that night when he first saw not Miss OU or the girl who won Sooner Scandals for the Kappas and Delts or the haughty oil heiress, but a little girl lonely, lost and unloved.

"You're so special," he could hear her saying to him under the green ash tree behind his little frame home on the old Roark place. Her voice was as pretty as Judy Garland's but sweeter, as she placed a hand against his cheek, the words more tender than ever before, her face like a mother's, but with more emotion. *"I... I would never want to damage something so precious."*

Hard coughs racked him.

"This is Showtime 1—the clouds you're seeing or breathing now are of the man-made variety," Clarke said.

He realized it was so as he turned on the defroster to try and clear the grimy fog from the windshield. He could hear the scores of bombs exploding in the city ahead from the Forts and Liberators. His eyes squinted through his canopy and goggles.

"Watch yourselves, boys, there's fires boilin' up as high as five thousand feet," Shanklin announced with even less radio decorum.

For a moment, everything broke open and he saw a blazing orange-brown inferno. Then he heard a roar and caught a glimpse of an FW-190, then another, race past toward the bomber stream—or where the bomber stream was supposed to be—but wasn't.

"Rodeo 1, let's get 'em," Clarke said, all transmission protocol apparently dismissed for the day.

As he readied to do so, he glanced a final time at the photo of his one true love. He reached a gloved hand to his masked face for the closest thing to a kiss he could give. Then he pressed the glove tenderly to her likeness. As he pulled it away, he was already diving into the flaming city, seeing no more the dancing black eyes that would forever thrill him.

TWENTY-FOUR

The visibility was a little better, 9/10 or maybe even 8/10, as he streaked up the Elbe River Valley behind only Clarke and Travis, squinting to keep sight of them. Now the heat fogged his goggles. The FWs were racing right down into—

Lord Amighty.

Roiling, dying Dresden reached up and snared him. It was hell come up to earth. He was tearing along the river now, less than fifty feet high. Wide and full, it was cluttered with debris, with bodies—*clumps o' bodies.*

Bombs were thundering all over the central "Old Town" of the city, off to his right.

One of the FWs exploded and blew back and past him in pieces.

"One down," Clarke said, coughing.

The other FW veered right, into the center of the city. Clarke or Travis yelped an instant before a torrent of airborne debris and particles spattered his own cockpit. It was like trying to plow a burning field through a tornado and a horde of locusts while astride a galloping horse. Clarke swung left and Travis right toward the city center to keep from flying into the most magnificent church he had ever seen. Its dome towered hundreds of feet over them.

Wonder what gospel they been preachin' in there past few years?

"Climb, boys, climb!" Clarke said.

"Lord, we're gonna get blown up by our own planes!" Travis said.

He followed Clarke, who climbed another hundred feet or so and back toward the open space of the Elbe. Travis found them again beyond the domed church as they followed the twisting river, which looked to him like a giant sewer littered with bodies—and pieces of bodies—with the lid blown off. It smelled that way too, as did everything in sight.

The FW was long gone.

Flames geysered up from below. He skittered out of the way and nearly crashed into Travis.

"Watch it!" Travis said in alarm.

"Let's hoof it on up the river a bit," Clarke suggested cheerfully, *"give ourselves some breathing room and see what we might get into."*

"Showtime 2 to Showtime 1," Travis said. *"Uh, sir, this place is a powder keg, we're still bombing it, for all we know there may be other groups coming in to bomb yet, delayed or couldn't hit their own primaries, and besides—what's to get into? This city is destroyed. Uh—sir, what the heck is that down there?"*

"That's a llama." Lance gaped. Indeed, the uninjured creature pranced down a ruined street, dodging corpses, some of them still smoldering, rubble to one side, burning structures to the other.

"All right, let's pivot starboard at that blue bridge up there and see where that llama came from," Clarke said. *"It must be someplace interesting."*

"Is there not one fighter plane left in this whole danged country?" Lance asked, disgusted.

"Hah, you're just upset 'cause you're going to owe me dinner at the Rainbow when we get back to Limey Land." Clarke led them across the river again and headed back towards the center of the city.

Rue filled him. *Even if there* was *any fighters in this city, we couldn't see 'em.*

"*I'm giving you a break, Parson,*" Clarke said. "*Since this bandit's on the ground, I won't count it in our little contest.*"

Before he knew what Clarke was talking about, the CO accelerated forward and down. Through the brown globs of smoke drifting northwest to southeast he saw...

A zoo?

Several fires raged around its grounds, blasted trees lay strewn about, and the buildings and other structures still standing were charred, damaged, and in some cases, burning. Animals of various sorts and conditions dappled the scorched, pockmarked area. A towering giraffe emerged from a swirling smoke ball, charging full blast away from an enclosure. Behind him thundered a cluster of stags. Clarke was already firing, and within seconds, the entire party splattered into a welter of flesh, blood, and bone. He wasn't prepared to credit Clarke for intentionally accomplishing the feat, but the head and neck of the giraffe spun off the rest of the creature's body and through the air. The body lumbered forward several more steps before collapsing in a crimson goo.

Clarke continued firing past the animals and into some structures beyond, one of which exploded, the force rocking Lance's plane as he flew over it.

"*You crazy fool!*" Travis said, his own plane nearly knocked out of the air.

"*What was that, Showtime 2?*" Clarke asked brightly.

"*You gonna kill us yourself to show off with some dumb animals?*" Travis asked.

"*See here, now, believe he's right, Parson,*" Clarke said as they flew on, still not a flak gun or enemy fighter in sight. "*I'd say it's time to call it a day, lick your wounds, and head to London for dinner. What say you?*"

Mighty white o' ya, jackass.

He had had his fill, but he spotted a German troop truck ahead. His heart leapt. Without a word he shoved the throttle forward almost to the gate, swooped past Clarke and Travis, and bore down on the truck, which he now saw carried bodies on litters.

Shouldn'ta come here today, boys.

He lined up his K-14. Just then he spotted a clutch of uniformed Wehrmacht soldiers on the front steps of a building next to the truck. Flames boiled from the back of the three-story structure and greasy brown smoke shrouded most of it. He pulled the control stick back just enough to set *Captain America* up for a nice pass over the building.

He had all six .50-cals churning by the time the smoke scudded aside just long enough for him to see the big, bold Red Cross sign painted atop the large structure.

"Happy Valentine's Day, boys," he said as he unleashed dozens of five-inch-long slugs which tore through the roof. Just as he cleared the building, its front portion, which had not been on fire, exploded, shaking his plane and showering debris in all directions.

That beats a goofy giraffe and Bambi.

Satisfied, he let Clarke pass him. Up ahead, he saw the domed church again.

"That the first baby hospital you ever shot up, Parson?" Travis asked.

"Huh?" he said.

"Surprised with your Jerry heritage you wouldn't know the big sign on the front corner of that Red Cross building said 'City of John Maternity Hospital,'" Travis said. *"Or maybe you did."*

Before that sunk in, he remembered Mama's voice saying, *"Your cousin Kati nurses babies in the Johannstadt Frauenklinik, the largest maternity hospital in Dresden, she faces constant peril from the Nazis as a member o' the outlawed Confessin' Church o' Bonhoeffer and others, and everone calls her 'the angel o' mercy.'"*

His mind stalled, all the more when something flashed in front of him, spawning a deafening roar and suck of wind. He jerked the stick back in reflex and squirted a run into his pants. His heart pounding, he steadied the trim and nudged the right rudder pedal.

The noise, confusion, and terror obscured much of Clarke's full-throated stream of obscenities, the first he had ever heard from him.

That's the Black Knight!

He couldn't take it all in—

The German was roaring down to the deck and away at one o'clock—fire spouting from the right wing-roots of Travis's Mustang and the wing shredding off—the plane spinning and crashing into a blackened open square already covered with debris and corpses—Clarke zooming after the German....

Why didn't he take me out, I was tail-end Charlie and I never saw him?

He lit out after the other two planes.

They roller-coastered at speeds approaching 400 mph across the Elbe into what his pre-flight group briefing said was the Dresden *Neustadt* or New City, fires blazing across it as well, then back toward the river, downstream along it for a mile or two, then turned port toward the blazing old city center. His mind raced.

Gotta 'member everthang 'bout 109s—murderin' Hun's days on earth're over—gotta grab ever advantage I can—attackin' three Mustangs in a has-been 109! Why'd he never switch to an FW?

The ME's disadvantages against the P-51 were too numerous to count. A much-earlier design that had already peaked. Tighter cockpit than even the Mustang, reducing what the pilot could physically make the plane do. No rudder trim control in the cockpit, meaning the pilot had to wear out his left leg on the left rudder pedal, affecting his port turns.

The Black Knight must be a physical specimen to accomplish what he did with his plane without exhausting himself.

Most of all—Clarke was lining up the German for a shot—especially in just this sort of situation, fraught with obstacles and peril in all directions, the ME-109 was no match for the Mustang's maneuverability, particularly on inside turns.

The Black Knight apparently wasn't privy to his thoughts, though, because he continued to juke, shift, and employ the turbulent terrain, visibility, and other elements just enough to keep Clarke from getting a comfortable shot.

Even he can only keep a great pilot like Clarke in a P-51D off him so long. There, he's got him!

Clarke opened fire on the German, but just as he did, the 109 wrenched right and over a wide boulevard, then leaped up into an enormous black cloud billowing forth from a fire in the upper floors of a large old brick building.

Whoa! One thang he's got's quicker climb rate at low altitude.

Clarke rocketed up into the roiling darkness after him, though. Lance wasn't about to follow him into it, so he raced down the boulevard on the deck. It had decent visibility low, and higher the farther he went.

According to *Captain America's* compass, he was heading south. The overcast and smoke veiled any semblance of sunlight. He made a gradual climbing turn in the direction that Clarke and—*Christian Schroeder, that's his name*—headed. He climbed to around three hundred feet, still able to see the ground, as he sailed around the southeast boundary of the vast cauldron. Ahead, to the north, he saw a vast park teeming with people, and Clarke and Schroeder over it—but the German was now on Clarke's tail.

What the heck—no—Clarke's smokin! Looks like his canopy's gone? Clarke's still in it, though.

Then the Mustang nosedived into a row of burning apartments just beyond the park and exploded.

Lance blinked once, then tore after the German, who had gone to the deck and shot toward the river again. If it took ramming the monster to bring him down, he was prepared to do it. He had no intention of leaving Dresden while the Black Knight still drew breath. He closed nearly to shooting distance on the 109 as they screamed past the domed church again. A statue fronted it, still standing. A man preaching.

Prollly ain't Menno Simons.

Then they were back over the messy river, heading over a bridge as he got within range.

No, he's goin' under it! Schroeder zoomed through an arch between the bridge above and the water below. How he'd managed to fit, Lance had no idea. He pulled *Captain America* up just in time to vault the bridge, which was covered with people. He opened his guns on the German even as he cleared the structure. Tracers streaked toward the 109's rudder, a chunk of which splintered off.

Yeah, I know, that 109 can take a hard lick and then some, but you ain't callin' the shots here, stud. I knew you'd head back into town, 'cause you can't outrun me in the open.

Electric with intensity and anticipating the move, he cut inside him as the inferno swept over them again, but the German swung up and away from him and into a wide, towering column of smoke. This time, he followed. Up and up the 109 climbed, increasing its lead. As the Mustang's supercharger kicked in and he closed the gap, he expected Schroeder to dive back down into the worst of it again and use it to try and make his escape. Instead, he leveled off around 3,000 feet where the visibility was somewhat better and headed east back over the city.

Crazy coot—

His thought ended when the German rolled to port, then, while upside down, split-essed into a dive and then under and past him, headed the opposite direction.

Holy cow, how's a 109 pull that this low without crashin!

He sailed straight into another towering column of stinking brown smoke, wincing and nearly groaning, his old head injury knifing him worse than ever before, and wondering with disgust if the column just happened by chance to be there. He banked right and away from the worst of the conflagration, then decided to gain some altitude and a surveillance advantage in hopes of spotting Schroeder before the reverse happened. A few seconds into his climb, the sixth sense that had failed him earlier near the hospital caused him to glance and see the Black Knight in his rearview mirror, bouncing him from above and behind.

Geez! How could he find me so quick?

Knowing bullets were on the way because Schroeder would know he couldn't stay with him long due to the Mustang's speed advantage, he yanked back the stick, then slammed it to 4 o'clock while punching the right rudder. The world spun around him and his stomach bounced like marbles as *Captain America* snap-rolled right on its longitudinal axis just like he had practiced it a hundred times. He spun again for good measure, went straight into a dive, then saw, to his shock, the black 109 had not overshot and was still on him, behind but slightly beneath him.

Schroeder opened up with his guns before he could accelerate away. The plane shuddered somewhere low. One more burst and he was a goner.

He reversed the snap roll, going to the left and this time straight into a dive. The Black Knight stayed right on him, firing.

This is it.

He closed his eyes and prayed.

Will You still take me, Sir?

He felt a jolt, followed by a loud crack, braced for pain, then opened his eyes.

Schroeder was hurtling straight for him, to ram at full speed. Quick as lightning, he punched the right rudder and ducked away, so close to a collision he felt the 109 pull at him as it passed. He also glimpsed a gloved hand against the ME's plexiglass canopy wrapped in—

Rosary beads? Purple *rosary beads....*

The German swung away to port and he saw he was pouring smoke out of a gaping hole in his black engine cowling.

What the—

A white puff of smoke behind and below him.

Well, I'll swan. So, there is one pea shooter in this whole wretched city showed up to fight today! A 20-millimeter on the ground, same ordnance FW-190s churned out at him in his *Hellfire and Brimstone* days.

Goodness, they get one stand o' junior Ack-Ack into play and shoot down one o' their own, one o' the greatest air warriors in history....

Something compelled him to follow his stricken foe. Schroeder at first climbed, with no apparent problem.

He's gittin' 'nough altitude to bail.

Then the German went into a smooth, controlled, banking descent. *What's he doin... headin' fer the deck on purpose?*

He followed him back over the tortured city, through clouds, smoke, fire, and intermittent spaces of decent visibility. Then it struck him.

He's lookin' fer a place to crash where he won't hurt nobody, ruther'n savin' his own hide and lettin' his plane smash who-knows-who-and what....

He let him go. Soon the German headed down into a broiling, wreckage-strewn range of what appeared to have been a complex of stadiums and athletic fields.

Think that was ground zero o' the Brits' first attack.

The Black Knight, flames now leaping from his ruined engine, dove straight into the clearest visible stretch of pitch—*wait, didn't that article say he was a soccer star in Dresden? He'd know where these fields are*—and exploded into a crimson ball.

Lance passed over him, then turned and came back. Gazing down, he felt closer to the man in the burning plane below than anyone on earth.

It's time.

He pushed the stick forward to dive and join him, but it jammed, and the plane refused to descend. Angry, he shoved harder, but he couldn't budge it. He swung around and came back once more. Still, he could not dive. Bewildered, his face solemn, he returned the salute.

He headed back toward the Elbe. The dome loomed ahead, but it looked strange—*like it's shakin....*

The entire structure began to tremble, then wobble, then collapse, from its three hundred-foot top to the statue on the ground far below. He kept his eyes on it as he veered away. It seemed to fall in slow motion and took a long time to do so.

May be more pea shooters down there—but what the heck? Looks like lotta activity on that big bridge.

He headed that way.

Hey, the stick ain't jammed now....

Humanity—dead and alive—covered the smoke-shrouded structure, along with wagons, carts, horses, and a few motor cars. Descending toward the deck, his burning, bloodshot eyes spotted a gaggle of dark gray Wehrmacht overcoats, the rearmost one pushing something. He frowned.

Prolly ammo or gold they stole from some Jew.

He gripped his fire button and took *Captain America* to within fifty feet at a steep dive. As he began machine gunning, the helmeted soldier in back turned and looked up at him, the overcoat unbuttoned in front. It was a very tall young woman with scarlet tresses streaming down both sides of her head from under the helmet, a long yellow dress, and an expression of "Why?" painted across her beautiful face.

A swaddled baby lay in the cart she pushed.

He let off the button and jerked the plane away. His brief burst of fire, judging by the tracers, had gone just right of the girl and other people, chewing up pavement on the bridge. Dazed, he didn't know how he could have missed. Something broke within him. He didn't care where he went now, and he hoped something larger than a 20-millimeter would find him.

Soaring along the cobbled streets of the *Altstadt*—Old Town Dresden—he saw rubble of every conceivable sort spread about, countless buildings still on fire, others smoldering, charred skeletons. Bare bodies lay everywhere, and parts of bodies, arms, legs, and heads. He kept seeing strange forms on the streets and sidewalks. He peered closer. They were jellied, melted, or vaporized shapes of former human beings, all shrunken. A human skeleton embraced the perfectly preserved head of a baby, the remainder of whose body was in a baby carriage next to them.

A chimpanzee ambled through the rubble of a street near the zoo. It looked up at him and waved with one arm—the hand was gone. On the zoo grounds just beyond, an enormous elephant lay on its back, impaled by an iron rail that had run him through, his intestines spilling to the ground on both sides as he wailed. Just beyond, two baby polar bears tried to crawl out from under their dead mother, who had shielded them and into whose back an incendiary stick had apparently scalded an enormous hole. In the great park beyond, globs of human bodies hung, oozing, and dripping from scores of trees, most of them leafless and many of them bomb and fire-blasted.

Neighborhoods of row apartments and houses burned or smoldered for miles. A large train station near the city center came into his view as the breeze cleared some of the thicker smoke away from it for a moment. Ruins stretched the length and breadth of it. A hospital train with red crosses painted on it peeked out of a colossal pile of broken stone, wood, and iron, what appeared to have been the train's white exterior charred nearly black.

Firefighters stacked eight-to-ten-foot-high heaps of debris outside two caved-in entrances to the station.

No, that's not debris. Those are dead bodies.

Lance descended nearly to eye level.

They're—he gulped—*children. All of them.*

Many wore costumes. The one being laid on the top of the nearer mound was a little girl dressed like a pink bear.

He turned toward home.

TWENTY-FIVE

FEBRUARY, 1945
FRANCE/TOFT MONKS/NEW YORK CITY

He made it almost to Normandy before getting a steer in to a Ninth Air Force fighter base just as his fuel tank went dry. While eating supper in the officers' mess, the base crew chief called him outside.

After saluting, the man fixed him with a steely glare. "See here, Major, sir, what's your angle?"

"Whadduya mean?"

"Permission to shoot straight, sir?"

"Yeah, shoot."

"Sir, you didn't fly in here from no Dresden, Germany. Your coolant system is riddled, in the most vulnerable spots. Looks like somebody used it for 7.9-millimeter target practice. Now, who'd be firin' a Mauser or flyin' a BF-109 within twenty miles of here, Major? Because that's as far as you could possibly o' flown this bird with them holes in it where they are. I seen one pop from a pistol on the ground into that liquid coolant system bring a Mustang down. It's your Achilles heel."

His head swam.

When Schroeder dropped under me, he musta fired up into them coolant lines. Bullseyes o' course.

"I flew from Dresden." He turned away, not giving a rip what the crew chief thought, but unnerved by the implications of what he had said. Implications impossible to contemplate.

—

Word that he had shot down the Black Knight reached Toft Monks before he did. A Mustang pilot chasing an FW that had attacked one of the bomber groups "saw" it.

He felt like Lindbergh at Paris in '27 when he landed. Men converged on him from every direction, on bicycle, Jeep, truck, motorcycle, motor car, and foot. Shanklin announced he was nominating him for the Distinguished Service Cross, which he could sport on his nationwide war bonds tour. "You're going to be the most famous ace in the Eighth Air Force. There's a lot more war debt left to pay off than *Luftwaffe* to keep fighting, though. You'll help the country most, the next several months, after your thirty-day furlough, by helping raise cash."

Lance was floored. " But I didn't shoot him down, sir. He woulda shot me down, he already shot heck out o' my plane, 'cept their own flak gun got him in the nick o' time."

"The good thing is, fella who saw it was under a lot less stress than you were when it happened," Shanklin insisted. "So, we'll go with what he says. And you'll be glad we did, too."

"But, sir—"

"And if we need a corroborating witness, I'm sure we can get that, too."

He stepped to within two feet of his group commander and stared him in the eye, tense.

"Roark?" The colonel was obviously unsettled by the other man's suddenly threatening manner.

"Don't do it, sir. I—I'll tell the world not only that I didn't shoot him down, but what you tried to pull."

"Roark, you don't mean that," Shanklin said.

"I—" He stopped, his brain unable to provide the words. "—I don't care, sir."

That was it, he realized as he wheeled and left Shanklin's office without saluting. He didn't care anymore, about anything. He was empty as a treeless shortgrass field the cattle had just been moved from after munching it to the nubs.

My war is over.

It was a revelation. He walked through a light snowfall to the infirmary to get an injection for the venereal disease that had flared up again. *I don't even care if I get my ashes hauled.*

Inside, medics hurried a young man hooked to an IV and lying under a blanket on a stretcher out a side door to a waiting ambulance. The unconscious face looked familiar.

"Who was that?" he asked an MP, who recognized him and saluted with gusto.

The MP shook his head. "Intelligence officer said he was a bomber pilot captured by the Swiss of all people. They, uh...."

"What?"

The MP looked around to make sure no one was in earshot. "Well sir, 'parently the Swiss been kowtowin to the Krauts all along to help keep 'em out o' their country. So, they slam our boys in their prisons when they land there. And I guess they got 'em a real hellhole they stick 'em in if'n they try to 'scape." He glanced around again and seemed sheepish to continue.

"So, what the blazes happened, sergeant?"

"Well, sir." The MP cleared his throat and looked down, "I reckon that feller there, well, some lowlife Commy Russian scumbag prisoners cornered him and—well sir, they 'tacked him—they committed outrages on his person, sir—repeatedly, fer days and weeks. Some Nazi slime runnin' the place didn't believe him or ignored him. He all damaged inside now, scumsuckers done it so much they messed up his plumbin', give him diseases, why, he got boils on him head to toe, sir. Saddest thing about it? He's a dad-blamed Quaker."

He stood there, stupefied. "Is his name... *Palmer?*"

"Why, yes, sir," the MP said, startled. "How'd you know that, Major?"

He was already almost out the door. He forgot about his shot. All he could think of was his loyal, soft-spoken Quaker co-pilot who had probably saved his life when *Hellfire and Brimstone* hit the drink after Schweinfurt.

—

He caught a lift back to the States a few days later, by way of Iceland in an old Fort the Army Air Forces was putting out to pasture. The "mind doctor" or whatever he was back at Toft Monks told him both his external and internal tanks were empty and ordered him to see an AAF doctor at an airbase outside New York City within forty-eight hours of landing.

Guess we'll see 'bout that.

He was numb. It took him 'til he landed in the States to realize the burning hate and desire to kill was gone. So was pretty much any passion or even interest in anything.

The nightmares, on the other hand, were back.

Liquor would quash them as before, but for the first time since Sarah died, he felt hesitant to drink. He still did some, but he didn't enjoy it like before, and sometimes he kept the bottle stoppered and just got up when the frights came and walked and walked, sometimes 'til the sun came up.

His mind seemed stuck in place, like the firing pin had been removed. He found himself napping some during the day, without the nightmares. By the time he had been in New York a couple days, though, he was on the brink of collapse from lack of sleep. That night, he conked out early in his quarters at the base, still in his uniform, but awoke around midnight screaming so loud that MPs had come to his room. He told them he was fine, settled himself until they left, then threw on an overcoat, airman's cap, muffler, and gloves, and took off on foot through a soft snowfall.

After two hours with his mind in neutral and taking little notice of his changing surroundings, he came to an all-night diner. The cold had numbed his hands and feet and his nose ran like a sieve, so he stepped in to warm himself.

Customers sat scattered around the place, including at a large corner table with three or four young naval officers, an attractive middle-aged woman with thick graying hair tied in a pony tail, and another man. A waitress directed him to a two-top a few tables away from the group.

The woman appeared to be the center of attention at the corner table. The officers, their uniforms thick with service decorations, peppered her with questions. He was cold and more interested in fishing a half-pint of Four Roses from his coat pocket. When the waitress brought him a cup of coffee, he held the already-opened bottle over it. On the brink of pouring, his hand froze, then began to shake. This continued for a full thirty seconds as the woman at the corner table laughed aloud with the men surrounding her. He felt a bead of sweat on his upper lip.

"Hey, Majuh!"

He whisked the half-pint out of sight as one of the young Navy men, one arm in a sling, the other holding a cane, marks and gashes on his face in various stages of healing, gimped toward him from the corner.

"Why, I believe I know you," the lean, handsome officer said, a Boston accent he recognized from a number of men he had served with during the war growing clearer. "Ahn't you Waddy Young's friend, the football playa from Oklerhomer?"

He looked down as if struck at the uttering of Waddy's name, then back up, said, "Uh, yeah," and slowly accepted the proffered "cane" hand.

"Shoah," the officer said, now hesitant after his reaction, "we met at the Stawk Club, befaw the wah. Ehr, Jack Kennedy."

He nodded, startled at the chance meeting and Kennedy's remembrance of him. His eyes twinkling, Kennedy touched him on the arm with the hand that held the cane and motioned him to come. "I've a feeling we'll make betta company faw you than you've got—ehr, Majuh."

He started to resist, but something about the man's countenance seemed so likable, he nodded. "Sure, what the heck?"

Kennedy introduced him around the table, coming last to the woman. "And this is Miss Dawthy Day."

The name seemed familiar as he nodded and shook her hand. He sensed the men at the table might normally favor the same sort of beverage that comprised the lump in his overcoat pocket, but in this setting, the coffee that the forlorn-looking waitress offered seemed as stout as he should go.

The group pitched back into their conversation with gusto.

"But what choice had we aftah the Japs attacked us at Pearl Hawbuh and killed thousands of ah people?" Kennedy asked Day.

"There are Pearl Harbors every day, Mr. Kennedy, in America and throughout the world," Day said. "Did you read in this morning's papers of the Negro who was shot and dragged by the bumper of a motor car through the streets while a mob cheered?" One of the other officers nodded. "Somehow, he still lived, so they drenched him with kerosene, set him on fire, and stood by as he screamed and burned to death. They left him lying in the street until a garbage truck removed him."

"That's awful—" Kennedy began.

"So, what of the negroes?" Day asked. "Were they supposed to 'Remember Pearl Harbor' and take to arms against us to avenge this and countless other cruel wrongs? No, we ask them to be pacifists in response to whatever happens to them."

Is this lady a pacifist, sittin' amongst all these sailor boys? From the looks o' their ribbons, Kennedy's git-up, and that little feller's facial scar, they sure's heck ain't. And what's she gittin' at 'bout colored folks?

As the other Navy men bit their tongues or squirmed in their seats, Kennedy stared out the frosty window into the night as snow, illumined by the glow of lights from inside the diner, gathered on the sidewalk. "Why, I don't believe I evah met a negro in person 'til I was in college, really. And I certainly didn't evah see... the sawts of folk comprising yaw Catholic Workers House this afternoon and evening. Theah smells, theah filth, pounding crazy-eyed on tables. Why I do believe if yaw friend, Hennacy heah, hadn't restrained that one poor devil, he would have wrenched yaw ahm off for turning down the radio. I don't honestly know how you can work, much less live—as you do—amongst such—conditions—Miss Day."

Catholic Worker... Dorothy Day... where've I heard these names before?

"Look, I love peace much as the next fella," a strapping redheaded officer said to Day, his voice starting to catch on him as his eyes grew filmy. "But our greatest leaders, all the way back to Washington and Jefferson, believed a strong defense was the best guarantor of peace, the best hedge against war."

"Oh, I'll go you one better than that." Day's blue-gray eyes twinkled. "Our best leaders in the Church—going almost all the way back—have believed the same thing. They've launched crusades, prayed over wars, and canonized knights and generals. But in the beginning, 'twas not so. From the time—the life—of Christ forward through three centuries, most of His followers and the church fathers were pacifists. They inveighed against the baptized even *joining* armies. If already in an army, they believed, he must shed no blood, including in time of war. As Tertullian declared, 'The Lord, in disarming Peter, unbelted every soldier.'"

"But how Christian is it to stand by while the innocent and defenseless are slaughtered?" the redhead asked.

"Jesus said all who take up the sword shall perish by the sword," Day said.

"But Miss Day," Kennedy said, "with respect, the Japs killed nearly three thousand Americans, without provocation. The Germans, who have tramped ovah half the world, declared wah on us. And who thinks the Russians will stop at Berlin now that theah winning?"

"'You have heard that it has been said', Christ replied, 'that you shall love your neighbor and hate your enemy,'" she said. "'But I say to you, love your enemies, do good to them that hate you, and pray for those who persecute and slander you.'"

"Yeah, I remember gittin' taught that in Sunday School back in Texas, and at home, too," the redhead said. "But don't the Bible say a fella's worse'n an infidel, if he don't protect his own?"

"Jesus said, 'To him that strikes you on the one cheek, offer the other as well,'" said Day. "And of him who takes away your goods, ask not for their return.'"

"But national defense—not attackin' others, mind'ja, jist defendin' our-selves—ain't mainly about material possessions, Miss Day," the Texan argued, "it's about life and death, 'specially women, children, and old folks who can't defend theirselves."

"'Be not afraid of those who kill the body and after that have no more that they can do.'" Day turned her gaze toward Lance, who yearned for even a prairie dog hole to crawl down into.

"But there is such a thing as a just wah, is theah not, Miss Day?" Kennedy protested. "Doesn't even Augustine and Aquinas teach that in certain situations, if it meets certain criteria, a nation has the right to decleah wah to defend itself?"

"Ah, yes, the sword of Constantine has indeed cast a long shadow." Day met the dark eyes of the Texan, whose burning gaze began to swim. "Even such great men as those felt compelled to burnish it for him. But Christ said, 'You have heard that it has been said, "An eye for an eye and a tooth for a tooth," but I say to you not to resist evil.'"

"Not to resist…." The scarfaced officer, who had said nothing during the dialogue, trailed off, partly because silence had fallen across the rest of the table.

"But, Miss Day," Kennedy said softly, not meeting her eyes, "I… *this*—" he said, moving his injured arm, with a grimace—"What was all this fah?"

Wait a minute… I remember now readin' in Stars *and* Stripes *that a Jap destroyer cut the PT boat he commanded in two during a battle, nearly killing him. Then he rescued several of his wounded crew, pulling one through the sea by a lifejacket rope clenched in his teeth, and swam for help, despite his injuries. And all I figured him as, back at the Stork Club, was a typical friendly, privileged rich kid….*

Sympathy filled her eyes. "I know… Jack. I also know your worst injuries are unseen—your back, your pain, walking at all. And I know… about your brother." The eyes of Kennedy and the rest of the Navy men dropped, as did his. His old crew chief Red McElroy later served in the same capacity for Kennedy's deco-rated older brother Joe, who died when the Flying Fortress he piloted, packed full of explosives and intended to serve as an enormous unmanned warhead, exploded in the air while he was still on board.

"What would you have us do, Miss Day?" Kennedy asked, his voice barely more than a whisper, looking her in the eyes, his own glistening.

She sighed, compassion shining from her face as she spoke. For the first time, he noticed her dress looked as worn as if she were one of the folk it sounded as though she helped. "We love our country, dear Jack. We have been the only country in the world where men and women of all nations have taken refuge from oppression. But if we are to emulate our Savior, and not oppose His work, we must be about the works of mercy rather than the works of war—no matter the cost to our own comfort or even lives. We must care for the sick and the wounded, devote ourselves to the growing of food for the hungry, continue all our works of mercy in our houses and on our farms."

"But it's crazy to expect that people—that men—can follow this pacifism!" the redhead blurted. "It's too much to bear, to stand by and not act."

Day's eyes warmed again, as though she had heard it all many times before and took no offense. "My friend Bob claims it places not so much a burden as does Catholic sexual morality with its day-to-day difficulties and the heroism it calls for from so many in such an unchristian age as this." She shot a brief glance at Kennedy, who blushed crimson and looked down at his plate.

Lance respected Day's intellect, conviction, and poise, but after she and her male colleague had departed he could not think of one significant point she made in his forty-five minutes at the table with which he agreed.

Niggers, bums, pacifist pansies... and screwball human beings tryin' to imitate what Jesus Christ did... what in the world is wrong with this lady? Who can abide such hogwash?

Your mother, came a still small voice that thundered down the depths of his tortured soul. He sat stupefied for a long moment.

Oh Lord.

The half-century-old woman slogged through the snowbound night, a cheap scarf over her uncolored hair.

It's her... the lady Mama told me about in California. "She's the most like Jesus o' any woman I evah saw."

A wave, hot and frigid, and altogether barren and despairing, surged through him. No one around the table in a uniform looked comfortable.

"Whadduya think, Jack?" the redheaded Texan asked Kennedy, who was staring out the window again, where the snow had stopped and lay in heaps on the ground.

Kennedy turned back to the others. "I think my parents sheltahed me from a lot. And I think we shall have wahs until such a day as the conscientious objectah enjoys the same reputation and prestige that the wahya does today."

—

After finishing the processing for his leave two days later, he got on the train for Chicago, and eventually Oklahoma. He felt tired and grumpy, partly because of his latest nightmare—of Waddy, Trigger, Patton, and others so roaring with laughter that sweat broke out on their faces and began to stream down them, along with finally the skin, too, all as they continued to howl with delight. He hadn't taken a drink since his raucous first night in New York, about which, he could remember little other than the headache and two feisty Italian girls it left with him in someone else's apartment the next morning. His head hurt worse now than after that, and all he'd had last night was a Coke after playing basketball with some other furloughed pilots in a base gym.

Gotta have me some.

He shook his head as he sat in his sleeper coach compartment and grabbed for the same half-pint he'd had at the all-night diner in New York City. He couldn't find it anywhere. Shaking with fury and frustration, he opened his mouth to scream an obscenity just as his coachmate stepped into their compartment.

Charles Lindbergh.

"Guess we're both older, wiser, and a bit thinner up top from our experiences," Lindbergh greeted him.

Lance blanched, not realizing his hair had thinned enough anyone else would notice, especially as short as it was cut. Remembering that no male he knew of anywhere in his family for generations back had ever suffered noticeable hair loss, he wondered for the first time whether the drunk Canadian flight surgeon he met his final night in London might have been right when he suggested the stress of combat was causing hair loss in some men.

"Dunno what I think anymore." He shook his head. "Maybe hearin' the wartime exploits o' Charles Lindbergh'll git me back on track."

Lindbergh's face took on a curious expression.

"What is it, Cunnel?"

Thus, began a quiet, devastating ten-minute chronicle of Lindbergh's experiences in the war. "As the awful truth of the German crimes against the Jewish people came out, here we were, doing the same thing to the Japs. *They really are lower than beasts. Every one of 'em ought to be exterminated.*' How many times I heard American officers in the Pacific say those very words!"

So much had Lance lost his fighting spirit that his next thought remained silent rather than shouted. *Stuff the cockroaches en masse into the darkest depths o' the lake o' fire and watch 'em sizzle and pop like strings o' Black Cats.*

Who didn't feel that way?

"'And why beholdest thou the mote that is in thy brother's eye but considerest not the beam that is in thine own eye?'" Lindbergh stared at him, as though he had divined his thoughts.

He winced, remembering Lindbergh privately divulging to him and Mary Katherine's father years before that angels visited and instructed him during his perilous historic first flight from New York to Paris. That the Lone Eagle might indeed receive special revelations from God was not, at this point in time, of particular comfort to him.

Lindbergh continued to speak, "...our boys shooting Japanese soldiers attempting to surrender so that their comrades would remain in the jungle and slowly starve... Marines firing on unarmed Japs swimming ashore at Midway... troops machine-gunning prisoners on a Hollandia airstrip... Australians shoving captured Japs out of transport planes over the New Guinea mountains... carving off Jap shinbones for letter openers and pen trays... burying Jap heads in ant-hills 'to get them clean for souvenirs'... 'the infantry's favorite occupation' of poking through the mouths of Jap corpses for gold-filled teeth...."

"What is barbaric on one side of the earth is still barbaric on the other," Lindbergh said, seeming to speak more to himself than to Lance.

Or to convince himself, or maybe just to discover?

"'Judge not that ye be not judged. It is not the Germans alone, or the Japs, but the men of all nations to whom this war has brought shame and degradation. But Christian men, we say, why they must be the exception, the salt of the earth, the city on a hill... and they have answered with inquisitions, pogroms, tearing people apart on the English racks, burning others and even each other at the stake, enslaving black peoples across the world, slaughtering the Indian race... incinerating German and Jap cities full of women, children, slave laborers, prisoners of war, and old folks, for the benefit of Christ and God."

Lindbergh's voice trailed off and his now-middle-aged head sank.

It is a long time since he flew the Atlantic.

Hopelessness and dread more filled him than the day he lost Sarah, as darkness descended on the Lehigh Valley.

TWENTY-SIX

When he reached Oklahoma, he had no idea where to go. He disembarked at the wind-swept Interurban Train Station in Norman, his one suitcase in hand.

No one is here. No one I give a hoot about seein', anyhow.

After putting on a checkered shirt, pinks, and his leather fighter-jockey coat, he borrowed a car from a lady just east of town who had worked in the OU Athletic Department since before he was in college and had always seemed to fancy him. Still not drinking, still shaky and numb, he drove west, the wan, almost-spring sun spangling the auto's dash through the leafless trees lining Boyd Street.

He crossed Highway 77 and passed the Monterrey Club on the left, closed until suppertime. The student union bell tower chimes tolled from the campus. He turned left on Asp and drove past the building. When he passed the library, he glanced to the left, where Mary Katherine's lonely little bench still sat. A couple blocks ahead, he turned left at the Kappa House and her porch. The street out front retained a small, faint, pinkish-tan stain of her red paint.

Heading south down College, pretty blonde, redheaded, and brunette sorority girls giggled as they walked with books in hand.

They're so young.

Wistful remembrances of college days pricked him. *Oh goodness... is that... no, but she looks enough like Sara Lee Cantrell, I wonder, is she a younger sister?*

He turned left at Lindsey Street, the southern boundary of Norman's developed area, and headed east, the campus to his left, pasture land to his right. The large wooden sign still stood at the near end of quiet, empty Owen Field, announcing *"Oklahoma Sooners—1938 Big Six Champions,"* its cream field peeling, crimson letters faded. He thought of Waddy and the Nebraska game and Mary Katherine. For a moment, he wasn't sure whether it was 1938 or 1945.

Soon, he headed west on two-lane State Highway 9, on which he had first come into Norman. The blustery open country where clover-like purple henbit weeds and Johnson grass festooned the raw roadsides and plowed red fields, and golden prairie grass stretched into the distance. How much once lay beyond.

Oklahoma never looks uglier'n March.

A half-pint of something would be good to help his melancholy and nurse along the road to Duncan and the old home place, which seemed as bad a spot as any to swing through. He probably wouldn't even stop there. After a while, he came to a simple crossing of lonely two-laned country roads east of Blanchard. Nothing greeted him but the wind and the big old post oak standing sentinel at one corner of the junction as it had since he first passed it when he was a little boy.

He slowed to a halt and a bold cardinal launched his melodious song from atop the tree.

Dang, you sound determined, buddy.

It was as close to being amused as he was capable of. The bird stared right at him, seemingly intent on announcing something of major importance. An old black Model A with a couple of dents approached from the west and stopped opposite him.

Sadie sat behind the wheel. One question flashed in and out of his mind spinning and breath got a lot harder to come by.

Why the hecks's she drivin' such a heap?

For a moment they stared at one another. She looked more beautiful than ever despite the years that had left crow's feet and other slight creases in her face and something else that he couldn't pinpoint.

And she lookin' at me strange, like somethin' wrong with me, almost like she's afraid er somethin'.

It was unsettling.

Shaking off such notions, he eased the car forward and unsmilingly motioned her to the side of the road. Feeling like someone else was controlling the movements of his body, he parked near the post oak, got out of the car, and stepped back to her, trying to act nonchalant while sucking for air. For several seconds, their eyes locked as though searching the other's for a place, an answer, a reason.

Then she seemed to find something in his and hurt entered hers. She reached to open the door.

Still saying nothing, his chest tightening, he looked down at the ground and stepped back. She got out slowly, glancing at him, then away, her face solemn. The wind ruffled her black hair, still thick and tending toward unruliness, but shorter than before. They walked side-by-side through a bar ditch and up into a long, fenceless, just-plowed pasture.

They walked for ten minutes without a word. Peeking at her from time to time, he finally realized, as they reached a treeline bounding the field, what was so different. Meanwhile, his eyes but not his mind saw the remnants of what had probably been a mountain lion laying a few yards into the trees, and he stopped and turned to her as a thin shaft of sunlight illumined her face and hair. A tuft of gray betrayed the latter.

"I'm awful sorry you're sad."

First words between them in ten years.

Her eyes met his, then filled with tears. She cupped his chin in her hand. "What happened to you?"

He stared at her for a moment, struggling for an answer. His expression evolved into a frown, then a burning glare that he fixed on her for many seconds. Finally, he looked down, stricken. He sank onto a fallen tree trunk. His shoulders slumped, and he gazed at the ground. He could not look her in the eye.

As gray clouds scudded in front of the sun and the breeze picked up, floating dust over them, she knelt by him and cradled his head, still scarred from the Hill barfight wound, in her arms. Rocking him gently, tears spilling out, she sang "Red River Valley" soft and sweet. Long quiet minutes passed with Oklahoma and their memories the only witnesses. His soul relaxed, feeling the approach of a safe harbor it had somewhere departed without ever meaning to.

She rocked him still, a half hour later, as the sun, peeking through again in the last vestige of day, dipped behind the western horizon. His head stirred, and she loosened her hold, as he looked up into her face, inches from his.

"Why'd'ju…." he asked, like it happened yesterday.

"Cuz you skeert me to death."

He thought about that for a few seconds, then nodded. His lips parted and his jaw tightened. "Am I good?"

Her eyes welled over again and she bit her bottom lip. "You the bravest…." Her voice cracked as tears streamed down her brown cheeks. "You the bravest, noblest boy I ever knew, Lance Ro-awk." She started to say more but stopped herself.

When she kissed his cheek, everything those lips still meant to him and stood for, everything they reminded him of who and whose he was and what his true country was came back into his heart. He knew now that he could never have her. Yet, he felt something spark within him. It was like a kindling of fire in a winter camp at night, but more so like life growing, from something that was sick and not yet healed, but like a dying that had stopped.

They said no more as they again crossed the darkening field to their cars. When they got there, he spotted another, bigger dent on the rear fender and squared up to her.

"Is he—did he ever—"

"I be awright," she said gently. "I'm a Stanton." He opened her door and she got in, started the engine, shifted the stick into drive, and smiled at him. "You be awright, too, Lance Ro-awk," she said before she pulled away, with a smile like long ago in the shortgrass country, and her eyes even danced a little, too.

—

Just after dark, as he headed south on State Highway 81 out of Chickasha, he spotted lanterns glowing up ahead in the middle of the two-lane road. As he slowed to a stop, he saw two Oklahoma Highway Patrolmen and their vehicles backstopping a makeshift wooden barricade. One of the pistol-packing, cowboy-hatted lawmen stepped to his window.

"Sorry, sir, this road's closed. Got a manhunt for a dangerous killer." The patrolman stopped and stared at Lance. "Well, I be hanged!"

The lawman smiled and extended his hand to shake.

"Hullo, Chief," Lance said, grinning.

"Lance Ro-ark," Quanah "Chief" Bailey, his best friend back at Duncan High, smiled and shook his head. "Didn't reckon I'd ever see you again, boy."

Chief had served in the famed Comanche Code Talkers, whom the US Army employed on the front lines against the Germans to radio important messages with Comanche code names. "Krauts never broke our code," Chief said with pride. "And ever one of us was from the shortgrass country. Even our commanding general Barton in the Fourth Division went to OU."

"Dang," he said, "you boys is famous. Didn't'chu fight at Normandy, the Bulge, Bastogne?"

"Yeah, though I caught me a German bullet at St. Lo and missed the last part o' that. Caught an infection, too, and they shipped me back here."

"Million-dollar wound," he said happily. "Good fer you."

"Yeah, Highway Patrol practically begged me to join 'em. So here I am, third week out on the road, on the lookout for Matt Kimes."

"Matt Kimes? Thought he died long time ago."

"Yeah, he 'scaped enough times," Chief said. "Shot him how many laws through the years and they go and let him out o' Big Mac for a few days release and he robs hisself a bank in Texas. Somebody's aunt's sister's dog's pet coyote supposedly saw him down near the river, headed thisaway."

"War could go on fer a hunnerd years and some thangs wouldn't change 'round this country." He remembered his brief but friendly face-to-face encounter with Charley Floyd long ago as the legendary Oklahoma outlaw eluded a nationwide manhunt, not many miles from where he now sat.

"Evthang alright?" the other cop hollered at Chief.

"Yessir, a-okay," Chief turned and jerked a thumb at Lance. "Just an ole buddy played football with at Duncan. Well, guess it's no time to be socializin." He turned back to Lance. "But I got to tell you one thing. After you left for OU, I kept a'plannin' to come see you, and you know I never did. I just hit that old bottle so hard and them... women... then it didn't help me feel any better, just made me madder at everone... 'specially white folks."

He peered up and down the road for approaching vehicles. In the distance, toward Chickasha, a pair of headlights dimly appeared. He sped up his talking. "So, one night at a gin joint out by the Meridian refinery, redneck fellow three sheets to the wind started a'callin' me Injun names, got me riled up. He ended up getting a knife in me. So, I fetch an old .38 out o' my boot, put it to his head, and pull the trigger. Nothing happened. I pulled and pulled it. Then two other yahoos got after each other with knives and I skedaddled."

He glanced back at the other patrolman, who was repositioning one of the lanterns, then hurried on with his story, but his voice grew thin and high. "Like to run over ole White Parker outside the place. He—" His voice faltered, and he caught his breath, striving to finish. "He said he knew you from all your work over to the Post Oak mission. He said you's the godliest young man he ever knew."

Chief's words struck him like a triphammer and he looked away. White Parker was the eldest son of Quanah Parker, the legendary Oklahoman and Comanche warrior, chief, and peacemaker, who had opened the tribe's reservation lands in the shortgrass country to the Mennonite missionaries a half-century before. To-pay, one of Quanah's seven wives, was one of the first and most devout Christian converts in the tribe, and a good friend of his. Chief's given name of Quanah was in honor of the Comanche leader.

"He been trying to share Jesus with me for years," Chief went on, talking so fast he was missing an occasional word. "At his Saturday afternoon street preachin' to our folks in Lawton, he come out the oil patch I roughnecked." The lawman began to weep as he spoke. "That night he said the Lord told him I might be at that joint, I needed Jesus worse than ever, so he had to go and git me, Lance. And, he didn't know the half o' it, 'cause I's headed to my truck to git my shotgun and stick it in my own mouth. And you know what I kept a'thinkin' as White laid out what Jesus did for me for the one hundredth time? I just keep a'thinking how you were always the happiest, kindest person I ever knew no matter what befell you. Thinking that you were the person best to me of anyone red or white, and I wanted so bad to be like you and I needed one thing to be thataway and that was Jesus. So… so I got down on my knees right then and there on the red dirt outside that hellhole, with yellin' and glasses smashin' inside and prayed for the Lord to forgive me and make me a new man, a Christian man. Didn't even go wild Comanche Indian when the army reburied Chief Quanah Parker at Fort Sill—even though his wives begged them not to—then confiscated the Post Oak church and property for an artillery range."

Memory of the latter, done after he left for the war, still stung him, despite his having come to share far more in common with the military than the Mennonites.

"Lights, Chief!" the other cop shouted.

"Well, I got to go, Lance," Chief said, grinning in a way he had never seen him do over something good, and backing away toward the barricade, "But thank you, my brother—all that hooey you put up with from me and a lot of others all them years paid off for someone—*me!* Look me up, I'm in Duncan. I wanna hear about all your exploits, boy, you famous, you in the papers a bunch! Shootin' down that famous German ace! You and Waddy Young, tearing up them Krauts and Japs like you did them teams at OU! Like you and me did at ole Duncan High!"

Two vehicles approached from Chickasha and he slowly turned his car around. The headlights illumined a signboard by the side of the highway. It read *"Future Home of the Chief Drive-In Movie Theater."* He stared at it, then back at Chief, then slowly upward. Like often in recent days, a feeling came over him that something was thawing out. He didn't know what it was or even how to wrestle through what all had just been said, but for the first time in a long while, he felt like he had somewhere to go. And it wasn't Duncan, though that would be next—*the Roarks are finished bein' run out o' our countries*—it was the Corning Mennonite Church.

TWENTY-SEVEN

He spent the night in a cheap Chickasha motel, intending to arrive in Corning before the worship service. His mental alarm clock had not failed him in years, but this time it did, and it took church bells from somewhere in town to wake him. He flew off the bed, threw on his clothes, rushed out the door and down to his car without washing, shaving, or anything else.

A bank of low charcoal gray cumulus clouds blanketed the town as he headed west, but the farther he sped, as cotton country turned to wheat, the more they thinned. By the time he reached the old drive up to the church, the winter wheat rose like golden pillars on either side of him and the sun gleamed off the whitewashed old frame church. He couldn't remember the last time such anxiety filled him. Pitching into a covey of FWs seemed inviting compared to this.

I know the older folks won't have me, they'll turn me away er I'll have to publicly repent er somethin'.

A silent voice within, for a long time nearly dormant, cried.

Who wants you to turn around—God or Satan?

Regardless, his heart pounding and his breath coming in gasps, he panicked and swung the car wildly around to leave. It got away and careened toward a pasture fence a few yards off the road. He slammed the brakes to the floorboard as the vehicle fishtailed and skidded up to the fence, dust and dead grass swirling, halting just as it touched. An old horse, tall but bent with age, his head looming over the fence and car hood, stared into his eyes.

Shaking, he stared back.

A few more inches, and....

Blood rushed through his head. The old horse kept staring, his eyes black and soulful, a tuft of hair limp over the white spot on his forehead. His heart knew before his mind, and then he jumped out of the car, at the fence, and cradled the grizzled old chestnut head in his arms and squeezed the soft snout. Movement for the animal seemed difficult, but his grunt came from somewhere deep and ancient and known.

"Oh, Jebby," he whispered, and his heart that had stopped dying, now began to beat again with life for the first time in a very long time. They clung to one another until he felt his friend's legs shaking. He could read Jeb's thoughts in his eyes as well as if the creature was speaking them aloud to him in English.

"I be right back, boy." He kissed him some more. "Somethin' I gotta go do, but then...."

There were no tears yet, but his voice wouldn't work anymore. But Jeb knew him better than he knew the horse, and the animal's eyes alit much brighter now that he knew he was staying and not just coming, and he half-snorted and tried to nod, too.

"I be right back," he said again, gazing at his old comrade as he pulled the car away and turned toward the church. Though still no words sounded, they didn't have to. He looked skyward, again, confused, wondering could there still be a God after all?

A moment later he pulled up to the church. They were singing a hymn preparatory to the Lord's Supper.

I missed the whole blamed sermon, nearly the whole service!

He almost turned and left, but instead sprang from the old borrowed car whose rationing-prolonged tires looked suspect for the return trip to Norman and hoofed it up the steps to the front door and into the church.

He stood in the rear for a moment, assaying the familiar old room. Strange? Cold? Welcoming? He wasn't sure. He wanted to sit at the rear, but there were no seats. Hearing whispers that he sensed concerned himself, he backed toward the wall. Then, gentle hands nudged him forward. Self-conscious, he began walking, trying to find the first available seat. More tense with each step, he caught surprised glances, some of them friendly, some not. *Oh, I gotta leave, I was a fool even to come here, they won't want me back after all I done—and I been in the papers doin' it—why they liable to church me!*

He turned to retreat, but men were coming down the aisle with the communion elements. One of them glared at him, shook his head, and started to speak, when another, a hulking, bearded elder, blinked in surprise, then passed the tray to his fellow and bear hugged him, lifting him off the floor. Blushing with embarrassment, he said softly, "Oh glory, Lance, it's good to see ya back, brutha."

He stood there for a moment, dazed, unable to process even why he was there, much less what all was now happening. Other folks recognized him, some nodding and smiling, others grim or stonefaced.

Oh, Lord, some are glad to see me, but others... what's gunna happen?

He crept forward again, nodding to folks, startled by the pew to the left where he and Daddy used to sit. Just before it was the spot where old Schmelzer always sat. His son and grandsons were there but not him.

He was real old when I left.

He never suspected the absence of the old man would bring him more pain than his presence and his many pinches of his ears, but it sure enough did.

Then folks were clearing a spot for him in his old pew, right on the aisle where he always sat. He realized with a jolt that a couple of them were moving in protest of his presence. His old buddy Klassen, square-jawed and broad-shouldered, blond, and tanned, reached a large strong hand over a pew to shake his.

Someone else patted him on the back, but he heard someone whisper, "After all our boys suffered, he shows up now?"

He sat down and Krehbiel, another old buddy, who he'd heard had faced down that rascal Council of Defense fellow from Corn when he showed up during the war trying to make trouble for the young Mennonite COs, sat next to him and gave him a firm handshake but a chilly nod.

They were singing "In the Rifted Rock I'm Resting" all the while and the rows in front of him were going forward to receive the elements from—

Lord in heaven, it's my Grandpa Schroeder. But he was retired and near death last I heard. Grandma Schroeder had passed a few years before. Grandpa Schroeder was distributing the bread and juice to the folks who came forward. *He looks like the Hunchback o' Notre Dame he's bent over so bad.*

Grandpa was staring at him, too, beaming with joy, tears trickling down his face that looked old, worn, and lasting as an erosion-sliced shortgrass country hill.

"Guess ya heard your Grandpa stepped up to guest preach today, did'ja?" Krehbiel asked him with a smile.

He stared at him, then spotted two other elders watching him and glancing at one another. *They fixin' to ask me to leave.*

His stomach was churning. Then came a dissonant sound from across the aisle among the females. He turned and saw a beautiful young woman with fair hair, the smooth, graceful neck of a swan, and glimmering eyes the color of the sea.

Oh, my Lord, that can't be... Younger girls on both sides of her nuzzled up to her, holding her. *They's a whole flock of 'em, just lovin' bein' with her. But it can't be....*

When she turned to him and smiled, he felt blood rush to his head and he had to grab the side of the pew.

"Emma?" he asked as the lyrical, full-throated paeon of praise to God went up acapella from the Corning Mennonite Church. She could not have heard him, but she read his lips, giggled a bit—in a graceful and elegant fashion—and nodded.

She had always been the tall, gangly girl a few years younger than him with freckles and glasses and a bird's nest of a bonnet who was sweet with the younger children in the nursery and helped the ladies with the children of the local girls who got in trouble. And who had the most painful, off-key singing voice he had ever suffered through. But he hadn't seen her in all the years he had been away, though once he met a German girl in Detroit who favored her and seemed perhaps to have been a distant cousin. What had been the odds of that?

Then Krehbiel was gently nudging him up to head forward for the Lord's Supper. Wild panic swept him.

I don't deserve it. The Lord'll be madder at me if I do take it than if I don't. And... so will them elders headed thisaway.

But Emma was looking at him as he hung there, half-seated, half-standing. She glanced this way and that, but her attention was on him.

"Well, git on up there, silly," she said, in a manner that he heard just fine but that no one else seemed to detect.

Then he was moving forward, Klassen in front of him like a shield as the congregation sang "Blessed be the Tie that Binds." But the two unwelcoming elders were closing in and hospitality was not in their eyes. The congregation quieted. Grandpa, joy in his eyes, but now steel, too, had raised his hands.

"*'And he arose, and came to his father,'*" the old man declared to the congregation, his voice again swelled to the sound of many rushing waters as in Lance's youth. "*But when he was yet a great way off, his father saw him, and had compassion, and ran, and fell on his neck, and kissed him. And the son said unto him, 'Father, I have sinned against heaven, and in thy sight, and am no more worthy to be called thy son.' But the father said to his servants, 'Bring forth the best robe, and put it on him; and put a ring on his hand, and shoes on his feet: And bring hither the fatted calf, and kill it; and let us eat, and be merry: For this my son was dead, and is alive again; he was lost, and is found.'*"

For a moment, the room was silent. Then, as if on cue, the singing resumed, more full-throated than before, the two inhospitable elders disappeared, and no more did he detect so much as a discouraging expression.

One by one, the men in line in front of him took the bread and cup, as did the women on the other side with another elder, as ever it had been done.

But I can't, I don't....

Panic struck him again as Klassen took the elements.

Then he was looking down into Grandpa Schroeder's blue eyes. Tears streaked the stooped old man's bronzed face as he marshaled his now-wavering eighty-year-old voice and said, his lips trembling with emotion, "My dear son...."

It was like standing at the judgment bar of God before the Almighty Himself, only to be found wanting. Never in his life had he felt more unprepared, more unworthy for anything than to take the little chunk of bread Grandpa held out.

As the congregation began to sing "There is a Fountain Filled with Blood," he could no longer look into Grandpa's eyes—and they looked so much like Mama's he felt it was she standing there peering into his soul.

Grief and loss overwhelmed him as his head drooped.

"What is it, my dear boy?" Grandpa asked.

He could only shake his hung head as all the bright, shining faces, so full of hope and promise, paraded across his memory. Trigger imitating Mussolini and Stalin on the Tannoy. Patton the only person recognizing the toll taken on him over Bremen, placing a gentle hand on his shoulder. DeLozier looking up to him, reverencing their old home places with him, and planning a gathering of their families when they returned. Mary Katherine with everything the world had to offer, giving her whole heart to him under the green ash tree, her cheek smeared with cottonwood dust. Waddy walloping the Nebraska Cornhuskers so he could score the greatest Sooner touchdown of their generation. Sarah crowning his long, lonely, loyal wait for love and completion with her sweet and gentle spirit, for so short a time. Mama before the lines on her face and California and...

...losin' me...

...and making sure he knew what was right, and how much it, sometimes, cost.

It must all be punishment for turning wicked and especially for turning away from the light that God had shined so strongly. His throat clutched.

I am beyond saving.

"It's too late fer me, sir," he gasped toward the floor in a choked voice.

"It ain't nevah too late when you His," Grandpa said.

But... can that be true? She... she'll know I'm a wretched hellbound cur.

He lifted his head just a shade. It was as heavy as though a boulder was sitting on it, but he knew why. He was terrified to see the pitying, knowing, satisfied look on her lovely sanctified face—the one face that suddenly mattered—her recognition of the utter justness and rightness of his lost estate and unspeakable destination.

But he had to see the look on that face, as a final confirmation and declaration of his richly deserved guilt, he had to, he needed to... he *wanted* to, so right did he know such a verdict was. The final stanza of the hymn flowed over him as with breathless terror beyond a thousand charging ME-109s he peeked around and saw her wondrous features—*Oh my, look how tall she's grown!*—tear-stained but smiling.

Smilin' at me... smilin' for me, oh dear Jesus... and noddin', tellin' me... tellin' me, yes! And hallelujah is in her eyes!

He turned back to Grandpa and looked into Mama's eyes and saw them happy and laughing finally, because she knew he had laid down his sword forever and that whatever came he might die but he would never again kill for what he believed. She knew that he would go back to Chickasha and confess his crime to the German POW warden there, and to someone else what he had done to the brave and trusting black soldier from Pampa. Knew that Jesus would be with him, and if He allowed, he would have many people to ask forgiveness from, and much restitution to make. And one day, if by God's grace he were permitted freedom, he would return to Dresden and do whatever the Lord empowered him to do to serve and love those people. Only then, did he realize that he himself was weeping tears of forgiveness and joy and thanksgiving to His Savior.

"But—" he still stammered.

"Take it, son," Grandpa said with the very voice of Matthew Haury and the shortgrass country as he accepted the bread. "It's fuh sinnas."

AUTHOR'S NOTE

Shortgrass and *Mustang* aim to take you the reader on an adventure through one of the most colorful and momentous eras in American history. We believe these books abound with nostalgia, patriotism, and memorable, sometimes larger-than-life characters. With the passage of time, however, language, racial and other social views, and the culture itself have progressed. Authentically conveying a past sense of time and place is challenging in numerous ways, not least the risk of offending contemporary sensibilities. Thus, we wish to clarify that where names, terms, or attitudes appear in the narrative that may do so, we do not intend to endorse them, but rather, as sensitively as possible, to portray truthfully the people, viewpoints, and events of the era.

Conversely, we have in some cases softened potentially offensive language and passages in care and concern for you the modern reader, particularly within scenes involving intense emotion (and sometimes alcohol), as well as wartime military contexts. Such language during the 1930s and 1940s was oftentimes much more tartly "modern" than is now realized. If you don't agree in full with our choices, we hope you will at least recognize our earnest intentions to respect both you and our forefathers, while at the same time deliver you an entertaining read.

John J. Dwyer is longtime Adjunct Professor of History and Ethics at Southern Nazarene University. He is former History Chair at a classical college preparatory school, newspaper publisher, and radio host. His books include the non-fiction historical narrative *The War Between the States: America's Uncivil War* and the novel *When the Bluebonnets Come*, both from Bluebonnet Press; the historical novels *Stonewall* and *Robert E. Lee* from Broadman & Holman Publishers; the two-book historical narrative *The Oklahomans: The Story of Oklahoma and Its People* from Red River Press; and the prequel to *Mustang, Shortgrass*, from Tiree Press.

John is a native Texan who grew up in Oklahoma. He graduated with a journalism degree from the University of Oklahoma, did post-graduate studies in history at OU, and earned his masters degree from Dallas Theological Seminary. He lives with Grace, his wife of 29 years. They have one daughter, Katie, and one grandson, Luke.

Find out more about John and his writing at www.johnjdwyer.com.

CPSIA information can be obtained
at www.ICGtesting.com
Printed in the USA
LVHW111345290519
618337LV00008BB/269/P